About the Author

British-born author, **Louisa Bennet**, studied Literature at
the University of London and went on to learn Canine
Linguistics from her golden retriever, Pickles, which is
how she discovered what dogs really get up to when
we're not around. Truth be told, Pickles came up with
the story for The Monty and Sidebottom Mysteries, and
Louisa just transcribed it. She's faster on the keyboard
and less easily distracted by food and passing squirrels.

Louisa worked in magazine publishing and climate
change consulting before her eyes were opened to
the world of woofers. She divides her time between
London and Sydney, Australia, and runs courses
on crime fiction and creative writing. Pickles runs courses
on wee-mailing, duck toppling
and drool management.

To stay in touch with
Monty, the sniffer super-sleuth, please go to
www.MontyDogDetective.com.

MONTY AND ME

Louisa Bennet

avon.

Published by AVON
A division of HarperCollins*Publishers* Ltd
1 London Bridge Street
London SE1 9GF

www.harpercollins.co.uk

First published in Great Britain by HarperCollins*Publishers* in 2015
This edition published in 2020

A catalogue copy of this book is
available from the British Library.

ISBN: 978-0-00-843525-7

This novel is entirely a work of fiction.
The names, characters and incidents portrayed in it are the work
of the author's imagination. Any resemblance to actual persons,
living or dead, events or localities is entirely coincidental.

Typeset in Bembo Std by
Palimpsest Book Production Limited, Falkirk, Stirlingshire
Printed and bound in UK by CPI Group (UK) Ltd, Croydon CR0 4YY

MIX
Paper from
responsible sources
FSC **FSC® C007454**
www.fsc.org

This book is produced from independently certified FSC™ paper
to ensure responsible forest management.

For more information visit: www.harpercollins.co.uk/green

To Ann Young, Zina Daniel and Maureen Larkin.

Chapter One

I bound from the car and, nose to the ground, zig-zag around the front lawn of my new home. I hoover up downy feathers that stick to my wet nose and I sneeze, sending the feathers flying. As a pup, I once tore a cushion to shreds searching for the duck inside. I found loads of feathers but never found the duck. I'm still searching. Can't be that many naked ducks about.

'So, what do you think?' Rose asks, smiling.

What do I think? I think those bitter white tablets the vet gave me were worth it after all. I can't feel my stitches and my paws seem to float above the grass as if I'm dreaming. I run over to Rose, tail wagging like a windscreen wiper in a downpour, and lick her hand. After being cooped up in a cage at the vet's, I need the wind in my fur, big time. So I charge up and down, leaning into each turn like a motorcycle at Brands Hatch, almost tripping over a faded wooden sign on the overgrown grass that once welcomed visitors to Duckdown Cottage. It even has a white duck painted on it.

Duck!

I bolt down the side of the house to where the duck droppings are so potent it's like fireworks going off in my head.

'Monty!' she calls. 'Leave the ducks alone.'

She can't be serious! Duck and pheasant retrieval is what I'm bred for. It's a calling.

I go into selective hearing mode and charge for the pond, revelling in the glorious combination of mud, poultry poo and stagnant water. It's the canine equivalent of Chanel No. 5. Most of the quack-pack sit serenely in the shade of a willow. A matronly mallard leads them in meditation.

'Om shanti,' the mallard intones.

'Om shanti,' they reply.

The others snooze, plump bodies balanced on one of their twig-like legs, eyes closed. It's too much. I can't resist. Time for a bit of duck toppling!

I charge at them, plumed tail held high like the battle flag of an invading army, and bark with excitement. The ducks panic, running around in circles, then scatter. Some head for the water, others bolt across the lawn, wings back. Before Rose can grab my collar, I dive for the pond, water splashing over me, cool and exhilarating.

'Monty, stop! Your stitches!'

Mouth open, I pounce on a black and white tufted dowager and come up with her in my jaws.

'Get off me, you slobbering fur-ball!' she quacks and kicks me in the muzzle.

I can't tell this squirming mass of feathers and webbed feet that I'm not going to hurt her, because I'll drop her if I do. Sodden but proud, I trot out of the pond and deposit the ruffled bird, unhurt, at Rose's feet. A gift. I am expecting praise, ears up, long pink tongue dangling, mouth turned up in what the big'uns – that's our term for people – often think of as a smile.

'Bad dog!' she scolds, trying to catch her breath.

The duck quacks out 'Tosser!' as she waddles off, a little wobbly.

I watch her go, my ears flat, head lowered, tail tucked in, confused by Rose's reaction. Not the duck's. They never take it well.

'This isn't going to work if you eat the ducks. You have to leave them alone, Monty,' she says, wagging her finger.

Even when she's cross she's softly spoken. It's like a gentle breeze whispering through tall grass.

I 'harrumph' and sit.

Detective Constable Rose Sidebottom is the alpha, the pack leader. My *new* pack. I can't quite wrap my brain around what a sidebottom is, since the ones I like to sniff are most definitely at the back. So I think of her as Rose. She's a trainee detective. I sympathise. I was a trainee guide dog once, and it's not easy having your every move watched and judged. On the way here I spotted her training harness in the back of the car. Who'd have thought detectives wear them too! Except she calls hers a stab jacket. Not sure why.

I peer up at her eyes, the colour of Blu Tack. How do I know? I tried eating some once. Very chewy, which was great fun. But not very tasty. Her mousy brown hair is pulled back in a long ponytail that reminds me of a bushy tail. I know she is not very tall because my head comes up to her waist, but she is strong, as I found out when I bolted from my cage and she grabbed my collar. She's not one for glinting, clinking jewellery and she dresses in monotones – today, it's a grey trouser suit. The only exception is an antique silver watch with narrow strap and diamonds around the tiny face that carries someone else's smell: a sickly person wrapped in blankets. Even this she keeps hidden under her shirt cuff. It's as if she doesn't want to be noticed.

Rose gnaws her lower lip. She looks worried. Is this because I chased the ducks? Oh no. I feel bad about that. I'll have to try not to. Will be hard though. Goes against my instincts. You know the Retriever thing.

I puff out my chest and sit tall, determined to ignore the little quackers.

I will be good, I will.

But I just can't resist a glance at the pond. The bird I've just released lifts her tail feathers and farts at me in defiance. Right, that's it! I'm not putting up with . . .

'Now we've got that clear I'll show you around, but take it easy, okay? You need time to heal.'

I focus back on Rose. Butter wouldn't melt in my mouth.

'Stand!' she commands.

I obey, quick-smart and walk to heel. I know how to do all this easy stuff. Sit! Heel! Drop! Stay! Fetch! All those commands – and many more – were drilled into me at guide dog school. Although I didn't know at the time, getting to guide dog school is like winning a scholarship to Oxford or Cambridge. And I got top marks there, too. I was destined for great things. It wasn't until my first posting that I disgraced myself and suffered the ultimate humiliation – but that's a story for another time.

Ahead is a tumbledown shed covered in ivy. As wide as a garage, its lopsided wooden doors hang open on broken hinges. The ancient black paint peels and curls. I sniff a door

post and pick up an old wee-mail – that's the doggie equivalent of an email. It's a message from a slightly deluded
Dachshund called Legless who believes she is named after
the elf in *Lord of the Rings* because of her exceptional speed.
On those little legs? Somehow, I don't think so. Wee-mails,
though brief, go one step further than emails: they convey
our mood. Hers is elation. She boasts she's finally bitten the
postman's ankles after three years of trying. That I can believe:
her head's at the perfect height.

'Aunt Kay used to love gardening. It helped her unwind,'
Rose says, staring at a dented green wheelbarrow just inside
the door. 'She could grow anything. She'd sing to the flowers,
you know.'

I look up and see tears in her eyes. I lean against her leg
and feel her sadness. It reminds me of my own. I don't
understand why big'uns' eyes fill with water but I do understand the pain of loss and Rose clearly misses this Aunt Kay
very much, just like I pine for Paddy, my old master. It feels
like I've lost a limb and although it will never come back,
the memory is agonisingly real. I howled each night at the
vet's, calling Paddy's name, but in my heart I knew he wouldn't
come.

I miss Paddy's hand stroking my head. I miss our fishing
trips together and how he'd never scold me when I scared
away the fish. I miss our evenings; he'd sit in his armchair
tapping away at his laptop as I lay at his feet, head resting
on his leather slippers. And I miss his smell: musty books,
Listerine, woollen cardigan, and liver treats, which he always
kept in his cardigan pocket, just in case.

'Should mow the lawn one day,' Rose mumbles, as she
walks away.

It takes me a while to focus on what she's said. Mow? Why? I prefer meadow. Love the way the dandelions tickle my belly and the bees scatter as I charge through the tall grass.

I place a wee-mail above Legless's ancient message. No need to sign it because every dog has a unique aroma. It's the same wee-mail I've left whenever I've had the chance to pee. It conveys my shame. I ask one question: who killed Professor Patrick Salt? I hang my head and tuck in my tail as I plod after Rose. She's investigating his murder, but little does she know, so am I. I failed Paddy in life and I have vowed I will not fail him in his death.

Rose waits for me.

'Poor boy,' she says, giving me a pat. 'I shouldn't get cross with you. It's not your fault I've messed up at work.'

It's early evening in September and summer came late this year so the air is still warm and the light has only just begun to fade. We stroll by a greenhouse with panes of glass missing and tomato plants laden with over-ripe fruit. I can smell their sweetness. I also detect a ratty scent. I clock it for investigation later, and follow Rose to the very end of the garden where a tall oak tree tickles the sky and a thick yew hedge marks the boundary. My heart races. This must be where the river is. Oh boy! Just like home. Then I remember *this* is now my home.

In the distance, there's a low rumble that becomes a clackety-clack. It gets louder as it draws closer. I feel vibrations through the ground. My nose is stung by a gush of air, ripe with hot metal, engine oil and rubber. I step back and bark a warning, then there's a fearful scream from the other side of the hedge. It tears by so fast it's gone in seconds, its bright eyes glaring at me through gaps in the foliage. My tail is up and curled over my back like a question mark, my legs wide set, then I charge forward and growl at the creature. I must defend us. I bark at Rose to move away, but she stands there laughing, her ponytail bobbing.

'It's all right, Monty, just a train. You're going to have to get used to it. The line's on the other side of the hedge.'

She strokes my head and I relax. Not sure about this train thing. Never met one before and until I've thoroughly sniffed it, I'll be on my guard.

Rose kneels down and looks me in the eye.

'The fence is pretty rotten and I can't afford to fix it. So I need you to promise me you won't run away.' She scratches behind my ear.

Oh yeah! Up a bit, that's it. A bit more. Ah yes, bliss!

'Okay?'

For you, anything! I promise.

Unless . . .

Truth be told, I have an Achilles Heel. My nose might be my greatest asset but it's also the chink in my furry armour. I'm a food addict. There. I've said it. An addict. Food's the reason I'm no longer a guide dog. The most embarrassing moment of my life. But then, that's how I met the Professor. Life's confusing, isn't it?

'Hungry?' Rose asks.

Something tells me we're going to get along just fine.

I walk back to the house, so close to Rose she almost trips over me. She unlocks the stable-style kitchen door. It scrapes the worn yellow and brown, diamond-patterned lino floor. I am hit by a smorgasbord of smells: some very old indeed. What better place to inhale the house's history than the kitchen? Rose's scent is the newest: vanilla and honey, pepper-mint and the sea. She must've spent her childhood near the ocean because the sea is part of her make-up now. But her clothes carry the odours of her work: bitter coffee, stale cigarettes, plastic chairs in over-heated rooms and someone else's sweat that's tinged with the vinegary smell of fear. Ever wondered why your dog sniffs you when you come home? He wants to know where you've been and who you've met.

There's a loud ringing coming from Rose's pocket. I feel her body tense. She answers.

'Sir?' Her hand trembles.

I look around, searching for the threat, ready to defend her.

A man yells down the phone. 'Sidebottom, get in here now!'

Chapter Two

If you asked Rose Sidebottom to describe herself she would say she was of average height with a forgettable face, had average mousy hair tied back in a plain ponytail, and graduated from police college with an average pass.

However, there were two things about her that were far from average. One was her embarrassing surname. She'd heard every single bottom joke ever invented. Her school days had been plagued by taunts, police college with practical jokes, and it was now proving a handicap in her struggle to be taken seriously as a trainee detective constable. The other unusual thing about Rose was her instinctive ability to know when somebody was lying. A tingling feeling, much like pins and needles, would spread from her hands and feet all over her body. As a child, it had sucked big time. Rose knew from a very young age that there was no Father Christmas or Tooth Fairy, that thunder wasn't God moving His furniture, that at twelve her best friend had betrayed her secret crush on a boy to a gang of girls who hated her, and that her father was cheating on her mother. Life would have been so much easier simply not knowing.

However, as a police officer, her in-built lie-detector had sent her conviction rate through the roof, and at one domestic incident, she'd saved the life of a woman whose polite and helpful boyfriend had claimed all was well, as the woman lay bruised and bloodied in the back room. Her skill for ferreting out the truth helped her earn a coveted position on the Major Crime Team, much to the surprise and envy of her uniformed colleagues.

But it hadn't saved her from committing the mother of all cock-ups earlier that evening, which is why she now stood in front of DCI Craig Leach, wishing the ground would open up and swallow her. Her boss sat behind his messy desk; his shaved snooker-ball head welded to a heavy-set, bull-like body without, so it appeared, a neck.

Rose tried not to fidget.

'Do you realise what you've done?' he said, his voice a low rumble, his Mancunian accent as strong as ever, even after twenty years working down South. He didn't wait for her answer. He yelled, red-faced.

'You've blown Operation Nailgun!' Boom! Like a volcano erupting.

Nailgun was a Drugs Squad operation.

He continued, 'DI Morgan's livid, and I don't blame him. Five months of surveillance up in smoke!'

The flats of his fat-fingered hands slammed down on the desk, the piles of files quivering. Rose jumped, and knew that through the glass wall behind her, DI Pearl heard every word. Why was he still here? They'd been working non-stop on the Salt case all weekend. Everyone else had gone home to get some much needed rest.

'Sir, I had no idea who he was. I'm not involved in Operation Nailgun.'

'You walked straight past two undercover detectives in their car, and then Gary and Meg in the pub. They couldn't believe it, and nor can I. What are you? Blind?'

'Sir, I barely know Gary and Meg.'

The Drugs Squad was on level four, Major Crime on two.

Rose naturally spoke quietly, with a soft West Country accent, unwilling to engage in the loud banter and often coarse language of her fellow detectives. She knew Leach found her voice irritatingly mouse-like, so she raised it as best she could. But it sounded more like a croak.

'I stopped at the pub to have a quick drink on my way home. To be honest, sir, I was a bit shaken up.' She paused. Was she sounding weak?

Leach nodded. 'Go on.'

'Sir, he started chatting me up. I was flattered. He's a good-looking bloke. Charming.'

'Ray Summers? The charming bastard deals in Class A drugs. The real nasty stuff. He's . . . no, he *was* our only lead in an international drugs trafficking ring. Summers was meeting the local gang leader tomorrow. One more day and we'd have had those scumbags behind bars. Do you see what you've done?'

'I'm sorry, sir.' Close to tears, she stared at the floor.

'What the hell did you tell him?'

'Nothing, sir. I didn't even tell him I was a police officer.'

Revealing her job sent any potential boyfriend running for the hills. It was a more effective turn-off than body odour, flatulence or a history of chain-saw massacres.

'Well, you blew their cover, didn't you! They raid his warehouse a half hour later and find a big fat nothing. No drugs, no computers, no financials, and he's disappeared.'

Rose swallowed hard. Her career was about to end before it had even begun, because of one stupid mistake. Why-oh-why hadn't she just picked up Monty and taken a bottle of plonk home with her instead?

'How did he know you were a detective?'

'When I went to the loo, I left my handbag behind. He must've gone through it and found my warrant card.'

Leach raised surprisingly bushy eyebrows, given his scalp was so hairless. They reminded Rose of furry caterpillars on a white cabbage. 'Never let your warrant card out of your sight, Sidebottom. This is your last chance.'

'Sorry, sir, it won't happen again.'

'Did he at least say anything that could help us find him?'

'He was on the phone when I got back from the loo. He ended the call when he saw me, but I heard him say something about a shipment. That it had to be stopped. Then he made his excuses and left in a hurry. I didn't put two and two together until Meg came over and gave me an ear-bashing.'

Leach had his hands clasped together on the desk so tightly that his puffy knuckles turned purple.

'So, the Super chews my ear off, Morgan wants you back on the beat, and God knows what your team will think of you. Great result!' He threw his weight into the back of his chair. The bags under his eyes were darker and puffier than usual. She felt sorry for him. 'If your colleagues don't trust you, you're no use to them or me. You need to fix this. Start by apologising to Morgan and don't put a foot wrong on the Salt case, you hear?'

'Yes, sir.'

Leach placed his hands behind his head and studied her flushed face.

'Rose, are you sure you really want to do this job?' His voice had softened. 'We get to see people at their worst. Doing terrible things. Murder, torture, abuse. It's long hours, the public and the media generally hate us, and it's hard on relationships.'

Rose glanced at his ring finger where a wedding band had once been, leaving a permanent dent in his pudgy skin.

'Yes, sir.' She looked straight into his eyes. 'I've always wanted to be a detective.'

Leach tilted his head to one side. 'God, you remind me of Kay when she was your age. Stubborn and naïve.' He smiled, which was rare and therefore unnerving. His teeth were surprisingly small for such a large head. Like baby teeth. 'She found it tough going at first, you know. She was sensitive, found the blood and guts hard to deal with. But she was dogged. Wouldn't give up. Became the best DI I've ever known.'

'I want to be like Kay, sir. I know I can do it.'

Leach nodded as he stood. 'Maybe. But this is a big cock-up, Rose. I'm increasing your supervision and assigning you to an experienced DI . . .'

Opening his office door, Leach beckoned Dave Pearl inside.

A slick dresser, fancied by most of the female officers and popular with the lads, he sauntered into the office as if it were his own.

'Dave is your new mentor.'

Just when Rose thought it couldn't get any worse, it just did. Dave's tanned forehead creased into a frown as his eyes, the colour of tarnished silver, looked down at her with contempt.

'All right with you, Dave?' asked Leach.

13

When Pearl realised he was being watched, he produced an affable smile. 'Of course, boss.'

'You do what Dave asks and nothing more, you got that?' said Leach, picking up his coat. 'Right, I'm off.'

He strode out, leaving Rose alone with Pearl. Pearl's smile vanished.

'Well, well, so the chosen one's fallen from grace,' he mocked.

Despite being almost a foot shorter, she squared up to him. 'Guv, I'm very sorry about what's happened and I'm going to work extra hard on the Salt case. I know I've got a lot to do to win back people's respect.'

He shook his head. 'You know, I just don't think it's going to be that easy. I mean, who's going to want to work with you after this?'

'If you give me a chance, the others will follow, sir.'

Pearl leaned closer. 'You're not up to the job. Never were.'

'I know what this is really about. Just because I didn't want to go for a drink with you . . .'

'You've got it all wrong, lady. Why would I want to go out with someone who drops her knickers for a drugs trafficker?'

She balled her hand into a fist but punching him would instantly end her career.

'How dare you!'

'Just because you're Kay Lloyd's niece, doesn't mean you've got any talent. Remember that.'

Chapter Three

Rose left me in the kitchen with a water bowl and a promise she wouldn't be long. She kept her promise, but the yelling man has upset her: Rose hangs her head like a dog that's been scolded. I nudge her leg and lean against her, wagging my tail in support. She bends down, taking me in a hug.

'What a mess!' she sighs into my fur.

Mess? From under her armpit I look around the kitchen. It's not *that* much of a mess and I've already tidied up a Marmite-coated crust I found under the table earlier. In the sink are some Chinese take-away food cartons that, thankfully, haven't been washed and could do with a good licking. I'm happy to oblige, all in the name of orderliness, naturally. Sadly, there's not a whiff of McDonald's – my absolute favourite. Every dog's absolute favourite, truth be told. I just wish McDonald's would sell doggie-burgers, or better still, open up separate doggie cafés. How about Big Barker burgers, Woofer Wraps and Puppyccinos? Oh dear, I'm salivating at the thought, all over Rose's shoes.

'Let's get you fed,' she says.

She sounds chipper, but her anxiety thrums like a dragon-fly's wings.

From a bag, she pulls out some dog food tins. How do I know they're for me? They have an ecstatic Labrador on the label, that's how! They only grin like that when there's food in the offing. When Rose opens a cupboard door, I smell wafts of joyful laughter, roses, ripe tomatoes and rich earthy smells. I wonder if this might have been Aunt Kay, as her scent is faint, and scents fade with time. However, the kitchen's surfaces hold a lot of stories. From the scratched skirting boards I pick up a whiff of Legless the Dachshund, mostly washed away after many years of mopping. A farmhouse oak table has deep gouges and is marked with ink, from a time when this house was full of children. The only thing that seems new is the washing machine that's winking its red light, stuffed full of clean washing waiting to be hung up to dry.

'How much should I give you?' Rose asks, peering into an open tin of meaty goodness. 'Never had a dog as big as you, Monty.'

How much? All of it!

She looks down at me and I lick my lips. She shrugs.

'All of it, I guess.'

We're really bonding!

She scoops out the gooey yumminess into a bowl, adds a white tablet, then places the bowl on the floor. She is surprised when I wait for the command.

'It's okay. Eat it.'

I wolf down my meal fast because you never know when another dog will turn up. I then lick the bowl until I swear

I can taste the ceramic glaze. Rose hangs her washing up on the garden line strung up between two trees and I help by stealing socks so she has to chase me to get them back. What fun! When the last sock is coerced from my mouth, Rose is breathless and laughing. She gets me in a playful head lock.

'You're naughty, but you've cheered me up no end.'

Glad to be of service!

Now to focus on *her* meal. She chops chicken breast and some vegetables. I breathe in the delicious sweet fleshiness of chicken sizzling in a wok and look up at her, eyes wide with hope. Her mobile rings just as I have her in my hypnotic gaze. Damn! I swear she was about to give me some.

Rose peers at the phone's screen and looks relieved. At least it's not the shouting man again. Instead, oinking noises are coming from the phone.

'Mum, that's never been funny,' Rose sighs.

Is her mother a pig? Surely not?

'Come on dear, what do you expect? You've joined the pigs.' Another oink.

I haven't seen Rose with a single pig so I have no idea what the crazy woman is talking about.

Rose's voice falters. 'Maybe not for much longer.'

'That's wonderful news! I can't wait to tell your father.'

'No it's not, Mum! I love what I do. But I've ruined a surveillance operation and my boss thinks I'm a blithering idiot. Can't say I blame him.'

Her heartbeat is up, her pale face flushed like sunburn. I nuzzle her leg.

'Don't you let those bastards bully you. I know what they're capable of, remember. I've been on the receiving end of their brutality.'

Rose rolls her eyes. 'Give it a rest, mum. You've never even been arrested.'

The succulent meaty smell is too much. Two long strands of my drool are competing to reach the floor first. But because I tilt my head, one stalactite of saliva lands on Rose's knee.

'Oh, Monty,' she says, wiping it away with paper towel.

'So you have a boyfriend? I was beginning to wonder if there was any hope.'

'Monty's a dog.' She lets go of the spatula and strokes my head.

A big sigh from the pig. 'Why aren't I surprised! You know, Allen still asks after you.'

'He has bad breath and doesn't wear deodorant.'

'Well, at least he has a conscience.'

The chicken is burning. This is terrible. I nudge her hand.

'Mum, gotta go. Just serving dinner. I'll call soon.'

She serves her meal and eats at the table. I lie at her feet and keep an eye out for any titbits she might drop by mistake. As we say, *If it's on the ground, it belongs to the hound.* But Rose is a tidy eater. Next time I'll be upping the cute factor and begging. Paddy always used to give me a little piece at the very end of his meal. Except when he ate curry. He used to say that curry made my farts smell like cow dung, which didn't seem a problem to me but made Paddy screw up his nose and make *Phwoar* noises.

As Rose works at her laptop, I lie at her feet. I hear claws scratching wood and see a squirrel peering in through the kitchen window. It stretches out a claw and taps a Neighbourhood Watch sticker on the glass. I lift my head and it bolts. What a strange little fellow! Distracted, I almost miss a photo of my beloved Paddy in a scientific journal

Rose is reading. He's looking mighty fine in his best suit. I love the way his eyebrows and moustache are dark, but his beard and hair are almost white. I guess it's the equivalent of a dog's muzzle going white with age. The corners of his eyes are full of wrinkles because he smiles a lot and his eyes are a rich brown and welcoming like hot chocolate. I hear a whimper and realise it's me. Rose looks down and strokes my head. It's very soothing. The photo disappears from her screen but his face stays with me.

I imagine Paddy's house all dark and lifeless, and my doggie duvet near the back door, complete with a very grubby, and therefore exactly-how-I-like-it, fluffy yellow duck. It pongs to perfection. Once, Paddy placed my manky friend in the washing machine. It was a front loader, so just in time I snatched it away and hid it behind some hollyhocks. Even worse, every now and again, Paddy would insist on washing my doggie duvet cover. We'd argue over it, as I held one end in my jaws and Paddy hung on to the other. Of course, Paddy was the boss so I'd let go eventually, but I could never understand why he'd want to wash away my blissful cocktail of stink. Let me explain.

My bed is an aromatic archive of my adventures, places I've been, animals and people I've met, and even old bones I've chewed. Ah, those bones! Most important of all, it's a heady history of Paddy himself. Every time he touched my bed, he left his loving scent, as well as details of where he'd been, who he'd touched and what he'd eaten. My short-term memory is as sharp as a puppy's canines. But, my long-term memory is as poor as a where-the-hell-did-I-put-my-nuts squirrel. So, my bed holds my long-term memories for me, which means I can revisit them whenever I wish. All it takes is a quick snuffle. Wash my bed and you wash away all those fond recollections – gone forever. The result? Olfactory amnesia. Very distressing. How I long to bury my nose in my doggie duvet and inhale all those happy times.

'Goodnight, Monty,' Rose says, startling me.

I open my eyes to find she has created a makeshift bed of cushions.

'I'll collect your old bed as soon as I can,' she says. 'This'll have to do for now.'

I sniff the cushions and jerk my head back. Lavender, moth balls and sickness and . . . oh dear. Someone was once very ill in this house. And sad. Sadness has a scent too; it's like decaying rose petals.

Chapter Four

I rest my jowl on one paw and try closing my eyes. I am tired, but can't sleep. I miss Paddy so much and want to be with him. My eyes spring open at the pitter-patter of tiny claws on the floor. I smell dustbins on a hot day, rotting fruit, greasy food wrappers and, strangely, a hint of hot metal, engine oil and rubber, just like the train. It can only be one thing, though: a rat. I creep towards the source of the sound. It is dark but I don't need lights to see where I'm going. There is a small hole in the skirting board to the right of the larder door. Sticking out of that small hole is a rotund rat's bottom. Its back legs are scrabbling on the lino's worn and slippery surface. I can hear muttering.

'Need to go on a diet,' she says, with a high-pitched squeak, tail wriggling like a worm. Or what's left of her tail. She appears to have lost half of it. I'm guessing in a trap.

I was a young pup when I discovered how much big'uns hate rats. I'd been fostered to a family who were preparing me for guide dog school. This was in Windsor and my foster dad, John Collum, was a gardener at the castle. You may know something about Windsor Castle's history – prisoners in towers, political intrigues, sieges, royal weddings, and the 1992 fire that was supposedly an accident; the canine wee-vine says otherwise. But most big'uns don't know about the doggie shenanigans both past and present. The royal Corgis are master conspirators and escape-artists who regularly make a break for McDonald's on the high street. The footmen have to disguise themselves as ordinary folk and catch them before they make headlines in the *Sun*. How do I know this? When the Family wasn't in residence John let me join him in the castle grounds. That was when I first met the royal canines and first saw rats in traps, many dead or dismembered. I'll never forget it.

'Are you stuck?' I ask the fat, furry bottom.

Her squeak is ear-splitting and she bursts out of the hole, stubby tail first, like a cork from a champagne bottle. She sees me and does the kind of turn I've seen stunt car drivers do on TV – a hand-brake turn I think it's called. Then she bolts.

'Wait! I won't hurt you. Just want to talk,' I say, jogging along after her at a leisurely pace.

She tries to escape through a gap under the door, fails, and makes a dash for it in the opposite direction. This goes on for a while, backwards and forwards across the lino until I decide to sit in the middle of the kitchen and just watch her scurrying to and fro, a bit like watching a tennis match. Eventually she stops darting about and leans against a table leg, gasping for breath.

'Mate, you're killing me,' she says.

'I'm not going to kill you,' I reply. 'I've been sitting here, just watching, in case you hadn't noticed.'

Her bulbous, ball-bearing eyes assess me. 'What do you want, then?' she asks, her nose and gossamer whiskers twitching constantly.

'Nothing, really. My name's Monty and Rose adopted me today.'

'What you done then? Got kicked out, did you? Sent to the pound?'

Her breathing is less frantic and she rests her pink paws on her pot belly. But her stare is penetrating.

I look away. 'My master was killed by another big'un,' I say. 'I tried to defend him. I really did . . .'

I howl. I have to. I don't know any other way. It's just what we do. In the distance, another dog hears me and howls back, in an Oprah-like, I-hear-your-pain way. When I look down again, the rat is sitting near one of my paws and stroking my fur. Because she is so small, it feels like a feather, and it's very relaxing.

'There, there, you poor thing,' she says. 'I'm really sorry to hear that. You lot are very loyal to your masters, so this must be hard for you, but I'm sure you did everything you could.'

I still can't find words. Careful not to squash my new friend, I place my muzzle between my two front paws on the floor. She continues to stroke my fur.

'Name is Betty Blabble. Nice to meet you, and look, sorry I was so suspicious earlier, but you're sorta big, you know. Even for one of your lot. Gave me a shock, is all.'

'I don't kill other animals. No need, since I'm always fed. Might have had fun chasing a few in my time, but that's all. You're safe with me.'

She peers into one of my eyes. It occurs to me that she can probably see her full reflection.

'You know, I think you're a good egg,' she says, nodding.

Her twitching whiskers touch my muzzle. My ears wriggle, as they do whenever I feel ticklish. She laughs, which sounds like nails scratching a chalk board, but it cheers me up.

'Just so happens you're in luck,' she continues. 'Rose might work for the filth, but she's a good 'un. First copper I ever met who is. I only moved here a few days ago so I'm still getting to know the place, but she always has enough food in the pantry and doesn't seem bothered with a few house guests, including yours truly.'

I lift my head, intrigued. 'Why don't you like the police?'

'Well now. That's a long story, but all I'll say is that I've had a few run-ins with the Law. In my Eurotunnel days. Turned over a new leaf since,' she announces, nodding once for emphasis.

'Which Law?' I can't help asking. 'French or English?'

I haven't met a Eurotunnel rat before but from her slight Kentish twang I'm guessing she's spent more time at the British end of the tunnel. Who hasn't heard of the vicious tunnel turf wars? Big'uns believed the damage caused by the bitter rodent rivalry was due to human vandalism. How wrong they were.

There's a hard glint in her eyes as she makes the zip-it sign across her mouth. I take the hint and change the subject.

'Rose is going to find the man who killed my master. She's working the case. *And* she rescued me from the vet's. So in my book, she's the best.' Betty nods, whiskers tickling my nose again, my ears twitching in response. 'I want to help her find Paddy's killer, but don't know where to start.'

'So, this killer. Did you get a good sniff of him?' she asks. 'A him or her?'

'Definitely male. And I got a good smell *and* taste. I took a chunk out of his arm.'

Betty holds up her tiny paw to high-five me. I lift mine, so my black pads hover near her. She smacks hers onto mine.

'Good on ya,' she says. 'Proud of you.'

'So if I could get near enough to sniff the suspect, I'd know immediately if he was Paddy's killer.'

'Now we're talking,' says Betty. 'Can't understand why big'uns don't use your lot more often to solve crime. Your super-snorters could save a hell of a lot of time. I say, let the police dogs get on with it and fire all those useless coppers.'

I decide not to point out that Rose would be one of those coppers getting fired.

'Paddy once told me we have the best sense of smell of any mammal, except for a bear.'

'I'll have you know, Mr Monty, rats can beat dogs in one sniffing category. Landmines.' She nods her head again for emphasis.

I am taken aback and shift my paws, unintentionally knocking Betty over, who tumbles like a roly-poly Weeble.

'I'm sorry, are you okay?'

She brushes her fur down. 'Take more than that to worry me. Just try not to do it again, will ya?'

'So what did you mean about sniffing landmines?'

'Rats are the best at finding landmines. Don't know why, but it's a scientific fact. I know 'cause a mate of mine works for the army and he finds them.'

'Never knew that.'

'So,' Betty says, sitting up on her hind legs, nose raised as if she has the scent of a plan. 'Next question: do they have any suspects?'

'I don't know. I've been at the vet's since it happened.'

Betty stares at the gash of seventeen stitches; my chest fur has been shaved.

'Well, mate, if we're going to catch us a killer, you're going to need to tell me *everything*.'

Seems like *we* are now a criminal-catching partnership. My heart lifts. I have a buddy to help me. Then it drops like a stone in a pond. I don't want to relive the worst moment of my life. It makes me feel sick. I get up and pace around the table.

'I can't.'

'Go on love, tell me what happened.'

Chapter Five

I look out of the window at the full moon. It reminds me of a triple cream brie I stole one Christmas from Paddy's nibbles platter. Betty and I sit close together on the kitchen floor, bathed in the milky moonlight.

'Go on,' she says. 'You can do it.'

I have relived the attack on my master many times in my head, always wondering the same thing. Could I have saved him? But I haven't told anybody about what happened. I lick my nose, psyching myself up. My heart races. I swallow hard and begin my tale.

'I knew there was something wrong, even before I saw the man.

Perhaps it was the way the car crawled down our single-track lane, like that creepy cat two doors down who stalks birds. I heard the tyres crunch on the gravel and thought it odd, since our elderly neighbour, Mr Grace, never has evening visitors, and we weren't expecting any. I should have paid more attention, but I didn't because I was up to my chest in cool river water, facing upstream, searching for fish. Once I'm fishing, I'm focused.

Paddy was sitting in the back garden working on his laptop as usual, sipping his after-dinner wine, the clink of the glass on the table top a familiar sound. Our home was a semi-detached, red-brick cottage, with low ceilings and narrow leadlight windows at the end of a cul-de-sac. The house was small – a two up, two down – but the garden was canine-heaven: quarter of an acre of lush green lawn, loads of flowerbeds to dig up, trees that dropped a plentiful supply of sticks to chew, and, best of all, on the other side of an easily jumpable gate, was the river.

So there I was enjoying the currents tickling my belly when I spotted a cracker of a fish no more than a few inches from my right paw. Just in time I remembered not to wag my tail. I've learned the hard way that the ripples frighten fish away. I opened my jaw, ready to pounce, grizzly-bear-style. Then I heard our front doorbell ring. Paddy didn't, but my hearing is much better than his. I should have gone to investigate then, but the fish was tantalisingly close.'

I drop my head, ears flattened.

Betty interjects. 'You weren't to know Paddy was in danger. Stop blaming yourself.'

I shake my head and whimper. I should have known. It was my job to protect him. I swallow and press on with my tale.

'I pounced, head into the water, mouth clamped down on what I hoped was a fish. But the slippery sucker zipped off and all I was left with was a mouthful of leaf litter and a nose full of water. When I'd stopped sneezing, I glanced up the garden path. I saw a man I didn't recognise walking down the side passage. His face was covered with some kind of dark sock with holes in it for his eyes and mouth. Paddy stood abruptly, knocking his chair backwards. I was too far away to smell his fear but I knew instantly he was in danger.

"What do you want?" Paddy said, his voice shaky.

The man said nothing but raised a single gloved finger to his lips. He was telling Paddy to be quiet, in the same way Paddy used to tell me to be quiet when I got carried away barking at squirrels.

I scrambled as fast as I could for the bank, but the water clung to me like porridge and I slipped on a stone. I got up, raced through the open gate and up the path. I detected the sour smell of Paddy's terror. I heard his heart beating too fast.

I bark. "Run," I told him, "Run"

But he didn't run. Perhaps because he was an old man: in dog years he was eight, in big'uns years, fifty-six. Or perhaps because he was paralysed with fear. I'll never know. I accelerated, my teeth bared, eyes locked onto the intruder, tail rigid and pointed at the sky. My growl was deep and rumbling.

The intruder saw me and his body tensed. Yet he didn't flee. I was not a surprise. Through the slit in his head-sock I saw him slowly lick his lips as if he wanted to eat me. For a split second I was confused about why he didn't seem afraid, but I kept coming. The man had a knife in his hand. He stepped forward and plunged the blade into my master's body. I roared in anger. As I leapt over plant pots to reach him, I inhaled his scent: the acrid tang of funny cigarettes, damp walls, some kind of stinky food not even I would want to eat, and a disease. One I have never smelled before. It reminded me of an insect, but I couldn't place which one.

Paddy opened and closed his mouth in shock. The attacker pulled out the blade. My dear master clutched his wound and fell to his knees.

"No!" I bellowed, as I jumped at the masked man.

He turned and swept his arm across my body. The blade sliced into my chest, slashing through skin and muscle. I yelped at the searing pain, but the force of my leap drove me forward and I crashed into him, knocking him onto his back. I rolled away as quickly as I could, afraid he would strike again. He missed by inches, and when the knife hit the ground I hurled myself at him. I bit deep into the arm holding the weapon and shook it with all my strength, tearing his flesh. It was his turn to yelp now. His flimsy jacket was no protection at all. I drew upon all my fury to dig my teeth deeper and deeper. The attacker dropped his knife, but then he kicked me so hard in the stomach, I had to let go. I managed to tear away part of his sleeve. I collapsed on my side, desperately trying to catch a breath. The left side of my face was sticky with blood oozing from my chest wound.

The man cradled his mauled lower arm. I noticed part of a tattoo. He spun around, searching for his knife. I was lying on it. I stayed still. He glanced at Professor Salt, who lay motionless, eyes wide open, as if the setting sun was the most beautiful thing he had ever seen. But I knew my dear master saw nothing. Those kind brown eyes were blind and cold, like marbles. The killer knew it too. Every time I breathed, it was as if I was being kicked again, but I managed to lift my head and snarl. I knew it was a weak snarl, but he didn't. He backed away, grabbed Paddy's laptop from the garden table, took his wine glass and entered the house. For the first time I noticed he was wearing a backpack. He slammed the back door shut, in case I followed. But I wasn't leaving my master.

I heard the killer move through the house to the study – I knew exactly which creaky floorboard he stepped on – and the rasp of desk drawers yanked open, then dull thuds. He was throwing something heavy in his bag. Then paper files slid against the fabric too. He moved to the sitting room, drawers thrown on the floor. Then the clank of metal.

I crawled over to Paddy and licked his face. Perhaps he was alive after all? I so wanted to be wrong. I did it again and again and his head jerked with each increasingly desperate lick. But his eyes didn't flicker.

I whimpered, "Wake up! Please wake up!"

I placed my snout above his mouth and sniffed for breath, hoping to feel the slightest waft of air. Nothing. I howled, my nose pointing to the darkening sky. I howled in pain and grief, as we have done for centuries. I howled because I can't weep like big'uns. I howled because I love my master more than anything.

I stopped when I heard the front door open and shut and the man's feet crunched on the gravel drive. A car door opened. But not quietly. It was metal screeching on metal. I smelt diesel as he drove away, and heard a tink, tink, tink of something rattling.

I grew weaker and dizzier as the pool of blood from my wound grew. But I would not leave Paddy. He was my world and someone had taken him from me. I howled again, but my head felt so very heavy. I rested it on Paddy's chest, his white shirt drenched in blood where the blade had pierced his no longer beating heart. I vowed to myself that if I was to live I would never rest until I found the man who took him from me.'

Chapter Six

A wall clock marks our silence as the second hand jerks around the face. I slump to the floor. Betty sidles up to me and lies, belly down, prostrate along the length of my paw, gripping it tightly as if it were a life raft in a big sea. Her head droops.

'You poor, poor thing,' she replies, stroking my fur, as if she is paddling her raft. 'And poor Mr Salt.' Then she peers up at me, nose twitching. 'Can you tell me what happened next?'

I return to my story.

'Some time later, I became conscious of an old, quivering voice. Sounded like Mr Grace next door, but my eyes were shut. I opened my jaw and made a sound, a whimper, or at least I thought I did. I lapsed back into unconsciousness and heard Paddy calling my name. He's alive! I rushed towards him and he knelt down and hugged me. I tucked my head into his chest and snuffled.

"It's okay, boy, I'm here," he said.

We walked side-by-side along the river bank. He threw a

ball into the water and I charged after it, enjoying the river's coolness. I was floating. No effort, no paddling, I was light as air. The surface glistened in the sun and I heard the words, "Fetch. There's a good boy."

A piercing and repetitive wailing burst into my dream. It threatened to drag me back to reality. I wanted to stay with Paddy. But the siren grew louder and more insistent. Then footsteps, urgent voices, big'uns shouting. I felt a warm hand on my neck. It was hesitant, the person, perspiring. She didn't like dogs, I could tell. Was she trying to hurt me? I managed to shift my head a little, which was still resting on Paddy's chest. The hand was withdrawn in an instant and the woman leapt backwards like a startled cat.

I mustered a weak growl. I wasn't dead yet and wouldn't let anyone touch my master if I could stop it.

"Dog's still alive!" the woman said.

Someone else bent over me. "Got to move him. The man could be too."

I opened both eyes, or tried to, but the lashes touching Paddy's chest were glued together with blood.

"No," I growled, and tried to sit up, but the growl came out as more of a moan.

I recognised the police uniforms and those funny chequered hat bands that look like reflective dog collars. My upper body was lifted from my master's chest, but my hind quarters stayed more-or-less where they had been. The result was I lay next to Paddy, my head facing him. The ambulance crew crouched over him searching for signs of life. A machine beeped and Paddy jolted, but his eyes still stared vacantly at the sky.

I heard, "Get a vet. Dog's bleeding to death by the looks of it. He's a surviving witness, poor fellow."

"Witness? It's just a dog!"

More voices. More sirens, car doors slammed, feet pounding up and down the side path. Someone issued orders in that sharp tone of a big'un in charge.

Another man kneeled next to me. His shoes were covered in blue booties and he wore a white body suit. He had black spiky hair and large hands. I knew he was a vet from the smell of disinfectant and various animals he carried on him. Several cats, a guinea pig, a tortoise (now, there's an odd creature), dogs, even a Jack Russell I think I recognised called Flash, and cows. Lots of cows. Always know when a vet's been near cows. That smell of shit stays with them for days. Of course, big'uns can't smell it after they've washed, but we can.'

Betty nods knowingly. 'Cows really stink.'

I didn't want to say that rats are high up on the animal kingdom stink-ometer, too. Best not to offend her. I go on with my tale.

'The vet patted my head.

"It's all right. I'm not going to hurt you," he said, then he lifted my lip. "Lip colour's not good. He's lost a lot of blood." He drew closer. "There's some fabric caught between his teeth. Could be from the assailant," he said, looking at Paddy lying next to me.

As the vet listened to my heart through a tube, a small female hand gently touched my brow. I liked her smell. It reminded me of a vanilla milkshake at the seaside. She stroked my face to relax me as she read my name tag. She was not afraid of me at all. It was Rose.

"Monty," she said, then glanced at the vet. "Malcolm, we need SOCO to swab his mouth."

She waved someone over, also wearing an all-in-one white suit and small white mask.

"Looks like he bit the killer," Rose said to the lady, then to the vet, "Can you hold his mouth open while we do this?"

"I'll give him some pain relief first."

I felt a slight sting in the scruff of my neck and within seconds I was drowsy again. Before I knew it, strong hands had prized my jaw open and the SOCO lady had removed something stuck between a canine and my back teeth.

Rose patted me, her disposable gloves bloody.

"It's okay, Monty, you've been very brave and we'll take care of Professor Salt now."

I looked up into a heart-shaped face and large blue eyes. I saw her properly for the first time. Her smile was genuine and in human terms she had a natural kind of translucent-skinned beauty. None of that greasy make-up stuff that many women wear. Doesn't taste good when you lick their faces, I can tell you. It's hard to tell the age of a big'un but I guessed Rose was no more than twenty-one. Much younger than everyone else there.

Distracted by her soothing presence, I didn't see the vet approaching with a muzzle until it was too late. I pulled my head back and managed to lift a paw to push the muzzle away, but it was already fastened. I struggled, trying to cry out, "No, I must stay with Paddy." But they didn't understand.

Rose said, "Must you use that? After all he's been through? He won't bite."

I tried to hold onto Paddy's shirt but I couldn't because of the muzzle. Malcolm placed his arms under me.

"Best to be safe," he replied as he lifted me, which is no mean feat given I'm thirty-eight kilos.

"Would you look at that!" Rose said, looking down. "Dog was lying on the murder weapon. Good boy."

I tried to wriggle out of Malcolm's grip, but the agony was too much, despite the painkiller.

"It's okay, boy, you'll be okay," Rose said, her voice soft as a puppy blanket.

As Malcolm carried me away I glanced back to see people in white suits walking towards Paddy. Rose was about to pick up the knife but stopped.

"Yes, take it," I urged.

"Sir, over here," she called.

People stepped out of his way. Eyes followed him. The man in charge. He reminded me of a Bulldog I once had a nasty encounter with. He placed the knife in a bag, nodded, and walked away.

A tall blond man with slicked-back hair like an over-groomed show dog shouted at her, "Sidebottom! Over here! Leave that mangy dog. And mind where you step."

She looked in my direction and sighed, then strode towards the man who'd called her name. She referred to him as "guv". He directed Rose into the house and as she walked, he stared at her backside. The alpha male claiming the female. All swagger. I didn't like him at all.'

Chapter Seven

I glance down at Betty who is up on her hind legs, shadow boxing.

'Nasty toe-rag!' she exclaims, punching the air. 'How dare he! You're not mangy, you're a bleeding hero. You wait till I meet this big'un. I'll give him a nasty nip.'

'I'm no hero, Betty, and I'd rather you help me find the killer.'

'With pleasure, Mr Monty. I need a project to focus on. Will stop me worrying about my pups.'

'You're a mum?'

I dumbly look around as if her brood is huddled behind her.

'All left the nest, doing their own thing now. Miss them terribly.'

Betty slumps against my leg. Her whiskers droop. She looks glum.

'Must be difficult to let them go,' I say.

'That's the hardest thing. I can't help wondering if they're okay. Makes no difference they're my fifth litter. I love them just as much as my first.'

'And their dad? Is he with you?'

She leaps up. 'You must be joking. He's the reason I left the tunnel. Bastard!'

I clearly touched a sore point so I stay quiet.

'Right, no point moping about. As my dear old mum used to say, "Don't get down, get up and at 'em." So, let's get on with solving this murder.' She scratches her head. 'The killer's scent? You'd know it again?'

'How could I forget?' I snort, reliving the smell. 'A stinky food, like rotten egg; damp walls; those funny cigarettes made from weeds; and a disease linked to an insect I've never come across before.'

'Do you mean he's been smoking weed?'

I look blankly at Betty.

'You know, makes big'uns giggle and eat lots.'

'I'm not sure about that. Sometimes Paddy would take me with him to the university and some of his students' clothes smelt of this weed.'

Betty nods sagely. 'And the disease? You think he's ill?'

'There is a sickness in him but I don't know what. It was like licking copper.'

'Do that often, do you?' Betty is giving me a worried look.

'Not really.'

'Okay, so we need to get your nose near some suspects. Sniff 'em out, so to speak. Hmm. How we going to do that?'

'That's my problem, you see. I'm not a police dog. I want to help, but how can I, if I'm stuck here?'

'Shush, shush, shush. Let me think. What has Rose said? Has she mentioned any names?'

I think back to earlier that evening when she collected me from the vet's. At first, all I remember is my excitement at being free of my cage and, once she was driving, all the amazing smells zooming past the open window so fast I could barely inhale them in time. I've always wondered why smells speed up when I'm in a car. Perhaps they're running, trying to keep up with the moving vehicle, a bit like dogs chasing a cyclist?

'Come to think of it,' I say, after the clock's second hand has twitched away a minute, 'someone rang Rose when she was driving. She said she couldn't believe a Larry somebody-or-other could be a murderer. Called him a . . . what was it? A small-time thief. That's it.'

'Larry who?'

I get up and have a good shake to clear my mind. Fur and slobber flies everywhere. Luckily the fall-out misses Betty but a few slippery blobs litter the lino floor.

'Larry Rice? Lice? No. Larry Ni . . . Nice! That's it. Larry Nice. I remember thinking he didn't sound nice at all.'

'Why's this bloke a suspect?'

'Not sure, but I heard the caller say they'd let him go.'

'Did they say where he lived?' she asks.

'Don't think so.'

'Then what we need is *The White Pages*. There's a copy on the hall table. We look up his address and pay him a visit.' Betty nods conclusively. But her brow slowly creases. 'Oops. We may have a slight problem.'

'What's that?'

'I've eaten the top right hand corner.'

'Of that big fat book?' I stare at her large stomach. No wonder she's so round!

She examines her claws, avoiding eye contact. 'I get peckish.'

I shake my head. 'It doesn't matter anyway. I can't leave here. I promised Rose I wouldn't run away.'

Betty tutt tutts. 'Oh you dogs are *so* domesticated. Think outside the square, will you? I get that you've been trained to take orders. But don't tell me you've never broken the rules. Come on! You must have.'

'I was a naughty pup. I mean, who isn't? Chewed a few shoes, stole food, peed on a trouser leg, that sort of thing. But I soon learned not to. And, okay, I'll admit to a few slip-ups since, but they weren't intentional. Not planned, like this. And they always involved food. I'm good as gold until I smell . . . well, anything meaty, to be honest. Then my mind gets fuzzy and I completely forget what I'm meant to be doing. It's a bit of a problem, really.'

Betty scurries up my leg and sits between my shoulder blades and whispers in my ear. 'There you go! Why's this any different? And finding Larry is for a good cause. After all, we're trying to catch a killer.'

I remember Paddy chuckling at a TV cartoon in which a tiny red devil sits on one shoulder and a little white angel sits on the other. Both are whispering in the big'un's ears. I glance round at Betty – my own little devil.

'Betty, you're asking me to break one of the canine *Ten Commandments*: Obey your master. I promised Rose I wouldn't run away. This is premeditated disobedience.'

She leans closer to my ear. 'But you're helping Rose solve the case. There are exceptions to every rule, Mr Monty.'

Betty just doesn't get it. Leaving Duckdown Cottage without Rose's permission is like *Mutiny on the Bounty*, *Spartacus* and *Rebel Without a Cause* all rolled up into one mega-pic of rebelliousness. It's all very well squeezing through the hedge, lapping up the left-overs of someone's lunch and then hopping back into the garden again. It's a whole other thing to travel far from home.

Betty scampers back down my leg and stands in front of me.

'You're not serious about these what-did-you-call-'em? Commandy things?'

'I am, Betty. *The Commandments* were laid down by our founding fathers, way back when the wolf nation first agreed to work alongside big'uns. They're our laws and are centuries old and every dog in the world is taught them as a pup. It's because of these laws that we have such a special relationship with people.'

'Yeah, but there's got to be a rule about keeping your master safe, surely?'

'That's number three: defend your master.'

'What's number one then?'

'Love your master.'

'Exactly!' Betty jumps up and down with excitement. 'So you did your very best to defend him. But now you need to demonstrate how much you love him and break the disobeying rule so you can hunt down his killer. You see where I'm coming from?'

I shake my head. 'If I run away to find this man, I risk being ostracised by my kind. Do you understand what that means?'

'Oh yes, only too well.'

Betty slumps against my leg like a deflated balloon and stares into space. Her moods go up and down very fast. I wait. Nothing happens, so I nudge her gently with my nose. No response.

'Are you an outcast, Betty?'

She looks sideways at me and sighs. 'Nah. Course not.' But she doesn't sound convincing.

Suddenly she jumps up and points a paw at the moon shining in through the kitchen window. I'm so surprised I rear up and bark.

'But you're not going to break any commandy things, Mr Monty, because Rose won't even know you've left the house. We've got all night, you see. This Larry bloke is bound to be a local, so you'll be back before she wakes up. So no harm done.'

I know what she's proposing isn't right but I'll never find Paddy's killer if I never leave the cottage.

'Look. At least let's find out where he lives before we make any decisions?' Betty urges. 'What harm can that do?'

I nod.

Chapter Eight

I position my front paws on a narrow hall table, my hind legs on the floor. A phone, notepad, mug of pens and a brick-thick copy of a phone directory lies, dusty and unused, on top. With my nose I push *The White Pages* until a corner of it hovers beyond the table top. Tiny bits of dust rain down on Betty and she sneezes, and again, and again. I take the big book in my mouth, careful to apply just enough pressure to keep it there, but not enough to tear the cover. It sure is heavy! As usual my mouth is full of slobber and there is a moment when I feel the directory slip, but I tilt my head just in time to stop it falling. Relieved, I quietly place it on the worn carpet.

'Allow me,' the rat says, spying the drool-coated cover. She slides on her belly across its surface, her fur like a cloth, wiping up the mess. 'Who needs Sainsbury's wipes when you've got me?'

She chuckles like raindrops on a tin roof.

I stare down at a well-chewed directory that's three years out of date. And it's not just the top right hand corner that's missing.

'I thought you said you'd only nibbled a corner?'

'Okay, so it's a little bit more than that.'

I give the book a shove with my nose and it falls open at the E section.

'Can you turn the pages? My paws are too big.'

'No problem, governor.'

Digging her front claws into the carpet, she kicks out her back legs, flipping the pages at lightning speed.

'Tell me when to stop. I can't read.'

'Slow down,' I say.

'How'd you learn reading then? The Professor teach you?'

'Yes, but don't tell anyone, Betty. Do you know what happens to animals that do anything out of the ordinary? They put them in cages and experiment on them. Betty, you've got to promise me you'll keep this to yourself.'

'I promise, on my pups' lives.' Betty is panting. 'This is like a bleeding workout, this is.'

She passes the Ls.

'Paddy was interested in how animals communicate, especially bees. He was a professor of bees, you see.'

'Didn't know they had such a thing.' She's slowing down.

'Paddy saw I was a fast learner, so he started teaching me the English language. I'm not talking about sounds and tones or basic commands. I mean letters of the alphabet.'

Betty stops kicking the pages and stares up at me, jaw open, her minuscule sharp teeth on display. I bet they could inflict a nasty nip. 'Bleeding Nora! Are you for real?'

'I got lucky; I had a brilliant teacher. But I get in a muddle when there are too many words, and Mr Google baffles me.'

'Who's Mr Google?'

'A very clever man who lives inside a computer,' I say. 'Can you keep going, Betty? We're nearly there.'

She turns round and kicks the pages again. She reaches the Ns.

'Stop!'

I follow the columns of names, addresses and phone numbers:

A Nice

Benjamin Nice

Mrs CE Nice

Then nothing. Just teeth marks and a circular hole.

'Oops,' she says. 'Did I eat Larry Nice?'

'Oh dear.'

'I never thought I was actually going to need to *use* it.'

Betty looks sheepish, if it's possible for a rat to look sheepish.

I sit and consider our situation. 'I guess we're going to have to use Rose's laptop, but I'm a klutz with the keyboard. I'm going to need some help.'

'Don't look at me,' says Betty. 'I can't spell and I wouldn't know one end of a computer from another. There wasn't much call for reading in them tunnels.'

'Then we need Dante. He's really fast with a keyboard.'

'Dante!' Betty laughs. 'Jeez, he must fancy himself with a name like that.'

'Well, he is a magpie.'

Betty jumps back as if she's touched hot metal. 'Magpie! What you doing being friendly with those devils? They're nasty buggers.'

'Dante's all right. He can be a bit snappy sometimes and he thinks he's a bit of an intellectual, but he's helped me out before.'

'A magpie?' Betty spits on the floor, although the gob is so small I can barely see it. 'Nah, I'll never trust one of them. They lie and steal and he'll probably try to eat me. Can't you use the laptop without him?'

'Why don't you give him a chance?'

'You guarantee my safety?'

'I'll keep you safe. But first we have to contact him.'

'So how do we do that?'

'A torch will do.'

'Where do we find one of them, then?'

'Paddy used to keep his in a cupboard under the sink.'

The kitchen cupboard doors have small circular knobs and I manage to pull them open, but there is no sign of a torch. There are two bins under the sink: everyday waste and recycling. Betty has crawled onto my shoulder and we both inhale the left-overs. Before I know it, Betty has dived head first into the general waste bin as if it were a swimming pool. I can't resist any longer and shove my nozzle in and ferret around for left-over chicken. I lick my muzzle. Now what was I doing?

I shake my head, realising I got side-tracked. Again.

'Betty, we must stay focused. Get out of there, will you?'

'You're one to talk,' she replies, part-buried under scraps.

It takes all my willpower to turn away but just as I'm free of the bins, the larder starts calling to me. Before I know it, my nose is stuck to the door as if it were a magnet. Ah, those biscuits smell so good.

'Come on,' Betty says, suddenly by my side, a little slimy with soy sauce in her fur. 'We'll have a big feast later. Let's keep looking for that torch.'

I plod from room to room, with Betty at my side. She has

to run to keep up. I discover a dusty dining room that hasn't been used for years; a cosy sitting room with faded sofa and armchairs; a very messy study with piles of books on the floor like mini skyscrapers; and an under-the-stairs loo. The toilet is making gurgling noises.

'Should it be doing that?' I ask.

Betty shrugs. 'No idea, mate.'

I peer up the stairs. I know they creak but I don't know where to tread yet to avoid the noise. I prick up my ears to check Rose is still asleep. Her breathing is slow and steady with the occasional little snore. Luckily, she's a deep sleeper.

'Best you don't come up, Betty. If Rose hears me, all she'll do is send me back to the kitchen. But, if she sees you, I'm not sure how she'll react.'

'I'll wait here then,' Betty replies, and plonks down on a threadbare section of carpet and starts licking the soy sauce off her fur.

I creep up, as quiet as a mouse – or a rat – although Betty has to be one of the chattiest rats I've ever met. I'm making good progress when the tread of a middle stair makes a rasping sound. I lift my paw and freeze. Rose's breathing is still a slow rhythm. She hasn't heard. I continue and hit another loose floorboard and this one makes a terrible screech. Again I freeze, paw raised. Rose's breathing pattern remains unchanged.

On the landing, I find only one door is shut: Rose's bedroom. There are three other rooms. One is a bathroom – I smell drains, toilet cleaner and fruity shampoo. I tiptoe in to find an ancient bath and basin in a very stylish yellow, something like the colour of vomit, and a toilet with a split wooden seat. Dangling from the chain-pull is a rubber basin plug instead of a wooden handle. There's a mirror above the basin, the surface mottled with damp. I peer up at some shelves littered with lotions. But I can't see a torch. A silvery face suddenly appears at the bathroom window and I jump backwards, almost knocking over the bin. It's that same squirrel again, tail flicking aggressively. What is his problem? To confuse me further, I swear I can hear him humming the theme tune for *Mission: Impossible*. I remember it from the time Paddy and I watched the movie together on TV.

I back out and am about to enter an empty bedroom when I detect something I've only ever come across once before: the smell of a human sickness that causes people to waste away and die. It's not easy to describe but it's like a mix of sunburnt human skin and rust. I back away. I really don't want to go in there and it takes all my willpower not to whimper. It's faint so I know the person isn't there any more. I pace round in circles, willing myself to get on with the search, and, holding my breath, I enter.

The room has curtains and a bedspread in matching florals. The double bed has a carved wooden bedhead. Dolls in dresses, with glass eyes and long eyelashes, are arranged on the bed near the pillows, and a tasselled lampshade over a reading lamp sits on the bedside table. On that table are two gardening books and on top of them are some reading glasses. I breathe.

I'm drawn to the many photographs on a chest of drawers, some faded, some in colour, some black and white. In them, the number of people gets fewer and fewer, as the woman who is in all the photos gets older and older. One particular photo stands out. It is of two women arm in arm and both look to be about Rose's age. One is tall with dark curly hair, wearing dungarees that flare out at the bottom. The other is of petite build, with mousy brown hair that flicks outwards on either side of a central parting, and pale blue eyes. She's wearing chunky gold earrings and a skirted fawn suit with huge shoulder pads. I am struck by the similarity between this last woman and Rose. But this image was captured a long time ago. I sniff this photo and pick up the aroma of decaying rose petals – the smell of sadness. The wardrobe is closed but I know that the clothes hanging inside belonged to a woman who smoked cigarettes and liked a particular perfume. I think she was Aunt what-you-me-call-it.

My head hangs and my tail droops. I am overcome by the room's melancholy. I almost give up my search when I spot a pair of fluffy slippers and a torch under the bed. Perhaps she had it there in case of a power cut? I take its long rubber handle in my mouth. It's a relief to leave the room. The torch is heavy and hangs at an awkward angle but I manage to carry it down the stairs and into the kitchen.

'Now what?' asks Betty.

I put the torch down and look out of the window at the full moon. 'We go outside and get Dante's attention.'

'Mate, door's shut, in case you haven't noticed.'

My mouth curls into a smile. 'Leave that to me.'

Chapter Nine

The stable-style back door has a wrought-iron handle that reminds me of a rawhide chew with a knot at one end. I jump up, place my front paws on the door, take the handle between my teeth and drop my head. Trouble is the door opens inwards so the first time I do this, I succeed in unlatching it, but my weight shuts it again. The next time I get it right. I use my paws instead of my mouth to push the handle down and teeter on my back legs, dropping to all fours as soon as I can. The door opens a fraction but that's all I need. I squeeze a paw and then my head into the gap, and force it open. I grab the torch and Betty and I walk out into the moonlit garden. I can see everything as clear as day, including the sleeping ducks and a couple of startled hares, eyes as wide as my water bowl.

'Now what? Now what?' Betty squeals, as she hops about with excitement.

I drop the torch in the grass and nuzzle the handle until I find the bumpy bit Paddy used to push to switch it on.

'Press this,' I say to Betty.

She does so, and jumps back as a powerful beam of light illuminates the middle section of the garden. The hares do backflips and dart for the nearest cover. I angle the torch so that the big oak tree is floodlit. It's like I'm calling Batman from his cave. I twist the handle a little, first one way, and then the other, so the beam shudders against the tree's tall branches.

'Oh wow!' says Betty, clapping her paws together.

I can't speak – I have my mouth full. I just hope that Dante is near enough to see it. He's very fond of bright lights and shiny things. Well, a bit more than fond. It's his obsession. Just as mine is food, his is all things glittery. It's landed him in all sorts of trouble, and I mean trouble with The Law. Big'uns' law.

'I say! You there! What do you think you're doing?'

I almost drop the torch in shock. I can't work out where the nasal voice is coming from. He sounds like he has a clothes peg on his nose.

'There!' Betty says, pointing at the oak's wide trunk.

Lowering the torch a fraction, I see an upside down squirrel clinging to the bark with its claws.

'I don't wish to be rude but this behaviour just won't do. This is a nice neighbourhood,' he continues.

Since dogs and squirrels have existed, we've always played Chase. We chase squirrels on the ground and they scamper into the trees. Gives us the opportunity for a jolly good bark. No harm done. But this squirrel is clearly in no mood for fun. I lay the torch on the lawn and go for the friendly approach.

'Hi there. Name's Monty, and this is Betty. What's yours?'

'Nigel. Your local Animal Neighbourhood Watch representative.' He puffs out his chest. 'Very important work.

Without my constant vigilance, this quiet hamlet would descend into anarchy.'

'It would?'

'It would,' says Nigel, flicking his tail. 'Look, I don't want us to get off on the wrong paw, but there are by-laws about this sort of thing.'

Betty and I exchange glances.

'What sort of thing?' I ask.

'Disturbing the peace, of course. You can't flash lights like that at this time of night. It's just not neighbourly. The hares are complaining of migraines already.'

'We won't be much longer. We're trying to attract someone's attention.'

'And what will be next? A rock band? Drunken brawls?' The squirrel scampers up the trunk and stops on a branch. 'Mark my words, young hound. Your actions tonight are the first step on the slippery slope to oblivion.'

In a flash of vibrating tail, Nigel disappears into the dark foliage. He's humming the *Mission: Impossible* theme tune again.

'Who does he think he is?' Betty protests.

'Let's get on with it, shall we?' I say, gripping the torch between my teeth and waving it about.

It's not long before I hear a familiar chattering in the distance. Initially, I mistake a large bat for Dante. Then I see the magpie, heading straight for the flickering beam. As he crosses it, his black and white plumage is illuminated – it's Batman in a white T-shirt.

'Bleeding Nora,' says Betty, as she runs under my body to hide. 'He's a big bastard!'

I lower the torch and bark, as quietly as I can, 'Dante, it's me, Monty. Down here!'

I glance at the upper windows but Rose's face doesn't appear. The magpie lands, claws outstretched, a few feet away. Betty cowers. In the torch's beam his striking features are visible – black beak and head, white above his wings and on his belly, and long dark tail feathers that shimmer a peacock green.

'Is this your idea of a joke?' he snaps, stomping towards me, his black, beady eyes angry. 'You're giving me a headache.'

'Dante, calm down, I need your help and had to get your attention.' I try to keep my voice to a quiet woof so that Rose doesn't wake.

The magpie goose-steps up and down. 'Oh for goodness' sake, Monty, find someone else to tap those bloody keys. I have better things to do.'

'No, no. This is important.'

'What? Doggie lost his bone?'

He's in a foul mood. Not good.

'My master's dead.'

Dante dips his head, as if scooping up water, and his tail lifts high. He then returns to his normal stiff posture.

'Dead? Oh dear me. I see.' He clears his throat. 'That explains what you're doing so far from home.' He resumes his pacing. 'I did wonder what all that commotion was about on Friday. Lots of shiny badges and glistening equipment.'

I step closer, forgetting my jittery friend sheltering beneath me. She darts to one side, before I tread on her.

'Did you see what happened?' My tail has gone berserk. It's going so fast Dante's feathers are getting ruffled by the breeze I'm creating. 'Do you know where the killer went?'

Dante has noticed Betty. His eyes sparkle. He darts forward, sharp beak open. I block his path.

'No! Betty is not a midnight snack.'

My teeth are bared. Shocked, Dante backs off. He knows that if I chose, I could break his neck.

'Fine way to treat a friend,' he complains.

'Betty is my friend too. I need you two to get along.'

Dante laughs, the kind of nasal, withering laugh I've heard from villains on the TV. 'Oh, please! You don't expect me to befriend my *food*, do you?'

'This one isn't food, okay?'

'This is preposterous! Who are you to tell me what I can and can't eat? I'm leaving.'

He turns his back on me.

'Wait! I need your help to find my master's killer.'

The magpie ignores me and is about to take off.

'You owe me, remember.'

I had vowed I would never mention this, but I'm desperate. It's not just about finding Larry Nice's address. Dante can be my eyes in the sky.

He turns quickly and screeches. 'I've paid that debt!' He's opened his wings wide and looks menacing. Betty darts behind a flowerpot.

I step forward but keep a safe distance from his sharp beak. 'Not yet. You help me find Paddy's killer, *then* the debt is paid.'

He folds his wings and tilts his smooth black head to one side, as if contemplating my offer.

'And you can have my shiny dog tag. You've wanted it for ages. Well, now you can have it.'

Dante stares at the round tag, a red and silver paw on one side, my name and the Professor's address engraved into the metal, on the other. This tag is the only thing I have to remember my beloved master by. It means the world to me. But finding his killer means more.

He nods. 'Throw in the torch, too.'

'No,' I reply. 'It's not mine to give.'

He opens his wings wide again and I think he's about to fly off. But he folds them.

'Oh all right. I'll help you find Salt's killer. You have my word,' says Dante. 'But, I want the tag now. Call it a down payment.'

'And you won't hurt Betty, or any other creature who helps me?'

Dante sighs. 'Yes, yes, okay, but try not to involve the whole wretched animal kingdom, otherwise I'll starve to death.'

I look over my shoulder at Betty. 'It's okay, Betty. Dante is a bird of his word.' She shakes her head and stays put. I focus back on Dante. 'The laptop's inside.'

Dante glances into the kitchen. 'What are you looking for?'

'A suspect's address in *The White Pages*.'

'That's it? Oh for goodness' sake! What a waste of my exceptional talent.'

I ignore his griping. 'That's just the start. Follow me.'

Dante flies behind me and deftly lands on the kitchen table. He focuses his steely stare on me. 'Whose laptop is this?'

'Belongs to my new master, Detective Constable Rose Sidebottom, who's working on the case.'

'Sidebottom? They have a coat of arms, you know. Ancient big'un family. Been around since the Norman Conquest of 1066. Famous for their prowess in the saddle and for their noble hunting hounds.' He cocks his head as if deciding whether I qualify as a noble hound. Unfortunately, a long strand of drool hangs from my mouth and one side of my jowl is tucked into my gums, having got stuck there from when I held the torch. Dante tutts. Apparently not.

'How do you know about coats of arms?'

'Bit of a history buff. Did you know my ancestors originally guarded the Tower Of London, not those wretched usurpers, the ravens?'

'We're pressed for time so can you get on with it?'

He sighs but positions himself so that his claws rest on the edge of the keyboard. He leans forward and taps a key with his beak. As the screen is illuminated, Dante becomes mesmerised, as he is by everything bright.

Betty has followed us at a distance. She tugs my fur. I drop my head so I can hear what she says.

'So why does he owe you?' she whispers.

I whisper back. 'I saved his life.'

Chapter Ten

Rose's laptop is demanding a password. Dante turns his dark, sleek head in my direction and blinks.

'Well? Any idea?'

Betty leans into me as if trying to hide in my fur: she's still fearful the magpie will try to eat her.

'Let me think,' I say. 'It wouldn't be her name . . .'

'Obviously,' says Dante, with withering condescension. All magpies sound arrogant, but Dante's exceptional intellect makes him particularly intolerant. 'Date of birth, something that's important to her?' he suggests. 'Humans are sentimental like that.'

'Duckdown! Try duckdown,' I say, wagging my tail, confident I've cracked it.

Dante taps in the word and up pops, Incorrect Password. 'Try harder, Monty,' he says, sighing. 'Only two more goes, then we get locked out.'

I feel Betty fidget. 'Oy, Mr Dante. Why don't you have a guess?' she says.

'Madam, I have an IQ in the top ninety-ninth percentile

in the world and I would be a member of Mensa, if big'uns allowed birds to join, which they don't, the stupid snobs. However, I don't know the owner of this laptop so your guess is as good as mine.'

'What about a car number plate?' I suggest. 'I know big'uns love their cars.'

The magpie nods. 'A possibility.'

'Wait here.'

I run out of the kitchen door, down the side passage to the front of the house where her car is parked. Betty comes with me, muttering something about not being 'left alone with that tosser'. I memorise the number plate and we race back to the kitchen.

But it doesn't work – Incorrect Password.

'One more try,' Dante announces.

My tail is drooping as my confidence wanes. I realise I know very little about my new master. Where does she come from? Somewhere by the sea, but that doesn't help. Is she a pack animal or, as I suspect, a lone wolf? I know she's a detective. I know she loves this house but is sad sometimes because the person who lived here before her has gone away. What was her aunt's name? I think back to when Rose and I stood outside the dilapidated shed. It's a bit hazy. Oh, hold on . . .

'Kay! Her aunt! Could she be the password?'

'A bit short for a password, and remember this is your last chance.'

'Okay then, try Aunt Kay. That's what she called her.'

My nose is dry so I lick it. I can feel Betty clinging to my leg. Dante taps in AuntKay. And . . .

We are in! I'm so excited I run around in circles. But I

collide with a chair on the turn and skid to a halt. Betty squeaks with delight. Dante ignores us. Colourful short-cut icons appear on the desktop, looking like tasty sweets in tiny jars. This reminds me of food. I peer longingly at the larder door, distracted by the mountain of deliciousness I know is stored within. My stomach rumbles.

'I'm in *The White Pages*. Who are you after?' Dante asks.

I tell him. A moment later we have Larry Nice's address: Block D, Flat 251, Truscott Estate, Greyfield Common.

Betty rubs her front paws together. 'I can get us to there.'

'And what, pray, would a *rat* know about directions?' says Dante. '*I* can use Google maps.'

She ignores his sarcasm. 'I know the railway tracks like the back of my paw. In fact, I ride the trains a lot, just hop on and hop off whenever I want. I happen to know that the Waterloo train stops here at Milford, and two stops later, hey presto, you're at Greyfield Common. If we take the train, we'll be outside Larry Nice's flat before you can say Bob's-your-uncle, Fanny's-your-aunt. Then, Mr Brainbox, it'll be up to you to find this Truscott Estate place. Think you can manage that?'

Dante rears his head up. 'What you fail to comprehend, madam, is that I have better things to do with my time. Something your tiny little rat brain wouldn't understand.'

'Piss off, Dante!' says Betty, hands on hips. 'At least I don't have a poncy name like you.'

'I am named after *The Divine Comedy*, I'll have you know. A masterful poem.'

'Yeah, I know The Divine bloody Comedy. Ate some pages from it once. Tasted like shit. You like to think you're all dark and menacing, don't you? Well, I've got news for you! You're just a grumpy old bird!'

Dante opens his wings and screeches, 'Harridan!'

'Stop it! Both of you,' I say. 'You'll wake Rose!'

Instantly silent and still, we listen, like cardboard cut-out silhouettes in the laptop's brightness. Rose doesn't stir.

'I like your idea of the train, Betty,' I say, quietly, 'but I'm a big dog. You can hop on and off unnoticed; I can't.'

'That's true,' says Betty, 'but the first train of the day is almost always empty and the driver is too sleepy to notice who gets on and off. Milford is a small station with loads of bushes. We hide until the train comes and then, just when the doors are about to close, we jump on.'

'When's the first train?' I ask, feeling uneasy.

'Five-thirty.'

'I can't do this, Betty. I don't know what time Rose gets up for work. It's too risky.'

Betty stands between my front paws, looking up into my eyes. I hang my head and our noses almost touch.

'What if Larry Nice *is* the killer and gets away with it, all because you didn't want to leave this house? You want to know the truth, don't you?'

I pace up and down, wondering what to do. Disobey Rose, or stay put and feel useless? I think of the Queen's Corgis and their secret night escapades from Windsor Castle. But they know they'll get a royal pardon. I won't be so lucky. I think of Rose upstairs who's been very kind to me and what it might mean to betray her trust. Then I think of the promise I made to find the bastard who took Paddy from me.

'Well?' asks Betty, her ball-bearing eyes gleaming with mischief.

'Let's do it,' I say.

'Rose won't know a thing,' Betty promises.

Famous last words.

Dante nods at my dog tag. 'We made a deal,' he says.

My tag says I belong to Patrick Salt. It still smells of him. I don't want to let it go but I am a dog of my word.

'We'll need you to guide us to the Truscott Estate tomorrow.'

'Fine. My tag?'

'Betty, can you use your teeth to free the tag from my collar?'

'You sure?' she asks.

'I'm sure.'

She scurries up my chest fur and before I know it, the tag clanks to the floor. Dante swoops down, picks it up in his claws and flies out of the kitchen window like a black ghost. I watch my only remaining memory of Paddy disappear into the night. But Betty won't let me feel down for long. She is squirming with excitement.

'We're going on an adventure, we're going on an adventure!' she squeaks, as she does The Twist.

'This could be dangerous. Are you sure you want to come?'

'Wouldn't miss it for the world. Besides, we're mates and I never abandon a mate.'

Chapter Eleven

It's five in the morning and it's dark. I have no idea why big'uns say it's raining cats and dogs, but it's pouring down on this particular dog as I squeeze through the garden hedge and follow a bedraggled Betty hopping along the railway track.

'Keep away from that. It's the live rail,' she says.

It doesn't look remotely alive to me, but I do as she says. Every now and again I look back, worried that the big screeching monster I heard last night will attack from behind. We pass an owl sheltering in a hollow tree, its yellow eyes piercing the blackness. It's reciting Shakespeare. Owls often do this to confuse their prey. And let's face it, *Hamlet* would confuse anybody. There you are going about your business and you look up wondering who's wittering on about death and dreaming, and then, Bam! You're skewered by a hooked beak in the back.

'One may smile and smile and be a te-wit,' the owl hoots.

'Does he mean us?' Betty asks.

'I hope not,' I say, starting to doubt our plan.

We reach Milford station, which is little more than two raised platforms, one on either side of the tracks, and a footbridge over the line. The ticket office is closed. I hunker down on sodden shingle, while Betty scampers up the platform ramp.

'All clear,' she whispers. 'We'll hide in here till the train comes.'

I follow her into a tangled mess of brambles laden with decaying blackberries and wait for the five-thirty train.

'Breakfast,' she says, and nibbles a berry. She stands beneath a wide leaf and uses it as an umbrella. 'So, tell me, how did you save Dante's life, then?'

I blink away a raindrop. 'It was nothing. Hardly worth telling.'

I sniff a blackberry and try one. Not bad. A bit furry.

'Oh go on. Tell me. We've got nothing else to do till the train comes.'

'All right then. Dante found a silver necklace at the side of the road. The main road into Geldeford. He was so busy trying to peck open the locket he didn't see a petrol tanker bearing down on him. He was going to get squashed. I was walking with Paddy at the time and I managed to grab Dante by the neck and pull him out of harm's way. He thought I was going to kill him so he kicked up a terrible fuss and tried to poke my eyes out. When the tanker hurtled past and nearly clipped the both of us he realised I'd saved his life.'

Betty stares at me with her piercing ball-bearing eyes. 'But why? Why risk your life for a magpie? Especially a miserable git like Dante.'

'I don't know. I like to help, I guess. That's why I wanted to be a guide dog.'

'Still don't get it.'

Betty eats in silence. Despite the pat pat of rain on leaves and the ting of water hitting guttering, I hear the train approach before it comes into view. As it lumbers into the station, the platform lights illuminate its bright colours – yellow, red (or it could be green as I get these two muddled up), white and blue. It doesn't seem fearsome at all, more like a colossal, brightly coloured centipede with gigantic eyes. Apart from the driver I only see one person in a carriage. Two men clutching hard hats run onto the platform just in time and board the front carriage. When the doors start to beep, Betty shoves me and we bolt into the last carriage.

I sniff the stale air. The floor's been mopped in dirty water – I detect a faint hint of cleaning fluid. Perhaps a thimbleful. Still smells of old coffee, stale chips, greasy hair and crumpled newspapers. I don't hear any coat rustling or throat clearing or human breathing. We are alone, for now anyway. I give myself an almighty shake, which starts from the very tip of my nose, then sets my jowls flapping, ears bouncing, migrates down my spine in a cork-screw fashion, before becoming a bottom wiggle and capping the whole performance off with a tail wave. Ever watched a slow-motion dog shake? Worth it, I promise you. Anyway, water, loose fur and slobber sprays outwards in all directions, blanketing the floor, nearby windows, seats and Betty. Boy, does that feel good!

She stands there glaring at me, a double-drowned rat. 'Thanks a bunch!' Betty does her own little shake and her fur fluffs back out.

'What now?' I ask.

'When we get to Greyfield Common, we run out the door and head for the tunnel.'

'Tunnel?'

'Yeah, under the road. Until then, we lie down between these seats and hope no big'uns see us.'

I follow her.

'Dante won't let us down, will he?' Betty asks.

I want to do another shake – one is never enough – and my ears tickle. Must have water in them. I waggle my head instead, so as not to soak Betty again.

'He'll be there.'

'So what I don't get is how come you and Dante are friends when he's such a patronising git and you're such a nice dog?'

I spot a cold chip, missed by the cleaners, under a seat. I extend my long tongue and snap it up. A bit soggy, but nice all the same.

'Some months after the locket incident, Dante set up a nest in Paddy's garden. At first he ignored me, so I left him to it. He was like all magpies: stand-offish. Then one day I found him in the garden shed using a stolen laptop. A shiny, silvery one, of course. He needed the power point, you see. When he realised I could read a bit, he warmed to me and showed me how to use the laptop. Even helped me set up on Twitter. He was my first follower. I felt a bit sorry for him, to be honest. He only has six Twitter followers, well, seven, counting me.'

'I'm surprised he's got any at all.'

'I don't think he has any *real* friends. And he doesn't realise it's his own fault. I think he's quite lonely.'

'Serves him bleeding well right. He needs to learn some manners.'

The brakes screech and we stop at Geldeford station. My

home is nearby! My *old* home anyway. I stand up, unable to fight the urge to leave the train and run to Paddy's place.

'What're you doing?' squeals Betty. 'Hide!'

I lie down just in time. A woman gets into our carriage. Fortunately, she sits at the other end and doesn't notice us, despite the puddle at the door and the paw prints. We are silent for the rest of the journey. At Greyfield Common we jump out, startling the woman, and run for the tunnel. Hidden in the darkness, we wait for the train to leave the station. We hear the flap of wings and Dante lands beside us.

'Listen up!' says the magpie, yelling like a drill sergeant. 'These are your directions to the Truscott Estate. Follow the tunnel this-a-way.' He points his beak into the blackness. 'When you come out, you'll see steep grassy verges either side of the line. One side has beech trees. Climb that slope. You'll cross a road and then follow the riverbank path. But you'll need to take the pavement for the last half a mile. It's lined with houses so you'll just have to take your chances. Follow me.'

'Yes, sir!' says Betty and salutes him.

He ignores the sarcasm and flies off.

'Best get going,' I say to Betty, 'and best you get up on my back. I know you're fast but you won't be able to keep up once I get into a run.'

She clambers up my back leg and along my spine, until she sits behind my collar and hangs onto it like a little jockey. I set off at a jog and then, once I'm following the river, I run. It's still bucketing and I have to blink away the rain as I peer up at my guide in the sky. We reach the final leg of our journey. I'm soaked. So is Betty. We sneak past front gardens and garages. If Dante sees a big'un coming, he squawks a warning and we hide until he gives us the all clear.

'What a racket!' Betty complains as we near the council estate. 'If I ever meet the bloke who invented that wretched Twitter, I'm going to bite him.'

There's a myth about the dawn chorus which I'd like to clear up. Big'uns assume the bird population is welcoming the new day in song, and that's certainly how it all began. These days, it's more raucous because they've discovered Twitter and they can't tweet without tweeting – out loud. Every message has to be accompanied by bird song.

Big'uns don't feel the need to sing when they tweet and I don't need to bark, so why do birds have to make such a commotion? I just don't get it.

We peer through the heavy rain at the Truscott Estate, which is a blur of street lighting and grey walls. Built on what used to be common land – a green open space everyone enjoyed – it now consists of four housing blocks in a row, fronted by garages, street parking and rubbish. Discarded appliances rust in the rain. Wrecked sofas, torn mattresses, broken glass and beer cans litter the pavement. Some cars have their wheels missing. Stairwells lead up to open walkways that connect each flat. Light grey breeze blocks, charcoal grey asphalt, blue grey gravel, silver-grey weathered timber fencing, gunmetal grey street railings. The whole estate seems to drip a dismal grey. It's as if the architect was asked to design the most depressing housing possible, in keeping with the area's name – Greyfield Common. The only hint of colour is from the angry graffiti and a child's merry-go-round, once painted red, now faded to rust. Somebody has spray-painted 'Release The Wolves' along the length of a concrete walkway. I sniff the air but can't detect any. Just a dog or two.

Dante lands next to me.

'Which block?' I ask him.

'Block D, over there,' he nods, 'Number 251. I'll meet you on level two, by the steps.' He flies off.

A few people, heads down, sheltering under umbrellas, race to their cars or duck through covered walkways. We make it to level two unseen, but just as we turn the corner a big man in a blue overall, who smells of car grease and toast, almost collides with us. Betty scarpers.

'What the . . .!' The man tries to get round me. 'Get outa here, you filthy stray!'

He attempts to kick me and I race back down the steps with him hot on my heels. I skid through a puddle and fall onto my side. I get up quickly and hide behind some industrial rubbish bins. The man squints in my direction, cursing and walks off. I wait a bit and then run back up two levels.

'What happened to the warning?' I ask Dante, panting. 'And where's Betty?'

'Here!' she says, appearing from a dark corner. 'Jeez, you're almost black. What happened?'

I realise that I'm covered in dirt from the puddle. The estate's greyness is rubbing off on me.

Dante is defensive. 'I can't watch you all the time. I'm not God!'

Then I see he's clasping a shiny beer bottle top in one claw.

'Got distracted, did you?' I tease.

He ignores my comment and nods to his right. 'Four doors down. Larry's in there. I've just seen him at his kitchen window making a cup of tea. So, what's your plan?'

Good question. In my enthusiasm to find Larry Nice, I

haven't thought about how I'm going to get close enough to smell him.

Betty and I creep down the puddle-riddled walkway and stop outside number 251. The door is shut and looks as if it's been kicked in at some point: the bottom panels have been replaced and the wood around the lock is splintered.

'Betty, you stay out of sight,' I say. 'Dante, use your beak to knock on the door. When you hear him coming, fly away.'

Betty conceals herself behind a drainpipe. Dante stands on the doormat and taps three times, but nobody comes. I hear the radio inside his flat. The weather forecast man is predicting showers. I could have told him that!

'Louder. Give it a good whack.'

'I'm doing my best,' he protests, but he bangs harder and keeps going.

I hear footsteps, Dante flies off, and the grimy lace curtains are pulled back a fraction. Larry's face appears at the kitchen window. He looks at where an average height big'un might stand if he were outside the door, and as a result he doesn't see us.

'Bloody kids!' I hear him say.

He disappears from view and Dante returns.

'Knock again,' I say.

'My beak's getting sore,' Dante complains, but follows my instructions.

I hear Larry, his voice angry. 'Right, you little bastards, I'm going to give you a bloody good hiding.'

The door opens wide and a skinny man, with a face like a whippet and legs like a chicken, stands there in his burgundy nylon dressing-gown. Larry Nice has been smoking weed and is enveloped by an acrid fug. Initially, that's all I can smell. It's

LOUISA BENNET

overpowering. I remember Paddy's killer smelt of it too, so I stand my ground, bedraggled, a filthy grey, on his soggy doormat.

Larry gawps at me. 'What the f—'

I jump up, pressing my nose against his skin, but he thinks I am about to bite and he squeals. I knock chicken-whippet man flat on his back. He lies winded on a carpet that stinks of beer, then struggles to push me off him. His slippery dressing-gown is short sleeved and in the struggle my claws scratch his arm, but he has no bite mark. He smells of cheap aftershave and pubs, Rich Tea biscuits and polystyrene. But not that weird, stinky food stench, and not the disease that reminds me of an insect, which I still can't place. As I charge out of the door and down the steps, I know for certain that Larry Nice did not kill my master.

Chapter Twelve

Rose helped PC Joe Salisbury raise the roller door to Larry Nice's lock-up on the Truscott Estate, wearing an unflattering blue rain jacket that made her look like a blueberry. Her shoes were soaked through from searching for Monty in the rain. She'd woken to find the dog gone and Kay's old torch in the garden. How Monty had escaped she had no idea since the exterior doors were shut.

'This is going to take a while,' said Salisbury, jolting her from her cogitation.

The garage was packed full of boxes.

Salisbury's uniform had attracted a small crowd of jeering teenage boys. The oldest, probably eighteen, shouted, 'Filth!' and threw a bottle, which hit Rose's arm, then shattered at her feet. Salisbury was a muscular giant whose mere presence was usually enough to cause troublemakers to think twice. He headed for the perpetrator, who turned to run but Rose got there first. Shoving him into the wall, she cuffed one wrist and then the other before the stunned offender knew what was happening. The rest of the gang scarpered.

'Name?' Rose demanded.

'I ain't saying nothing.'

'Hold him,' she said to Salisbury. She searched his pockets and found a wallet and driving licence. 'Damien Flannery.' Rose looked at the young offender. 'I'm Detective Constable Rose Sidebottom and you're going to apologise for throwing that bottle at me.'

'Get fu—!'

'Language!' snapped Salisbury.

'If you apologise,' Rose continued, 'I may change my mind about charging you with assaulting a police officer.'

Salisbury gave Rose a questioning look. She ignored it. 'Well, I'm waiting.'

'No way.'

'I'm still waiting,' she said, cupping an ear.

'You got it all wrong. The bottle fell. I didn't throw nothing.'

'Don't make me do it,' she warned.

'All right, all right.' Flannery scanned the carpark, checking nobody was within ear shot. 'Sorry,' he muttered.

'Right. Consider this a warning. Now you leave us alone to get on with our jobs, okay?'

'Yes, detective.'

Salisbury undid the handcuffs and Flannery shuffled off, hands in pockets.

'Are you sure that's a good idea?' Salisbury asked. 'Not even a formal caution?'

'We don't want a riot on our hands, and anyway, he's young. I want to give him a second chance.'

Salisbury shook his head but didn't argue.

'Best we get started,' she said and tore open a box.

'You handled yourself well just then.'

'Thanks, Joe.'

Rose had always considered Salisbury handsome, despite a potato-shaped chin hidden beneath a thick beard. At Police College she had developed a crush on him, but it became obvious he was in love with a local nurse so she'd resigned herself to the role of friend. Now he was married, a devoted father to a baby boy, and her closest mate at the nick.

The first few boxes contained flat screen TVs, the next, iPads.

'Must've fallen off the back of a lorry,' Salisbury joked.

Rose plonked down on a box of a dozen bottles of shiraz, rubbing her arm.

'What's the matter?' Salisbury asked. 'Are you hurt?'

'No.'

'Is this about Operation Nailgun?'

Rose nodded.

'It's no secret Leach laid into you. But look on the bright side. He gave you a second chance.'

Rose leaned forward so her forearms rested on the tops of her thighs, and stared at the concrete floor. Leaves from a nearby elm tree blew into the garage and swirled around her soggy shoes.

'I've been a complete idiot, but I'm going to show everyone I can do this. I know I can.' If she kept telling herself this, perhaps it really would come true? 'My problem is Pearl. He's made it clear he wants me gone from Major Crime.'

Salisbury opened a wine box next to her. 'Gotta say he doesn't seem very supportive.' Earlier, Pearl had taken Salisbury aside and loudly instructed him to, 'Make sure she doesn't turn this into a bloody fiasco.' He'd intended her team mates to hear.

'And he's supposed to be mentoring me. How perfect is that? Who's the boss going to believe? Him or me?'

Salisbury moved on to the next box. 'You're just going to have to make sure you don't put a foot wrong. Don't give Dave any reason to push you out.'

She shook her head. 'And to cap it all, the dog I rescued from the vet, you know, Monty, has run away.'

'That dog's a survivor. I'm sure he'll turn up safe and sound.'

She covered her face with her hands. Tears were welling up in her eyes. *Stop it, you baby!* she said to herself.

Salisbury gave her shoulder a reassuring squeeze. 'Rose, I think you need a cuppa and some breakfast. Knowing you, you haven't had anything to eat. How's about I go get us some?'

Rose couldn't help but look at him and smile. Salisbury was a firm believer that a cup of tea could help solve almost any crisis. 'Love a bacon and egg sarnie, and tea would be great. Thanks, Joe, you're a real mate.'

As Salisbury strode off to the café round the corner, Rose continued the laborious task of opening every one of Larry Nice's boxes. She shoved yet another wine box aside to get to the back of the lock-up when she heard a clank of metal on metal. Kneeling, she discovered a black backpack that seemed out of place in a sea of cardboard. She unzipped the top of the pack, her hands in disposable gloves. She glimpsed polished silver plates, a silver teapot and candelabra. She immediately called Pearl.

'That inventory from Salt's insurer. Any chance it listed some silverware that's now missing?'

Rose heard him yell across the room to Detective Sergeant

Kamlesh Varma, who confirmed that some silverware was indeed missing from Salt's house and that the fastidious professor had photographed all his precious possessions and sent the images to his insurance company. Varma had these photos.

'Can you send the photos to me via WhatsApp, sir?'

She received them within seconds and compared them to the contents of the bag. Identical.

'Well, I think we may have found the missing silver,' she said to Pearl, spotting Joe returning with breakfast.

'Don't touch anything else. I'm on my way,' said Pearl.

Chapter Thirteen

Later that morning, Rose watched Leach and Pearl interview Larry Nice through a video feed to a TV in the monitoring room. She felt sixteen again and banished from the in-crowd. She longed to prove she could squeeze a confession from a suspect, but that dream seemed about as unlikely as Pearl helping her to achieve it.

Nice was shaking his head, hands on the table, fingers splayed. His wide-eyed terror reminded her of those greetings cards when animals have disproportionately huge, glassy eyes that never blink.

'No way!' Nice said. 'I don't know this Salt bloke.'

He hadn't been hard to find: sitting in his council flat watching soccer repeats with a packet of crisps balanced on his stomach and a joint smoking away in the ashtray. He'd mumbled about a dog-attack. Said his nerves were shot to pieces. For a fleeting idiotic moment Rose wondered if the dog attack was in fact Monty. She dismissed the idea as ridiculous but couldn't help worrying about him.

'So how did his silverware find its way into your lock-up?

Flew in, did it, on a magic carpet?' asked Leach, crossing his arms and leaning back into a plastic chair too small for his bulky frame.

'It's a set-up, that's what it is.' Nice leaned forward. 'I never been to his house. Honest, Mr Leach.'

'Yeah, and I'm Prince bloody Charles!' Leach snorted.

Nice smirked as if he were contemplating the rough-as-they-come detective as the future King.

Leach continued, 'Show me your arms.'

'What?'

'Your arms. Show them to me,' he said, patting the table top.

Nice looked baffled but did as he was told.

'Got a few scratch marks there, Larry. Looks like a large dog paw to me. How did that happen?'

'As I told you, Mr Leach, a dog attacked me this morning. I opened my door and the vicious brute just went for me. No reason. Needs shooting, if you ask me.'

'Really? Anyone else see this attack?'

'Dunno. Neighbours could've heard me shouting.'

'Did the dog bite?'

Nice squinted at his arms. 'Nah, don't think so.'

'We'll get you checked out at the hospital, just to be sure.'

'Very nice of you, Mr Leach.'

Pearl leaned in, his wrist watch hitting the table. It was a showy piece with a thick metal band that he wore one link too loose so it jangled when he moved. 'Larry, you've got no alibi for Friday night. Home alone just doesn't cut it.'

Their suspect shrugged but the sweat in the cleft of his upper lip and the damp patches under his arms betrayed his agitation. There was a knock at the door and an officer handed Leach a note.

'Well now, isn't this a surprise,' he said, as he showed it to Pearl.

Pearl tutted. 'You're in deep shit, now.'

Nice started to fidget. 'What ya talking about?'

'Can you explain how your fingerprints ended up on Salt's wine glass? Huh? The same one he'd been using just before he died,' demanded Leach.

'They can't be my fingerprints.'

'Give it a rest, Larry,' said Pearl. 'We know you were there.'

Larry crossed his arms. 'I'm not saying another word till you get me a lawyer.'

Leach gave Pearl a got-him-by-the-short-and-curlies look. 'Come on, Larry. You've been caught red-handed. Why don't you tell us where you hid Salt's laptop and iPhone? You know it'll be better for you if you cooperate.'

Nice stared at his stained old trainers in sulky silence.

'You probably didn't mean to kill him, right? Did Salt grab you or something? Did you panic?'

Nice's only response was, 'Lawyer!'

Leach stood, followed by Pearl. 'Okay, we'll get you one, but he won't save you, Larry. Confessing could make things easier for you. Think about it.'

They left the interview room but Rose continued to observe Nice through the video feed. She'd watched and listened with every ounce of her concentration and hadn't experienced a moment's tingling. Not even a minor itch. As far as she was concerned, Larry was telling the truth. But it was obvious her superiors thought differently. Was she the only one to think this was all too easy and way too neat?

She left the observation room and found Leach and Pearl in the corridor.

'We've got the little prick,' said Pearl, ignoring her.

'But no bite marks,' Leach said.

'That we know of. Could be somewhere else on his scrawny body.'

Leach shook his head. 'I need a confession, or a DNA match from the dog's teeth.'

'But, boss, the wine glass puts him at Salt's house and he's got Salt's gear in his lock-up. It's a burglary gone wrong,' said Pearl.

'Not sure. It seems all too . . .'

Rose interjected, 'Easy?'

Leach shrugged. 'Perhaps.'

Pearl raised his eyes in frustration.

Rose persevered. 'Sir, this doesn't feel right. Larry has been in and out of here for the last ten years and it's always been about dealing in stolen goods. Not even an assault, let alone murder. And he's never actually committed a robbery before. He might be a creep but he's not stupid, so why would he leave the silver in a lock-up he knows *we* know about? That really is too dumb. It feels like a set-up to me.'

Leach squared up to her, his body filling most of the width of the corridor. Rose made a mental note not to get stuck behind Leach if the fire alarm went off. He didn't move as quickly as he used to.

'Rose, I'm an old-fashioned plod and I'm all for a bit of gut instinct, but it's not looking good for Nice. We find a DNA match, he's going down for murder.'

She could feel Pearl standing close behind her; she was caught between them like meat in a sandwich.

'Rose, it's not enough to *feel* he's innocent,' Pearl mocked. 'Feelings can let you down, as you well know. You didn't pick up on Ray Summers' lies, did you?'

'Shut it,' Leach snapped, surprising Pearl just as much as Rose. His rebuke encouraged her to go on.

'What if this isn't about a robbery?' Rose persevered. Pearl would never listen to her. At least Leach might hear her out. 'What if it's about something more complicated, like what the Professor knew? Like what's on his laptop?' Her voice had gone high-pitched and squeaky with nerves. 'The silver-ware theft could be a smoke screen.'

Leach folded his arms. 'Go on.'

She cleared her throat. 'I find it odd that Professor Salt was our leading expert in apiculture . . .'

Leach looked blank.

'Bees, sir.'

'For crying out loud, just say bees then,' he growled.

Rose nodded. 'He was trying to understand why the honey bee is dying out. So, isn't it a bit odd he's murdered just when he's about to announce a major breakthrough?'

'What breakthrough?' Pearl challenged. 'His department head never said anything about a breakthrough.'

'I checked academic journals and media on background. He was highly regarded and there's lots of support for his theories. His work is sponsored by Flay Bioscience, and their PR depart-ment has been whipping up a frenzy over a cure for whatever is killing bees. The big launch is in two weeks' time.'

'Oh, come on,' said Pearl, 'you don't seriously think someone is going to commit murder over sick bees?'

'Why not? Flay Bioscience is big money. It's in the Footsie 100 and makes hundreds of millions in profit each year. People have killed for far less.'

Leach ground his teeth as if he had marbles in his mouth to contend with.

'Look, Rose, if there's a choice between a conspiracy and a cock-up, I'll bet on a cock-up every time.' Leach tapped his chin with his pudgy finger. 'Is it likely that a high-profile corporation orders a hit-man to kill their star researcher? I don't think so. However, Larry-the-loser cocking up a burglary? Now, that I can believe.'

'But, sir . . .'

Leach held up his hand. 'Dave, has Flay Bioscience given us permission to see Salt's files and emails?'

'No, sir. The company won't allow access, claiming confidentiality and patent issues.'

'Have you gone after a warrant?' asked Leach.

'Not yet.'

'Get one. We should cover all angles.' Leach directed his next order to Rose. 'Talk to the neighbour, Francis Grace. He was muddled when we spoke to him on the night. He might be clearer today.'

'Sir, I'd like to interview Salt's colleagues at Flay Bioscience,' Rose said. 'I think we should know more about this product launch.'

'Do the neighbour first, then go see Salt's boss at the university. Some guy with a poncy name.'

'Bomphrey, sir,' said Rose.

'That's it. You and Pearl interview Bomphrey *before* we go rattling cages at Flay Bioscience. They've got more lawyers than we've got officers. See what you can find out about this big announcement and if it's still happening.'

'Thank you, sir,' Rose said as she walked away, ecstatic at her small but significant victory.

Chapter Fourteen

My cage is one of fifteen in a row with concrete floors and no natural light, just glaringly bright electric light bulbs that hang, unshaded, at regular intervals from the ceiling. I have water and a cheery grey breeze-block wall to stare at. The place reeks of bleach, poo and desperate wee-mails that only the prisoners are ever going to read. If I was dressed in orange overalls you could've mistaken this for Guantanamo Bay, otherwise known as Gitmo. No wonder this place is known as 'Dogmo' by my brothers and sisters in captivity. I wasn't read my rights when I arrived and I haven't had my one phone call. And nor has any other prisoner by the sound of it. There is a constant cacophony of barking as my fellow canines call out for their owners to save them.

I'm here because I disobeyed Rose. Fair cop, guv.

But there's a rumour circulating on Cell Block D, my block, that I'm in for murder. Every dog here knows about Paddy's death and how I tried to save him. News on the wee-vine sure travels fast. But the rumour within the pound's perimeter is that I took my revenge on Paddy's killer and ate his leg.

While he was still alive. I suspect the gossip started with Lola, the Chihuahua, who sits on her pink cushion all day nattering to anyone who'll listen. She's the dog world's answer to a tabloid sensationalist with not an ounce of truth in it. To be honest, the thought of chewing chicken-whippet man's leg makes me feel sick. Regardless, I feel I need to set the story straight. Where's a lawyer when you need one?

In a cage on my right is a heart-broken Staffordshire Bull Terrier, whose master threw him out of a moving car because he was 'allegedly' a lousy guard-dog.

'But nobody ever proved nothin',' he told me.

He barely moves and avoids all human contact. He's been here longer than most, recovering from his operation. With no microchip and no collar, he's been given the name of Ralph. He now has three legs and, according to one of the girls working here, is a 'lifer': he has no chance of finding a new home.

On my left is a black and white mongrel – a bit of Terrier and a bit of Border Collie, called Taz. He leaps against his cage door and howls constantly, swearing at the big'uns, effing and blinding in doggie-speak. His nose gets grazed and bloody from the repeated impact with the bars. The guards take him away, patch him up, so he can do it again. He tells me he's suspected of aiding and abetting a terrorist. The terrorist turns out to be Molly, a rogue sheep, who made a bid for freedom from his master's farm. Instead of rounding her up, he 'allegedly' opened the gate for her. His master dumped him at Dogmo. I'm not sure which one of my neighbours is the more heartbreaking to watch.

How did I end up in this place? The car-grease man must have dobbed me in.

When Betty and I ran from Larry's flat earlier this morning, I bolted down the steps and across a kids' play area that looked and smelled more like a landfill site, when a council van screeched to a halt, blocking my exit. Out jumped The Dog Catcher. I skidded on sodden food wrappers and came to a standstill. There was no mistaking him in his council khaki, clutching his net in one hand and, in the other, a long pole with a noose at the tip. I almost had a heart attack, remembering my mum warning us as pups to run like hell if we ever saw The Dog Catcher. Betty scarpered. I tried to do the same, but he threw his net and almost caught me.

I darted behind a graffitied see-saw. He stood on the other side. We eyed each other in the pouring rain. This was it: pistols at dawn. It was either him or me. I knew The Dog Catcher wouldn't clamber over the see-saw so he had to go around. I shot to my right, and he headed towards me. I switched direction, and so did he. This went on for a while, then he pulled out a bag of liver treats. Now that's below the belt! He opened it, waving it in my direction, calling me.

'Here boy! Good doggie.'

Did he think I was that stupid? Okay, I was drooling, I'll admit. The liver treats did smell good but I wasn't falling for it.

I did a one-eighty and ran back into the estate, only to discover there were two dog catchers, this one a female. I was trapped. I looked around for a way to escape. A mum with three kids, all in raincoats, were heading my way. If I could dive through them I might escape. Surely The Dog Catcher wouldn't risk throwing a net or using his noose on them? I was about to spring in their direction when my pursuer opened a plastic container and pulled out . . . Oh no!

'Look what I've got for you. Cheese!' he said.

I was lost then. Anybody who knows about dogs can tell you that cheese is like cocaine for dogs. Once tried, your dog's addicted. It all started very innocently when Melissa Collum, the five-year-old daughter of John Collum who fostered me as a pup, decided it would be fun to tear cheese slices into strips and feed them to me. The Dog Catcher waved the cheese at me. Despite the rain, there was no mistaking its gorgeous creaminess. My brain was telling me to run, but my stomach said, Sod that, go get the cheese. Before I knew it, my legs were moving and just as I was about to take the cheese slice in my salivating mouth I was caught in a noose.

After that, I was bundled into a van and brought to Dogmo. Not that the people here haven't been kind: there is a very nice lady with red cheeks and a plump figure called Gina who reminds me of an apple and smells of cats (she spends a lot of time in Cell Block C, the cattery, but I won't hold that against her).

'Been through the wars, haven't you?' Gina said when I arrived. 'Seventeen stitches and look at the state of you!'

During my struggle to free myself from the noose, I'd rolled in a burst rubbish bag. So not only was I covered in mud, but glued to my matted fur was potato peel, sweet wrappers, the remains of a rogan josh and a shepherds pie, used teabags, shredded paper, the contents of a vacuum cleaner and, my old favourite – chewing gum. The only way to get that out is to cut my fur so I have a particularly unattractive bald patch on my haunches. At least licking my foodie attachments made the journey to the pound a little less dismal than it might otherwise have been. When I arrived, Gina and

LOUISA BENNET

another woman checked me over and then washed me. What an insult!

Want to know why we don't like being washed?

Firstly, it's embarrassing. How would you like it if a perfect stranger dragged you off to the showers? Secondly, we're quite capable of cleaning ourselves, thank you very much. Thirdly, you take away our smell. Our identity. Without our smell we might as well not exist. And lastly, in this case, I had several good snacks planned as I worked my way through the deliciously stinky items caught in my coat.

My big mistake was giving my dog tag to Dante. Probably about as stupid as the time I tried stealing a royal Dorgi's breakfast – yes, Dorgi, a Dachshund and Corgi crossbreed. The Queen has two, the biggest goes by the name of Vulcan. Her Majesty is a secret *Star Trek* fan.

'Off with his head,' Vulcan yelped when he caught me finishing off his food.

I really did think I was for the chop that day. He made such a racket, a security guard came running, pointing one of those guns at me. Taught me a big lesson, I can tell you: never assume a dog has finished his meal. There could be hell to pay! Especially if that dog has the power to behead you! Anyway, back to my name tag. I'm sure if the big'uns at the pound had seen Patrick Salt's name on my tag, they would've contacted the police. His murder has been all over the news. But as I don't have a tag and because my microchip is damaged, they don't know I am *that* dog. I've tried telling them I'm Monty and live with Rose at Duckdown Cottage, but they just tell me to stop barking. I overhear Gina saying she will call the local vet and notify the police in case anyone is looking for me. I get excited and pant enthusiastically. But she seems very busy and can't have done it yet, because wouldn't Rose have turned up by now to claim me if she had?

Oh no!

What if Rose doesn't want me back? What a terrible thought! She asked me not to run away and I disobeyed. She's probably angry. Well, if I'm splitting hairs, I'd argue I was on my way home when I got nabbed, but Rose won't know that. She'll think I can't be trusted. I sigh loudly and lie with my head between my front paws as I consider my options. Wait and hope, or make a break for it?

I'm interrupted from my dilemma when three big'uns enter our block carrying leads. Lola pauses mid-gossip with a Dalmatian-crossbreed called Bubbles, and then resumes her chatter. She's clearly not an outdoors girl. Bubbles, however, stands and wags her tail. Charlie, a mongrel with some Jack Russell in him, runs in little circles yipping, 'Me! take me!' Nelson, an old Staffie crossbreed, moves arthritically to the front of his cage. I lie still and say nothing, as does Ralph. I don't want to go anywhere, in case Rose shows up. A tall lanky teenage boy chewing gum – please don't drop it, I know it'll end up stuck to me – ambles to Taz's cage. He has enough metal in his ear, lip, eyebrow and on his fingers to drive a metal-detector berserk. Dante would find his shiny bits fascinating. Taz snarls and leaps at the door, fangs bared.

'Let me out, you son-of-a-bitch!' says Taz.

The teenager jumps back, shocked. I can smell his fear, sour like vinegar. He looks at the report card on my cage door, then at me placidly waiting, and shouts out, 'I'll take this one instead. Goldie.'

Goldie? Is that the best they can come up with? And do I look like a girl to you, mate?

'But he's only just arrived,' Gina says, the apple-cat lady. 'He doesn't need a walk.'

'Don't care. Not taking that one. It's vicious.'

Taz snarls again.

Gina sighs. 'Okay, Mike. Take Goldie. Carol, you happy with Nelson?'

Carol, a tall woman in wellies that smell of cow manure, nods.

Mike opens my door. I aim for the gap between his skinny legs and the side of the cage. But he's too quick. He grabs my collar and clips a lead to it which he pulls up sharply and I choke. He ignores this and pulls me close to his knees, forcing me to walk to heel, almost on tip-toes. In single file we leave through the back of the pound and turn right onto a road through an industrial estate, then, left into a country lane. I sniff the air all the way, but nothing is familiar. The rumble of traffic dies away. The lane has no pavements and the steep hedgerows on either side slope up to beech trees. We face oncoming traffic, not that there is much. The rain has stopped and from what I can glimpse through the leafy canopy, the sky is clearing to a wispy blue. I wonder where we are going, but I don't get that far.

I hear a car door shut. A rasping sound – metal on metal. Then a car engine starts. It rumbles and the smell of diesel is familiar. My ears flatten, my tail goes high, my fur stands up on end. It's him! It's the killer's car.

'Whoa, boy!' Mike says, with panic in his voice.

I strain at the lead and crouch low as if I am stalking my prey. My nose pulsates, desperate to detect the killer's scent. I hear that tink tink tink I remember so well. The car is faulty. It's coming towards us. I snarl and leap forward, determined to be free of my leash. I can see it now. It's a white van, the kind that tradesmen use with two seats at the front and equipment in the back. I lunge again, growling and snapping. I choke and cough as the collar cuts into my throat.

'Stop it!' yells Mike. 'Stop!'

I veer out into the middle of the road, using all my weight, dragging the boy with me. My muzzle is peeled back into a ferocious snarl.

The van is so close I can see the person driving: but he's not what I expected. He has white hair and looks to be in his late fifties. His window is wound down and his chubby arm rests on the doorframe. No tattoo. He's not the athletic man in black who killed my Paddy. The van swerves to avoid us. He looks startled but doesn't stop. I go quiet and stare at the receding rear bumper, blinking in confusion. I am convinced that's the very same van the killer used, but the driver isn't him. I don't realise I'm standing in the middle of the road until Mike pulls me to the side.

'Psycho dog!' he yells at me. Then at the other dog-walkers. 'Did you see that? He's crazy.'

Carol replies. 'He ain't gonna last seven days. Too aggressive.'

Seven days?

'Take him back, Mike. We can't re-home aggressive dogs and if we don't find his owner, he'll have to be put down. Shame, though. He seemed so docile.'

What? No way! I know what that means. Something I learned from the other dogs at guide dog school. We all knew the story of an Alsatian that mauled her trainer and she was taken to be 'put down' and never came back. I'm too young to die and, anyway, I have to find my Paddy's killer.

I know now what I must do. I can't wait for Rose to find me. I must do a runner.

Chapter Fifteen

Patrick Salt's lawn edges were perfect, as were the expertly pruned roses and the neat rows of winter lettuce, green cabbage, wild rocket and spring onions in his vegetable garden. He had been a meticulous man, Rose thought, as she searched the garden for Monty.

On the way to interview Salt's next-door neighbour, it occurred to her that Monty may have tried to find his way back to his old home. The house was locked up so Salisbury followed the path along the riverbank and Rose checked out the garden.

'Monty!'

She heard a clatter next door, turned and almost tripped over an empty, porcelain water bowl decorated with dog paws. Next door, Francis Grace was watching her from an upstairs window. She held up her warrant card and mouthed 'Police'. The old man disappeared. Rose picked up the bowl and filled it with water, just in case Monty was around and feeling thirsty. She popped it back where she'd found it.

'Where are you?' she said, double-checking the back door was locked. It was.

She peered through little square glass window panes into the sitting room. The SOCOs had left their mark on the room. Furniture had been shifted, drawers left open. Poor old Salt would not have been happy. In their search for fingerprints they'd left white dust on several surfaces including the key and lock on an antique walnut display cabinet, now devoid of its silverware.

Rose pulled out her mobile and phoned the vet who'd treated Monty. The receptionist transferred her through immediately. When he picked up she could hear a dog yapping in the background.

'Malcolm, I'm sorry to bother you. It's Detective Constable Rose Sidebottom.'

'It's no bother. Lovely to hear from you. How can I help?'

'Monty's run away and I can't find him. He hasn't . . .'

A small dog squealed and then gave a fierce and high-pitched growl. There was a loud clank as Malcolm dropped the phone.

'Malcolm, hello?'

He picked it up again. 'I'll call you back shortly.'

Salisbury stepped over the garden gate as if it were a child's toy and strode up the lawn towards her.

'No luck,' he said. 'I asked a few people walking dogs if they'd seen him, but nobody has. At least we tried.'

'I'll call the pound.'

Salisbury glanced over the wooden fence and caught the old man watching them from an upstairs window.

'Rose.' He nodded in Grace's direction. 'We should get on with the interview, hey? If Dave finds out we've been searching for a dog instead of interviewing a potential witness, we'll both be in serious hot water.'

Ah yes. How could she forget Pearl, who'd sent Salisbury with her so he didn't have to deal with the 'mad old coot' himself?

'You're right. I'll phone as we walk.'

They wandered down the side passage and as she started to dial, Malcolm rang her back.

'Sorry about that,' he said. 'The Yorkie doesn't like needles. So Monty's run away?'

'Yes, some time during the night. He wasn't brought in by any chance, was he?'

'No, I haven't seen him. Try the pound, and I'll call you if I hear anything. Or if I don't. Um, do you . . . ?'

They had reached Francis Grace's porch.

'Malcolm, got to go. And thanks.'

Rose put her phone away and rang the doorbell. Her hand trembled.

She was nervous, not because she hadn't done this type of interview many times, but because she knew she couldn't afford to put a foot wrong.

'Don't worry, you'll get through your probation. I know you. You're a fighter.' Salisbury gave her an encouraging smile.

She half-smiled back. 'I know. That's why I have to make a difference on this case. That's if I can keep suntan man off my back.'

Salisbury laughed. He knew she was referring to Pearl who'd recently returned from a week in Ibiza. 'So why's he gunning for you?'

'He asked me out and I said no. A mortal sin, in his book.'

Salisbury glanced at her. 'There's got to be more to it, surely?'

'Maybe he thinks I've got it too easy. He spent five years on the beat before making DC. I did it in two.'

An arthritic hand twitched back a lace curtain, then a man in his mid-seventies, not much fatter than a twig, opened the door. 'Yes?'

Rose showed him her warrant card. 'Detective Constable Rose Sidebottom and Police Constable Joe Salisbury. We'd like to ask you some questions about Patrick Salt.'

'Terrible business,' the old man muttered. 'What is the world coming to?'

As Salisbury and Rose walked through the house and into the sitting room, she was struck by the heat, its excessive cleanliness, and the unexpected Oriental furnishings, vases and artworks. From the exterior it had appeared the mirror image of Salt's English gentleman's home, but inside it couldn't have been more different.

The wallpaper was a deep red with golden birds she guessed were cranes. A white porcelain vase with long, narrow neck caught her eye. It was decorated with colourful birds she didn't recognise.

'You like that do you?' Grace asked. 'Made in the Qing Emperor Qianlong period.'

Rose had no idea when that was but she guessed it must be a very long time ago. Either side of it were two blue and white porcelain plates on stands. Each one depicted a blue dragon.

'And these?' she asked.

'Ming.'

Was he serious? They must be worth a fortune.

On the wall, an exquisitely embroidered yellow silk robe, decorated in swirling dragons, was encased in a glass-fronted frame. It looked as if it had belonged to an emperor.

'That's Qing dynasty, eighteenth century,' said Grace.

'Very beautiful,' said Rose.

Her hand brushed a radiator on full-bore, even though it had turned into a warm day. She glanced at the windows which were shut tight. The old man sat in a cushioned electric recliner chair and directed them to sit on an intricately carved rosewood bench with dragons' heads for arms. Stunning-looking but uncomfortable. Salisbury pulled out his notebook.

'Mr Grace,' Rose began, 'you called the police and an ambulance Friday night at two minutes past seven. Can you tell me how you came to discover Patrick Salt's body?'

'One of his lot asked me the same question that night,' he replied, nodding at Salisbury's uniform.

'You were naturally in a state of shock then, and I'm sure having to identify Patrick's body must have been very upsetting for you. So we want to see if you remember anything more, now you've had time to think about it. So how did you know Professor Salt was in trouble?'

Mr Grace grinned, with oversized false teeth that appeared to dominate his gaunt face. She half-expected the teeth to pop out and bite her.

'Heard the dog making strange noises. Never heard him do that before. I hear the odd bark, perhaps, but it's hard to mistake the cry of an animal in pain.'

'So you went round to take a look?'

'I peered over the fence and saw them both lying there. All that blood. Terrible.' Mr Grace shook his head.

'Did you see the killer?'

'Dear me, no.'

His gaze flickered over her shoulder. Rose felt a tingle

that started in her feet and hands like pins and needles and spread up her spine. She shuddered.

'Are you sure? Perhaps you glimpsed someone leaving?'

Grace's skull-like grin disappeared. 'Are you calling me a liar, Detective Bottomly?' His voice was too loud. He was trying to bluster through his lie.

'No, sir, and it's Sidebottom.'

'Really? Sidebottom? Oh dear me.' He burst into sudden laughter and his eyes disappeared into the folds of his wrinkled lids.

For the millionth time, Rose regretted not changing her surname to something nice and forgettable, like Smith or Jones.

'Did you see anyone suspicious in the area before hearing the dog whining?'

'Who said he was whining? No, it was more a yelp of pain followed by a cry of despair.'

Salisbury gave her a we've-got-a-right-one-here look. Rose, however, understood perfectly and realised this man was no fool.

'Thanks for clarifying that, Mr Grace, but did you see or hear anything suspicious in the area prior to the dog's cry of despair?' she asked.

'I thought I heard Patrick shouting, but I couldn't make out what he said. Hearing's not as good as it used to be.'

'Did you catch any of his words?'

Grace's sparse eyebrows drew together and he pinched the bridge of his nose as he considered the question. 'No, I'm sorry.'

'Did you hear other voices?'

'Don't think so.'

'Do you recognise this man?' Rose said, giving him a photo of Larry Nice.

He fumbled with his bifocals and then stared so closely at the image she expected him to go cross-eyed.

'No,' he replied, handing it back to her.

'Did you at any time go round to check if Patrick was alive?'

Grace shook his head fiercely. 'Oh no, I was too frightened and I could see he was dead. I mean, there was a great big blood stain on his shirt and his eyes were staring at the sky. I rushed into the house immediately and dialled nine nine nine.'

'Can you tell me about Patrick's routine on a Monday?'

Francis Grace leaned forward. 'I didn't spy on him, you know. But he was a man of habit, a precise man of science, and truly brilliant, of course. A great loss.' He collapsed back into his chair cushions and lapsed into silence.

'His routine?' she prompted.

'Ah yes. Well, he'd work at the university on weekdays, although I believe he spent time at that big biotechnology company as well. What's their name?'

'Flay Bioscience?'

'That's the one. Patrick always left the house at eight and was home by six. He walked the dog before and after work, along the riverbank. Apart from that he sometimes went to apiculture conferences.' He fixed his gaze on Rose. 'Bees, to you.'

Rose ignored the implication that she was too dumb to know what apiculture was.

'He travelled a lot,' Grace continued. 'Oh and on Sundays, without fail, he'd go fishing. Even in the rain. Took the dog, naturally.' He looked deep into her eyes. 'Dog's like a bear, I'm telling you. I've seen him in the river, fishing. Watches the fish for hours and then pounces, mouth open wide, like those Alaskan bears catching salmon.' He shook his head. 'That dog will miss him terribly. They were very close and had a special understanding, you know.'

'How do you mean?' She had an inkling, but wanted to be sure.

As a child Rose had always found it easier to connect with animals than people. Her mother's two Yorkshire Terriers – Mo and Jo – disobeyed her parents constantly, but Rose just had to give them a look and they'd know what she wanted. And they obeyed. Likewise, she recognised their mischievous moods. Her parents ran a guesthouse and she'd saved many a tourist from an ankle bite, sensing her wily companions were about to attack.

'Look, I don't want you thinking Patrick was a nutter or anything,' Grace said. 'A bit eccentric, maybe. But he was probably one of the greatest scientists of our time. He was researching the drastic decline of the honey bee. And before you mock,' Grace said, wagging a crooked finger at both of them, 'it's a very serious problem indeed. No bees, means no flowering plants, *ergo*, no food.'

Once again, he lapsed into silence, but appeared remarkably calm considering the impending apocalypse.

'You were explaining about the close relationship he had with Monty?' Rose urged.

'Monty? Yes. Patrick would talk to the dog, as if he were a person. I mean full-blown conversations, and the dog would respond.'

Salisbury's jaw dropped and he stopped taking notes.

Then, realising his mouth was wide open, he shut it and studied his boots, not wishing the old man to see his incredulity.

'I often heard them through our adjoining wall, or when they were in the garden. That dog does more than just sit and fetch, I can tell you. He can open the front door, even flick the kettle switch with his nose. I swear he understood what Patrick said.'

Salisbury's pen hadn't moved and this time he couldn't stop himself staring at Grace. But Rose knew assistance dogs could be trained to do incredible things. Take cash from an ATM, roll somebody into the recovery position, pick up the phone. If Monty could open doors perhaps that was how he escaped last night?

'It appears the dog tried to defend Professor Salt,' she said. 'Do you think he would know the killer if he met him again?'

'Without a doubt!' replied Grace, slapping his hands down on the fabric arms of his chair.

Salisbury was now staring at her as if she had joined the cuckoo club.

She ignored him. 'Did Professor Salt have any enemies that you know of?'

'I don't think so. I mean, the academic world can be a nasty one. Petty jealousies and all that. But he never mentioned anyone he was worried about.'

Rose handed him a card with her contact details. 'Thank you for your time and please call me if you think of anything else.'

He nodded and took the card in his crooked fingers. Then Grace pointed at her eyebrows.

'Do you know you frown when you're concentrating?' Grace asked her.

'Um, no, sir.'

'Shame. Makes your pretty face look quite fierce.'

Rose went beetroot red and stood to leave. She had one last question. 'Your furniture and artworks are stunning. Are you a collector?'

Grace pressed a button on his electronic armchair which slowly tilted him forward, making it easier to stand. It reminded Rose of Wallace being mechanically tipped from his bed, then sliding down a chute to the kitchen, where the long-suffering Gromit served breakfast.

'I worked for many years in banking in Hong Kong. In the glory days, before we gave up the colony, which we never should've done, if you ask me. Anyway, I became a collector. I have a passion for Chinese history and art. Know a little about it, too. More than those idiots on the *Antiques Roadshow*.' He glared at the television as if it were all its fault. 'When I retired, I decided to return to England, and I brought all this with me. Reminds me of the good old days when life was fun,' he said, his face genuinely sad.

Outside, and out of earshot, Rose said to Salisbury, 'I think he knows more than he's saying.'

'Here we go,' said Salisbury, shaking his head.

She glanced up at her friend. 'I'm usually spot on . . . but after Ray Summers, I'm not so sure I trust my instincts. I mean, how could I not know that slime-bucket was telling me porkies?'

'Maybe Summers wasn't lying. Maybe he really did like you. Or perhaps you'd had one too many. Who knows? But why do you think Grace is lying?'

'Fear.'

Chapter Sixteen

Rose was on her way back to base when Pearl phoned, telling her to meet him at the university's School of Life Sciences building. Salisbury was called away to join his search colleagues.

The university campus was large and notoriously difficult to navigate. It had been nicknamed The Geldeford Triangle because visitors and new students had been known to disappear, only to be found, hours later, dazed and confused. Satnavs weren't much help because the roads were numbers, rather than names. To make it worse, students had removed road signs for a bit of a laugh. Pearl gave her the building number, known succinctly as D542SLS.

Twenty minutes later she parked her unmarked pool car next to Pearl's. He hadn't waited for her and was already inside the building which, from the front, resembled the white bow of an icebreaker with porthole-style windows. It was four-storeys of glass and metal, and it glinted with newness. A sign outside proudly proclaimed The Flay Building was opened in 2014 and sported a large Flay Bioscience logo.

From the list of faculties, Rose could see Biotechnology was by far the largest. Evolution, Environment and Behaviour, where Salt had worked, was the smallest.

As she walked through the sliding doors into the air-conditioned lobby Pearl greeted her.

'Took your time.'

Before she could respond a man of slight build, who looked to be in his mid-twenties even though he was thirty-four, wearing jeans and a pale mauve V-necked jumper, bounced his way towards them in black barefoot running shoes. With separated toes, the shoes made his feet look like they belonged to a goose. His goatee was clearly his most prized feature, trimmed to a degree of perfection that suggested he had way too much time on his hands.

'Dr Deakin Bomphrey,' he said, and heartily shook Pearl's hand, then Rose's.

His palm was hot and clammy and she wiped away his sweaty residue on her trousers. They were shown into an office dominated by an enormous Victorian twin-pedestal oak writing desk with red leather inlay, that seemed at odds with all the other, IKEA-style, light pine and powder-coated metal furniture in the room. Bomphrey sat behind the mono-lithic desk, which only served to make him look smaller than his five foot six inches. Rose and Pearl sat in two leather and chrome chairs which forced them to lean so far back they were almost horizontal. To keep upright they had to perch on the metal bar at the front. *A triumph of looks over function*, thought Rose.

'I can hardly believe it. Patrick was a friend as well as a colleague. We're all shocked and devastated.'

Pearl flicked back a blond lock of hair that was disturbingly close to a kiss-curl. Rose recognised the mannerism; he always preened his hair before an interview. She suspected that deep down he believed his good looks would win them over. Suddenly conscious of her own mannerisms, she realised she was frowning. She relaxed her brow.

'Dr Bomphrey, thank you for your time and we're sorry for your loss,' Pearl said. 'I have a few questions.'

Bomphrey nodded, his boyish face serious. 'Please. Anything I can do to help. I understand he was attacked by a burglar?'

Pearl side-stepped the question. 'Dr Bomphrey, what can you tell me about Professor Salt? We understand he has no family, except a daughter in Australia?'

'Yes, I believe that's correct. His life was his work, and of course the dog.'

'What about friends?' Pearl continued.

'Beyond his university pals, I'm not sure. When my wife and I invited him to dinner, he always came alone. No girl-friend or boyfriend that I know of.'

Pearl's lip twitched up in disdain. 'You saying he was gay?'

'No, not at all. No, no, no. He'd been married once and was divorced. No, that's just me rambling.'

'What about enemies?'

'He wasn't the sort of man to make enemies. Quiet, kept himself to himself, always pleasant.'

'What was his role here at the university?'

'Research and teaching. He was pre-eminent in his field, lectured all over the world. Published eighteen books and thirty peer-reviewed papers.'

'All about bees?'

'Yes.'

The corner of Pearl's mouth twitched again. Bomphrey didn't appear to notice.

'As you may know, the honey bee is an endangered species. Whole hives are dying, just like that.' Bomphrey clicked his fingers. 'Patrick was trying to isolate the cause, and was working on a solution with Dr Martinez from Flay Bioscience.'

Pearl had a glazed look in his eyes. Rose saw this as her chance to butt in. 'Why would a professor of apiculture work with a biotechnologist? That's unusual, isn't it?'

Bomphrey tapped his nose. 'Not bad for a plod. They must be upping the entry qualifications.' He chuckled at his joke.

God, what an annoying little turd! she thought. Even Pearl bristled.

Bomphrey continued. 'It was a joint project, requiring both sets of skills and they worked well together.'

Before Rose could speak again, Pearl cut in.

'Ever seen the Professor with this man?'

He produced a photo of Larry Nice.

'Is this who . . . ?' Bomphrey asked.

'Just a line of enquiry.'

Bomphrey shook his head. Rose watched a flicker of disappointment cross Pearl's face.

'I'd like to see the Professor's office.'

'Certainly,' said Bomphrey. 'Follow me.'

He led them up to the biotechnology floor, through a laboratory and then unlocked the door to a tiny, glass-fronted office. On one wall hung numerous framed awards and certificates. Patrick Salt was an Honorary Member of the Zoological Society of London, winner of the Frink Medal and the L.J. Goodman Award for insect biology. The other wall was covered in shelves, piled high with books and document files.

In a corner stood a tall white metal filing cabinet. The top drawer was open a few inches. Squeezed into this claustrophobic space was a white melamine desk, with a monitor, phone, power cables and mouse mat on it. The rest of the desk was clear.

'Is this door normally locked?' Rose asked.

Pearl seemed surprised by her question.

'Yes, his work was highly confidential. He'd lock it, and the door to the lab, every time he left. He was very security-conscious.'

'So who has keys to his office?' she asked.

'Er, Patrick, naturally. The cleaner, security and me.'

Pearl took a step forward, blocking her view of the man. 'Dr Bomphrey, can you take a look around and tell me if anything is missing.'

'Why should there be?'

'Please, sir, just have a look,' said Pearl.

The department head gazed around the room, absent-mindedly tugging at the hairs of his designer goatee. 'Doesn't look like it.'

Rose, being of petite build, squeezed through the narrow gap between Pearl and the wall so she could see Bomphrey again.

She asked, 'Did he have a work computer and if so, where is it?' she asked, looking at the disconnected monitor and cabling.

'He took his laptop home every night so he could continue working. We didn't like it, but we couldn't stop him.'

'So the laptop stolen from his home was his only laptop?'

'I'm not sure.'

'Can you look through his filing cabinet and tell us if any

documents are missing, or USB sticks,' she said, before Pearl could talk over her.

'I can, but not now. I have a meeting to attend.'

Those pins and needles again. Quite acute this time.

'So where are the back-ups for his electronic files?' she continued.

'Our secure server is with a company in Birmingham. Patrick was good at remembering to back-up his data. Did it daily, so thankfully all his hard work isn't lost.'

'We'd like to see those files,' said Rose. It was worth pushing. It would save them having to go to Court for a warrant.

'I'm afraid not,' replied Bomphrey. 'As I've said before, they are highly confidential. We can't afford his pioneering work to become public knowledge. Our sponsor simply won't allow it.'

'Flay Bioscience?' said Rose. 'But, as I understand it, Professor Salt worked for the university, so surely if *you* give us permission, then there's no problem.'

Bomphrey had been sitting on the edge of the desk playing with his goatee. Now he stood abruptly.

'It's not that simple. You have to understand that without Flay's generosity, we wouldn't have this magnificent building.' He gestured around the lab. 'And we wouldn't have the funds to work on our honey bee problem. I can't have our sponsor upset.'

Rose persevered. 'Sir, we appreciate your confidentiality issues, but we are investigating a murder and we need to know what was on the stolen laptop.'

'Murder?' Bomphrey snapped.

'Yes, sir,' said Pearl.

'Why do you need to see Patrick's work?' His tone was no longer conciliatory. 'Isn't this about the theft of some valuables?'

'That's a possibility, sir. But—'

Bomphrey didn't let Pearl finish. 'Then get a warrant. If you can. Flay holds the patents to Patrick's and Maria's work and I'm sure they'll protect their property. Now if you'll excuse me, I have a meeting.'

'Maria?' Pearl asked.

'Dr Maria Martinez. Now I really must ask you to leave.'

Bomphrey began to usher them from the room. Before she left, Rose noticed the framed photo of Salt in black tie at a dinner function. He was holding up his award – the Frink Medal. Next to him was an attractive woman with olive skin and dark eyes and hair, wearing a red dress. But she wasn't smiling. Her large lips were pursed and her eyes had an angry glint. Was this Dr Martinez? Rose made a mental note to talk to her.

Glancing once more at the open filing cabinet, she wondered why a fastidious man like Salt would leave the drawer open. And where was the key? It wasn't in the cabinet lock and it wasn't on the key ring they'd found at Salt's home. Bomphrey had just lost his prize professor and a laptop with confidential work on it, but seemed completely unperturbed by either.

They left the building.

'Next time, keep your mouth shut. Got it?' Pearl said.

Chapter Seventeen

Rose finished typing her report and said goodnight. Only her sarge, Kamlesh Varma, looked up to wish her a good evening in his perfectly enunciated public school voice. Everyone else ignored her.

Varma was known for his good manners, even when he was punched or spat at during an arrest. A 'Paki bastard' insult didn't stop Varma from his usual 'please', 'thank you', 'sir' or 'madam', and he would always refrain from correcting his assailant even though he was of Indian, rather than Pakistani, descent. Six foot tall and square-jawed, he dressed immaculately in bespoke suits his brother-in-law, a Savile Row tailor, made for him at a family discount. He reminded her of Roger Moore's James Bond, except, as Varma used to point out with a smile, he was a café latte Bond. At least he seemed to have forgiven her for messing up Operation Nailgun.

Pearl had his back to Rose, his feet propped on his desk, and was sharing a dirty joke with a male detective. He waited until she was almost out of the room and then shouted:

'Hear your mutt got picked up by the pound.'

Rose had been worrying about Monty all day. She'd checked with the local nick up the road, but no Golden Retriever strays had been reported. When she'd phoned the pound, she'd been left on hold for so long Pearl had laid into her for wasting time, so she'd hung up.

'Oh, thank goodness!' She beamed him a huge smile. 'Have you got the address?'

'Sure,' he replied, dangling a yellow post-it note from a finger, forcing her to fetch it.

An unidentified Golden Retriever had been picked up at the Truscott Estate that morning. She frowned. If this was Monty, how on earth did he get there and was it possible he knew Larry Nice? Larry claimed a dog attacked him. It couldn't be, could it? Was this a sign Larry was indeed the killer? She was about to pick up the phone when she noticed the time of the message.

'Two fifty-five? Why didn't you tell me earlier?'

Pearl shrugged. 'Because we're here to solve a murder, not chase after bloody dogs.'

Rose knew her face was pink with fury. 'But you could've told me.'

'Just have.'

He turned his back on her and carried on with his raiding-a-brothel story which she'd heard too many times before. It took all her self-restraint not to slap him across the back of his head. Her hands trembled as she dialled the Peasemarsh Pound. She was near boiling point when she heard the answer machine tell her the pound was closed and would re-open at nine the next day. Poor Monty would have to spend the night there. Rose left a message anyway, asking if someone could call her as soon as possible.

She headed for the door.

'Hey!' Pearl called across the room. 'You apologised to DI Morgan yet?'

Everyone stared. 'Not yet, sir. On my way now.' She had been avoiding it.

'Off you go then. We'll have a stretcher waiting.'

With dread, Rose climbed the two flights to level four, but the Drugs Squad rooms were empty. Relieved, she raced to the car park at the back of the building where she'd left her fifth-hand, dented, silver Honda Jazz.

'Sidebottom!'

A stocky man with a crew-cut in a well-worn leather jacket left his motorbike and strode towards her. Shit! Andy Morgan. He had more tattoos than most of the biker gang members he'd arrested, including a black widow spider and web on his neck. She'd always wondered about that tattoo because in prisons it often symbolised a drug addiction.

'Are you screwing Craig or what?'

He stood too close intending to intimidate. Had he been waiting for her?

Rose flushed pink. 'Sir, I can't apologise enough for messing up Nailgun. But how dare you imply I'm sleeping with my boss!'

'Why else would you still be working Major Crime?'

His face was contorted with fury, his body rigid. Rose pushed her hand out and placed it firmly on his chest.

'Step back! Now!' she said, trying to keep her voice calm. She placed her other hand on the pepper spray in her belt.

He glanced at her outstretched arm, then to her hand resting on her belt. He took a few paces back.

'Jesus!' he said, shaking his head. 'That was out of line. Sorry.'

Rose stood her ground. 'I should've noticed I was walking into a sting. I won't make that mistake again. If there's anything I can do to make up for it, I'll do it, sir.'

Morgan kicked the tarmac. 'Any idea where Summers might've gone?'

Rose thought back to her conversation with him. 'I don't know. We talked about the coast. Living by the sea.'

Morgan gave her a cold stare.

'Brighton. He mentioned Brighton. Sounded like he'd spent quite a bit of time there.'

'What? Recently?'

'I can't be sure.'

'Did he talk about any mates?'

'No.'

Morgan shook his head. 'Still think you should be back on the beat.'

He jogged over to his bike, pulled on his helmet, turned the ignition key and sped away.

Trembling, Rose dived into her car and left the car park. But she wasn't afraid of Morgan; she was furious with him. And insulted. She wound down the windows to let the night air in, taking deep gulps. As her anger dissipated, her self-doubt grew. Perhaps Pearl and Morgan were right? Maybe she wasn't cut out for the job? If only Aunt Kay were here to advise her.

At a red light, Rose rested her forehead momentarily on the steering wheel, remembering one summer holiday at Duckdown Cottage. She'd been thirteen. At her feet, Legless the Dachshund snapped at imaginary flies. She was shucking home-grown peas into a colander. Kay was making chutney, stirring the contents of a large saucepan. Rose broke the companionable silence.

112

'I told mum I want to be a police officer like you.'

Kay glanced at her. 'And what did Liz say?'

'Over my dead body.'

'Ah. Didn't think she'd like the idea.'

'She wants me to study tourism and take over the guest house. I can't think of anything worse.'

Kay turned off the gas burner and sat next to Rose. 'Liz and I have very different views of the world . . .'

'Is that why you fell out?'

'No, it was over you. At Glastonbury, when you were six.'

Rose's parents had left her alone all night at Europe's largest music festival and she'd gone looking for her mummy. Kay, on policing duty at the festival, had found her, lost and crying, her dress sodden, feet caked in mud. It wasn't until the next morning that Liz reported her daughter missing and there had been an almighty row.

Kay continued. 'All I can say is that you must do what makes you happy and be true to yourself. Don't ever pretend to be someone you're not, especially to please others.'

'How do you mean?'

'Well, for a while it seemed like I was never going to make it. Being a woman didn't help, so I overcompensated. Tried to be one of the lads, tougher, harder than the male officers. It wasn't until I stopped pretending to be someone else, and started using my head, that I made detective.'

A car horn jolted her from her memories. The traffic light was green. Rose accelerated and headed for home.

It was barely light when Rose drove through Farley Green and up the gravel drive of Duckdown Cottage. Still shaken, she stepped out of the car and leaned against it. She stared up at the four front windows – two up, two down – which were the only parts of the house still vaguely aligned. Everything else was at an odd angle, including a collapsed section of guttering, the uneven floors within, and the leaning outhouses. The front door, which had once been dark blue, had lost patches of paint to reveal the bare wood beneath. It was so badly warped with water damage, it was stuck shut. A solitary solar panel, a token to modernity, sat on the slate roof that leaked in the rain. She hoped the buckets inside had caught most of the morning's downpour. She simply didn't have the money to deal with the roof right now.

Rose looked at the untended rose bushes lining the front wall. They stood crooked but proud, like veterans on Poppy Day. Her aunt would be saddened if she knew her garden was running wild. But she'd be livid if she knew how Pearl and Morgan had treated her. Rose had already decided reporting them was pointless – her word against two senior and respected officers. No, she'd keep her head down and prove the bastards wrong.

'I just need something to go right for a change,' Rose said aloud.

Since she'd moved here, life had become complicated. Rose had just graduated from police college when her aunt died from throat cancer, leaving Rose the cottage in her will. She'd sought a posting to the Geldeford station and got it. Everything went downhill from there: her parents refused to speak to her, embarrassed their daughter was joining The Filth. It was against their hippy principles. When Rose arrived at the cottage, she was shocked at how dilapidated it was. She'd walked through every room feeling like an intruder, touching Kay's favourite leather armchair, a mug with her name on it that Rose had made for her in pottery class, and

Kay's clothes, still hanging in the wardrobe. Rose had little time to mourn, though; she was starting a new job the next day, the phone and electricity had been cut off, and there was a hole in the roof large enough to see the sky through. That was two years ago and she was struggling to keep the house from falling apart.

Rose didn't bother to lock the car. It wasn't worth stealing. On the kitchen bench top she found a note from the plumber: 'Gave drains a good flushing but willow root has cracked pipe. Will email you a quote, but it's a big job. Will need an excavator. Garry Smithson.'

She was too tired to worry about it. Instead, she emptied the buckets full of rain water, opened a bottle of cheap red wine, made a simple spaghetti bolognese, and ate in the back garden. A train rumbled to a halt at the nearby station, breaks screeching, but Rose had got used to the noise and found the trains' regularity comforting. A couple of ducks waddled up to her and pecked the cracked pavers, hoping for scraps. Apart from the occasional quack, the place was too quiet. No excited barks, no patter of dog paws, and no soft warm head leaning against her leg. She hoped Monty wasn't too miserable at the pound.

'What am I going to do with you?'

Rose couldn't take a dog to work, and there were too many gaps in the fence to keep him at the cottage. She could shut the wooden cross-bar front gate — at least that was still standing — but she needed to secure the perimeter. She flipped open her laptop lid, turned it on and checked the state of her bank account. Not good. Fifty-seven pounds and ten pence till pay day. She got out an old address book of Kay's and dialled the handyman she used to use.

'Yes?' he shouted down the phone.

Ed was easily in his seventies and hard of hearing but refused to wear a hearing-aid. She remembered he'd lost a finger to a horse.

'Ed, this is Kay's niece at Duckdown Cottage.'

'Bit late isn't it?' he replied. It was 8:42p.m.. 'I'm in bed.'

'Sorry to call so late but I wondered if you could help me out? I need the holes in the fence fixed and something to stop a dog getting through the hedge. I know Kay thought very highly of you.'

'Kay? Ah, yes Kay. Now she was a lovely lady. Yes, indeed. Who did you say you were?'

'Rose, I'm Kay's niece. I live at Duckdown now.'

'Ah yes, I remember you as a girl. A tiny little mouse you were, with a squeaky voice.'

Rose felt like stating she was all of five foot three and three-quarters now.

'I have a dog and I need to make sure he doesn't escape. Can you secure the fence for me?'

'The fence you say?'

'Yes, I think there's a couple of rolls of chain link fencing in the shed. Perhaps you could use that?'

'A dog, you say? What kind of dog?'

This was turning out to be a longer and harder conversation than she'd hoped. She took a deep breath.

'A Retriever.'

'That's all right then. It's them small dogs that bite. Kay's Dachshund was a vicious little bugger. Nipped my leg on more than one occasion and dug up my asparagus.'

Rose exhaled loudly. 'So, Ed, are you still doing handyman work?'

She hadn't seen him since she was a teenager, and he'd appeared old even then. His trousers were always too baggy and he had to constantly pull them up despite a piece of rope around his waist.

'What? Course I am! On my pension? I've got no choice. Miserable buggers.'

'Any chance you could come round here early tomorrow? I'm sorry to give you such short notice, but my dog ran away today.'

'Dog ran away, did it?'

'Yes!' Now Rose was shouting.

'Probably escaped through that broken fence,' said Ed. 'You should get that seen to.'

Rose was tugging at the end of her ponytail in frustration. 'That's why I need you here tomorrow morning. To mend the fence.'

'Right you are then. I'll be there at sparrow's fart.'

Suddenly their conversation was back on track. All she needed to do was establish when sparrows farted. 'When is that, then?'

'Will six do you?'

'That's great, but I have to tell you I can't pay you very much. I can do fifty quid but that's all I have till pay day. If you need more after . . .'

'That'll do for now,' Ed replied and ended the call.

Rose gulped down the glass of wine and poured another. Her mind turned to Patrick Salt. She just didn't buy into the idea that Larry Nice was a murderer. Was it really a burglary gone wrong? Or did someone want Salt out of the picture? Was it revenge? Jealousy? Or maybe greed?

She logged into her personal laptop. She was keeping her

notes on the Salt case there. Private notes. More like questions and hypotheses; ideas she'd never want her workmates to see. She opened a picture of the murder weapon. No prints on it. A folding knife, but nothing like the angular compactness of a Swiss Army Knife. The blade was shaped like a tear drop with a very sharp point. The steel had tiny wavy lines through it. The handle was black, possibly resin, and reminded her of a slim aubergine. Something was written in Mandarin or Cantonese on the handle and she'd asked a translator to look at it. Where on earth would small-time crook and general loser, Larry Nice, get an exquisite knife like this?

She Googled speciality and hunting knife stores and found nothing even remotely similar available in the UK. Then she trawled through Chinese knife distributors. She was about to log off when an image caught her attention. A Shilin Cutter. A traditional Chinese knife only made by one family in Taiwan, highly prized by collectors and very difficult to buy outside of that country. The handle wasn't resin, it was buffalo horn. The blade was Damascus steel, layered and folded in production to make it strong, resulting in an intricate wave-like pattern on the surface. Nice didn't even have a passport so the only way he could have got hold of such a knife was as a gift, or by stealing it. Such an unusual murder weapon had to be a clue. She wanted to know more about the knife, and knew the perfect person to ask.

Francis Grace.

Chapter Eighteen

Luckily for me, most people underestimate dogs. And we prefer it that way. *The Commandments* restrict what we can and can't show big'uns, for the sake of peace and harmony between our two species. Number six says we must never reveal we understand big'un language. But that's how I know I'm due for the chop – and not the lamb kind. I've been categorised as 'aggressive' and, as Rose hasn't claimed me, I'm going to have to take my life into my own paws and break outta here.

The last big'un has just left for the night. I wait and listen. Have you ever had a theme tune stuck in your head and it won't go away? Well, thanks to the humming squirrel I met the other night, I've got the *Mission: Impossible* theme on a loop. It's driving me bonkers. My fellow inmates are sleeping. Ralph, whose jaw's been broken in the past, snores. Some whimper in their slumber, others jerk their paws and utter closed-mouthed barks, dreaming of running wild and free. Even Lola, the Chihuahua, has stopped her day-long yapping and is curled up on a cushion. The lights are off and, with no windows in the cell block, it's very dark. Perfect. Time for action.

I stand and place my right forefoot into the gap in the criss-cross metal bars. My paw is too big to fit right through, but I can get it far enough to feel the hook of the latch against my toes. The stitches in my chest pull a bit but I ignore it. I focus hard and lift my paw. The latch pops up and out of the metal loop. The door falls ajar and with my forehead I push it wide open.

'How the flying-ferret did you do that?' asks Taz from the next door cage. He has gone from being sound asleep to totally alert in a matter of seconds.

'I leant a few tricks from the Queen's Corgis.'

'OMG!' yaps Lola, lifting her head. 'Get outta here! How do you know them royals?'

'It's a long story.'

Outside my cage, I indulge in an almighty shake, from the point of my nose all the way down to the very tip of my tail. Everything is moving and flapping. It's the best feeling. A great stress-reliever.

By now most of my fellow prisoners are awake and lined up at their cage doors as if awaiting an inspection by the screws.

'Anyone want to come with me? I can get you out of here, but after that you're on your own. I'm going to find my new master and I can't turn up with a whole pack.'

They all bark at once.

'Quiet!' I say. 'Big'uns will hear us. Now *be quiet*.'

Silence, except for a whimper from cage fifteen.

'I'm leaving right now, so stay close to your door if you want to be freed. If not, step back.'

Lola stays on her pink cushion. 'No thanks, I'm a high-maintenance kinda gal. A stray's life is sooo not my thing.'

Taz, on the other hand, has his face squished against the door so that his fur is indented with metal squares. 'I'm in. I'm in. Oh yeah, I'm in.'

I lift his latch and he charges out, bolting up and down the concrete corridor with glee.

'What about you, Ralph?'

The Staffie hasn't moved. He has his back to me, his head on his paws, his shoulders slumped.

'What's the point?' he says, his voice as rough as sandpaper. 'You're never getting out of here.'

'It'll all be over tomorrow,' he sighs.

I don't understand and look at his report card. Tomorrow at ten he's being 'put to sleep'.

'Ralph, mate! Save yourself! Come with us.'

Ralph shrugs. His spirit is broken. I don't have time to argue so I lift his latch, just in case he changes his mind. Other dogs are barking at me to free them, so I flick their latches. There are eleven of us including Charlie and the old fella, Nelson. Apart from Lola and Ralph, only Bubbles the Dalmatian-cross decides to stay and take her chance at adoption.

Professor Salt used to tell me that humans don't know if dogs talk to each other, or whether the barking is just demanding attention or issuing a warning. I guess by now you know the answer. But we keep verbal communication simple. We're not into long-winded conversations. Lola may well be the exception to that rule. Some of my kind understand other creatures up to a point. I'm lucky, I guess. I find it easy to pick up the lingo. I speak squirrel, mouse, rat, rabbit, magpie, small bird, several insects, and of course, cat, although a conversation with a cat is usually short, punctuated with expletives and ends in a fight.

Ever wondered what dogs are saying when they bark at cats? It generally starts out with, 'Get thee gone, demon!' and goes on from there. A touch old-fashioned, I'll admit, but basic Cat is one of the few languages mums teach their pups and the same ancient phrase has been passed from one generation to another for centuries. I guess cats and dogs regard each other in the same way as the British and the French. It's a love-hate relationship based on deeply ingrained suspicion that goes back as far as the Battle of Hastings in 1066.

Legend has it that Harold II was killed by an arrow in the eye. Not true. *The Dog Chronicles* – our oral history – tell us that it was Harold's trusty hunting hound who took the arrow, so his master could live. The archer who fired the arrow was said to always have a cat on his shoulder for good luck. Harold was later killed in battle, so the dog died in vain. But word spread throughout England of the hunting hound's heroism and loyalty, and that the cat had directed the archer to aim for the dog. And so the animosity began.

'How do we get through this door?' asks Taz, head-butting it repeatedly.

The doorknob is a long smooth stainless steel handle that you push down to open. I shove Taz aside, raise my forepaws and stand tall against the door. I bring my chin down on the handle and *click*, the door opens outward and I fall into a dark corridor. I land with a thud on the slippery floor and yelp. My chest wound feels torn. I look down, but from what

I can see the stitches haven't changed since Malcolm put them there. I stay still for a moment, panting away the sting. The other dogs go berserk and stream past me. There's a bottleneck of furry bottoms and wagging tails at the other end of the corridor where there's another closed door. I get up and open it.

A tsunami of dogs bursts into the reception area with destructive force. Taz slams into the reception desk, turns around, hits a wall and does it again, loving every minute. Nelson, a bit unsteady on his old legs, collides with a chair on wheels, which then smacks into shelves of medication. Pharmaceutical packets rain down on him. Charlie crashes into shelves of dog food, bags of treats, bowls, collars, leads and muzzles and sets about tearing at the bags of dried food. Some even smash into the main entrance doors, which appear to be of steel with glass panels protected by bars. I try and stay calm and look around me. On the reception desk are computers, phones, notepads and pens. Against the wall is a row of visitors' chairs and a large weighing machine. My fellow inmates have picked up on the heady aroma of kibble and are helping themselves. They've forgotten we're trying to escape.

I pad over to the entrance doors, which look out onto a small car park, now empty. I sit, my head cocked to one side, as I contemplate the sturdy double doors which stand between us and freedom.

In my twenty-one dog years of life, or three human years, I have come across many different doors. Wooden, glass, sliding, steel, roller, folding, you name it. Almost all of them have locks. What is it with big'uns? Why must everything be locked, gated and fenced?

Most locks have keys, some have bolts or little knobs you turn one way or another, and others have a keypad with numbers on them. The doors I am staring at are key-locked. But there is no key. Hurrumph. This is not good. I hear the crack of a dried pig's ear and inhale the delicious oily smell. I can no longer resist. A quick snack will do me good. Feed my brain cells, or so I tell myself. I crunch my way through a couple of porky triangles as I consider the problem. My master hid a spare house key under a plant pot in the back garden. It was wrapped in a plastic bag so it wouldn't rust. That's it! I must find the spare key.

Taz is ripping apart boxes of flea treatment and then spitting out their bitter contents. Behind the reception desk I find lots of cables (if I had time they might be worth a chew), a waste-paper basket – unfortunately empty of titbits to eat – a filing cabinet, but no keys. I keep looking, nosing my way through packets of medication, loads of paperwork with 'Invoice Paid' stamped on them, even find a dog biscuit in a jacket pocket left hanging over a chair. But no keys.

I start to panic, grab my tail and chew it. There must be another way out? An open consulting room door beckons me. I release my tail and investigate. I give a howl of joy when I see a casement window is ajar above the examination table. I feel an unexpected breeze behind me and turn quickly, ready to attack. But it's only my own tail whirring with excitement.

'In here!' I call.

They stampede towards me. The small room becomes a sea of seething strays. Now to get onto the examination table.

'Can you all step back?'

The dogs move aside. Some end up back in reception. I hear growling but ignore it. In normal circumstances leaping onto a table this high wouldn't be a problem, but my wound is still tender. I do a full circle to ready myself and then jump, landing on the long slippery table. With a paw, I lift the casement stay and nudge the window wide open and look down. I see a low and springy box hedge and muddy flower bed bordering the tarmac of the car park. Nothing we can't handle.

'OK, this is it. One at a time. Up on the table and then out the window. I see shrubs and an empty car park. Then a busy road. So watch out for cars.'

I feel like their mother.

Taz is first. He leaps through the window and zooms off down the street yelling, 'Oh boy oh boy oh boy!' The other dogs follow, except Charlie, whose little Jack Russell legs are too short to leap up that far. He tries several times and fails.

'I'm done for,' he says and hangs his scruffy head.

I hop down.

'Can you jump onto my back and then the table?' I ask.

His little tail wags so fast it blurs and his bushy eyebrows bristle. 'Can I ever!'

I position myself as close to the table as possible. He leaps onto my back but falls off the other side.

'Flippin' hell!' Charlie mumbles.

On the fourth attempt he manages to reach the table top. He dives out of the window, bounces off the box hedge and lands in the car park.

'Thanks, mate,' he yaps. 'I owe you one,' and runs off.

Finally, it's my turn and I dive through the open window.

The pound's car park has no lighting but the street lights bathe everything in an iodine-orange glow. Stars shine in a clear sky. Traffic rattles by. I sniff the air, hoping for a clue to where I am. But none of the smells are familiar: petrol and diesel fumes, beer and wine, and the tantalising smell of pizza.

'Wait!'

Ralph's broad, scarred face appears at the open window. Despite his missing back leg, he fearlessly jumps into the box hedge, rolls over and rights himself, leaving a deep dent in the shrubbery. He stands stock still, staring at me, his expression glum. Seconds pass.

'You ever need help, leave a wee-mail, and I'll find you. Name's Jake, not Ralph, by the way.'

Then he skips off at surprising speed for a three-legged fellow. I squeeze through a hole in the perimeter hedge and poke my head out the other side. Yup, there is a pub opposite and next to it, a café, which is closed. Further down the street is a pizza place with one of those little delivery scooters parked outside. Marco's Pizzas, the sign says. Ah, mozzarella, bacon, ham, pepperoni . . . I am lost for a while, and then snap out of it. I know those hypnotic aromas! I remember the name on the box! Paddy used to order home-delivered pizza from here, so I can't be too far from Paddy's place.

I had planned to find my way back to Duckdown Cottage and beg Rose's forgiveness, but I have no idea where the train track is, let alone which direction to go. But I can find Paddy's house. I long to sniff the comforting smell of his old cardigan. I want to relive all those wonderful memories in the smell of my bed. I crave my familiar world.

I wait until there is a gap in the traffic, run across the road and down a narrow alley. The back door to Marco's Pizzas is open, so I lie down near it and listen to what the people in the kitchen are saying. My nose pulsates at the pizza pong wafting my way. I salivate – I mean, who can blame me? It's a huge effort to stop myself rushing into the kitchen and stealing those heavenly discs of dough. I am dreamily sniffing an egg and bacon pizza (one of my many favourites!) that's just come out of the oven, when I hear someone mention Christchurch Road. Pepperbox Lane, Paddy's street, is just around the corner. I sit up, peer round the doorframe and see a teenage boy placing piping hot pizzas into a red, insulated satchel.

'Sixty-one Christchurch Road for those two, and thirty-three Ash Hill Drive for the extra-large pepperoni. Okay?'

The boy nods, places funny white blobs attached to wires in his ears and disappears from view. I charge down the alley and follow the boy to the main road. He is cut off from the rest of the world by loud music and doesn't notice me. The scooter has gone. He opens the door to a vehicle more like a roller-skate than a car. He slides the pizza bag onto the front passenger seat, goes round to the driver's side and opens the door. His mobile phone rings – I'm surprised he can hear it above the music. He wanders away from the car for a chat. I hop onto the driver's seat unnoticed, and squeeze through to the backseat where I lie flat on the floor. The teenager gets in and drives off at high speed. I find myself licking the edge of the pizza bag through the gap between the front seats. When I realise what I'm doing I pull my head back. Some time later, he opens his door and gets out. I leap out too. He swears and drops the pizzas.

I bolt, knowing instantly where I am. I can smell the rich aroma of flowing river water, mud and tall grass. The river is that-a-way, and so is my old home.

Chapter Nineteen

Why I'm surprised there are no lights in the windows, I'm not quite sure. Rose told me my beloved master was dead and I knew his heart had stopped when I lay next to him. But as I trot down Pepperbox Lane and see our home, my heart lifts. I half-expect Paddy to open the front door and say, 'There you are! Was wondering where you'd got to.'

But the door remains shut.

I stop short of our front gate because there is yellow plastic tape across it and the driveway. Paddy's Volvo Cross Country Estate is trapped behind it. I jump the low gate and sniff the car tyres. Ah, fond memories of our adventures together: the woodlands, beaches and pet supply shops we've visited. I can even detect a whiff of his parking spot at the university. The chocolatey smell is from the flowerbeds bordering the car park, which are covered in cocoa shell mulch.

I creep down the dark side passage, wondering what I will find when I turn the corner. I stop and sniff the air. The smell of sun-baked blood on brick pavers hits me like a whack across the snout with a rolled up newspaper. I freeze, then pull myself together. I take the plunge and turn the corner into the back garden.

More yellow tape. The chair is still where it fell when the killer startled Paddy. His wine glass has gone. I step onto the patio, one hesitant paw after another. I look at the exact spot where he died, and recognise the scent of both my blood and Paddy's, mixed together. I whimper. I'm short of breath. I long to be with him and need to howl. But I daren't. Someone might hear me. So I pant fast instead.

My water bowl is exactly where Paddy left it, wedged between the back doorstep and the hedgehog-like boot brush. Running has made me thirsty and I take a hearty drink. I'm surprised my bowl carries Rose's scent, but I guess she must have spent a lot of time here at the crime scene. Refreshed, I place my front paws on the back door. Time to get into the house where Paddy's smell is strongest. I know how to turn the round doorknob. But it won't budge. Somebody has locked it. I whine, desperate to be near Paddy's things. I nudge over an inverted flowerpot where he hid his spare key, but it's been removed. I run around the house, but the windows are shut and the front door deadlocked. Defeated, I lie as close to him as I can be – next to his blood. The pavers still hold the scent of musty books, his cardigan and, where his head hit the bricks, Paddy's oatmeal shampoo. I breathe it in and close my eyes.

I hear a tapping on the pavers and sniff. I open one weary eye.

'Dante?'

He stands very close and scowls at me. 'So you made it back safely? Thanks for bothering to let me know.'

I open the other eye.

'Didn't know you cared,' I tease, but I'm touched he has bothered to check up on me.

'Don't be absurd.' Dante shudders at the thought. 'So where've you been?'

'I got taken to Dogmo but managed to break out,' I explain.

'Ah, that was you, was it? Dogs have been yapping all night about "the great escape". Exceedingly annoying.' He juts his head forward. 'Rose know?'

'Don't think so.'

'As usual, humans will be the last to know,' he says, sighing at what he regards as one of the big'uns' many limitations.

'Can you help me find Rose's house tomorrow?'

'I might do.' Dante tilts his head to one side. 'Would you open the garden shed door for me? There's a good fellow.'

I feel a pang of anger. 'So you're really here to get power for your laptop?'

Dante dips his head as if scooping up water in his beak. He's embarrassed. 'And to see you, naturally.'

I drag my weary body to a stand. 'This doesn't feel right. It's somehow disrespectful to Paddy.'

'I don't understand why. I used his power point when he was alive. Why can't I now?'

Dante has never shown a moment's empathy and has upset many creatures who could have been friends. I'm too exhausted to argue. I just want to sleep.

I plod over to the wooden shed, turn the circular door-knob and the door swings open on well-oiled hinges. I gulp back a sob. Paddy's tools are displayed neatly on three shelves and the lawn mower's body glints, it's so impeccably clean. His leather gardening gloves and straw hat are on the middle shelf. I sniff them and whimper. They trigger memories of happy days: Paddy weeding as I roll on the grass enjoying a good scratch, Paddy mowing the lawn as I bark at the lawn-mower, Paddy in his deckchair, admiring his handiwork as I snap at flies.

Dante watches in silence. I take a glove in my mouth and carry it back to where I was resting. I lie down, place my head on the glove and shut my eyes.

I wake with a start. The sun is up, and from its angle I know it's early morning. A car door just slammed shut at the front of the house. I blink and rise quickly. My heart is racing. Has the killer returned? He won't get away this time. I hide behind a rhododendron bush to the side of the patio and wait, ears forward, listening, hackles up. I hear the tap of shoes coming down the side passage. I brace to pounce. Then Rose appears, calling my name. Her hair is wet and loose, as if she has only just finished a shower. Her eyes immediately lock onto the blood-stained bricks. She sees the glove, frowns, then looks around the garden.

'Monty, where are you, boy? It's okay, you're safe now. Monty?'

I stay hidden. I had expected to bound up to her, tail wagging. But fear grips me like the dog catcher's noose. I disobeyed her. What if she doesn't want me any more and sends me back to Dogmo? I can't go back there. I watch as she walks the length of the lawn. She stops at the garden gate and peers along the riverbank.

'Monty!'

I find it hard to resist. She strides back up the garden, notices the shed door is ajar, looks inside, shuts the door and frowns. She pulls from her pocket some liver treats. It's a new packet, too. Fresh and delicious. She sprinkles a few on the ground.

'Monty! Look what I've got.'

Oh boy! My favourite, well one of many, actually. I'm salivating, especially as I haven't had breakfast. Rose waits a moment and then heads back towards the front of the house. She's leaving. I can't resist any longer. I crawl from my hiding place and snaffle the tasty morsels. So focused am I, that I don't hear her walk up and grab my collar. I pull away immediately, front legs stretched forward, head and shoulders low as I tug backwards, hoping my weight and strength will force Rose, who is slightly built, to let go. But she doesn't.

'Monty, stop pulling! I want to take you home. Don't you want to live with me?'

I immediately sit still, tongue out, tail slapping the ground. She wants me back! I'm so happy!

Rose clips a lead to my collar and kneels so we are face to face. That's a brave thing to do with a dog you don't really know. She gives me a good scratch behind the ear.

'You're a real escape-artist, aren't you?'

Well, compared to those wily woofers at Windsor, I am but a mere pretender.

'Gina from the pound called. She was hysterical. Going on and on about a break-in. But it wasn't, was it, Monty? It sounds more like a break-*out* to me.'

Rose laughs like water tinkling over rocks and scratches me under my chin.

'How ever did you manage it?'

I close my eyes. I'm putty in her hands.

'It must have been a terrible place, you poor boy.'

I lick her bare arm and taste ducks, grass and shower gel.

'Let's go home, shall we?'

I walk over to the back door and bark at it. I want to take my dog bed, my toy duck and something of Paddy's with me. I stare fixedly at the door.

Rose checks her watch. 'Not now, Monty. I'm running late. I've got to drive you home and then get to work by eight-thirty. Fat chance!' she sighs.

I reluctantly give in and follow her to the car.

'Let's hope Leach doesn't notice my absence.'

I'm guessing this leach is the big boss. Sounds like a slippery dude to me. I don't think I'd want to lick him. Leaches taste horrible. So do snails. Pah!

I leave a wee-mail with my news at the front gate, and then jump onto the car's back seat, which I fill completely. I pick up a faint whiff of squirrel, which always cheers me up. They are playful sorts, always up for a game or two, although Nigel seems to have forgotten how to have fun. Have you ever seen a squirrel dew-skate? They do this on the wet surface of car roofs and bonnets. It's even better when frosty, when they use their claws like ice skates and slide round and round.

Rose winds down the back windows and, as we set off for Duckdown Cottage, I stick my head out, allowing the buffeting air to flap my ears and wobble my jowls. My nose pulsates, sucking in breakfasty aromas, kids' packed lunches, cars, buses, taxis, people walking, cafés cooking. I bark a 'Hi there!' to a Cocker Spaniel on a morning walk and howl at the big McDonald's sign.

'Hungry?' Rose asks.

I bark.

'Me too.'

She pulls into the drive-through and orders two bacon and egg McMuffins and a coffee. She unwraps one, blows on it and then hands it to me. I devour the salty, sugary, sticky yumminess and spend the rest of the journey licking my lips.

Life is good!

Chapter Twenty

Rose arrived at police HQ ten minutes late and missed the early part of Leach's briefing. He scowled as she crept into the room.

'Good of you to join us.'

Everyone turned and stared. Rose went beetroot and slunk to the back of the room.

'We're still waiting to find out if Forensics has anything conclusive from the scratch on Nice's arm. But he hasn't been bitten. Which says to me we've got the wrong bloke. Or he was working with someone else. Dave – check out Nice's known associates and see if they've got alibis. Do we have their fingerprints on file?'

'On it, boss.'

'Varma, anyone confirmed Nice's home-alone story?'

'His neighbours claim they didn't see him go out, but no alibi.'

'Joe, any news on the torn jacket?'

'We've searched his flat, the estate, including bins, his lock-up and Salt's house. Nothing yet, sir.'

'Keep looking. Search the river path and the roads near Salt's house. Rose, anything new from old man Grace?'

'He claims he didn't see the offender and he didn't recognise Nice's photo.'

Pearl snorted dismissively. She wanted to say she thought the old man was hiding something but knew she'd be laughed at.

Rose continued. 'Grace said the Professor was a man of routine. He'd leave for the university at eight and return home at six. He walked the dog before and after work. I'd hazard a guess the killer knew he'd be home by seven. Rather than being surprised to find Salt there, I think he expected him.'

She glanced at Pearl, who gave another snort. This didn't fit his burglary-gone-wrong theory.

'Right,' said Leach. 'Spread the net wider. I want fingerprints from the victim's neighbours, friends and workmates. Tell them it's just routine and for elimination purposes. I want to know if any of them had reason to kill Salt. Got it?' He glared around the stuffy room. 'Varma, you drive this one.'

'Yes, boss.'

'Anything else?'

'Yes, sir,' said Rose. 'I think the murder weapon is a Taiwanese Shilin Cutter.'

She received a murmur of interest as she filled them in.

'The little git probably nicked it, like everything else in his lock-up,' said Pearl.

'But Shilin Cutters are made by one Taiwanese company only. They're very rare and very expensive. It's hardly the sort of thing a bloke like Nice is going to get his hands on.'

'So who does it belong to, then?' said Pearl, crossing his arms.

'Likely to be someone who's travelled to Taiwan or is from that region. Grace is a collector of East Asian artefacts. Bit of an expert, it seems. I think it's worth finding out more about this knife from him.'

'Nice work, Rose,' Leach said begrudgingly, still irritated by her late arrival.

The briefing over, Rose was assigned the job of trawling through Salt's personal phone and banking records, which meant she was desk-bound for the morning.

'See if you can talk the solicitor into giving us Salt's will,' said Varma, leaving for Court to apply for a warrant for both the will and Salt's work files. 'Will save me the trouble.'

Pearl dragged another detective with him to rattle some of Nice's dodgy mates, hoping to discover a potential accomplice, while Salisbury and another uniform continued the hunt for the killer's torn jacket.

Rose checked Salt's phone and banking records, but everything was boringly routine. Next, the solicitor. Rose recognised her name: Sylvia Blight had been Kay's lawyer. She dialled the number.

'Rose, my dear, how aaaare you?' boomed Sylvia. 'Still at Duckdown?'

Rose recalled Sylvia's frizzy red hair, startling green eyes and plump body draped in a kaftan of vibrant colours. She ran an equally alternative legal practice from her home.

'I am and the house is still standing. Just,' she joked.

'Good for you. And I hear you made detective. Congrats, darling! I always knew you'd follow in Kay's footsteps. Good to see more female detectives, I say.'

'Thanks, Sylvia. I'm afraid this isn't a social call, though. You're executor of Patrick Salt's will, aren't you?'

Sylvia went quiet. 'I am, and you want to know who inherits?'

'I do. This is a murder investigation.'

'Yes, I'd heard. Poor Patrick was the nicest man. But you know I can't tell you without a warrant.'

'Sylvia, we're getting one, but time is of the essence. How about helping me out here? If I guessed Rebecca Salt was the main beneficiary, would I be on the right track?'

'You might say that, but I couldn't possibly comment.'

'Thanks, Sylvia.'

'She lives in Australia, you know. She can't have had anything to do with Patrick's death, if that's what you're thinking'

'I couldn't possibly comment.'

'Touché,' said Sylvia, amused.

On the way out, Rose knocked on Leach's door. He glanced up from his monitor. 'Yup?'

'It looks like the daughter inherits.'

'Nice work. Find out when she arrives in the country, will you? And drop by Grace's house? See if the old man knows anything about those Shilin Cutters.'

Pulling up outside Grace's house, Rose noticed a white Vauxhall Corsa parked in Salt's driveway, nose to tail with the deceased's Volvo. The yellow crime scene tape had been run over and snapped in two. The car had a Hertz sticker in the window and had clearly just been picked up: clean interior and exterior, except for some mud on the tyres. Was Rebecca already in Geldeford? A flicker of movement through the dining room window caught her eye but she couldn't see if the person was male or female. She used her Airwave radio to call it in, requesting back-up, and pulled out her baton, in case the killer had returned. She heard the back door open so she stepped quietly down the now familiar side passage. As she snuck a quick look around the corner, a blonde woman of Amazonian build and healthy tan stepped out of the back door. Rose showed herself.

'Police, stay where you are!' Rose shouted, holding up her warrant card.

The woman jolted to a halt. 'Jesus, you scared the crap out of me! What're you doing here?'

From the accent, Rose instantly knew who she was.

'I'm Detective Constable Rose Sidebottom.' *Forget the trainee bit*, she thought. 'And you are Rebecca Salt?'

'Who else would I be?'

The woman in figure-hugging jeans was one high-heeled boot away from contaminating the blood-stained pavers.

'Can you move away from the tape?'

'All right, all right. Keep your hair on.'

Rebecca stepped back and lifted her large-lensed Calvin Klein sunglasses onto her head, revealing bloodshot brown eyes. She looked Rose up and down, taking in the cheap cut of her suit and the drool stain on her trouser leg. The glamour girls at Rose's high school used to look at her the same way, sneering at her plain jeans, T-shirts and trainers. All these years later she still felt the sting of this woman's silent criticism.

'Can I see your ID?'

'Jesus! You must be joking?'

Rose waited. Rebecca sighed loudly.

'Passport's in my bag. Find them yourself.'

Rebecca shoved the bag into Rose's hands. There were

two passports: one UK and the other Australian. Both confirmed her identity.

'Thank you,' Rose said, handing them back to Rebecca, who snatched them away. 'We didn't know what time you were arriving.'

'So?'

'I'm sorry for your loss, Ms Salt, but you can't stay here. This is still a crime scene.'

'Look, Rose whatever-your-name-is, I've just got off a long flight, I need a shower and something to eat, and quite frankly, I don't need you telling me what to do. This is my dad's house and this is where I'm going to stay.'

In the distance, a police siren wailed. Rebecca raised her eyes.

'Oh great! What now? You going to arrest me for being in my own home? I have a key, you know.'

Rebecca held out her hand and shook a set of keys as if she were ringing a bell. 'See?'

'Ms Salt, I'm not sure if you know much about the circumstances of your father's death . . .'

'I can't deal with that right now.'

The police car stopped outside the house, the siren on full bore.

'Jeez, welcome back to Old Blighty!' Rebecca complained.

Salisbury and another male officer appeared.

'Everything okay?' Salisbury asked.

Rose made the introductions, then focused back on Rebecca Salt. 'I'm sorry, but until my DCI releases the crime scene, you'll need to stay somewhere else. Is there anyone you can contact? A friend? A relative?'

Rebecca opened her mouth to object.

'Sorry for your loss, miss,' said Salisbury. 'This must be very difficult for you, but you really can't stay here. I can drive you to a nearby hotel if that helps.'

Rebecca's demeanour changed. She gave him a blindingly bright, obviously expensive, white-toothed smile.

'You can take me anywhere, officer!'

Salisbury looked down and shuffled his feet, embarrassed. An angry mob didn't faze him, but a flirtatious woman floored him every time.

'Only joking,' Rebecca continued. 'I'll drive myself.'

Rose had clocked the chunky wedding and engagement rings on her hand. 'Did your husband come with you?' she asked.

Rebecca frowned. 'Already here on business. London and Southampton. He'll join me at the weekend.'

'And his name is?'

'Troy. Troy Fratting.'

'You haven't taken his surname?'

'No. Why should I? I've worked hard to establish my business, Salt Executive Search.'

'We'll need to know where you're staying. Here's my card,' Rose said. 'In the meantime, do you have a UK mobile number?'

With another sigh, Rebecca gave it to her. 'Can I go now?'

'Thank you, we'll be in touch.'

Giving Salisbury a flirtatious wink, she swivelled on her heels to leave, then stopped as if she had just remembered something.

'So when can I bury him?' Rebecca asked, as if enquiring when the next bus was due.

'We're not ready to release the body yet, I'm sorry. We'll let you know as soon as we can.'

'I can only stay in the UK a week. I've a business to run and I need to get back. So can you get a move on?'

As Rebecca drove away, Salisbury said, 'She's clearly grief-stricken.'

'Yeah, and I wonder how long her husband's been in the country? Interesting she didn't mention he was here when we notified her of her father's death. You'd have thought he'd have contacted us on her behalf.'

'I'm guessing she didn't get on with her dad,' said Salisbury.

'Or perhaps he didn't get on with her?'

Chapter Twenty-One

Francis Grace greeted Rose with his skull-like grin and ushered her into his hot-house sitting room. She handed him an enlarged photograph of the murder weapon and observed his reaction. At first he just squinted. But when his reading glasses were on, he gawped. The old man's skin was normally pale but Rose was convinced he turned a shade of grey.

'Oh my God!' he exclaimed, one hand touching his heart.

Rose leaned closer. 'Mr Grace? Are you okay?'

He nodded.

'Do you know this knife?'

He looked from the photo to Rose's concerned face and back to the photo. 'Is . . . is this . . . this killed Patrick?'

'We believe so. What can you tell me about it?'

'It . . . well, it's mine.'

She hadn't expected that.

'Yours?'

'It's priceless. Over a century old. I bought it in Taiwan.'

'Are you sure it's yours?'

Grace pointed to the Chinese symbols along the buffalo horn handle. 'This, here, is more than the signature of the maker, the Chiu family. It's a unique number. Mine's especially lucky because it includes an eight – number 85.'

'So how did the killer happen to have your knife?'

He removed his glasses. 'It was stolen a few weeks ago. I just haven't got around to reporting it. The thought of dealing with police reports and insurance companies . . . too exhausting. I just can't be doing with all that palaver at my age.'

'Can you recall the date it was stolen?'

His head shot up. 'How the hell would I know? It was there one minute and gone the next.'

Rose took a deep breath. It was like pulling teeth. 'So when did you first notice it missing?'

Grace wrung his arthritic hands. 'Let me see.' He seemed to be staring at his slippers for a long time. 'It was the morning of that wretched bank holiday. Yes, that's right. I remember that terrible music festival was on. What a racket! All those layabouts and hooligans wandering about, up to no good. Wouldn't be surprised if one of them stole it. The whole thing should be banned.'

'You mean the August bank holiday?'

'Yes, yes. I know it's a while ago, but I find I get so tired. Just too much effort to report it.'

'What time did you notice it missing?'

'Oh I don't know.'

'Have a guess.'

'I'm old and it takes me a long time to get ready in the morning, so it must have been around ten when I came in here and saw the knife wasn't in its case. I hate weekends and public holidays, you see. Nothing for me to do. It's all very well for you young people. You've got someone to be with. But us old folks are left all alone.'

He was right. She hadn't been alone on the August bank holiday. She'd been with the body of a woman found beaten to death in an abandoned warehouse.

'So why didn't you tell us about your stolen knife when we last spoke to you?'

'I don't like your tone, young lady!' he snapped. 'Why would I presume that it was my knife that killed him?'

Rose was losing patience.

'Mr Grace, you need to make a statement. I'll have to take you to the station.'

'Must I? Can't we do it here? I don't really like leaving the house.'

'I'm sorry, sir, we need to do this right. I'll look after you, don't you worry. I'll give the station a call and let them know to expect us. And we can take your fingerprints then, too. For elimination purposes.'

Rose called Pearl from the hallway. When she went back into the sitting room, Grace was peering out of his front window as if searching for somebody.

'Expecting someone?' she asked.

Grace turned too quickly and stumbled, but steadied himself by grabbing the corner of a Chinese black-lacquer table, inlaid with mother-of-pearl. 'Stop creeping around! You nearly gave me a heart attack.'

'Where did you keep the Shilin Cutter, Mr Grace?'

He nodded at a black-lacquered tray with a glass lid, shaped like a butter dish, on the same table Grace was gripping. 'In there.'

Rose noted the flick-over window locks were not being used.

'I need to bring it with us.'

She bagged the tray and lid.

'We'd best be on our way,' she said. 'Let me help you.'

Rose went to take his arm but he pulled it free, grumbling about the inconvenience. He shuffled off to get his thick woollen coat, even though it was warm outside.

'Now where are my keys?' he mumbled.

After some minutes searching, they were found in his coat pocket. It took another five to locate his wallet. Rose had almost walked him to her car when he remembered his walking stick.

'Can't go anywhere without it. Doctor says I could fall again, so I have to use my stick.'

It was clear he found anything outside his routine difficult to manage. Rose was inclined to believe him when he said that reporting the theft was simply too daunting.

'Any idea who might've stolen the knife, apart from the people at the music festival?' she asked, as she drove off.

'No idea.'

Rose's fingertips tingled. Grace shot a nervous look out of the car window.

'Is something bothering you?' she asked.

'Don't be ridiculous,' he snapped.

Rose had a feeling that Francis Grace knew something but was too afraid to admit it.

Chapter Twenty-Two

Pearl got to conduct Grace's interview. Rose, yet again, got to watch. She'd asked, but Pearl had said no, pulling in Varma instead. The old man took an instant dislike to Pearl, which cheered her up no end. It was like watching a dried-up old puddle and an oil slick – the two just didn't mix. Grace continued to claim he hadn't seen the killer and he didn't know who'd stolen his knife. He was a convincing liar and Pearl fell for it. Rose didn't. There was something important Grace wasn't telling them. And why was the old man suddenly scared, when the theft hadn't seemed to bother him at the time?

She was doing a background check on Troy Fratting when Leach called his detectives together. As usual, Rose sat at the back.

'Listen up. We have the DNA results on the cotton fabric found in the dog's mouth. The DNA does *not* belong to our prime suspect.'

Rumblings of disappointment spread through the team.

He continued. 'And Salt's killer is not in our DNA database.'

A few moans.

'But we do know something about him. Male. Blood group A, Rhesus negative. And . . .' He paused until he had everyone's full attention. 'There was enough blood at the scene to establish he's had malaria.'

Approving murmurs.

'So he must've worked or travelled somewhere tropical,' commented Varma. 'Asia, Africa, South America, India. Almost anywhere near the equator.'

Like Grace, Rose thought, but she wasn't dumb enough to say it out loud. There was no way the fragile old man could've attacked both Salt and the dog. Unless he had an accomplice.

Rose cleared her throat and was about to speak, when Pearl waded in.

'Boss. It still doesn't rule out Nice,' he said. 'There could've been two of them. He nicks the goods, the other bloke stabs Salt. I mean, let's face it, the Truscott Estate is full of scum who'd nick their grandmother's commode if they thought they could get some cash for it.'

'Careful, Dave,' Leach warned.

'Sir, it's a fact. I've arrested most of 'em.'

'Since you know the estate so well, find out if any of Nice's contacts have had malaria. And get Nice to give us some blood, will you?'

'On it, guv.'

'Any news on the jacket?'

'Nothing yet,' Varma answered. 'Nice claims he wore the jacket to The Hog and Hare a few weeks ago, and was so pissed he left without it. But the publican doesn't remember it.'

'I still say that little toe-rag is involved,' said Pearl. 'He's burned the jacket or dumped it somewhere we can't find it.'

He won a few nods of approval.

Rose couldn't bear it any longer. She spoke up, but it came out as a croaky whisper.

'Speak up, Rose,' said Leach.

She cleared her throat. 'Sir, I think this East Asian link is promising. Our suspect has malaria and used a Taiwanese knife.'

A few nods around the room encouraged her to go on.

'Why use Grace's knife? It's so distinctive. Why not just any old kitchen knife? Is he somehow connected to Grace?'

Leach nodded. 'Good call, Rose.'

'Sir?' said Varma. 'Grace is not the only suspect to have done business in the tropics. Rebecca Salt's husband, Troy Fratting, sells millionaire's yachts and his main market is South-East Asia. We should pay him a visit and get a blood sample.'

'Rose, where is Troy staying?'

'He's at the Southampton Boat Show, staying at the West Quay Grand. Rebecca is joining him this weekend,' she replied.

'Good. We now know Fratting arrived at Heathrow two days before the murder so he had opportunity. But what's his motive?' asked Leach, peering around the room like a school teacher challenging his pupils.

'Money?' Rose piped up, but it sounded like a suppressed hiccup. Everyone turned to look at her. 'His wife is the main beneficiary. The house must be worth four hundred thousand and our Professor had around fifty thousand in savings. Fratting runs a Sydney-based boat-building business. The kind with a price tag of fifty million and up. But the global financial crisis has hit even the super-rich, which means sales are down and he's in trouble.'

'Interesting,' said Leach, crossing his chunky arms.

'Who else gets a slice?' challenged Pearl.

'The dog gets some money so he's cared for, but I hardly think Monty stabbed his master in the heart and then himself for dramatic effect, just so he could inherit an allowance. Dumb mutts aren't clever enough to plan murder,' she replied, fed up with the way he tried to put her down all the time.

This comment earned some snickering. Pearl glared around the room and everyone went quiet.

'Sir,' said Pearl, 'I'd like to interview the daughter,' he paused for a second too long, 'and her husband.'

Leach gave him a wry smile. 'That would have nothing to do with her blonde hair and large *assets*, now would it, Dave?'

Rose had to suppress a groan.

'No, sir, not at all.' Pearl grinned.

'Fratting was Kamlesh's suggestion, so Kamlesh, you go to Southampton and interview him. Rose, you go too. And get Fratting's permission for a blood test. Got it?'

'Got it,' replied Varma, giving Rose an encouraging nod.

'Dave, check out the malaria connection. Then move on to Rebecca. But try not to drool. Not a good look.'

'On it, boss,' said Pearl, licking his finger and using it to chalk up his victory in the air. The Pearl fan club laughed.

'What are you all doing standing around?' boomed Leach. 'We have a case to solve. Get a bloody move on!'

Chapter Twenty-Three

They arranged to interview Troy Fratting at the West Quay Grand in Southampton. An unmarked white Ford Focus was assigned to them.

'Why don't I drive, sarge?' said Rose. 'You can relax.'

'You can't use the blues and twos, so I'll drive,' Varma replied, taking the keys. Trainees hadn't earned such privileges.

'What will we need them for?'

'You've never been to the boat show, have you?'

He smiled knowingly and opened the passenger's door for her. She blushed with embarrassment. His manners were impeccable, but it made her feel awkward.

'Oh, James, you're such a gentleman,' she said breathily, doing her best Miss Moneypenny.

'You know me. Licensed to thrill,' he said wryly, as he hung his jacket on a hook at the back, picked a hair off the lapel then bent down and dropped it on the asphalt to ensure it didn't sneak back into the car on a gust of wind.

Soon they were cruising down the M3 motorway towards Southampton. Varma talked through how he wanted to handle the Fratting interview. Then he changed the subject abruptly.

'It's not easy being a female detective. Even these days,' Varma said.

'Why do you say that, sarge?' she asked.

Their eyes met for a second, then his were back on the road.

'Because it's not easy being a cop of Indian descent, either. But it's worth persevering.'

Rose took a long look at her DS. Neatly ironed shirt, suit trousers with crisp creases, polished black leather shoes, closely shaven face, cool-looking sunglasses, classy aftershave, jacket hanging at the back. He looked more like a fancy-pants City banker than a cop.

'I probably shouldn't say this but for the life of me I can't understand why you're not a DI. You're just as good as Dave,' she said.

'Ah, flattery. It goes a long way.'

'No, I mean it. You stay level-headed whatever happens and you don't jump to conclusions.' *Like someone I can think of*, she thought. 'And your attention to detail is incredible.'

He grinned. 'Thanks, Rose, but Dave's got a real knack, and his informants' network is second to none. You know he was brought up on the Truscott Estate? But don't tell him I told you.'

'No, I didn't, but it makes sense. Explains how he knows so many people there.'

'His schoolmates have all done time. Scum-of-the-earth, most of them, but they give him what he wants to know. In return . . . well, that's between him and them. But it's one reason why he's an Inspector and I'm not.' He fiddled with his sunglasses. 'Look, Rose, I know you're going through a rough patch right now, but don't give up. Between you and me, I almost threw in the towel many times. So many times I wondered why I was doing this wretched job. I've been punched, spat at and abused way more than the others and I'm always the outsider.'

'So why do it? You've got a degree in economics. Why be a detective?'

'Corny as it sounds, I wanted to make a difference. And now I'm a detective, I have to prove someone like me can make it to the top. But I have to work harder and be smarter.' He nodded his head at her. 'You have to do the same. Be better than them. Don't expect them to make it easy for you either. That's never going to happen.'

'I know that. But my biggest problem is the very reason I joined the Force in the first place. My Aunt Kay. Everyone assumes I got into Major Crime so young because of good old nepotism.'

They zoomed past the turn off for Fleet Services near Basingstoke. Its only claim to fame was 'Loo of the Year' back in the nineties.

'Hey, you can make it, Rose. But you've got to convince them you've got the balls for the job.'

'I'm not very good at that.'

'Well, start practising.'

Rose wondered how much she should confide in Varma. 'I'm giving the Salt case my all, sarge. But I don't think the boss rates me and after the Nailgun disaster I get the feeling Dave isn't keen on me staying around.'

He looked over the top of his sunglasses at her. 'You ballsed up a major surveillance op, Rose. All things considered, I think Craig went easy on you. He wouldn't have done that if he didn't rate you.'

'Really?'

'Don't mistake his gruffness for dislike. That's the way he is.'

'And Dave?'

'My advice? Get back in his good books.'

Easier said than done, she thought.

As they left the motorway and joined the A33, traffic slowed to a crawl. At the Chilworth roundabout it was grid-locked. They'd made good time up to that point: forty-two minutes. The remaining six miles could take just as long.

'Time for the blues and twos,' said Varma. 'Told you.'

'Got it,' said Rose, slapping a blue flashing light on the roof and switching on the siren.

Varma accelerated hard and she was thrown back into her seat. He wove skilfully in and out of traffic, following signs to The Docks, until they reached the hotel car park. The West Quay Grand had once been a stunning cream-painted Georgian building with tall rectangular windows and stone steps leading to polished brass double doors. But it was now fronted by a four-storey-high pyramid of steel and glass, which housed the reception and foyer, as well as the bar and restaurant. To Rose it looked as if the misguided architect had returned from Paris desperate to find any excuse to mimic the Louvre's pyramid and unfortunately this hotel had been his next project.

Inside the hotel, they spied a man who must be Fratting lounging in a high-backed wicker chair next to a stone pot of miniature palm trees. In his thirties, he had shoulder-length wavy grey hair tied back in a short ponytail. His pink shirt was unbuttoned enough so you could see his tanned chest and he wore a pair of navy Bermuda shorts and navy Crocs that looked like rubber clogs with heel straps. Nursing a pint of beer, he couldn't have looked more laid-back if he'd tried. He waved them over.

'You've gotta be cops. Bit warm for a suit, isn't it?' Fratting held out his hand. 'Take a seat.'

As Varma made the introductions, Rose removed her jacket. Varma unbuttoned his but kept it on, preferring to remain formal however hot it was.

Fratting turned his craggy, tanned face towards a waiter, clicked his fingers in the air and ordered two beers before they'd even settled into their chairs.

'On duty, sir,' said Varma. 'I'm afraid we can't.'

'Just two tap waters, please,' Rose said to the waiter, who wandered off in sulky silence. She saw him turn on the charm for a group at the next table who were noisily working their way through bottles of Moët.

'So,' Fratting said, 'what can I do you for?'

Varma kicked off the interview. 'Mr Fratting, we're sorry for your loss. We just need to ask you some routine questions.'

'Go ahead.'

Troy sucked on his beer. His eyes wandered around the room, occasionally resting on an attractive woman. He was clearly mourning his father-in-law.

Varma waited. Fratting's gaze returned to Varma.

'What're you waiting for?'

'You're an exhibitor here, I understand?' Varma asked.

Fratting picked up some salted peanuts and threw them in his mouth like a performing seal catching fish. 'That's right.'

'Tell me about your business.'

'I run Fratting International.' He tapped his chest. 'I *am* Fratting International. We custom design, build and distribute motor yachts between seventy and a hundred and thirty feet. I'm showing our new skylounge model, *Sassy 11*. She's an absolute ripper. Want to take a squiz?'

'Must cost a pretty penny to exhibit here,' said Rose, nodding in the direction of the marina where hundreds of boats of all shapes and sizes glinted in the sunshine.

'Sure, but this is how I do business. Get 'em on board, get 'em excited. Maybe even get 'em pissed. No better way to bond with someone, you know,' Troy replied, saluting them with his pint. 'It's all about getting them to like me and trust me.'

I'd rather trust a second-hand car salesman, Rose thought.

'Sold any?' Rose asked.

He winked and clicked his tongue. 'Too right.'

Three teenage girls in shorts and tank tops giggled as they walked by, momentarily distracting Fratting.

'Sir?' prodded Varma. 'Where were you on Friday night?'

Fratting's smile faded. 'Now wait a minute. Am I a suspect?'

'It's a routine question, sir. To eliminate you from our enquiries.'

Fratting put his beer on the table slowly, giving him time to think.

'Here, of course. Friday was the second day of the show. We were real busy that day. Took a few orders, too. And in the evening, I was wining and dining a client.'

'The client's name?' Kamlesh asked.

'Matilda Rutter. You'll have heard of her.'

Rose had. Rutter hotels and luxury holidays. A formidable

businesswoman and one of the richest in England. Varma jotted down the details, seemingly unimpressed.

'When did your dinner start and finish?' he asked.

'Well, the show doesn't end till six-thirty, so I guess I met her here around seven for drinks, and then we ate at the hotel restaurant at eight-thirty.'

'And she can verify this?'

'Why don't you ask her yourself?' Fratting replied as he waved at a slim, smartly dressed woman with a black bob, who, from a distance could pass for thirty, but close up, was clearly into her fifties. She wore a white linen jacket and trousers and a shimmering silk blouse in gold. Her gold handbag was Chanel and the diamond hanging from a chain round her neck looked big enough to buy the hotel. Or perhaps she already owned it? Rutter sauntered over to Fratting on high-heeled, strappy Jimmy Choos, also in gold.

'So sorry to interrupt,' she said, air-kissing Fratting. 'I've just bought *Sassy 11* from this adorable Aussie.' It sounded like Ar-sy, in a poor attempt at an Australian accent. She waved her hand around, unintentionally almost clocking Rose with a sapphire large enough to gouge an eye out. 'You really must have one! It's simply divine!'

Without being invited, Rutter sat in a vacant chair at their table and waited to be introduced.

'Matilda,' said Troy. 'These are detectives Varma and Sidebottom. They're investigating my father-in-law's death.'

'Really! My, my, Her Majesty's police force has really smartened up. There was me thinking you were buyers.'

Rutter gave Varma the once over. 'Nice cut. Who's your tailor?' she asked.

'Matilda, my dear, they need you to confirm we had drinks and then dinner here on Friday night.'

She blinked twice, but kept her eyes on Troy's face. 'Friday night? Let me see. It's been so busy. I'm a sponsor, you know.' Finally, she fixed her gaze on Varma. 'Yes, we had drinks, then dinner at Oceania, the restaurant here.'

No, you didn't. The tingling in Rose's feet had shot up her body so fast it felt like a mouse scampering up her spine.

'What time did you meet for drinks?' asked Varma.

'I can't recall exactly. But I know dinner was at eight-thirty. Troy had a booking.'

She stood.

'What did you eat?' Rose asked.

'What? I don't recall. Oh yes I do. The salmon en croute. And oysters as entrée. Now I really must dash. I hope you find the killer, officers. Poor Troy has been distraught.'

She turned to leave.

'Mrs Rutter,' said Rose. 'A moment, please. How can we get in touch with you if we have further questions?'

She opened her handbag and gave Rose a business card. 'Call my secretary, Natalie,' she replied, nodding to the bar's entrance where a young woman in a suit, with an iPhone glued to her ear, was deep in conversation.

Rutter left the bar a touch faster than she'd arrived, grabbed Natalie's arm and steered her out of the hotel.

'There! Told you,' said Fratting, slapping his thighs. 'Ask the restaurant staff. They'll confirm the booking.'

Maybe, but will the bar staff remember you? thought Rose.

'Do you have a car?' she asked.

'Yes, a hire car.'

'I'll need the model and registration please.'

Fratting frowned, pulled out a key from his shorts pocket and gave it to her. An Avis tag told her it was a black BMW 428i coupé and the licence number.

'Sir, do you know the details of Mr Salt's will?' Varma asked.

'No, but I'm hoping my wife gets everything. I mean, who else is the old bastard going to leave his money to?' he joked.

'Did you get on with him?'

'Didn't see him much. A bit of a stuffy old bugger but he chilled out after a few drinks.' He paused. 'We weren't enemies, if that's what you're implying.'

'When was the last time you saw him?' Rose pitched in.

'Must be a year ago.'

'Why didn't you contact us when you learned of your father-in-law's murder?'

'What would be the point?'

'Well, you could've identified his body, helped us with our enquiries.'

Poor old Mr Grace had to do it instead.

'I wouldn't have had time.'

'One more thing,' said Varma. 'We'd like to take some blood and fingerprints. Just routine, so we can rule you out.'

'Now wait a minute! What do you mean rule me out? How can I be *in* in the first place? I was here in Southampton.'

Rose said, 'Blood was found at the crime scene that doesn't belong to your father-in-law. We need a sample so we can rule you out of our investigation.'

'No way.' Troy shook his head. 'I'm not doing anything without a solicitor.'

Troy opened his smartphone and dialled.

'Got nothing more to say. This meeting is over.'

They thanked him for his time and left the bar.

'He's not telling the truth and Mrs Rutter's covering for him,' she said, in the hotel foyer.

'Why do you say that?'

She hesitated. 'Mrs Rutter was vague about the pre-dinner drink and scarpered as fast as she could. But what I don't get is why she'd give him a false alibi.'

'That's up to us to find out. I'll question the hotel staff. You start going through the CCTV security footage.'

'Oh goody,' she said. 'Hours of fun.'

Hotel security was little more than a stuffy windowless cupboard in the basement next door to the laundry. It had two chairs, a console and some screens relaying live footage from numerous CCTV cameras around the hotel. A small oscillating fan perched on top of a filing cabinet feebly attempted to keep the claustrophobic space cool. A tall, skinny security guard in his early twenties had gone out of his way to help, excited to assist a real live detective. He sat way too close to Rose as she combed through footage from the day of the murder and kept asking her distracting questions about her job.

'Please go about your duties as normal,' she encouraged.

'Nah, they can wait. Wouldn't miss this for the world,' he replied, sidling even closer. 'Two cameras cover the car park. This one covers most of it,' he said pointing at one monitor. 'What time do you want to see?'

'I'll handle it from here,' she said. 'I've used these before, thank you.'

'It's no problem. Really.'

'I'm sorry but this is confidential. You'll need to leave.'

He looked as if he were about to cry. 'You sure?'

She nodded. 'But I'll let the hotel manager know how helpful you've been.'

He perked up. 'That'd be great. Could do with a pay rise.' He shuffled to the door. 'Use the two-way if you need me,' he said pointing at a radio, recharging on a rack.

'I will.'

Rose waited till she could hear his footsteps disappearing down the dimly lit corridor, then she turned up the fan to top speed and watched the car park footage from mid-day Friday. Given the boat show was huge, Fratting could have easily left, unnoticed, before his supposed date with Rutter. She spotted his black BMW parked not far from the boom gate. She fast-forwarded. The car didn't move and there was no sign of Fratting. Until 5:58p.m., when he got in his car and drove off.

'Got you!' she said.

Excited, she called Varma on his mobile. A few minutes later, he'd found his way through the labyrinth of basement corridors.

'Show me,' Varma said.

She replayed the footage.

'So where did you go?' said Varma, watching Fratting leave. 'We'll need street footage, from Southampton to Geldeford.'

'No problem, sarge,' she said. Her finger hovered over the fast-forward button. 'Let's see what time he came back.'

The hotel car park was busy that evening but at 8:26p.m. Fratting's BMW 428i coupé reappeared. All the parking spaces were full, so he left the car next to some large bins outside the hotel kitchen, ignoring the No Parking sign. He half walked, half ran into the hotel, in a real hurry.

'Two and a half hours unaccounted for,' said Rose.

'That's just enough to drive to Geldeford, kill Salt and still make his dinner at eight-thirty.'

'But why would someone like Matilda Rutter lie and say they had drinks together first?'

'I don't know but I asked the bar staff and they don't remember seeing her, and let's face it, she's not easy to forget with all that bling.'

'Sarge, what if they're lovers?' said Rose. 'They could have easily snuck off for a quick shag. Mrs Rutter wouldn't want news of an affair leaking out, so maybe that's why she lied for him?'

'Looks like we're watching some more footage.'

Chapter Twenty-Four

Ed and I have reached an understanding. I stop peeing on his fence posts, and he stops poking me with his walking stick.

By the time Rose had dropped me off at Duckdown Cottage that morning, Ed was already putting up a chain link fence. Well, to be exact, he was doing a lot of pointing. The real work was being done by a teenage boy in a black T-shirt and torn blue jeans who swung a pick into the dry, compacted earth with the ferocity of wolves fighting over a carcass. Regardless, I greeted our visitors with tail wagging, tongue hanging out. After all, I need to prove to Rose that I'm worth keeping. But the old man took one short-sighted look at me and said:

'Looks a vicious brute. You keep him away from me, miss.'

Somehow Ed must have mistaken my smile for a snarl. So, I shut my mouth and sat, quiet as a butterfly, doing my best to look as harmless as possible. The boy glanced in my direction. His hair and eyes were as dark as a blackbird's feathers. I can usually read a big'un's eyes. Paddy could flick a look at the TV remote control and I would instantly bring it to him. Or he'd look at me with sadness in his eyes after speaking on the phone to his daughter, who lives far, far away. But not this boy. There was nothing in his eyes. Like watching the TV when it's switched off. I had never met a big'un like him.

'This is Finn, my neighbour's grandson. He's helping me today.'

I could tell that Rose had also sensed Finn's anger. It was like static electricity. If you got too near, it zapped you. She kept a safe distance from the boy.

'Nice to meet you, Finn,' she said, but she didn't sound too sure.

Finn continued swinging the pick as if she hadn't spoken. Rose gave the old man a questioning look.

'What can I say?' Ed shrugged. 'Teenagers, hey?'

'But shouldn't he be at school?'

'Phyllis asked me to keep him busy today. That's all I know, miss.'

I saw indecision ripple across Rose's face. She looked as if she was about to ask another question and then changed her mind.

'I've got to get to work,' Rose said, checking her watch. 'I'll put Monty in the kitchen, but as soon as you're done, can you please let him out into the garden. He can't stay inside all day.' Rose handed Ed a back-door key. 'Pop this through the letterbox when you go, will you?'

Ed doffed his frayed tweed cap. 'Right you are then.'

'Oh, and here's fifty quid,' Rose said, pulling the only remaining note from her purse, the leather of which appeared as sunken as Ed's face. 'I get paid next week, so I can give you more then. What do I owe you?'

Ed rubbed his chin. 'Another fifty and we'll call it quits.'

Rose looked relieved. I dutifully followed her into the kitchen where she left me and drove away. I drank from my water bowl and then, bored, shoved my muzzle part-way into the hole in the skirting board and called for Betty. She wasn't home, but I could tell she had been around recently because her distinctive combination of smells was strong. I dozed for a bit, then woke and contemplated chewing a corner cupboard but decided that didn't live up to my 'good dog' aspirations. So I let myself out of the back door, having first checked that neither Ed nor Finn could see what I was doing. I shut the door behind me. I wasn't going to run away. I simply wanted some company.

Ed didn't see me approach from behind so – to reassure him I had no vicious intentions – I gave his hand a soft lick. Clearly, he has good reason to fear being bitten, having already lost a finger. The old man jumped at my touch and raised his walking stick, as if to hit me. But Finn stepped forward and gripped Ed's scrawny arm. I can only guess Finn's age – perhaps fifteen – but he has the height and strength of a man.

'What are you doing? The dog's dangerous,' complained Ed, trying to pull free.

I had fled to a safe distance, observing them. Finn simply shook his head, released his grip, then picked up a spade and started digging again. I wandered off and left wee-mails on the posts already in the ground. They announced Larry Nice's innocence and pleaded for new leads.

'Cheeky sod!' Ed shouted, spying me with leg cocked.

He tottered after me and tried to whack me with his stick, but I was too fast. As I sped off across the lawn I caught Finn laughing and felt his anger dissipate. But not for long. The emptiness flooded back into his eyes, like a roller blind drawn down over a window, and, once again, the pick smacked into the earth with brutal force. For the rest of the morning I watched them work, always far enough away to avoid Ed's stick, but near enough to pick up Finn's curious scent of boxing-gloves, gym sweat and sheep gut. As he hammered hooks through the chain link fencing into a wooden post, I noticed the faintest whiff of somebody else's skin coming from his hands, and that his right-hand knuckles were grazed and bruised.

The sun has now tipped its head towards the afternoon, and the fence unravels like a very long snake. Every now and again Finn looks at me lying in the grass and I lift my head, ears pricked expectantly, tail slapping the ground, but the boy never responds. And he doesn't say a word to Ed the whole time. With the key to the house, they go inside and help themselves to mugs of tea, and, as the sun grows warmer, I doze on the lawn.

My whiskers twitch as they are fanned by the flapping of minuscule wings. I ignore it. Just the garden insects going about their business.

'Hey, big boy,' I hear, the voice female and husky.

I open my eyes to discover a seven-spotted ladybird standing on a blade of grass, not far from my nose. But she is no ordinary ladybird. I blink slowly. Am I dreaming? Nope, she is definitely wearing thigh-length black boots on four of her six legs. She looks straight at me fearlessly, almost provocatively. She emits a scent that's making me slightly giddy, but would be enough to blow a male ladybird's mind.

'Got your wee-mail,' she says. 'Name is Celeste, and you must be Monty.'

I nod, careful not to squash her.

'I think our two cases could be connected,' she continues.

'Cases?'

'Yes. I run the Celestial PI Agency. I put the "I" back into "PI",' she says, raising the red and black domed casings that hide her wings. She unfolds her wings at lightning speed and spreads them wide too. It's like I'm watching my own mini carnival parade of vibrant colours and extravagant costumes. She winks at me.

'I see,' I say, although I don't really. 'What does the "I" stand for?'

With a barely audible click, her wings are stowed away again. 'Insects. I solve *insect* crime.'

'Is there much insect crime?' I ask.

'Is there? Of course there is! Death by drowning – get a lot of wasp complaints in the summer when loved ones drown in beer. Messy business. Returning the bodies can be a problem. Stag beetle disputes – now, they can get very nasty if they're not sorted out quickly. Stag beetles tend to go in for fights to the death, which means I sometimes don't get paid if my client dies. And there are loads of ant wars – I managed to stop a huge territory dispute the other week. Got them to agree on hunting ground boundaries. Oh, and black widow spiders – they're very enterprising. They hitch rides here in banana crates, you know. Well, I can't tell you how many marital disputes I get dragged into. She's usually trying to eat him, you see, and he doesn't like it.'

'Never thought about it that way.'

I lift a back leg, intending to give my ear a good scratch whilst I consider my next question.

'Careful! You could swat me.'

I try scratching *carefully* but it doesn't work. I miss my ear twice because I can't get the right rhythm going, so I give up.

'Have you worked on a big'un murder case before?' I ask.

'No I haven't, but that's exactly why I'm here,' she says, her voice bubbling with excitement. 'Patrick Salt is what both our cases have in common.'

The calendar girl of the insect world's PI business has just dropped a bombshell. It takes a while to sink in.

'Celeste, if you know anything about Paddy's death, you've got to tell me. Please!' I'm panting fast.

'Yuck! Keep your doggie breath off me, will you? It stinks.'

'You're kidding, aren't you? Everyone knows that ladybirds have the smelliest . . .'

'Rubbish!'

Celeste folds her top legs across her body. I think I've offended her.

'I'll do my best not to pant over you,' I say, 'but what's wrong with my breath?'

'You've been to that culinary cess-pit, haven't you?' She taps her antenna knowingly.

'Huh?'

'You know, that burger place on the high street. Have you any idea how many insects die of food poisoning there? More deadly than insect spray! They're dropping like flies. Including the flies. There's a petition going round to close the place down.'

I try not to get distracted by the idea of flies campaigning outside the local fast food restaurant.

'Celeste, please tell me what you know about Paddy's murder?'

She lifts off the blade of grass, wings flapping furiously. 'Oh no you don't! Not so fast. I need your solemn promise that you won't try to steal my client. Word gets around, you know.'

'What word?'

'That you're setting up your own detective agency. On *my* patch. Well, that's what the rat world is saying.'

Betty Blabble. Of course. That rat loves to chatter.

'I don't know what Betty's been saying, but I don't run a detective agency. All I care about is finding my master's killer. That's all.'

Celeste hovers above my muzzle, her wings fanning a trickle of cool air across my face. She lands on a dandelion head and peers deep into my brown eyes. I have to suppress my natural instinct to snap my jaws at her. I've caught a good few flies in my time like that, but the wasp was a big mistake. Ouch!

'God, you're a handsome brute,' she says in her breathy way, flashing her scarlet wing covers at me flirtatiously and doing a mid-air pirouette. She lands on my nose, which sends me cross-eyed and for some reason makes me want to sneeze. 'Just so we're clear, I'm happy to collaborate with you and your team on this *one* case. But remember that Four Zero Zero Four is *my* client.'

Four Zero what?

'When can I meet your client?' I ask, trying not to breathe, which is well nigh impossible if you need to speak.

'Here. Tonight. When your new master is asleep.'

She shoots into the sky like a glistening red and black rocket. I exhale and sneeze at the same time.

Four Zero Zero Four? What kind of creature has a number and no name?

Chapter Twenty-Five

Rose arrives home after dark to find me peering over a rusty wheelbarrow. Next to it is a slatted wooden bench. They span the gap between the new fence and the side of the house, placed there by Finn to keep me in the back garden. I could easily jump the barrier, but choose not to.

Rose looks exhausted; her eyes are bloodshot and her walk is limp, like a week-old lettuce.

'Fence looks good,' she says, squinting into the darkness.

Good isn't exactly how I'd describe it. Reminds me a bit too much of Dogmo.

She moves the wheelbarrow aside and I race over, tail wagging and lean into her as she gives me a good scratch under the ear. Ah, that's perfect. Bliss! She tells me she's been in Southampton watching footage of Troy Fratting who's been 'a naughty boy'.

Where do I know that name from and has he been chewing socks or stealing food?

'Not only has he lied to us, but he's having an affair with

his alibi. I reckon he's a better suspect than Larry Nice,' Rose says.

I bark in agreement. I know Larry didn't do it.

'Hungry?'

Always, but that's not what I meant.

We go inside and, as I wolf down my dinner, Rose pecks at her toast and Marmite, leaving half-eaten crusts on the plate. She can barely keep her eyes open as she sinks into the sofa, fires up her laptop and researches malaria on the Net. This is a new word for me so I read up on it too. I jerk my head up. It hits me like I've just jumped into freezing water. Whoa! The disease I smelt on the killer has to be this 'malaria', spread by mosquitos, the insect I couldn't identify. But big'uns can only get this disease in countries around something called the Equator, which looks like a huge dog collar encircling the planet. I paw the screen. I want Rose to know this is important.

'Hey, don't scratch it,' Rose says, placing my paw back on the floor.

She senses my excitement.

'What is it, Monty?'

Dogs don't read, and I can't let Rose think otherwise. I've gone too far, so I lick the back of her hand and ignore what's on the screen. She peers deep into my eyes. I take back what I said about hers being the colour of Blu Tack. Her irises are more like bluebells with darker flecks radiating through the pale blue.

She frowns, then glances at the photo of a mosquito.

'Don't like mosquitos, hey? Is that it?'

I wag my tail, slapping the carpet. Once more, she peers straight into my eyes, which most of my kind find quite challenging. But I hold her gaze.

'I'd love to know what you're thinking.' She strokes my head. 'That'll do for tonight. I'm pooped. Bedtime, what do you say, Monty?'

She yawns and so do I. As she turns off the lights, I wonder if this Troy Fratting bloke has been to the Equator. Does he have malaria? I have a good shake, hoping to get my brain working. His name is familiar but I still can't place it.

The lead-light kitchen window is open and through it I watch clouds float across the moon and the big oak tree's branches scratch the sky. Rose is in bed asleep as I wait for Celeste to appear.

'Evening, governor.'

I look down to find Betty sitting on her chubby back legs, peering up at me.

She chatters fast. 'What happened to you, mate? I was bloody worried, I was. That so-called friend of yours, Dante, was no use what-so-ever. He just buggered off! Did they take you to the pound? I've heard it's terrible. They kill dogs there and turn them into dog food and . . .'

'Betty, stop!'

She takes a breath.

'I'm fine,' I say. 'I was taken to Dogmo, but I escaped.'

Betty hugs my leg. 'It's good to have you back. I missed you, mate,' she says.

I tell her about my jailbreak, how Rose found me at my old home, and meeting Celeste. Betty squeaks at the scary bits of my story and her grip on my leg gets tighter. It's now feeling like a compression bandage.

'I'm supposed to be meeting Celeste's client, here, tonight.' I glance at the window again, and then down at Betty. 'I wonder if Troy Fratting has anything to do with Paddy's death?'

She releases me from her embrace and looks up at me, confused.

'Who's Troy Farting, when he's at home?'

'It's Fratting, and he's Rose's new suspect. The strange thing is, I think I know him. Or Paddy did.'

Betty nods but she's distracted. Her nose is twitching and her head swivels towards the table. She's smelt the Marmite crusts.

'Fancy a snack?' she asks.

Before I have time to answer, she scampers across the floor, up the table leg, and has one of the four crusts in her mouth. She drops another one over the table top edge.

'Seeing as we're mates . . .'

With one snap of my jaws, the crust is gone. Betty sits in the middle of the plate and chows down on hers.

I hear a distant thrum of wings and Celeste flies in through the window. She lands next to the plate Betty is sitting on, with the grace of a ballet dancer.

'Get your filthy mitts off my grub!' Betty snaps, baring her teeth.

Celeste places two of her four legs on her hips, her dark compound eyes – all of them – glaring at the rat.

'Madam, if you think I'm remotely interested in dry old crusts, then you are sadly mistaken. I only eat gourmet.'

'Oooh, get you, Mrs la-di-da.'

Not a good start. I intervene.

'Celeste is the private investigator I was telling you about.'

'Geth I better be nithe to her, then,' Betty says, unintentionally spitting out crumbs, which she then shoves back in her mouth.

174

'This is Betty Blabble,' I say, then pause, realising I don't really know much about her.

'So, Betty,' says Celeste, 'what are your skill sets?'

Betty has almost finished the last crust. 'My what?'

Celeste sighs. 'I mean, how are you going to help us find Patrick Salt's killer?'

'Well, why didn't you say so?' Betty swallows the last morsel. 'How's about climbing, swimming, biting and stealing? Can hold my breath under water, too. That do you for "skill sets"?'

Oh dear. This isn't going well.

'Add to that French-speaker.'

'Really?' Celeste looks impressed. 'Eurotunnel?'

'Correct.'

'You're far from home.' There's a hint of suspicion in Celeste's voice.

'Nah, cause this is my home now,' says Betty, suddenly crouching on all fours as if about to pounce. 'So, let's be clear. Monty's my mate, and I'll do anything for a mate. I'm gonna help him find his master's killer. If he wants you around, that's his business. But I'm not gonna be bossed around by no bug. Got it?'

She slaps the table for emphasis with the end of her truncated tail.

'Fine by me,' Celeste replies. 'But there have to be ground rules. Everyone has a task and they do it. Otherwise, it gets messy, and I hate mess.' She stares at the pinhead-sized breadcrumbs scattered around Betty.

Betty hisses. Celeste starts to unzip a black, shiny boot. Oh no! She's going to release her terrible stink.

Yup, you got it – ladybirds have disgustingly smelly feet.

I'm not talking 'Who's got cheesy feet?' smelly, I'm talking weapons of mass destruction, mortally malodorous. One whiff and anything smaller than a dragonfly keels over. A rat, like Betty, will feel like she's been squirted by a skunk.

'Betty,' I say, keen to prevent Celeste from releasing her chemical warfare on us, 'I think Celeste should be pack leader. She knows how to investigate. I don't.'

'MI5 trained,' Celeste adds. 'Surveillance, interrogation, self-defence . . .'

'Give me a break! Bugs don't get to join MI5,' scoffs Betty.

'Correct, but we've infiltrated MI5 and spy on their training sessions. Usually upside down from the ceiling,' Celeste replies, with a firm nod.

'So, you're a spy. Whoopee doo. What's the point of learning about guns and terrorists and stuff? What we need is good old-fashioned instinct and animal cunning, which is what dogs are best at.' Betty tutts at me. 'Oh Mr Monty. You're more than a dog that follows orders and does clever tricks. *So* much more. You should be leading this pack. You gotta learn to trust your instincts, mate.'

'I'm a follower, not a leader, Betty,' I say. 'I can help by using my nose and teeth.'

'Someone has to lead this investigation, and I'm the only professional,' Celeste says.

Betty ignores her. 'Monty, you've been trained to think you can only follow orders. But, that's not true. You found your way to Larry's flat, and you led all those dogs to freedom. That shows real leadership.'

I shrug. 'I was lucky.'

'Rubbish! And I ain't taking no orders from bug-eyes over there.'

Celeste is tapping her boots on the table with impatience. 'I lead this investigation, or I leave. So, what's it to be?'

'You lead,' I say. Arguing is getting us nowhere.

Betty shakes her head in disapproval.

'Shall we get on with it?' Celeste says.

She then does something I've never seen before – she shoves her two front feet in her mouth and wolf-whistles!

I hear a deep droning sound, like those World War II buzz bombs I've seen in a documentary. A round fluffy bee, carrying a miniature red hot-water bottle, lands next to Celeste.

'Monty, Betty, this is my client, Four Zero Zero Four.'

'Please, just call me Four,' says the bee.

Betty looks confused, just as I am. What a peculiar name. I am about to say, 'Pleased to meet you,' when the bee bursts into tears.

'Pull yourself together, Four,' says Celeste. 'How can we help you if you keep crying all the time?'

'Oh you poor love,' says Betty. She scuttles over and strokes the bee's fur, careful to avoid her sting. 'There, there. We're here to help.'

'I'm sorry, it's just so awful,' Four manages to gasp.

'What is?' I ask.

'Oh Mr Monty, your master was a saint,' Four says, sniffing. 'He tried to save us, he did. He was our only hope.' More sobbing.

'This could take a while,' says Celeste, sighing. 'Come on, Four, tell the nice dog what you know. He's lost someone very dear to him too, remember.'

'Of course, how selfish of me. I'm so sorry about Professor Salt. I really am. You see, I think he died because of us.'

I am so taken aback, I snap my head up and bump the

table which sends Four and Celeste tumbling. Betty hasn't moved: she's dug her claws into the wood.

'What do you mean?' I say, a little sharper than I'd intended.

Four cringes. Celeste has dived between us and taken up some kind of martial arts stance, leaning back on four legs and holding two in front of her eyes. She looks like a Ninja wearing a round spotty backpack.

'Take no notice of him,' says Betty, mothering the bee. 'He's a big softy.'

I step back, giving Four some space. 'I didn't mean to scare you. I just want to know what you mean,' I say, trying to stay calm.

'Oh dear, where to start?' Four takes off and flies around in small circles just above my eye-line, which makes me dizzy.

'At the beginning?' I suggest. 'Why don't you sit here so I can hear your story.'

I gesture to the edge of the table nearest to me. The loud buzzing of her wings is drowning out her voice. 'I promise I won't hurt you.'

Four does as I suggest and hugs her hot-water bottle, which is clearly cold and empty, but it seems to comfort her.

'Okay, here goes. My hive is one of ten at Cherrywood Farm, about four miles away. In my hive, there were fifty thousand of us. But my colony started dying a month ago. In August! Our busiest time! The older bees die off during winter, so the young ones can help the Queen get the colony going again in spring. We expect that. But we've never had whole colonies die off in late summer. It was frightening. Every day we carried more and more bodies away from the hive and every day, fewer and fewer of us came back from pollen collection. One by one, everyone got ill, except me. I'm the last one left of ten hives.'

Four bursts into tears again and it is all I can do to stop myself whimpering in sympathy.

Betty cuddles her. 'You poor little love.'

'You must be very lonely,' I say.

Four nods. 'I was worker bee 4004. I had a purpose. I was happy. I had friends and a job and a nice home. Now, I have nothing. I can't make honey all on my own and if I can't make honey, I might as well be dead.'

'Don't talk like that, Four, my dear,' Celeste says. 'You are very much needed, I promise you. Now, tell Monty what you know about Professor Salt.'

'All right.' Four takes a big breath. 'I heard on the big buzz about this wonderful big'un who was trying to discover the reason why so many of us were dying. Then, eight sunrises ago, when there were only a few of us left, I overheard the farmer talking to a man he called Professor Salt. I heard your master say that the farmer should stop using pesticides in his fields and try a new type of hive that puts less stress on us. This didn't go down well with the farmer, I can tell you. The professor was explaining he had designed and built some new hives he was testing somewhere away from pesticides, with a new breed of strong, healthy honey bee. It sounded heavenly.'

Four pauses and looks directly at me. 'Do you know where this place is, Mr Monty? I have to find it. Otherwise I'll die of loneliness. I know I will.'

'Bees can't survive alone,' says Celeste, in a hushed tone.

I know how Four feels. If Rose hadn't adopted me, I might've given up. I want to help her and look around for my bed, but it's still at Paddy's place. Its smell might help jog my memory of the beehives. Instead, I try the next best thing to get my brain cells working: I chase my tail for a few seconds. It's a bit like using jump-leads to start a car.

'What's he doing?' Four asks Celeste.

'Search me,' she replies.

By now I have my tail in my mouth and look like a ring doughnut covered in fluff. Somewhere in my past, I see Paddy driving through a forest, with me in the back sniffing the rich aroma of pine and fox, then hearing the deafening sound of thousands of bees. But I have no idea if this is real or one of my dreams. I let go of my tail.

'Sorry, Four. I need my bed with all my memory smells. If I had that, I'd at least know if I've been there.'

'Okay, the doggie needs his bed. I get that,' says Celeste. Clearly, she doesn't.

She continues. 'But can we get on with Four's story? I've got other clients, you know. Time is money.'

Four clears her throat. 'Mr Salt gets kitted up so he can look inside the hives. He scoops up some of the bodies and puts them in a circular dish. He's about to drive away when a man in a red sports car arrives – the kind of car that goes very fast and splatters lots of my bee friends on the wind-screen. This man demands to know what your master has told the farmer. He's angry. Professor Salt says he hasn't betrayed any secrets, but the project has to stop. The other man says it's too late and the trials have proved their new super bee is safe.'

'Super bee?' asks Monty.

'That's what the angry man said – super bee. The professor then gets angry too and says he will never allow its release. And this is the bit that really frightened me. The professor said these super bees were killers.'

'Killer bees?'

'I don't like the sound of this,' says Betty.

Four continues. 'Mr Salt had a special name for these killer bees. Now, what was it? That's it! He called them Frankenstein bees. Any idea what that means?'

'Frankenstein was a mad scientist who created a monster using body parts from dead big'uns,' I say. 'I've seen the movie. One of Paddy's favourites. He used to say whenever people tried to play God, they upset the natural order of things and end up creating monsters.'

Four stares at me blankly. 'What did he just say?' she asks Celeste.

'Don't worry about it,' says Celeste. 'So, Monty, I think our first move is to find the driver of this red car. He sounds like he had motive to kill Mr Salt.'

I pant as if I've been running, tail pointing up, stance wide, ready for battle. I have completely forgotten about Troy Fratting, Rose's new suspect.

'We have to find him. Whatever it takes.' It comes out like a growl.

Both Celeste and Four back away. Even Betty looks unsure of me.

'I promise you, Four, I'll help you find Paddy's bee sanctuary. But I need your help in return. You've seen the man driving the red car. Will you help us find him?'

'I will.'

Chapter Twenty-Six

A dark shape descends from the cloudy night sky and lands on the kitchen windowsill. He cocks his glossy black head and his eyes glint a disturbing orange as they reflect light from kitchen appliances. He surveys the room's interior before hopping onto the sink drainer.

Celeste and Four have frozen. Dante hasn't yet noticed them, but he will. I don't want them to become the entrée on his dinner menu, so I quickly make introductions.

'Oh, perfect,' scoffs Dante. 'First a rat, and now a ladybird and a bee. Why don't you recruit the whole wretched insect and rodent world and watch me starve to death?'

'Celeste has her own PI agency and she's . . . well, she's no ordinary insect.'

'Hello, handsome.' I hear a seductive purr.

Celeste has flown over to Dante and is hovering just above the drainer, displaying her magnificent red and black colouring. Her intoxicating scent, much like a lily of the valley, fills the air. She winks at the magpie and then drapes herself across the hot tap handle, her shiny black boots arranged to show off her slim legs. It's hard to know who is more taken aback: Dante or me. Four is still paralysed with fear. For a split second, Dante is speechless; he tucks his long beak into his chest and looks puzzled. I bet he's never had a potential meal flirt with him before.

Celeste extends one of her non-booted legs towards him, as if expecting him to do what the humans sometimes do, and kiss her foot as though it were a hand. 'My name is Celeste. MI5-trained. Solving crime's my game.'

She opens out her wings and displays the red and black casings, Rio carnival style.

'I run the Celestial PI Agency.'

Dante repeats the name of her agency as if hypnotised.

'That's me, you gorgeous thing. And a little bird tells me that you're famous. Or should I say infamous? Your reputation precedes you, Dante. I've been absolutely *dying* to meet you. There's something so terribly sexy about a creature with the intellect and cunning to bring humans to their knees.'

My mouth is hanging open, and so is Dante's beak. The short silence is broken by Betty faking vomiting.

'Trollop!' Betty is mumbling. 'I've never heard the like.'

Dante is deaf to Betty's ranting. He shakes his fine head, extends one black leg forward and bows.

'At your service, madam.'

'Such a gentleman,' Celeste enthuses and gives him a nod. 'Now tell me about the Rothschild diamond. It was you, wasn't it, you clever boy?'

Dante doesn't answer immediately. 'Madam, you are a detective, so please understand I am disinclined to incriminate myself.'

'No, no, you've got me all wrong. I'm a huge fan. Whatever you say is off the record. You have my word.'

She bats all her eyes at him.

'Then it would be a pleasure,' replies Dante. 'It's not often my talent is appreciated.'

Is Dante being nice? Surely not?

Betty yawns loudly and then leans against the rim of the plate, looking thoroughly bored. She starts to pick her teeth with a claw.

'So you *are* the Black Devil!' Celeste jumps up from the tap with delight. 'I thought it must be you.' She looks at the rest of us. 'This is incredible! Have you any idea who Dante is? He's one of this country's most wanted. He's the jewellery thief that big'uns can't catch. And you know why?'

She doesn't wait for an answer.

'Because they assume this country's most wanted burglar is a big'un. And they are so very wrong, aren't they, Dante?

Dante extends his wings wide, revealing his stunning black and white plumage. His chest puffs out, and with head back, he gives an almighty squawk. I don't think I have ever seen him so happy.

'Dante, keep it down will you? Rose is upstairs.'

Dante nods and folds his wings. 'Celeste, you must promise you'll keep my identity secret. Now, promise me, my dear.'

'Let me assure you that I only work on insect crime. Well, until my case overlapped with Patrick Salt's murder. Regardless, I have no intention of betraying you.'

Betty pipes up. 'Hold on a mo. You pinch bling? Mr I'm-all-terribly-clever-and-intellectual is nothing more than a common burglar?'

Dante stomps over to her. 'I'll have you know, ratty, that

the jewellery I take is worth millions. The homes have state-of-the-art security. One job takes months of surveillance and planning to execute.'

Betty has her paws on her hips. 'But why do it? Risk getting yourself killed for a few shiny baubles?' She shakes her head. 'That's dumb, if you ask me.'

Dante charges at Betty. I intervene.

'There's a good reason why Dante does what he does,' I say. 'But it's up to him to tell you. All I'll say is that he does it to help others, not himself.'

Celeste swoons and almost falls off the tap handle. She recovers just in time.

Betty nods. 'Ah, I see. A modern-day Robin Hood. Now you're talking my language. But I gotta say, I never took you for a charitable sort.'

Celeste bats her eyes at Dante. 'I could do with a creature of your exceptional skills at my agency. Together, we would be invincible.'

Betty bursts out laughing.

'I am very honoured, Celeste,' replies Dante. 'But I work alone. It's safer that way.'

I catch Dante winking at her. This is doing my head in.

'U-hum,' I say, clearing my throat. 'I hate to interrupt, Celeste, but perhaps Dante can help us find the red car?'

'Would the Black Devil do that for us? Would you?' purrs Celeste.

'I can't say, madam, until you brief me. Why don't you tell me about this car and I'll see what I can do?'

Dante sidles up to the tap handle where Celeste is reclining. As she briefs Dante, I notice that Four has fallen asleep. Betty chews a crumb stored in her cheeks and mutters.

'I'm clever too,' she says. 'Cleverer than rabbits, hamsters, mice and guinea pigs, that's for sure. But nobody coos over me. That's what happens to a female past a certain age. Nobody even notices her.'

Celeste stops talking.

'I see,' Dante says. 'I don't like the sound of this at all.'

'That's not all of it,' I say. 'Larry Nice isn't the killer. Wrong smell. Somebody has gone to a lot of trouble to frame him. So we're looking for a new suspect.'

Celeste takes control. 'As the angry man is likely to be a colleague, we should look for this red car at the university. Dante, can you fly over the campus in the morning, say around ten, when most staff will have arrived, and look for a red sports car?'

'I can, but I need more information. Make, model, registration, is it a soft-top?'

Everyone turns and looks at Four who is fast sleep on her cold-water bottle. She looks so serene.

'Four!' Celeste bellows. 'Wakey wakey.'

The poor bee almost rolls off the table with shock. 'What? Who? Where?'

'Four, you remember the man who argued with Professor Salt?'

The bee looks blank.

'You know, when the Professor talked about killer bees?' Celeste prompts.

'Ah, yes,' Four replies and has a good stretch.

'Can you remember anything more about the red sports car he was driving?'

'It was red.'

Dante swears under his breath but Celeste keeps going. 'If

we showed you pictures of cars, would it help jog your memory?'

Four picks up her cold-water bottle and hugs it, silent.

'Poor thing's terrified,' says Betty. 'Let me have a go.'

Betty sits next to the bee and gives her a hug. 'I know this is very scary, but just do your best, okay? Do you think you can tell us anything about the angry man who shouted at the nice Mr Salt?'

Four shakes her head. 'I'm sorry, I can't tell one big'un from the other. They all look the same to me.'

'Perhaps you know more than you realise. He was definitely male?' I ask.

'Yes.'

'Tall? Short?'

'I can't tell the difference.'

'Young or old?'

Four lifts off the table and buzzes around in a figure of eight as she ponders. 'Well, he wasn't a child and he wasn't an old man. He walked easily.'

'Dark hair or light?'

Four lands in a ball of despair. 'Oh dear, I'm so stupid. I just don't know.'

Betty places a paw around the bee. 'Don't say that. You're not stupid at all. You've done well, my love.'

'Really?'

'Yes. So stop being so hard on yourself,' says Betty.

'Right then,' says Dante. 'We should look at male colleagues in the same department as Professor Salt.' He looks around the kitchen. 'So where's the laptop?'

'I'm not sure. I'll go find it. Best if I search alone,' I say.

I creep into the hallway. Following my nose, I find Rose's

handbag and satchel leaning against the leg of a narrow table near the stairs. I prod the larger bag with my paw and feel something flat and rectangular inside. The buckles are undone. With my nose, I slide the leather flap up and over, revealing the inside pockets. The laptop is a snug fit and I won't be able to pull it out alone. So I trot back to the kitchen and ask Betty for help. She gives me a toothy grin and points to herself.

'Oh, so you want me? Little old me?' she says, to emphasise that I haven't asked the others.

Betty follows me back to the hallway, where I nudge the satchel over on its side.

'Can you crawl into this pocket and get behind the laptop? Then, as you push it up, I'll pull it out.'

'Easy peasy pudding and pie,' Betty sings.

She wriggles inside the bag, its soft leather lifting and falling over her back like a Mexican wave as she moves deeper into the pocket. I wedge my nose far enough in so I can clamp my jaw around the laptop edge. I pull, but its surface is slippery and I don't want to scratch or dent it with my teeth. After a few tugs, the laptop shifts towards me. Once I have it on the carpet, Betty scrambles out of the bag and gives me a high five.

I carry the laptop into the kitchen and place it gently on the floor.

'Yuck!' Celeste says, eyeing the slobber pooling on the lid.

'Oh for goodness' sake!' says Betty, who then belly-flops onto the lid and propels herself across it with her back legs. Her thick fur soaks up my drool. When she reaches the other end, she stands, paws on hips, her stomach fur wet, matted and gooey.

'There you go. Good as new,' she says.

Dante lands on the floor, opens the lid and taps at the keys with his beak. Celeste moves close to watch him work.

'We're in the university website. Which faculty did your master belong to?'

'Life Sciences,' I reply.

'Okay, here we go. Now, Four, take a look at these photos and see if you recognise the angry man.'

Dante taps through each and every image, including Dr Bomphrey, Paddy's boss. Four keeps shaking her head. I suddenly remember Troy Fratting, but his name isn't on the faculty list. We are all disappointed, most of all Four who starts crying again.

'Well, sorry I couldn't be more help. Must be getting on,' says Dante, clearly uncomfortable with a sobbing female. He starts to shut down the university system when Four screams, 'Stop! Go back.'

Dante returns to a Home page image shot outside the Dean's office. Several cars are parked to the right of the main entrance. Third car along and, partially obscured by a white BMW, is a red Bentley Continental GT convertible. The soft-top has been folded back and we can see the cream leather seats through the sloping windscreen.

'That's it!' shrieks Four. 'The red car!' She bounces up and down.

'Are you sure?' asks Dante, positioning his beak close to the yo-yoing bee. 'Look, I don't mean to cast aspersions on your visual skills, but if you can't recognise the man, how can you recognise the car?'

'I, um . . . I, well . . .'

Celeste comes to her rescue. 'Dante, there are some things

even a magnificent mind like yours simply can't fathom because it's just not logical. It simply is. Bees find it next to impossible to differentiate between one human and another, but a red car – a big, shiny lump of deliciously bright red – that's something a bee can recall. Bees respond best to strong colours.'

'I bow to your superior knowledge of bees, madam,' Dante replies.

Transfixed, I move closer to the screen. I can just make out the number plate. I read it out loud.

'GN1US.'

Chapter Twenty-Seven

Rose heard Rebecca Salt yelling even before she stepped into the police building on Wednesday morning. In fact, the whole street would have heard her, and probably the next county. Possibly, even the French would have glanced across the Channel at the ruckus and nodded in agreement with Rebecca's description of the British police as 'arseholes'. If Rebecca's executive search business ever folded, she could make use of her powerful voice box and take up town crying. But she wasn't objecting to Varma and Pearl interviewing her husband. No. Rebecca was furious because Leach wouldn't release her father's body.

'I don't have time for this,' screamed the grief-stricken daughter. 'I've got a business to run!'

Salisbury was on his way out when he bumped into Rose in the car park. 'Get a load of that.'

'If shouting becomes an Olympic sport, she'll win gold,' said Rose. 'Does she know Troy lied to us?'

'Not yet. God help him when she finds out.'

He grinned and went on his way.

Rose jogged up the stairs to Major Crime. At least Larry wasn't their only suspect now Fratting was in the mix. She was about to enter the monitoring room to take a quick peek at the interview in progress, when Leach stormed down the narrow corridor towards her as if he were spoiling for a fight.

'*Who's in charge here?*' Rebecca bellowed from somewhere on the ground floor.

'Jesus! Is that woman ever going to shut up?'

'Doesn't look like it, sir.'

'I'm on my way to see the Super, so this has to be quick.' He patted her on the back but his arm was stiff like a paddle and he kept his distance. 'Good job, Rose. Looks like Fratting has some explaining to do.' He cleared his throat. 'And since you're on a run of good luck, I'd like you to work your magic at Flay Bioscience. Their MD, Chadstone Flay, is refusing to let us see Salt's files.'

'The warrant didn't come through, then, sir?'

'No, got knocked back. Insufficient grounds or some such bollocks. More likely this Flay bloke has friends in high places. Bet the bastard's a Mason. They stick together, even if it means bending the law. *Especially* if it means bending the law. I'd like to shove their little trowels up their tight ritualistic arses!'

Do Masons really have trowels? she wondered, trying not to imagine where Leach wanted to shove them.

'But if Flay has refused, what can I do about it, sir?'

'Use your charm. Try and see him without his lawyers.'

'You sure you want *me* to do this?'

'Dave suggested the idea. He thought Flay would be less, you know, threatened, if we don't send in the heavies. Do it like a casual chat. Keep it light.'

Rose looked down the corridor at the interview room door through which she could hear Pearl's sneering drone being met with Fratting's stony silence. What was Pearl really up to sending her to interview a bigwig like Flay?

'Appreciate this opportunity, sir, but given the potential importance of these files, I'd feel better if a senior officer came too.'

'Everyone's busy, so off you go. And by the book, Rose. Can't have them claiming police harassment. Got it?'

Leach darted down the corridor towards the Super's office.

Rose didn't know whether to be happy or troubled by Leach's order. He was clearly pleased with her at the moment, but this would be a difficult meeting, assuming she could even get to see Flay. What troubled her most was that Pearl had suggested it.

Despite her misgivings, she just had to get on with it so she rang Flay Bioscience and asked to speak to Mr Flay. As expected, she was transferred through to his Executive Assistant, Sophie, who, also predictably, refused Rose an appointment.

'Sophie, can I be honest with you?'

'Of course.'

'I'm new to this job and my boss asked me to make this appointment.' She lowered her voice. 'I think it's a kind of test, you see. So I really need to get this meeting set up. Please?'

'Mr Flay is really busy. Perhaps in a few weeks?'

'I won't have a job in a few weeks if I don't get to see Mr Flay. Oh come on, Sophie. Please? Give me five minutes.'

Sophie was quiet. Rose knew when to keep her mouth shut and wait. 'Look, why don't you come by in half an hour?

He's got a gap of a few minutes between meetings. I'll explain you said it was urgent. Does that suit you?'

'Thanks, Sophie. I really appreciate it.'

She grabbed her notebook and raced down the stairs and out into the car park. She headed for the same Ford Focus Varma had driven yesterday. A tall red-brick wall separated the car park from the busy road on the other side. As a result, Rose could hear Rebecca laying into her husband, who'd just been released. But because they were standing on the pavement on the other side of the wall, they couldn't see her.

'Mrs Fratting, I urge you to keep your voice down.' Another voice, which had to be their solicitor.

'I'm not Mrs Fratting, and you've done your job. So piss off!'

'*Mr* Fratting, you're a suspect in a murder . . .'

Before Troy could speak, Rebecca waded in. 'So what were you doing Friday night? Hey? Screwing some cheap tart, were you? God, you're pathetic!'

'Babe, you know I love you, but sometimes I have to wine and dine the ladies to close the deal. You know how it is?' Troy simpered.

'You don't have to screw her!'

There was no mistaking the sound of the slap. That must have really hurt.

'Please! This has to stop,' cried the agitated solicitor.

Troy whined. 'If you'd just given me the money, none of this shit would've happened.'

'Oh, so it's all my fault you're such a waste of space! Well, you're not dragging me down with you. I'm in Hong Kong at the end of next week and I don't give a rat's arse if they throw you in a cell. That's *your* problem.'

Rebecca stormed off.

'Babe, I need a ride.'

'Go ask your girlfriend!'

As Rose got into her pool car she was in no doubt Rebecca was referring to Matilda Rutter. Rose had found footage of Troy and Matilda sneaking into his room at 4:02p.m. on the day of the murder. She was in the middle of divorcing her second husband for adultery. It wouldn't help her case if word got out she was no better than him.

Fifteen minutes later, Rose pulled up at the security gates of Flay Bioscience. The high perimeter fence surrounding the huge site, the armed security guards and excessive number of security cameras reminded her of a prison. The only building that seemed 'corporate' was the ultra-modern ten-floor main building that looked like the silver nib of a giant fountain pen pointing at the sky. All the other buildings were one or two storeys in breeze-block grey. The place gave her the creeps.

Sweet-talking her way into an appointment had proved relatively easy. Getting through security, however, was proving more difficult. She held out her warrant card.

'Sorry, miss,' said the guard through the security hut's window as he ran his finger slowly down his clip board. 'You're not on my visitors' list.' He did little to hide a smirk.

'Call Sophie, Mr Flay's EA. She arranged the appointment.'

He took his time making the call and opening the boom gate. 'You weren't on the list. What can I say?'

'How about sorry for wasting my time?'

As she drove off she heard him mutter, 'Don't get arsy with me, bottom-wipe!'

She slammed on the brakes and reversed.

'You want me to arrest you for obstructing a police investigation?' she said to the guard.

'But, but . . . How did I do that? You weren't on the list. I mean, what can I do?' he blurted out, his puffy eyes wide with shock. 'Sorry, officer.'

Rose drove off without responding, knowing next visit, if there was a next visit, he'd drop the attitude. As she pulled up outside the giant fountain pen, her mobile rang. It was Varma, letting her know that Salt's body was being released for burial. The distraught daughter was leaving the country next week because, apparently, her company couldn't function without her. A second, independent post-mortem was to be carried out before the burial, the details of which would go to the defence lawyer, once they had a real suspect.

'Got a date for the funeral?' she asked.

'Monday, apparently.'

'God, that's fast.'

Her mind immediately turned to Monty. Should she take him to the funeral?

Rose announced herself at reception. Sophie tottered out of the lift in her platform shoes and all six foot of her beamed such an over-the-top cheery welcome that Rose almost asked what happy pills she was on, and if she could have some. As the lift shot up to the top floor, she felt like a midget, and a pretty plain midget at that. Sophie was immaculate in stockings, short skirt and silk blouse, with twin-set pearls. Rose felt shabby in her roughed-up moccasins and ill-fitting navy suit.

She was ushered into an enormous office, the centrepiece of which was an L-shaped glass and chrome desk. On it was an iPad and an iPhone and a framed family photo: mum, dad, girl and sulky boy with a grumpy-looking pony. The rest of the desk was clear. Behind it, the electronic blinds were down even though there wasn't a peek of sunshine through the cumulonimbus clouds. Seated in a black leather chair, Chadstone Flay studied her, and she, him.

In his early forties, he had a large aquiline nose, striking bone structure and dark brown eyes, deep set under bushy greying eyebrows. As a result he reminded Rose of a hawk. He removed his bifocals and stood to shake her hand. His pinstripe suit jacket was open, therefore revealing a dark red silk lining. The buttonholes on the jacket cuffs were real, the bottom button on each sleeve undone. The suit was bespoke. His silk tie had diagonal stripes in varying tones of red, his white shirt was stiff as if it had been starched and his cufflinks were stunning rectangles of what appeared to be lapis lazuli. On the walls were framed photos of Flay at Eton, Flay at Cambridge, Flay with various famous industry moguls, Flay with the Prime Minister. The one that really caught her eye was the photo of Flay with the Chief Constable. Rose swallowed what felt like a peach stone. This man was connected up to the eyeballs. Why on earth would Leach send a trainee like her here alone? With a sinking feeling, she wondered if it was because she was expendable? If Flay complained, they could get rid of her with little compunction.

'Detective Constable Sidebottom, it's simply marvellous to meet you. Please do take a seat.'

He gestured towards a circular table, again glass and chrome, at which one man and one woman sat completely still, both pale complexioned in dark grey suits, their shoes polished to a mirror shine, their closed-lipped smiles as fixed as shop mannequins. Rose couldn't help but wonder whether if they went outside on a sunny day they might burst into flames. Her hope for a one-on-one chat with Flay was obviously out of the question.

'Dreadful business,' said Flay, joining them at the table and reclining in his chair, fingers touching, as if in prayer. 'I was horrified to learn our beloved Professor Salt was dead. He was a wonderful scientist and an all-round lovely chap,' he simpered. 'I simply can't imagine why anyone might want to kill the poor fellow.'

'Could it have something to do with the work he was doing for you?' Rose asked. 'His laptop is missing.'

Lawyer One suddenly came to life. He leaned forward.

'Can I just correct you there, *Trainee* Detective Sidebottom? Patrick Salt wasn't employed by Flay Bioscience, rather, by the university. This company sponsors the Life Sciences faculty and provides the funding for student scholarships. Our involvement is entirely philanthropic.'

And I'm the Prime Minister, thought Rose.

'I'm a big believer in giving back to the community,' said Flay, waving his right hand as if riding in a royal carriage, 'and I want to give young people a chance to work in this world-saving industry of the future.'

Flay smiled, but his eyes didn't. His pronounced grey teeth reminded her of gravestones.

'We understand Professor Salt was researching the decline of the honey bee. We also understand that you have patented the work he did with Dr Martinez. Given Professor Salt's untimely death, will you continue with your product launch?'

'I see you've been very diligent. As to the launch, that will go ahead as planned. Sadly, the global problem of the honey bee's decline won't go away just because Patrick is no longer with us. We must soldier on, and I'm sure dear Patrick would have wanted his work to bear fruit.' He tilted his head and grinned. 'Apologies for the mixed metaphors.'

'So Flay Bioscience will be manufacturing some kind of cure for the honey bee problem?'

Lawyer Two leaned forward.

'We do not see the relevance of this speculation to your case,' she said. 'Nor are we willing to discuss Patrick Salt's work. It is highly confidential, and if leaked, could cause considerable commercial damage to Flay Bioscience.'

Rose stared for a moment at the woman's mouth. Her gash of red lipstick looked uncomfortably like blood. Rose really had to stop watching vampire movies.

'We are honour-bound to protect Patrick's work,' Flay said, with all the sincerity of a magician who claims the bunny really has vanished.

The walking-dead hadn't shared their names with Rose. Instead, each one's business card had been neatly placed on the table. Rose picked up the card opposite the female and read her name.

'Caroline, this is a murder investigation. We are trying to establish a motive and this scientific breakthrough might be that motive. Perhaps a rival company wanted to stop him? We don't know yet, but that is why we need to see Salt's files.'

'Come, come,' said Flay, 'this terrible business is surely nothing more than a burglary. I hear Patrick's antique silver was stolen and has been recovered in someone's garage.'

How do you know that?

'I mean, saving the honey bee is hardly the stuff of corporate espionage, now is it?' Flay continued. 'Nobody's interested in Patrick's and Maria's breakthrough, except us.'

'Mr Flay, if you're concerned about data leaks, we can go through the files here at your office.'

'The answer is no,' replied Flay, emphasising the last word. 'Is there anything else I can help you with, because I have a meeting with Cancer Research UK, one of the many charities we support. We're sponsoring their fund-raising ball. You might like to come along, but, well . . .' he leaned towards her and laid a sympathetic hand on her sleeve, 'sadly tickets are five hundred pounds each, and it's a terrible shame we don't remunerate our constabulary as well as they deserve. Don't you think?'

Rose calmly moved her arm away.

'Mr Flay, did Patrick Salt have any enemies?'

'I have no idea, but I'd doubt it. He was a quiet, good-natured chap.'

'To your knowledge, has he ever been threatened?'

Flay shrugged. 'Not to my knowledge.'

A painful tingling shot up her arms to her shoulders, as if she'd been stung.

'Did you have a disagreement with Professor Salt?'

Flay flicked such a quick look at Lawyer One, she almost missed it. 'I relied on Dr Bomphrey to manage the Professor. I had little direct contact with him.'

The tingling continued.

'Mr Flay, doesn't it bother you that confidential data has been stolen, along with Patrick's laptop?'

'Naturally, but we won't be beaten to market. It takes years, not weeks, to achieve what Patrick and Maria have done. So, yes, we're not happy about it but we trust you'll do your job and recover it.'

'That's Dr Maria Martinez?' She waited for Flay to nod. 'What was their relationship like?'

Flay frowned. 'Professional and amicable. Now is that all?'

Rose knew she should stop there. She'd tried and failed in her task. But if Flay had fallen out with Professor Salt over the cure-all for bees, he might have motive to kill him.

'Not quite, sir. Have you ever had malaria?'

His eyes almost disappeared under his frowning bushy eyebrows. 'Malaria?'

Layer One stepped in. 'Mr Flay's medical history is confidential.'

Rose ignored him. 'It does no harm telling me, if you have nothing to hide?'

'How dare you treat me like a suspect!' Flay seethed, the tone threatening.

In for a penny, in for a pound. 'We're asking all Professor Salt's colleagues for their fingerprints so we can eliminate them from our enquiries. We'd like yours, sir.'

'This is preposterous!' Flay said. 'I'm phoning your superior.'

'Sir,' said Lawyer Two. 'Can I have a private word?'

Flay glared at her for a moment, then nodded. 'Will you excuse us?' he said to Rose. Lawyer One showed her out.

'Everything all right?' asked Sophie from behind her desk, looking worried.

'Yes, great,' Rose lied.

The sound-proofing was too good. Rose didn't hear a thing through the thick frosted-glass double doors. A few minutes later Caroline, Lawyer Two, called her back into the room.

'Mr Flay has kindly agreed to take time out of his very busy schedule to assist with your investigation. He'll provide fingerprints so long as they are destroyed at the end of this investigation.'

Rose couldn't give that guarantee herself. 'Give me a moment,' she said, turning her back on the group and phoning Leach, who agreed to the terms.

'You have Detective Chief Inspector Craig Leach's word that your fingerprints will be destroyed when this investigation is concluded, providing, of course, you haven't done anything you shouldn't. Please drop by Geldeford Station as soon as you can.'

She gave them a fake smile, secretly enjoying Flay's stunned expression.

'By the way, sir, how did you know about the silverware? Those details haven't been made public.'

Flay's eyes narrowed. 'I don't recall.'

Rose felt their icy stares on her back as Sophie escorted her out. She stayed calm until she got into her car. Then she slammed her palms down on the steering wheel. It took a lot to get Rose angry and her blood was boiling.

Flay's superior tone had really got under her skin, but she was furious with herself for walking straight into Pearl's trap. She had pushed Flay too hard. She knew that. Which was exactly what Pearl had expected. He knew she was desperate to redeem herself and that she'd get easily riled.

Well, she was going to be taken off the case as soon as she walked into police headquarters, so she might as well do her best to solve it while she had the chance. It was time she followed her gut instinct, and her instinct told her Salt's murder was related to his work. Her next stop was Dr Maria Martinez.

Chapter Twenty-Eight

Dr Maria Martinez was possibly the smiliest woman Rose had ever met, and after her chilly reception at Flay Bioscience, it was a welcome relief. Martinez worked at two locations. Today she was at the university's Life Sciences building.

'Come in, come in! How is it going? Have you caught him yet?' Martinez said, her Spanish accent strong, and her voice naturally loud, as if she were addressing a rally without a microphone.

Her dark eyes, rimmed by long thick black lashes, were so perfectly positioned on her olive-skinned, heart-shaped face that she might have been called beautiful if her mouth hadn't been so wide and her lips so full. It was truly a Mick Jagger mouth. But Rose had no doubt that this curvaceous woman turned heads wherever she went. Red hooped earrings, the diameter of coffee mugs, swayed as she moved. She wore a white lab coat and her long, thick chocolate-brown hair was tied up in a French twist, secured with a clip that looked like a red rose. Her court shoes were a matching red. Rose guessed that in a world of clinical whiteness, Martinez was keen to inject some vibrancy.

'I cry for three days, you know. I loved that man!' she said. 'He was a special human being. A joy to work with.'

'That's what I'm hearing,' said Rose, 'so why would anyone want to kill him? Could someone have been jealous of his work or, maybe, threatened by it?'

Rose deliberately attributed their work to Patrick alone, to see how Martinez reacted.

'It is so tragic. He was to be famous. Oh yes. Famous! He had phone calls from all over the world, you know. Farmers. Peers. Governments. Even the US department of agriculture, they phone him.'

'Why would a US department call him?'

'You see!' Martinez exclaimed, raising her hands in exasperation. 'Everybody, they think, this is just a bee. Who cares? But imagine a world with no flowers! All the beautiful colours – pink carnations, red roses, yellow daffodils – they are gone without the bee. Pouf!'

She opened one hand as if throwing something into the air.

'If flowering crops are not pollinated, we have a global food shortage. No apples, strawberries, potatoes, tomatoes, cauliflower and so much more. Farmers cannot feed their animals, so meat, it becomes very scarce. This is a huge problem for governments. Did you know that in the US they have very few honey bees left? Hives are sent across the country on trains so crops can be pollinated. But it is very stressful for the bees, especially as they are already sick. Many, many die.'

Her wide smile hadn't left her face despite her grim prediction. It was as if she had only one facial expression.

'So why haven't I heard about this? I don't think I've seen anything in the media.'

'Panic! The government, they no want the people to panic. But in secret, they worry and plan. They want a solution to this *big* problem.'

'And why are the bees dying?'

Martinez fiddled with an earring. 'Ah, there are many theories. Some say the pesticides kill them. Some say it's genetically engineered plants that make the bees sick. I work ten years in bioscience so I say, I do not think so. Others, they say the hives are not a healthy home. Patrick, he thinks this. He believes pesticides poison bees and make them susceptible to attack from the Varroa mite. Here, I show you.'

Martinez pointed to a microscope. Rose peered into a petri dish and saw dozens of bedbug-like creatures shaped like brown buttons with many legs.

'So where do these mites come from?' Rose asked.

'Varroa mites have always lived in hives and they provide food for hatching bee larvae. This was a good thing. But now the mites multiply. They grow too strong. So when the baby bees hatch, they are attacked by the mites. They are over-whelmed and die.'

'So you worked with Salt on a way to control the mites?'

Martinez's smile vanished.

'I cannot speak about this. Flay Bioscience, they make me sign a confidentiality agreement.'

'Maria. I need your help to catch the Professor's killer and this information could be useful.'

'*Si, si,* I understand,' Martinez said, glancing at the door. It was lunchtime, so they were the only ones in the lab. She dropped her voice. 'I would like to help. Truly. But I want to keep my job.'

Martinez didn't ask her to leave. Instead, she sat on a stool and waited for further questions. A good sign.

'If I was to assume you and Salt had found a chemical solution to the mite infestations, would I be on the right track?'

'You would not. Patrick did not like the chemicals. At Flay Bioscience, we have scientists working on a chemical solution. But there is a problem with this option.' Martinez leaned forwards and whispered. 'So far, the chemical that kills the mites, also kills the bees. You understand?'

Rose nodded. 'Then, is your solution a genetically engineered one?'

Martinez glanced at the door again. 'You could assume that, given my area of expertise.'

Rose smiled. Martinez was a smart woman.

'Can I also assume that this work is behind the product launch in two weeks' time?'

'You could assume this if you wish.'

'And it was your only joint project?'

'Si.'

'What other projects was the Professor working on?'

Martinez spoke so quietly, Rose strained to hear. 'He was testing ordinary bees in a new design of hive. This is something Mr Flay does not know, so you did not hear this from me.'

'I understand. Go on.'

'You see, Patrick believed we have forced bees to live in hives that make them weak and vulnerable. He wanted to change beekeeping. This upset many people.'

'Who specifically?'

'Beekeepers. I do not know specifically.'

'Did the Professor build his alternative hives?'

'Dr Bomphrey would not fund the project.'

Rose's hands were clammy and her heart raced. If Salt's and Martinez's solution worked, then Flay Bioscience would make millions. That was undoubtedly worth killing for. But if a rival company had stolen their work to claim it as their own, why kill Salt and leave Martinez alive? Or was it possible that Martinez murdered Salt so she could take all the glory? Rose didn't think it likely. Martinez's admiration for Salt seemed heartfelt. Rose liked her warmth and was convinced that, so far, Martinez had been telling the truth.

'Was Salt ever threatened?'

Martinez hesitated.

'Any recent arguments?'

Still no response.

'Maria, if you know something and you don't tell me, you're obstructing a murder investigation.'

Martinez exhaled loudly. 'The day Patrick died, he was very angry. An argument on the phone. But I don't know who with, because he was in his office and I was out here. But he shouted very loud.'

'What did Patrick say?'

'I am not sure. The door was closed.'

Rose's hands and feet were tingling – Martinez had told her first lie. 'Maria, you said he was shouting. You must have heard something?'

'I think he say something like, "You can't do this . . ." Oh, I don't know.'

Rose stepped closer so it was harder for Martinez to avoid

eye contact. 'Maria, you can remember. I know you can. Patrick said, "You can't do this," and then what?'

'I think he say, "I want my share," but I am not certain.'

Was the tingling Rose felt from Martinz's earlier lie or this statement? Rose couldn't be sure.

'What else did he say?'

'That is all I can remember.'

Rose pointed at Patrick's goldfish bowl of an office. She noticed that the filing cabinet drawer was shut. It had been ajar two days ago.

'Is the office kept locked?'

'Yes, always,' Martinez replied.

'And who has a key?'

'Patrick, of course. Dr Bomphrey. I think the cleaner, too.' She twisted her mouth into a grimace. 'And me. But please don't tell Dr Bomphrey. He does not know this.'

Indeed, he apparently did not. When questioned, Bomphrey had not listed Martinez as one of the key holders.

'So how did you get one?'

'Patrick, he gave it to me. He sometimes go home to work and then he forget something. I often work very late, so he call me and ask me to check something for him in his office. I swear it is true: Patrick gave me a copy of his key.'

As Salt was dead, there was no way of checking her claim, but why tell Rose about the extra key if she had something to hide? And besides, there were no tingles this time.

'What about the filing cabinet? Do you have a key for that?'

Martinez hesitated. 'Yes.' She whispered, 'Am I in trouble?'

Rose shook her head. 'Not with me. Since Patrick's death, have you removed anything from his office?'

'No, I touch nothing.'

Sharp tingling shot up Rose's arms.

'Your joint project? Where is all the data?'

'In a password-protected folder. Only a very few can access it, including myself and Patrick.'

'Nowhere else? Would Salt have made copies?'

'Absolutely not. Patrick was meticulous about such things. I am also very careful.'

Tingling in her hands. Maybe Martinez wasn't quite as careful as she was making out?

'Was your work to be published jointly?' Rose asked.

'It was. Equal credit.'

Bomphrey and Flay had made it clear that she could not see any of the Professor's files without a warrant. But they hadn't said she couldn't follow Martinez into his office. It was risky, but worth a punt.

'Can you let me in? I won't touch any files. I just want to look around. Get a feel for the man.'

'I am not sure if . . .'

'But you want us to catch Patrick's killer, don't you?'

She nodded, the hoops in her lobes swinging. She pulled a key-ring from her lab coat pocket and opened Patrick's office door.

'Please, be quick.' Martinez's voice was shaky.

'A framed photo of you and the Professor is missing. Do you know who took it?'

Her eyes widened. 'No, I do not.'

Tingling. Had she taken it as a souvenir?

'Has anyone used this phone since his death?'

'No, I have not seen anyone in here.'

'And his angry phone call was when exactly?'

'Um, it was Friday, just before he left for the evening. I think five-thirty. Something like this.' She paused and then leaned forwards conspiratorially. 'You could dial 1471.'

Rose took the hint, put on disposable gloves and picked up the receiver and dialled. She jotted down the number and the time: 5:17p.m.

'What the hell do you think you're doing?' demanded Deakin Bomphrey, charging across the laboratory in their direction.

'Oh *mierda*!' Martinez muttered.

Rose calmly replaced the receiver. 'Dr Martinez has been helping me with my enquiries, and, as you requested, I haven't touched any files.'

'But the phone! And, how did you get in here, for Christ's sake?'

Rose didn't want to land Martinez in trouble but she couldn't lie.

'I have a key,' Martinez confessed, looking up into Bomphrey's sour face. 'Patrick gave it to me.'

Bomphrey's mouth puckered as tight as a cat's bottom. He held out his hand and Martinez removed the key from her key-ring and handed it to him.

'Who were you calling?' he asked.

'I was checking the number of the last phone call received.' She told him the phone number. 'Any idea who it belongs to?'

'It's mine. So what?'

'Yours was the last phone conversation before he died. Why did you call him, Dr Bomphrey?'

'None of your business! I want you to leave right away and do not talk to anyone in my department without my permission. Do you hear me?'

'I repeat, why did you phone Professor Salt?'

'Just everyday work stuff. Now leave!'

'I need to inform you we are asking all Professor Salt's colleagues for fingerprints, for elimination purposes. If both you and Dr Martinez could pop by Geldeford Station, I'd be most grateful.'

'Out!' snapped Bomphrey.

Rose was almost at the laboratory door when Bomphrey yelled, 'I'm ringing your superior. You won't get away with this!'

Join the queue, she thought.

Chapter Twenty-Nine

As soon as Rose walked back into the building she went to see her DCI. She recounted her meetings with Flay and Martinez. Leach listened in deadpan silence.

'I shouldn't say this. It's not PC and all that bollocks,' Leach said, rubbing his snooker ball-like head until it shone. 'But for a mouse of a girl, you certainly know how to stir up a shit storm!'

'Sir, I did nothing wrong and I'm looking for your support.'

'You've got guts, I'll grant you. Most people would've been intimidated by that rich git.'

'Seems he's mates with the Chief Constable.'

Leach nodded. 'His solicitor's already phoned me.'

'And?' Silence. 'Sir?'

'I said I'd look into his complaint. I have to follow protocols.'

Rose sighed. An official complaint would have to be thoroughly investigated. It would go on her record.

'Sir? Why did you send me to see Flay alone? If he claims harassment, I've got nobody to back me up.'

'Get your report written and I'll make some calls.'

'Sir, please tell me why you sent me? Why didn't I have a senior officer with me?'

Leach tapped a pen on his desk. She waited for an answer. 'You're non-threatening, that's why. I thought maybe you could sweet-talk him round.' He grinned. 'I wish I'd seen his face when you asked about the blood test.'

'So you'll back me up, sir?'

'I always back my people, Rose. Write up your report. Leave nothing out and I'll put in some calls. Off you go.'

Rose didn't make eye contact with anyone as she went to her desk. Despite Leach's reassurance, she knew she'd been hung out to dry. Pearl wasn't in, which was probably a good thing. She might've said something she'd regret. She started writing her report but couldn't concentrate. Something Dr Martinez had said was nagging at her. What did Salt mean by, 'I want my share'? Did he ask Bomphrey for more money? As Bomphrey wasn't cooperating, she was relying on Martinez's recollection of events. What if she misheard Salt's conversation?

Rose found Rebecca's mobile number and rang it. Not surprisingly, she was frosty.

'What do you want now?'

Rose kept her voice low. She didn't want to be overheard. 'First, I'd like to ask if I can come to your father's funeral.'

'Oh. Right. Yes, if you want to.'

'And I'd like to bring his dog, Monty. I think he would've liked it. They were very close.'

'He liked that dog more than he liked me. Maybe I needed a tail to wag or something,' she sighed.

'Can I bring him then?'

213

'Why not? Seems like half of Geldeford's coming. Shit! I better get the catering sorted. Know anybody good?'

'Afraid I don't, but ask Sylvia. She knows everybody.'

'Thanks.' Rebecca sounded weary. 'There's so much to organise and I'm not sleeping. Bloody jet lag.'

'Um, Rebecca, do you know if your father wanted a pay rise?'

Silence. 'How did you know that?'

'A lucky guess.'

'Well, to be honest, I don't know for sure if he ever got round to asking for a raise, but I encouraged him to. He hated doing things like that. Never wanted to make waves. But Flay was going to make billions off him, so I told him to demand a share of the profits. Quite honestly, they were ripping him off.'

'Was Flay paying him or the university?'

'The university paid a salary. Flay paid a set sum bonus. A token amount. It was insulting.'

She was interrupted by her red-faced boss booming across the room, 'Rose! In here. Now!'

'Thanks, Rebecca, you've been very helpful. I'll see you at the funeral.'

Rose tried to appear confident as she shut Leach's door behind her, but she was shaking. It didn't help that Leach flung his pen across his desk as he sat down. It bounced and landed on the floor.

'Sit.'

She did.

'As you predicted, Bomphrey's gone running to Flay, complaining about your snooping. His words, not mine. Says you tried to look at Salt's files without a warrant.'

'He's lying. I used the phone. That's all.'

Leach held up his hand. 'Flay's flipped his lid and phoned his golfing buddy – yes, you guessed it, the Chief Constable – claiming you harassed him.'

Rose's stomach felt like an escalator that had just gone into freefall. 'I deny both accusations,' she croaked.

Head jutting forward, knuckles on the desk, Leach looked as if he were about to charge at her and send her flying. She gripped her chair's arms, ready for the impact.

'The little prick!' Leach bellowed.

Rose wasn't sure if he was referring to Flay, Bomphrey or the Chief Constable.

'What a social-climbing tosser!'

She still wasn't sure, but at least it wasn't her. Nobody could accuse her of that.

Leach cleared his throat. 'I made it clear to the Chief Constable that you were doing your frigging job and you were *not* harassing anybody. Nor did you search for files. And if he thinks he can bully me, he's got another think coming!' Leach scowled at his desk, his face still flushed and blotchy.

Perhaps she was wrong about him? Standing up to the Chief Constable was usually not a good career move.

'Rose, I have to ask you one more time, are you absolutely sure you didn't look at any university documents?'

'I did not, sir. I dialled 1471 to find out who had last called Salt on his direct line. That was all. Flay and Bomphrey are lying and their over-the-top reactions tell me they have something to hide.'

'Did you threaten Mr Flay?'

She hesitated. 'All I said was that his fingerprints would

215

be destroyed providing he hadn't done anything he shouldn't. I was simply clarifying the arrangement.'

Leach flung his weight back into his chair and burst out laughing. 'I bet that went down well!' His whole body shook. 'I'd have done the same thing, you know.' Just as suddenly, he was serious again. 'I'll get that bloody warrant if it kills me. They're sure as hell hiding something and I'm bloody well going to find out what it is.'

'Thank you, sir. But what about Maria Martinez? Could she be in danger?'

'Why do you think that?'

'If a rival company stole Salt's data on this cure-all for bees, then Martinez is a threat because she is the sole-surviving inventor. Sir, somebody stole a photo of her and Salt from the Professor's office. It could be used to identify her for a hit,' Rose said.

'Unlikely, but I'll send a car to watch her home.'

'Thank you, sir, I think that's a good idea. And what happens about the leak?'

He lowered his voice. 'Rose, there is no leak, other than someone chatting with his mate over a beer at the golf club bar. Not that I have any idea who that could be, mind you, and there's nothing I can do about it anyway.' He stared at her in silence for a moment. 'You know, it's just possible Flay is jumpy because he's diddling his taxes or something like that, and Bomphrey, the little doormat, is crapping himself because he doesn't want to lose his sponsorship deal. Whatever their reasons, we need to get to the bottom of it.' He looked her straight in the eye. 'Until Tweedledum and Tweedledee calm down, I want you to stay away from them. Best for you. Best for us.'

'But sir, I . . .'

'There'll be an investigation into their complaints, but just tell the truth and you'll be fine.' His phone rang. 'Stick to desk duties for now.'

Her bubble well and truly burst, Rose shuffled out of his office. Pearl was back at his desk and smirked like a cat that's just got the dog thrown out into the rain.

Chapter Thirty

I always pick up on the subtle shifts in big'un moods, but this morning it's like full-volume, surround-sound. It's Saturday and Rose is sitting at the kitchen table, wearing her trackie pants and baggy T-shirt, sipping from a strong mug of tea that went cold ages ago, her long hair dishevelled, head bowed, looking very hang-dog. She hasn't said a word all morning or even commented on the magnificent hole in the lawn I dug earlier. I like to shove my nose into the cool damp earth and smell all the burrowers down there, like moles, badgers, rabbits, mice, and feel the worms that tickle my muzzle as they wriggle.

I nudge Rose's leg and leave behind a splodge of soil on the fabric. Oops. She looks down but doesn't seem to notice. Instead, she places a hand on my head.

'Oh Monty, all I do is shuffle paperwork. It's pointless.'

Apparently she's been doing this for the last few days and doesn't like it. She sighs and goes silent again. I glance at her uneaten toast but even a food-a-holic like me knows now is not the time to beg.

'That jumped-up arsehole!'

I lean my head against her leg to reassure her that I'm here, whatever happens. Her anger vibrates through her body. But I don't understand what she's just said. Has someone jumped up somewhere they shouldn't? On the sofa? Or the kitchen table? Paddy would never let me get on the furniture. It was off-limits. And, why is she talking about his bottom? Dogs are fascinated by other dogs' bottoms, but I didn't think big'uns were.

'At least Leach is on my side.'

Not in my experience. Leaches suck your blood and then dump you. Nasty creatures.

Rose gives me a hug.

'Should I call it quits? I'm never going to be like Aunt Kay. She was such a brilliant detective.'

Okay, this is bad. I know Rose will be a great detective because she has an animal instinct. A gut instinct. Most big'uns have forgotten how to tap into it. Not Rose.

I want to help her, but how can I prove Larry Nice is innocent and point her in the direction of Mr GN1US? I bark and head for the back door. I want her to come with me to Larry's flat. Too late, I remember that I'm not supposed to know where he lives.

'Sorry, Monty, I'm not in the mood for a walk.'

No, I don't want to go for a walk either! Frustrated, I sit back down next to Rose, whose unopened laptop is on the kitchen table. What I would give to see her recent case notes. Does she know about the argument between Paddy and Mr Genius?

Her pale blue eyes are pink and watery. She pushes the mug away, crosses her arms on the table and rests her head there.

'I'm such a failure.'

She sounds like she's in another room. I lick her hand.

'Thanks, Monty.'

She stares at the phone for a while and then dials.

'Hey, mum.'

'Oh, it's you. Hold on a minute.'

There's a bang as if the phone has been placed on something hard. Then I hear her mother talking to somebody else.

'I'm very sorry you've had to park down the road, but this is Mousehole, and we don't have multi-storey car parks. That's the point of coming to a quaint Cornish village.'

Her mother lives in a mouse-hole? Must be a big one.

I can't hear the reply, but a man is speaking with a strange accent. Rose's mother grunts something unintelligible. I hear footsteps recede.

'Bloody Belgians. Always moaning.' She sounds far away.

Another clank and the phone is back in her mother's hand. 'Rose, darling, what a lovely surprise! How are you?'

Rose is silent but a tear drips down her cheek. I stand and whimper, desperate to make her feel better.

'I'm not doing very well.' Another tear. She grabs a paper tissue and blows her nose.

'Oh dear,' her mother says. 'What's the matter?'

'I don't know what to do.' Sniff. 'I seem to be making a right mess at work. My colleagues hate me and now I'm being investigated for an illegal search.'

'Well, did you?'

'No! Thanks for the vote of confidence.'

Her mother is about as comforting as a cactus plant. Tried scratching myself against one once. Never again!

'Well, how would I know what those beasts have you doing?'

A full-blown sob.

'Look, Rose. You're not Kay. I do wish you'd stop trying to be her.'

'Mum! How can you say that? Aunt Kay was a trailblazer. If it wasn't for women like her, I wouldn't have even been considered for detective work.'

'And look what it did to her,' her mother shouts. 'It killed her!'

Rose recoils as if she's been stung. Both are silent. They are talking about the woman who died of cancer in this house. I watch Rose's face and see mixed emotions: sorrow in her eyes but determination in the tightening of her lips.

'One case,' says Rose. She pauses. 'Every detective has one unsolved case that haunts them, mum.'

'And what happens to you when you work that one case? It made her ill. Killed her in the end. I don't want the same thing happening to you.'

'It won't.'

'Really? You're already sounding miserable.'

Rose closes her eyes. For once, I have to agree with her mum. Rose isn't happy and she doesn't look well. Perhaps she needs to chew on some grass? I always find it makes me feel better.

'Why can't you be proud of her? And me?'

'Well, I . . .'

A moment of hope brightens her face like sunshine breaking through a storm cloud. '. . . I can't. I just can't,' her mother says.

Rose stares at the floor, her face in shadow. 'What I need

right now is someone to cheer me up. I'm feeling pretty depressed.'

'Don't be ridiculous, Rose. Depression is a figment of your imagination. Don't get depressed, get active, as we always used to say on the campaign trail.'

Rose suddenly sits up straight, her eyes wide and bright. What just happened?

'You know, mum, that's good advice,' she says, the surprise clear in her voice. I am surprised too. 'Thanks.'

'Look, I have to go, rooms need cleaning, beds need changing, Belgians need kicking. Bye for now.'

With a click, her mother is gone.

Rose scrolls through her mobile's phone list and dials.

'Rebecca Salt? This is Rose Sidebottom.'

'I'm in a hurry. Can you talk fast?'

I instantly recognise the voice. Paddy's daughter. She could out-howl most dogs.

'I'm sorry to disturb you but, as you know, I've adopted Monty.'

'Yes.'

Rebecca never liked me. The feeling was mutual.

'I was wondering if I could pop round to your father's house and pick up his dog bed and a few of his things?'

Rebecca says it's fine as long as we don't take anything else. Rose thanks her and says goodbye. Then she rummages in her handbag for a set of keys.

'Shouldn't have these,' Rose says, then grins. 'Oops.'

They are Paddy's house keys. I bark with excitement. Rose stands, and rushes about the kitchen.

'Okay, boy. We've got a vet appointment first.'

My tail droops.

'Then we'll fetch your things and I'll take another look around.'

My tail wags.

'I'm going to solve this case. Whatever it takes.'

I bark. Now you're talking!

I'm instantly at the kitchen door, pawing the floor. Rose throws on a coat, grabs her bag and charges down the side passage towards the car with me on a lead, when I hear a familiar thrum of ladybird wings.

Celeste races to catch up with me. 'Where are you going?' she asks.

'My old home,' I bark as quietly as I can.

'Give me a chance,' Rose says, looking down the length of the lead at me. A creature conversation with Rose around is always a little tricky. Misunderstandings abound.

'I'm coming with you,' Celeste says. 'I want to see the crime scene.'

Chapter Thirty-One

Celeste follows my wagging tail as I jump in the back of Rose's car. The rear seats have been flattened so I now have the entire space to myself. It's the doggie equivalent of a stretch limo. Wooferoo!

Rose drives off, the back windows down. I stand, steady myself, ready for bumps and jolts, and then put my head out of the window. Immediately, my ears fly back, the fur along my head and chest flutters and my jowl wobbles. I feel like I'm flying! Rose notices me in her side mirror and laughs.

'You like wind in your fur, don't you?'

Oh boy! Yes, I do! My tongue lolls out of my mouth and my tail wags at great speed.

Celeste finds the buffeting wind too much so she nips into a gap between the two flattened back seats. We turn onto a big roundabout. Oh yeah! Have I told you how much I love roundabouts? I suspect it's how big'uns feel at fair grounds when they're on those machines with seats that swing round and round. I lean with the motion of the car and howl out of the window.

'Where's he going in his knock-off shirt?' Rose says.

I follow her line of vision. She's looking at Larry Nice, who's wearing a blue and white Chelsea home shirt over his bony frame, cigarette smoke trailing behind him as he shuffles along the footpath leading to Sainsbury's.

'Somebody forgot the G,' she says, meaning the 'Samsun' on the front of Nice's shirt. She grins at me in the rear-view mirror.

Larry Nice! I bark fast and loud, with real urgency. Stop the car! Stop!

We pass him by. I'm still barking, my head jutting as far out of the window as I can get. Larry doesn't see or hear: he has headphones over his ears and an iPod on his belt. He looks down, oblivious.

'Sit down, Monty,' yells Rose. 'You'll cause an accident.'

I don't stop.

'I'm pulling over. Now stop barking!'

I obey but only until she parks and opens the back door to see what's wrong. I bolt, lead trailing behind me.

'Wait!' she calls after me, but I am gone.

Ears back, tail out, I take long galloping strides along the footpath towards Larry. I hear Rose chasing me, yelling my name, frantic. Pedestrians jump out of the way. They see my focused stare and flattened ears, and mistake my speed for aggression. I am only a few strides away when Larry looks up, sees me and drops his cigarette. He freezes, mouth open, then raises his arms to his face: big'uns always protect their faces. I skid to a stop at his feet. He has his back to a wall and says with shaky voice, 'N . . . nice doggie.' I can smell his vinegary fear.

'No, Monty!' Rose screams.

I look up at him and wag my tail. Larry peers down at me through a gap in his fingers. I sit and wait. I put on my best smile. After a few seconds Larry lets his hands drop to his sides. 'N . . . nice doggie.'

I lick his hand. He yanks it away, afraid I'll bite him. I wait, tongue hanging out. Then Larry lets me sniff the back of his hand. I lick it, and he pats me. Smells of those weedy cigarettes. He clearly doesn't recognise me as the filthy dog outside his flat.

Rose has caught up and is watching us. She is breathless but manages to say, 'Well, I'll be . . .'

Larry's eyes seem to hover over Rose's heaving chest. 'This your dog, detective?'

She nods, still trying to catch her breath.

'Police dog, is he? Very friendly, considering,' says Larry.

Rose steps closer. 'Considering you're a suspect in his master's murder, yes, he is incredibly friendly to you.'

Larry kneels down and is about to rub my furry chest when he notices the shaved patch around my blue stitches.

'Poor bugger.' He strokes my back instead and I nuzzle him. Larry looks up at Rose. 'You think the dog would let me pat him if I had anything to do with Salt's death? Do ya? Course not.'

Rose shakes her head. 'Larry, this dog's probably the best alibi you've got, although I'm not sure it would stand up in a court of law.'

'Can you tell Mr Leach the dog says I'm innocent? Come on, give me a break, will ya?'

'I'll tell him, but not sure he'll take any notice.'

Larry stops patting me and stands. He's staring at Rose's chest again. Why is he doing that?

'Got time for a beer? I can do me food shop later.'

'No thanks, Larry. See you around.'

Rose takes my collar and leads me back to the car. She phones Leach, even though it's his day off, and explains what just happened. She says she doesn't want anyone complaining she's hassled a suspect. I hear him tell her not to worry.

We set off again.

'Good work, Monty,' says Celeste, peaking out of the gap between the flattened seats. She speaks at a pitch Rose can't hear. 'When we get there, I'll search for the really minuscule details even SOCO might've missed.'

We make a quick trip to the vet hospital, where a nurse removes my stitches. As we leave, Malcolm opens his consulting room door, sees Rose, and comes over.

'Monty's looking well,' he says, not actually looking at me at all. He can't take his eyes off Rose.

She is blushing and tugging her coat together, apparently trying to hide her baggy T-shirt and trackie pants.

'His wound's healed well. Thank you. Um, I better get going.'

'Yes, of course. Well, um. Yes.'

Malcolm calls in his next patient and watches us leave. Rose bundles me into the car as fast as possible, then drives off at breakneck speed. What is going on?

'Why do I always bump into people when I'm looking like crap?' Rose says to the rear-view mirror.

I stay out of it.

Soon I can smell that combination of aromas that is my old home: sun-bleached fences, lavender and sweetpeas mixed with the wet, muddy, reedy odour of the river. Soon we are parked outside and I jump from the car, followed by Celeste.

The crime scene tape is still there, like a bandage that can never make things better.

Rose opens the front door and walks in. Celeste is sitting unnoticed in the fur on my back. I hesitate. Everything smells so familiar. But Paddy isn't there. I take one step, then another, into the hallway, my tail between my legs. I sniff familiar musty books, and the residue of Paddy's favourite aftershave and the last meal he ate – a chicken korma. I recognise my fur on the carpet and a couple of twigs that must've hitched a ride into the house on my tail. Paddy hadn't yet vacuumed them up. Nor will he. Rose looks back at me.

'Come on, Monty. Show me your bed.'

Celeste flies off to the back garden and I lead Rose to the kitchen. My bed is like a thickly padded duvet with a faded and slightly grubby, navy-blue cotton cover. I sniff it, inhaling its comforting smells. Memories come flooding back: Paddy giving me a good morning pat, every day without fail; Paddy chasing me around the garden so he could wash off the 'stink' of manure I'd just rolled in (ah, we had such fun, I can tell you!); Paddy and I huddled under a large umbrella, fishing in the rain; our trip to the sea when a crab pinched my paw and Paddy shared his fish and chips with me to make me feel better. I am lost in happy memories. When I look up from my bed, Rose is gone. I pick up my toy duck and follow her scent to the study. She's opening and closing desk drawers. I sit at her feet, offering her my most prized possession. It was once yellow and fluffy, and is now matted and grey. Which is just the way I like it: tasty and well-loved. She leans down and I open my mouth enough for her to take it without it dropping or snagging on my teeth.

'Thanks, Monty. This your special toy? We'll have to bring it with us, then. Now what about your food?'

At the mention of food, I would normally race to the cupboard where my tinned meat, kibble and treats are kept. But I see Paddy's cardigan hanging on the back of his swivel chair. It's grey wool, with big black buttons and two baggy pockets. In one pocket is Paddy's handkerchief. In the other, some liver treats. But for once, I'm not interested in food. This cardigan is intensely evocative of the Paddy I love. I want it to come with us.

I take it gently in my mouth and pull. It stretches but gets caught on the chair arms. Rose lifts the cardigan free and lets me drag it along the floor to my bed in the kitchen. I then go back into the office for my duck and place that, too, on my bed. I lie on them. Where I go, they go.

'It's okay, boy. They're coming with us. Now show me where Paddy kept your food.'

I trot over to a cupboard that is high enough so that I can't open it. I sit and look up at it. Rose opens the door.

'Clever dog,' Rose says and pats me. 'I swear you know what I'm saying.'

She finds a couple of hessian shopping bags and puts everything from the cupboard in them as well as my food bowl. She then rolls up my bed like a sausage roll, with Paddy's cardigan inside, and carries everything to the car. I follow, my duck in my mouth. Once the car is loaded, Rose returns to the house. She wanders from room to room, as I do, but gravitates back to the study. She sits at Paddy's desk and feels underneath the table top, then takes drawers out and checks their exterior surfaces. She scans the bookshelves, then removes books and feels behind them too. She even looks behind a framed print on the wall of irises by some big'un called Van Gogh.

'You'd think he'd keep a back-up somewhere,' Rose says to herself. 'On a USB or something.'

I harrumph and lie at her feet. As my eyelids begin to droop I hear a crashing sound next door. I am instantly alert, head up, ears raised. The wall to the office adjoins Mr Grace's sitting room. Rose and I stand. We both know something is wrong.

She looks at me and whispers, 'Quiet.'

I understand and follow at her heel.

Leaving Paddy's front door ajar, Rose steps over the low picket fence between the two gardens and peers through Grace's sitting-room window. I do the same, paws on the windowsill. A man in black jeans and T-shirt is crouched over the old man, who lies motionless on the carpet. The intruder has his back to us.

A sharp intake of breath and Rose croaks, 'Police!'

I bark savagely, eyes wide, and paw the window frantically. There's a second when the intruder glances round, his face in side profile, then he pulls on a black head-sock, and he's gone from sight.

'Oh my God!' Rose breathes. I can hear her heart pounding and smell the adrenalin. Her hand trembles as she flicks open her phone and makes a call.

'This is Detective Constable Rose Sidebottom. I'm at two, Pepperbox Lane. I need urgent back-up and an ambulance, a man has been attacked . . .'

She grabs a brick that's framing the flowerbed and smashes the lattice window.

I hear a sound Rose can't – the click of a deadlock. He's

using the back door. For a split second I am torn – do I follow Rose inside the house, or the noise at the back? I decide on the noise, because that's where the danger is. I charge down the side of Grace's house, in time to see a man jumping the fence and hurtling off along the river bank in the direction of Geldeford.

I bare my teeth. I want to taste blood – his blood. I tear through the garden and bound over the fence. I run as if my life depends on it. I ignore my chest muscles screaming. My paws pound the ground. I am silent, no barking this time: no warning for him. He shoves a female jogger out of the way, who screams as she falls in the river. Only then does he notice me. He takes something shiny from his coat pocket and throws it into the river, then jumps a stile and races towards a car. He winces; one arm is clearly painful. He's fast and agile, like a gymnast, and his movements are familiar. I'm closing on him. Every second counts. If he gets in that car, I'll lose him. I can't lose him, not again. I'm not close enough to get a good sniff but I'm convinced this is the man who killed my master. My muscles burn, but I find more speed. I am at the stile, but it's too high for me to jump, so I squeeze under it. This slows me down. I hear a car start. No! I see his dark image inside the car and I reach it just as he begins to accelerate. My paws and snout hit the window and my claws scratch the paint. I bark and snarl, the whites of my eyes visible. He has removed the sock that covered his face and we look at each other for a brief moment before I tumble to the ground, leaving a smear of drool over the glass.

His car tears off down the country lane and disappears round a corner. I will never forget his sweaty face and cold eyes.

I lie in the dirt, panting. The air is thick with dust, churned up by car wheels. I consider chasing it, but know it's hopeless – I can't keep up with cars for long.

A siren is getting closer. I shake the dirt from my fur and stagger back along the tow-path. A couple are helping the young woman out of the water. They don't even see me. I look toward the middle of the river, where the killer threw something shiny. The water is dark and deep and I am not sure I can reach the bottom. I have only ever fished in the shallows.

'No,' a voice says, close to my ear.

I look around confused.

Celeste buzzes in front of my face. 'Don't do it. It's too deep. Let the big'uns find it.'

'But they won't. Only I know where he threw it,' I reply, still panting with exhaustion. 'Was it a knife?'

'Yes, but we can find him without it. I saw his face too.'

But I'm not listening. I must find the weapon.

The water is cool and I feel the squelch of mud and scratch of reeds under my paws. I wade out into the river. If there are fish nearby, I don't even notice. I am trying hard to work out where the knife hit the surface. I line myself up with a willow tree on the opposite bank and swim towards it. As the river gets deeper, the water gets colder, the current stronger. I keep my nose just above the surface and sniff all the time, hoping the man's scent will have followed the knife. The current is tugging at me, dragging me downstream. I fight it, just as I have fought the drag of a lead many times. My muscles ache but I battle on until I'm where I think the knife must have landed. I circle the area and take a few deep breaths, but my stitches restrict my chest movements and make it painful. I dive.

I open my eyes. The sun penetrates through the murky green water and I look down to the mud, pebbles and dead foliage on the riverbed. I spot something glinting, but half-buried. It is far away. I head for it, paws paddling against the current. I need air, but keep heading downwards. I open my mouth and scoop up the shiny object, mud and all, and almost choke. My lungs are heaving and I feel light-headed, but I keep pulling at the water and head towards the sunlight. I burst through the surface, still clinging to something metal. It is almost impossible to breathe with it in my mouth but I take some shallow gasps and swim to the bank. Water blurs my vision and I realise Rose is calling and beckoning to me, with real panic in her voice.

I hear wings hum by my ear. 'It's a Coke can,' says Celeste. 'Let it go. Take a breath.'

I ignore her in disbelief. It can't be!

Celeste perseveres. 'Monty, you need to breathe. I promise you, it's not the weapon.'

I am almost at the riverbank and Rose is knee deep in the water, ready to grab me.

I spit out the crushed can and do a u-turn.

'No!' Rose screams. 'Monty! Come back! Please, you'll drown!'

'It's not worth dying for,' Celeste urges.

I have to try one more time.

I am growing tired but I paddle back out to the middle of the river. Rose is screaming, her voice growing hoarse. I sneeze some water from my nose and pant as I once again swim in circles, trying to get my bearings. A deep breath and I head back down to the riverbed, my legs pumping as fast as I can move them. I swim quickly to the bottom and peer at the mush, leaves, twigs and rubbish littering the bed. I almost swallow water in shock when my paw hits the red handle of a partially buried shopping trolley. Caught in the trolley is a long-bladed kitchen knife. The handle is dark and I take it in my mouth and pull. But something catches and it won't move. I have to get some air. My ribs feel crushed by a huge weight, as if the water is solidifying into concrete. I wiggle the handle back and forth. It comes free. I look up. The sunlight dancing on the surface seems so far away. I am light-headed but one thing I know for sure: I have the weapon. I extend my front legs upwards and claw at the water, but my strokes get weaker and weaker, my head fuzzier and fuzzier. I have no energy left. I won't make it to the surface in time.

Chapter Thirty-Two

A hand grasps my collar and yanks me upwards. I am almost unconscious, my vision blurry, my body limp, except for my jaw which is clamped down on the knife handle. I must not drop it. Not now. Rose has dived down to reach me. Her head is surrounded by air bubbles and her ponytail floats above her. Her pale grey trackie pants and white T-shirt billow in the green river water. As I am hauled the last few feet to the surface, I almost drop my prize, and, just in time, Rose takes the knife from my mouth. Her head disappears underwater as she struggles to keep us both afloat.

'I'll take the dog,' a man says and grabs me.

I spit out water and mud, spluttering and gasping, still unsure what is going on. He pulls me towards his black uniform and rests my upper body on his broad chest, then he swims on his back towards the riverbank. It's Joe, the nice policeman. I know his smell. I relax and let him take me. He's strong and propels us easily along. I now hear shouting. I glimpse Rose swimming freestyle next to us. Has she got the knife? She's a strong swimmer and reaches the shore moments before we do. Joe stands and carries me like a baby to the shore, as my head lolls over his arm. I hear splashing as another person runs into the river and helps Rose to dry land, where she collapses on all fours coughing, her sodden hair covering her face like seaweed over a breakwater.

I am placed on the tow-path on my side and retch up some water. I open my eyes and see several faces I don't know staring down at me. I try to lift my head. Joe leans over and water drips from his concerned face onto mine. Rose crawls over to me and places her wet face so close, our noses touch. Hers is small and pink.

'You all right, Monty? Hey, boy. Don't die on me.'

I wag my wet tail once, but the sodden feathers of my fur feel like lead. She strokes my face and sits back on her haunches.

Rose's boss – the Leach – takes off his coat and places it around Rose's shoulders. She is shivering.

'Get a paramedic down here,' he yells to someone.

Rose is still gripping something in her hand. Is it the knife? I sit up and whimper, then vomit watery bile. Not pretty, I know, but I feel so much better.

'There you go, sir,' she says to Leach, as she lifts her clenched hand and opens her palm. In it sits a kitchen knife. She coughs, then clears her throat. 'I'll lay any money this was used on Mr Grace.'

Leach calls to the over-groomed pooch, otherwise known as DI Pearl. He struts towards us and takes his time. He oozes alpha male pretensions but I reckon if it came down to a fight with the Leach he'd roll over onto his back in a flash, yelping for mercy. Pearl places the knife in a plastic bag and walks away, without saying a word to Rose.

'That has to be the stupidest and bravest act I've seen in

a while,' Leach says to her. His voice is gruff but he gives her shoulder a gentle squeeze and his small eyes, like two amber beads, have lost their hard glint. 'Well done, Rose. Proud of you.'

Is it river water or tears I see in her eyes?

'Thank you, sir,' she sniffs. 'But Monty found the knife. No wonder they're called Retrievers!'

Flattered, I vomit watery gunge.

'Hey!' shouts Leach at Pearl. 'Get that vet down here. You know, the one from Friday. And hurry!'

I don't want to go back to that vet hospital, even though Malcolm is very nice. I struggle to stand. I'm leaving, if I can muster the strength. Rose crawls towards me and cradles my head.

'It's okay, Monty, Malcolm'll just make sure you're not hurt. But you're staying with me. I promise you.'

I believe her and rest my head in her soggy lap.

'Rose, you'll need to make a statement and explain what you were doing here. But for now, I have to know if you can identify the assailant?'

'I only got a glimpse of his face. Side profile. Black hair. East Asian appearance. Muscular build, five-ten.'

'It's a start.'

'He was cradling his arm, sir. He has to be Salt's killer.'

'Write down everything you remember, as soon as you can.'

Rose nods. 'How's Grace, sir?'

'He's lost a lot of blood and on his way to the hospital. You probably saved his life.'

Rose is too proud to speak. Two compliments from a man who rarely gives them.

'Did Grace say anything?' he asks.

'He did, but not much of it made sense. He said it was his fault. Said "they" killed Patrick by mistake. They were after him because of something he did in Hong Kong. Mumbled about a suicide and a son taking revenge.'

'A whole new avenue of investigation,' her boss concludes.

He stands up slowly, his knee joints stiff. I hear a crack.

'Sir, I can't be certain but I expect you'll discover Nice was at Sainsbury's when Francis Grace was attacked.'

I can't help sighing with relief.

Chapter Thirty-Three

As soon as we enter Rose's kitchen, the smell hits us. And believe me, with my super-hooter, it gets right up my nose. Sewage.

'Phwoar! Monty! Was that you?' She laughs.

Excuse me! My farts aren't that bad!

It's early evening, I've had the all-clear from Malcolm, and Rose has my dog bed and Paddy's cardigan rolled up under one arm and bags of my food in both hands. I have my toy duck by the neck and gently drop him on the kitchen floor. Rose leaves her things on the table and heads straight for the downstairs bathroom, which is little more than a toilet and a hand-basin, barely large enough to wash a rat. Speaking of which, I wonder where Betty is?

The toilet bowl is full to the brim with brown water, shredded toilet paper and . . . well, I'll leave the rest to your imagination.

'Oh fantastic!' says Rose, raising her hands in despair.

'Oh disgusting!' says Celeste, who is sitting between my shoulder blades. She makes retching sounds and flies off.

'That's all I need,' Rose says. She looks at me and sighs. 'All I wanted to do was relax, and now this happens.'

Well, I was hoping for a whopping-enormous dinner. After retrieving that knife from the river, I am super hungry. Could eat my weight in food. No, the weight of a car. No, a truck!

She rummages under the kitchen sink and comes up with a rubber plunger.

'This should do it,' she says, holding it up as if she were carrying the Olympic torch.

She rams the rubber, dome-shaped end into the toilet bowl and pumps it up and down. The smelly toilet water splashes all over the tiled floor. We both jump back.

'Oh shit!'

Exactly!

On go the pink washing-up gloves and poor Rose mops up the wet floor. Then she rings Smithson Plumbing.

'Not surprised,' I hear Garry Smithson reply. 'It's that willow. Roots are blocking the pipe. You'll need new pipework and you might want to cut that tree down, and all.'

'I'm not cutting the willow. It's been here ever since I can remember. Can't you lay a new pipe away from the roots?'

'Possibly. Either way, it's an excavation job and I can't do it straight away. A week or two.'

Rose holds the phone away from her ear and tries to strangle the receiver. Not sure why. I'd be happy to gnaw it, if she likes. Haven't tried eating a phone yet.

'Is there no other solution?' she asks.

'Not long-term, no.'

'How much will it cost?'

'Ah, I'd have to quote it properly but I'd say a couple of grand.'

'A couple of thousand! But Garry, I simply don't have that kind of money. Can't you come out here and do something temporary to fix it?'

'I don't work weekends. Can't you cope till Monday?'

'No, Garry, I am not living with raw sewage and I'm not weeing in the bushes, okay?'

What's wrong with weeing in the bushes? I do it all the time.

'I'll have to charge it as an emergency call-out.'

She sighs. 'That's fine,' she says, when she doesn't mean it is fine at all, 'please just get here as soon as you can.' The call ends.

Rose looks down at me and I sit looking up at her.

'Bet you're hungry?'

Oh yeah! I lick my lips.

'You know what this shitty kind of day calls for?'

Dinner? Now?

Rose rings a number, orders pizza and then opens a bottle of red wine. Garry turns up half an hour later and uses some kind of foul smelling chemical in the blocked toilet that makes gurgling noises and my nose sting. Within a few minutes the brown liquid has drained away.

'This stuff could strip the tarmac off a motorway,' he says. 'But it won't work for ever. Here's me quote for laying new pipes.' He hands her a hand-written piece of paper. Rose glances at it, shakes her head and puts it in her pocket. 'And that'll be sixty quid for unblocking your toilet. Cash.'

Rose goes to the kitchen to fetch her purse. I guard Garry. His eyes are too close together and I don't trust him. Any animal with eyes that close is usually two-faced.

'What you looking at?' the plumber snaps at me.

I bark a few times, just to show I won't be pushed around.

'Hey, lady! Can you keep that dog under control?'

Rose returns. 'What's he doing?'

'Barking at me, all nasty-like.'

I sit, mute, and look at her with big innocent eyes.

'He's a big softy, Garry. His bark is far worse than his bite.'

Not true, but I'm not going to contradict her.

'Sorry, Garry, it'll have to be a cheque. I don't get paid till Monday.'

He grumbles but accepts it and leaves, watching me all the way as he walks to his van. Rose then feeds me an extra-large dinner – I am growing very fond of her. She has a bath and puts on pyjamas covered in flying pigs. There is some sort of connection between her family and pigs that I can't quite make out.

I join her in the sitting room as she curls up on the threadbare chintz sofa and sips her wine. Her laptop is on the low coffee table. I gnaw at one of my rubber chew toys thinking of pizza, but soon grow bored. I squeeze into the gap between the sofa and the coffee table and she plays with my ears.

'You were very brave today, Monty, chasing that horrible man. And those currents were really strong. How on earth did you learn to dive like that?'

I lift my paw and she shakes it, in a how-do-you-do way. Then she plays with my toes.

'Your webbed feet must help, I guess.'

Yes, that's what I was trying to say.

It almost feels as if we're having a conversation. I want to explain that I've been swimming in rivers since I was a pup and caught loads of fish too.

She has emptied her first glass of wine and pours another. Her phone rings and I recognise the voice – Joe Salisbury.

'I rang to see how you were,' he says.

I hear music and traffic noise in the background. Sounds like he's driving home.

'Hospital gave me the all clear.' She swallows. 'It's nice of you to call. Really.'

'You were amazing, Rose. The station is buzzing with the story.'

She blushes. 'Any news on the knife?'

'Word is it's the weapon used on Grace and – this is the best bit – it looks like the assailant cut himself. There might be just enough blood to get a DNA match to the fabric from Monty's mouth.'

'Even though it's been in water?'

'So I'm told.'

'When will they know?'

'Monday, maybe Tuesday.'

'So whoever killed Salt could've stabbed Grace too? And Larry Nice was at Sainsbury's when it happened. So it can't be him. Someone is definitely framing him.'

I woof with joy.

Salisbury hears me and laughs. 'Sounds like the dog agrees.' There's a pause. 'Are you going to Salt's funeral on Monday?' he asks.

I prick up my ears. Funeral?

'Yes, I'm going. I want to see who turns up and how they react.' Rose glances down at me. 'And Monty needs to know where his master's buried. I'm taking him along.'

'Poor fellow,' says Salisbury. 'Well, I'm almost home. See you Monday, after the funeral.'

Rose ends the call but continues to stare at the red button on the phone. Her fingers stroke the keys. She has gone into some kind of trance and I'm worried she's ill so I rest my chin on her knee.

'Just my luck he's taken.'

Taken? Taken where? I may have to add finding Joe to my list of mysteries to solve. But Joe sounded pretty relaxed so perhaps his rescue can wait until after pizza?

The front door bell chimes. It's a real bronze bell with a rope dangling from it. I've tried jumping up and grabbing the rope when I'm bored but haven't managed it yet. I'm instantly standing, tail up, barking a warning. I get to the front door first, ready to defend her. Rose peers through a small side-window at the pizza delivery boy.

'Hi, can you come round the back? This door's jammed.'

Oh dear! It's the same delivery boy I scared half to death the other night. I decide to hang back and keep myself hidden. I lie down in the hallway and wait. I feel my ear being tugged and hear a squeaky voice.

'Keep some for me, will ya?'

It's Betty Blabble.

'If she leaves any crusts, I'll let you know,' I say, keeping my voice down so the delivery boy doesn't hear me growl.

'Here she comes. I'm off.' Betty races into a hole in the skirting board.

Ah, pepperoni, ham, cheese, tomatoes, mushrooms. I start drooling even before Rose has taken a bite from her first slice. She notices and wipes my face with the complimentary serviette. Embarrassing! Treating me like a baby! I'm relieved Betty isn't here to see it otherwise the whole doggie neighbourhood would be laughing at me.

'So how is Mr Snotty Nose linked to all this?' she says, deep in thought.

Who is this person and why does he have a runny nose?

'Maybe he's just an arrogant tosser trying to protect his investment in this new bee? On the other hand, he could easily afford to have poor old Salt taken care of.'

I shut my jaw like a trapdoor. Bee? She said, bee! I jump up and bark, almost knocking the pizza box over.

'Monty, behave yourself. I know you want some, but you'll just have to wait and see if I leave any. Now sit!' she commands.

No! I mean yes! Leave me some pizza. But, no! That's not what I'm excited about. I decide to sit and keep quiet. I want to know more about the bees and this arrogant tosser man. But I don't remember anyone looking after my Paddy, except me. She has totally lost me. I wait for more clues but Rose doesn't say anything more about them. Instead she Googles 'Francis Grace private equity'. Frustrated, I give myself a good scratch and then lie down and chew my paw. Rose finishes the pizza, all bar a few crusts. She gives me just one.

'Don't want you getting fat.'

No chance! She leaves the box on the sink drainer, lid closed, then returns to the sofa and her research. Bored, I manage to get my back to the sofa and my head on her knee so I can see the screen.

It seems the old man was once a hot-shot investment banker, who got into private equity when he moved to Hong Kong in his thirties. I don't get the private equity bit, but I know banking involves lots of money because that's where Paddy used to go when he wanted cash.

'Sounds like our Mr Grace was pretty ruthless,' Rose says.

She looks down at me and sees my eyes glued to the screen. 'Anyone would think you're reading this.'

I look up at her. *If only you knew.*

We continue reading in silence until we come to a news story from twelve years ago about the Yelong family.

'Oh dear,' says Rose. 'This is very sad.'

Shortly before Grace retired, he led a 'raid' on a family-run carpet manufacturing company called Yelong Carpets. This takeover was apparently worth hundreds of millions of dollars. The head of the family, Mr Yelong, put up a good fight but Grace forced him to sell and fired the top executives, including Mr Yelong, who committed suicide with the shame. Loads of workers lost their jobs and the remaining Yelong family members lost their home.

We stare at a Yelong family photo taken in happier times. Mother, father, two daughters, grandfather and a seven-year-old boy, Yelong Li, in school uniform: red and grey striped tie, white short-sleeved shirt and long grey shorts.

'I wonder,' muses Rose.

I look up at her and cock my head. Wonder what?

'He must be around nineteen now.'

She picks up the phone and dials the UK Border Agency. She gives them her name and rank, and asks if a Yelong Li from Hong Kong is in the UK at the moment. I hear a man say he'll call the main police switchboard to verify her identity and call her back.

In the meantime, Rose does some more digging into Yelong Li's history. She goes from one site to another until she has a mountain of data on Yelong Li. She discovers a photo of him at eighteen, about to run in the Hong Kong marathon. He's posing with some other contenders. I move in closer to get a good look. He's wearing a singlet so his arms are bare. He is thin and muscular, with dark-rimmed, rectangular glasses. He has a red birthmark across the left eye. I visualise the killer's face through the car window, his eyes mocking me. Unless Yelong Li has somehow removed the birthmark, no longer wears glasses and now has a tattoo, he did not kill my master, nor did he try to kill Mr Grace.

'That could be our killer,' says Rose. 'Right height, athletic build and certainly has motive.' She looks straight into my eyes. 'What do you reckon, Monty? Has Yelong Li taken revenge on the man who destroyed his father and killed your poor old master by mistake?'

I shake my head.

'Itchy ear?'

She gives them both a good rub.

I sigh and lie down on the floor. Only Celeste and I have seen the killer's entire face, but how do I tell Rose about the birthmark?

The phone rings. It's the man from the Border Agency.

I hear him say, 'Yelong Li arrived at Heathrow nine months ago, claiming he was on holiday. He's allowed to stay here six months without a visa. He's overstayed and we're on the look-out for him.'

Rose responds. 'Any idea where he is?'

'None, but we've flagged his details. Can I ask what your interest is in him?'

Rose swallows. 'We want to question him in relation to a murder investigation.'

What about the arrogant tosser and his bees?

Harrumph.

Chapter Thirty-Four

Betty and I enjoy the left-over pizza crusts. I can't believe Rose – who is snoring softly upstairs – doesn't like them. How is that possible? Betty nibbles fast and methodically, working from one end of each bit of dough to the other. I simply wolf each piece down whole. It takes all my strength of will not to snaffle the lot, but Betty is my friend so I wait patiently as she tucks into the next crust. A long piece of drool swings from one side of my mouth and slaps Betty across the head.

'Oops! Sorry about that.'

Betty rubs herself against the fur of my leg to remove the globule. 'If I need a shower, I'll ask for it,' she says.

I hear Celeste fly in through the lead-light kitchen window. She lands on a tap, keeping a safe distance from Betty and her crust. Moments later, Dante arrives and positions himself on the draining board, unnervingly close to Celeste. Has Dante got a crush on her?

'I've briefed Dante on today's events,' Celeste says. 'We had a pre-meeting meeting.'

'And I've filled Betty in too,' I say.

Betty mimics Celeste's husky voice, 'Pre-meeting schmeeting.' Then realises she is being glared at. She senses she's gone too far and changes the subject. 'So, where's our little bee?'

'A bit depressed, poor thing. Survivor's guilt. I thought it best to leave her alone tonight,' Celeste replies. She ups the volume. 'I would like to congratulate Monty on his bravery today. Monty, you deserve a medal.'

Celeste applauds by rubbing her legs together, Betty claps and even Dante taps his beak on the drainer. If I could blush, I would.

'You're a real hero, mate,' Betty says.

'Ah-hem,' says Celeste, clearing her throat. 'Okay, listen up. Time to focus on our case.'

'Slave-driver,' Betty mutters.

'Let's review what we know,' begins Celeste, walking up and down the tap handle. 'Today, Monty and I saw the suspect's full face. Unfortunately, Rose only saw his side profile and very briefly. I can tell you the man who attacked Mr Grace has black straight longish hair, shaggy cut. Dark eyes, distinctive eyelids. He's from East Asia, possibly Korea because he's tall, about five ten. Muscular, fit, but round face. Wearing black. He drove a silver, four-door Ford Fiesta, which happens to be one of the most popular cars in this country.'

'That'll make it hard to find, but impressive observation skills, Celeste,' remarks Dante.

'Helps to have these,' she says, pointing at her compound eyes. 'And his clothes carry a distinctive food smell. I think I know what it is.'

'Like rotten eggs?' I ask.

'Exactly. A few months back, an Asian spotted wing vinegar fly asked for my help. They're new to this country and have fruit growers up-in-arms. Anyway, she was very chatty and was telling me what a relief it was that stinky tofu isn't popular here. Just inhaling it sends them loopy.'

'So you think our suspect eats this particular tofu?' Dante asks.

'I do.'

My mind wanders back to the Ford Fiesta. 'He's changed vehicles.'

I get confused looks.

'On the night he killed Paddy he had a white van,' I clarify. 'Now he's driving a silver car.'

'Both are probably stolen,' says Dante.

'And neither were red and sporty, so they don't belong to GN1US,' says Celeste.

'Did you see a birthmark on his face?' I ask her.

'No. Why?'

'Because Rose believes a big'un called Yelong Li from Hong Kong is the man we saw today.' I explain the connection between Yelong and Francis Grace. 'But Yelong doesn't look like the killer or have a tattoo, plus he has a red birthmark across his left eye.'

'The man we saw today didn't have a birthmark,' confirms Celeste. 'Which means it can't be Yelong Li.'

'Hold on,' says Betty. 'We're getting side-tracked here. Forget this Yelong bloke. What about the tatt on the killer's arm? He could be part of an Asian gang. Maybe we can find him that way?'

'It looks like a star,' I say. 'Not a normal one though. It had more points. Seven, I think.'

'Now that could help,' says Betty. 'We search for gangs with star tattoos in the area. There's some pretty nasty gangs out there, I can tell you. Came across one in me Eurotunnel days. Smuggling drugs, they were. But we sorted 'em out.'

Dante and Celeste stare down at the rat in disbelief.

'What?' Betty shrugs, looking uncomfortable.

'How did you and your ratty friends stop them?' Celeste asks.

'Not something I care to share.'

Celeste's red and black wing casings lift a little in annoyance. Oh dear. I get us back on track.

'Dante?' I say. 'Can you look into local gangs tonight?'

'If you have a laptop.'

I lead them to the sitting room where Rose's laptop lies on the sofa. In no time at all we have found a star tattoo matching the one on the killer's arm. The Death Stars gang. I read the information out loud for Betty, who can't read.

'I don't like the sound of this lot. Real nasty buggers, they are,' she says.

I read on: 'They run a drug trafficking syndicate from South Korea, and they're moving into the US and the UK. They've been linked to numerous murders.'

'Why would they kill an entomologist?' Dante asks. 'It doesn't make sense.'

'Huh?' Betty says.

'He means Paddy,' I say.

'Why didn't he flipping well say so?' She gives an exaggerated sigh, then folds her arms. 'Gangs like them kill for two reasons. Revenge or money, and I'll back money any day.'

'How do you know what motivates them?' Celeste asks.

Betty avoids eye contact. 'We live at the dark and dirty end of town. We hear things. You know.'

We wait for an explanation, but don't get one. She moves on.

'Maybe these super bees are worth a bundle and someone didn't want Paddy opening his mouth.' She glances at me. 'Sorry, mate, but I'm just telling it as I see it. Whoever owns that red sports car could've paid one of this gang to sort him out.'

'She's right,' says Celeste. 'And I think the link to drugs is important. I found this stuck between the pavers where Paddy died.'

She unzips the top of one of her boots. We all step back, wary of her stinky feet. She pulls out a leaf fragment so tiny I can barely see it.'

'What's that?' Betty asks.

'From a cannabis leaf. I'm assuming Paddy didn't smoke pot?' Celeste looks at me.

I look blank.

'Weed, grass, hashish . . .'

'Funny cigarettes? No way.'

'Then I'm guessing it must've fallen from the killer's clothing.' She peers at each one of us in turn.

'So it looks like we have two lines of enquiry. One, we find where the Death Stars gang hangs out. Do they grow cannabis locally or import? Two, we find out who the GN1US number plate belongs to. The two may well be linked. It's possible that Mr Genius wanted Paddy dead and employed an assassin to do it.'

'I think so too,' I say.

'Let's focus on tracking down the Death Stars first,' says Celeste. 'Any thoughts?'

'I'll put the word out through wee-mail,' I say.

'I've got a few contacts in the Geldeford sewers I can ask,' says Betty.

'Good,' says Celeste. 'Dante, I need a list of lock-ups and storage facilities where people can come and go, no questions asked. Oh, and stores selling hydroponics.'

'As you wish,' says Dante.

'And how do we find the very humble Mr Genius?' Celeste asks.

'It's obvious he has something to do with this super bee project,' says Dante. 'So he either works at Flay Bioscience or the university. Might I suggest surveillance? A mind-numbingly tedious task, but once he's parked his car, we can follow him and ascertain his identity.' He yawns.

'Sounds boring,' says Betty, 'but as long as we've got lots of nibbles it won't be so bad.'

'Perhaps we don't need to,' I say. 'Paddy's funeral is on Monday and Rose is taking me. GN1US will probably be there.'

It suddenly strikes me this will be the last time I'll see my beloved Paddy. Even though I'm surrounded by friends, I feel very alone. I hang my head and drop my tail.

'Don't you worry, mate, I'll be there for you,' says Betty.

'You can rely on me, Monty. I've got your back,' Celeste says.

I look up to see her taking up a Ninja stance.

Dante fidgets from one leg to another, his sharp claws tapping the metal draining board. He finds emotions – especially someone else's – embarrassing.

I sit up tall, chest out, and pull myself together. This is about finding Paddy's killer, not wallowing in my grief.

'Paddy's funeral is our best chance of finding Mr Genius. I'll need you all to look out for the red car. Dante, you'll have the best vantage point from the air. If you see GN1US, call to me.'

He nods once.

'Betty, can you steal a Flay security pass? It's a rectangular plastic thing with a barcode and a photo on it. Paddy used to wear his around his neck on a long cord, but they could be left in cars or in pockets.'

'Easy peasy lemon squeezy.'

'Ah-hem, sorry to interrupt, but I'm running this investigation, so I should be giving instructions, not you,' says Celeste, tapping her boot, annoyed.

'Oh, give it a rest,' snaps Betty. 'Monty's plan is a good one. Let him get on with it.'

Celeste opens her wings and takes off. I am about to call her back when she lands on the table. 'Okay. I agree it's a good plan. I'll go with it. Just this once.'

Trouble is I don't really have a plan. I'm making it up as I go along.

'Celeste, I'll probably be on a lead and my view will be restricted. I need you to watch big'uns' faces. You know what the assassin looks like. He might turn up too.'

'I will. And if I spy him?'

'Alert me and don't let him out of your sight.'

'Do you think he'd be dumb enough to go?' asks Betty.

'If he does, he'll regret it.'

Chapter Thirty-Five

I open one eye to discover Rose plodding around the kitchen in her dressing-gown, her pink open-heeled slippers flapping on the lino. It's Sunday morning. I shut my eye and drift off again. The smell of bacon wakes me. I might be tired after yesterday's adventure, but bacon is irresistible. My nostrils quiver, I open both eyes and lift my head.

Rose looks at me and laughs. 'You look like how I feel. Like crap. What's with the tucked-in jowly look, Monty?'

I realise that one side of my jowl is curled inwards, caught in my teeth. Not a good look, but easily rectified with a big yawn.

'Thought bacon might get you moving,' she says.

I leave my bed and stretch, doing what is often described by yoga buffs as a downward dog. I can also do a doggie doughnut – when I take the tip of my tail in my mouth. But there's one yoga pose I'll never do and that's the cat pose. Pah! My stretch finished, I position myself as close to Rose as possible. I need her to know I'm ready for my bacon.

'Careful. The fat spits. Might burn you.'

She tries to shove me away but as far as I'm concerned the nearer to the bacon the better. So I don't budge. She serves her bacon and eggs with toast and sits at the table near her laptop, which is switched on.

Oh no! Did we move it last night and forget to switch it off?

Rose starts to read the news, and I relax. She must have brought it in here when I was sleeping. She finishes her breakfast, leaving a bit of bacon uneaten which she drops into my waiting jaws. Yum. Salty, chargrilled, crunchy, smoky, meaty. Heaven. I lick my mouth over and over again, savouring it.

'So, Monty, what are we going to do today?'

Eat some more.

Walk.

Chase squirrels.

Go fishing.

Play Frisbee.

Dig holes and sniff for moles.

I can think of loads of things to do and wag my tail very fast.

'I probably should do some chores. There's washing and cleaning to do, and the leaves need raking. Are you any good at chores?'

Chores don't sound like much fun. I decide to take control. I walk over to where Rose has hung my lead on a hook and stare fixedly at it, my body pointing in its direction. I learned this technique from my Pointer friends.

'Oh I see. You want a walk?'

Oh boy. Rose really gets it!

'Why not?' she says. 'But I have to have a bath and get dressed first.'

Why can't she walk in her dressing-gown?

She places the frying pan and her plate in the sink and climbs the stairs. Some time later she arrives in the kitchen with wet hair, smelling like strawberries. She's wearing black Nike trainers, sporty three-quarter-length training trousers and a figure-hugging fleece top with hood that zips at the front. She clips the lead to my collar and I drag her towards the back door. Walkies!

'Monty, wait! Keys and poo bags, first.'

She picks up the things she needs, including her mobile, and then we are off. At full speed. No idea where I'm going, but I'm going. Oh boy, am I going! In the interest of preserving her hand, she lets me off the lead. I charge through oak and ash woodland, picking up loads of tantalising rabbit, fox and squirrel smells.

'Monty! Don't stray too far. I don't want to lose you,' Rose shouts as I cock my leg and leave a wee-mail on a tree trunk.

It says, 'Know who drives a red Bentley GN1US? Monty@ Duckdown Cottage.' Then on another I ask, 'Seen Korean man with seven-pointed star tattoo and bite wound in arm? Monty@Duckdown Cottage.'

As I wait for Rose to catch up I wonder if I should put something on Twitter. But wee-mails are probably the best way to reach the locals.

Just as Rose gets close enough to give me a pat, I pick up a whiff of water. I dance around her with excitement, and then, with nostrils working overtime, I race to find the source. The closer I get, the richer the reedy, silty, fishy smells get. I know it's a river because now I can hear the water gurgling along the bank. The woodland comes to an abrupt halt as the land slopes steeply down a grassy bank to a small muddy beach. An alder tree has dipped its roots into the water and there is an abundance of great reedmace, with its big brown bullrushes sticking up like spears. I careen down the bank and sniff the water's edge. It's fresh and clean. Even better, I can smell fish. Might be European Perch or Ruffe. Either way, I'm ecstatic. But if I'm going to catch one, I need to be stealthy. Charging about in the river is great fun but it scares away the fish. I've learned this the hard way.

I choose a spot where the water is fairly still. I place one paw, then another, into the weak tea-like liquid, trying not to cause ripples. I move further out and it remains fairly shallow – only up to my chest – and I freeze. I sniff the surface and even though my tail won't stop its wagging, I keep it raised up so it doesn't send vibrations through the water.

'There you are,' I hear Rose say, breathing heavily.

I don't move an inch. My paws are firmly planted in the mud. Only my head, tilted downwards, moves from side to side as I search for a fish.

'You really do love water, don't you?' Rose says.

I have my back to her. I hear her sit on the bank. 'Oh look, policeman's helmet,' she says. 'How ironic.'

I know she's referring to a pink flower. I glance round to check she is okay.

'Are you really fishing?' she asks, frowning in disbelief.

I spot an arched spiny dorsal fin and see the red whoosh of a tail: a European Perch is almost within striking distance. It moves closer, its round eyes scanning from side to side searching for food. Just as I open my jaw and prepare to pounce, I hear my name called and recognise Nigel's nasal tone. I ignore him. The Perch is about to swim between my front legs – perfect. I slam my open jaws into the water and scoop up the wriggling fish, sneezing water. I head for the river bank, head held high, sporting my prize.

'*Lass mich los!*' the Perch demands, slapping me in the eye with his tail. '*Schweinhund!*'

Rose stands up. 'I don't believe it.'

Nor do I. I didn't expect to be abused in German. But I guess he has a point. I *am* about to eat him.

'Excuse me,' says the squirrel, hanging from a weeping willow that dips its branches into the river. 'Monty of Duckdown Cottage?'

I look up, the fish still wriggling in my mouth. I nod once.

'Have to ensure one is speaking to the correct dog of the house. Well now, I'm not one to interfere, and I'm certainly too busy to waste my time, unless I think it important . . .'

I want to say, *Hurry up*, but can't open my mouth. The fish slaps me in the eye again. Ouch!

'. . . but as your Neighbourhood Watch representative I feel it's my duty to inform you . . .'

I reach the muddy bank and drop the fish near Rose's feet.

'Clever boy,' she says.

'Um, actually, before I go on, and I don't mean to be rude, but do you have a fishing permit for this stretch of river?' asks Nigel. 'I'm a stickler for rules, you see. Rules are there to be obeyed and bureaucracy is what makes England, well, England! So, have you? A fishing permit, I mean.'

All I want to do is eat my fish. I can't wait a moment longer. I place my paw on the Perch to stop him squirming away and am about to tuck in.

'Ah, ah, ah! Not if you don't have a permit,' says the

squirrel, dangling just above my head. 'I'll have to report you, otherwise. You're leaving me no choice.'

The Perch pipes up. '*Beeil dich!*'

'I'm trying to get on with it,' I bark at the fish in frustration.

'Monty!' calls Rose. 'Put it out of its misery or I'll throw it back.'

Oh great! I peer up at the irritating squirrel.

'I don't need a permit, you goose. I'm a dog. Dogs don't need permits.'

'Wrong on two counts. Rules apply to dogs too, and I'm not a goose.'

Clearly this guy is a real pedant.

'Look, if you have something important to say, just say it.'

'Of course. And I will. But while I think of it, I'm canvassing for votes. Want to stay on as committee chairman and truth be told, they need me. I sometimes think I'm the only one who takes this job seriously.'

Frankly, I'm not interested. I just want to EAT MY FISH!

'So, Monty old chap, can I rely on your vote?'

'Yes!' I say to shut him up. 'Now, what did you want to tell me?'

I swear I hear the fish sigh.

'Ah, yes. Well, as your Neighbourhood Watch—'

'Nigel, you've mentioned that already.'

'Righty-ho then. I wanted to inform you that at this present moment there is a stranger with a damaged arm wandering around Duckdown Cottage peering in the windows. Seemed suspicious . . .'

I shudder. Fur up, tail up, I growl ferociously. The fish is forgotten. I know exactly who it is.

The squirrel is terrified and darts up to the highest branches. I bark at Rose, wanting her to follow me, and then I race like a Greyhound through the woods.

'Monty, what's the matter? Your fish!' Rose calls after me. I hear a plop and guess she has put it back in the river. Luckiest fish in England, that one. She runs after me. 'Monty! Wait!'

I don't. I can't. I leap over fallen branches and dodge tree trunks. I burst out of the woods and onto the road, narrowly dodging a car driving down the lane towards Geldeford. I don't even look round. I turn the corner and charge up our cracked concrete drive. Ducks scatter, quacking with indignation. I can't see him.

I run down the side of the house and into the back garden, leaping over the decrepit wheelbarrow. I sniff the air and know he is here. I stand on my hind legs and grab the back door handle, and open it. I'm inside in a flash, snarling with fury. I hear footsteps coming from the lounge room and the rasping sound of an old window catching on the frame as it's forced open.

No! I see a figure squeeze out of the narrow lounge window and run away. He's wearing blue jeans, a grey sweatshirt and baseball cap. Without even thinking, I leap through the same window, land badly in the flower bed where some terracotta pots lie at odd angles. I yelp. My wrist is bent back as one paw hits the edge of a pot. I stumble but gather myself and charge after him. He glances round. He has a scarf wrapped around his face and is wearing sunglasses.

Rose is running up the drive and falters when she sees the man tearing towards her with me in hot pursuit. He deliberately slams into her, his shoulder turned to meet her chest and she falls back heavily. She recovers quickly, rolls to one side and scrambles to stand. I race past her. A silver Ford Fiesta is parked just inside the entrance to a private road leading to a farm. The man gets in and drives off towards Farley Green. I watch the car speed down the single track lane and round a blind corner. I pace up and down, howling. I've failed, yet again.

It was the killer: I recognise the smell of dampness and funny cigarettes and the peculiar insect odour which I now know to be malaria. I don't detect the really stinky food (I guess he doesn't eat it every day) but there are some new smells surrounding him. One is faint, as if someone has touched him and left their unique signature behind. It's a chemical mixed with a musky scent used in aftershaves and perfumes. The other is pus. Yes, I know that fishy smell, because Flash, a Terrier I met at the vet's, had an infected leg and the nurses had to keep wiping away the pus. So the killer has an infection – and a bad one. Could it be where I bit his arm?

Rose calls to me and I limp over to her.

'Are you all right?' she pants. 'Did he hurt you?'

I am panting too. I lift my hurt leg. She takes it, looks at it. 'Do we need to see Malcolm? Again. At this rate you're going to need a daily appointment.'

Rose looks towards the lane. 'Who was it?'

I snarl between pants. How else can I tell her Patrick's killer was here?

'Similar build, but surely it can't be,' she mutters.

I pull away from her and hobble into the house.

'Monty, wait. I need to see if he's stolen anything.'

I hear her use her mobile to call the police. When she

catches up with me, I'm in the kitchen. I grab my food bowl, holding it up high. She laughs.

'You want a reward for chasing him away? Of course. In a moment.'

No, that's not it. I drop the bowl and then pick it up again, this time making sure that the words painted around the outside rim of the bowl are clearly visible to her. I whimper. She looks puzzled, and then comes closer.

'You're trying to say something, aren't you?' she says, kneeling.

Have I gone too far this time? Am I breaking commandment six? We're never supposed to show we understand big'un language. But in *The Dog Chronicles* there are numerous stories of my brethren breaking this one. What about Fala, President Franklin D. Roosevelt's black Scottish Terrier? It's well known that Fala went everywhere with FDR. It's also well known FDR was furious when the Republicans made up lies about Fala.

'I am accustomed to hearing malicious falsehoods about myself . . . But I think I have a right to resent, to object, to libellous statements about my dog,' said FDR.

What isn't so well known is that Fala tried to warn his beloved master about the impending attack on Pearl Harbor. The wartime wee-vine was flashing red hot with news from a Japanese sea-faring hound who'd stowed away on a freighter before landing on US soil. He'd overheard his master, a Japanese naval captain, talking about the planned attack. So Fala broke commandment six and picked up a toy plane and placed it on a map of Hawaii, barking repeatedly at his master. FDR kept removing the plane but Fala kept putting it back on Hawaii. Eventually, the President conveyed his fears that

Pearl Harbor was a Japanese target but his generals and admirals dismissed the idea. You know the rest. My point is that in extreme circumstances dogs have revealed more than they should about their abilities. Surely I must warn Rose that Paddy's killer has been in her house?

I give the bowl a shake. It's cumbersome and I drop it with a clank.

She picks it up. '*Paddy's Place*,' she reads aloud. 'What does that mean?'

I run to the open door and look outside, barking ferociously, and then race back to the bowl again and nudge the rim that says *Paddy's Place*.

She sits back on her haunches, her eyes locked on mine. 'Are you trying to tell me the intruder has something to do with Patrick's murder?'

I bark once and sit with my back very straight, as if to attention. That's what I'm trying to say! That man is Paddy's killer!

'My God, if that's true, then what the hell was he doing here?'

My thoughts exactly.

Chapter Thirty-Six

While a policewoman chats to Rose and takes notes, I busy myself checking wee-mails. There's a message from Jake, the three-legged Staffie. He must have stayed in the area after our escape from Dogmo. Good to know he's doing okay. It reads:

'Picked up your wee-mail. Heard rumours of local gang with seven-pointed star tattoos. Will investigate. Your mate, Jake.'

Great news! I thank him and then leave a general wee-mail asking for intel on our intruder's Ford Fiesta, last seen heading through Farley Green. My wrist is feeling better, and I don't want to go to the vet again, so I lie under a tree to rest. I watch a second car arrive, this one unmarked, and out steps the overgroomed pooch-man I don't like, and Rose's boss, the Leach. Rose will need my support, so I limp over to where they're talking.

'So, nothing missing?' asks Leach, wearing a loose grey T-shirt and faded blue jeans that are baggy on the bum. There's dark stubble around his jaw and lip, and I try to imagine what the Leach would look like with a full head of dark hair. He's wearing an old pair of Dr Martens boots, the soles of which are worn on the outer edges. I guess he didn't expect to work today.

'Cupboard doors are flung open and he's emptied a few drawers but as far as I can tell, sir, no. Monty disturbed him, so he probably didn't have much time. And it feels like he was after something specific.'

'No need to call me sir, given the circumstances,' Leach says. 'Now, what makes you think it was Salt's killer?'

I am sitting to heel. I look up, just as she looks down. Our eyes meet. She clears her throat.

'He was of similar build. He ran with the same athletic agility.' She pauses.

'Was he wearing the black clothing and balaclava?'

'No, sir.' Rose describes his new attire. 'But, I don't believe in coincidences. First Salt, then Grace and now me. The only thing we all have in common is Salt's murder. It has to be him, sir.'

When Pearl thinks nobody is looking, he looks Rose up and down and runs his tongue along his lower lip. He clearly likes her sporty outfit. The creep. He's dressed like a clothing catalogue model: hair so excessively gelled that a tornado couldn't budge it, brown leather jacket slung over one shoulder, white shirt open at the neck, skinny jeans and brown loafers with tassels. As he flicks back some hair from his forehead, the metal links in his watch band jangle. As I said, far too groomed. Like a Poodle. Don't get me started on those show-ponies.

Rose flicks a look at me. Is she going to tell them what she really thinks? She shuffles from one foot to the other, then focuses back on the Leach.

'Look, this is going to sound barmy, but this dog – *Patrick's* dog – appeared to recognise the intruder. He gave chase, just as he chased Grace's attacker. I believe the same man who killed Salt and assaulted Grace is, for some reason, now after me. I'm guessing he thinks I can identify him or I have something he wants. Possibly the dog.'

Pearl snorts with derision.

'Rose,' says the Leach. 'I'm sorry to have to tell you Francis Grace died this morning as a result of his injuries. So we've now got a double homicide on our hands.'

'Poor old bloke.'

'We don't have time for sentimentality, Rose. We need to find Yelong Li, and quickly, before he hurts anyone else.'

Pearl frowns. 'What would he want with you? And please, don't say the bloody dog. Is there something you haven't told us?'

'Well, as I said, this is going to sound weird . . .' Rose begins.

Pearl raises a blond brow as if to say, That's no surprise. You *are* weird.

I feel the urge to pee on his designer jeans but I resist the temptation. It'll just get Rose into trouble.

'Monty gave chase until the intruder got into a silver Ford Fiesta and drove off.'

'Yes, we know that,' grumbles Pearl.

'Then Monty ran to the kitchen and picked up his food bowl.'

Both men's mouths have curled very slightly at the edge. They clearly think she's losing it. I bark once and wag my tail in support. She continues, her voice growing more hesitant. 'On the outside rim of the bowl it says *Paddy's Place*.

Monty kept insisting I look at the words. I think . . . I think he was trying to tell me that he'd just chased away Salt's killer.'

Pearl guffaws, head back. If only some bird would shit in his mouth.

Leach shakes his head. 'He's a dog, Rose. They don't read. In fact they don't really think. They just obey commands.'

'But sir . . .'

'He probably wanted feeding, that's all.'

Rose persists. 'But he knew Larry Nice wasn't the killer and . . . and he showed me Larry was innocent by licking his hand. And now I believe he's trying to t . . . tell me that Salt's killer was in my home.'

I can hear the desperation in her voice. It's getting high-pitched and strangled. She looks like she's about to cry.

That's it! I've had enough of these buffoons. I'll show them!

I run into the kitchen, trying hard to mask my limp. I pick up my bowl so that *Paddy's Place* is clearly visible and then, once outside again, I sit and hold it up for the Leach.

He leans down, hesitates, and then holds the other side of my bowl. I release it into his hands. 'Okay, he's a bright dog, but he can't possibly know what's written on the rim.'

'Stupid mutt,' mumbles Pearl.

My leg quivers, desperate to soak his trousers in a stupid mutt's urine.

'Let's test him,' says Leach. 'Rose, bring some food out here and I'll prove that's what this is all about.'

'Sir, put food in front of any dog and he'll wolf it down immediately. It's not a fair test.'

'I'm losing patience, Rose,' frowns Leach.

She tells me to stay, so I remain still, but I can already feel my mouth filling with saliva at the thought of a meal. This is going to be torture. I know that to prove Rose is right, I mustn't touch the food. But food is my Achilles Heel. It's the reason I failed as a guide dog. Will it be my downfall again? I wish I had joined a local DWFA group (Dogs With a Food Addiction). But it's too late for that.

By the time Rose returns with an open tin of meaty goodness I am dropping slobber on her boss's boots.

'No chance,' scoffs Pearl. 'He's drooling. God, that's disgusting.'

Rose takes the bowl from Leach and forks the chicken and vegetable mix into it. I hear the squelch of the gloopy gravy. Divine! Ahh, that cooked bird smell! Rose swallows as she places the bowl in front of me.

'Stay!' she commands.

Normally, an army wouldn't have been able to stop me eating it. But I have to prove Rose right. Her happiness depends on it. Straight backed and chin up, I repeat to myself, *I must not eat the food. I must not eat the food.*

Drool is cascading from my mouth and my head is dropping. Those heady aromas are mesmerising, hypnotic, intoxicating.

'There he goes,' mocks Pearl.

I jerk my head up, furious with myself. Only ten seconds have passed but it feels like a lifetime.

'Okay, this isn't what I expected,' says Leach.

I snort deeply, unable to stop my nose sucking in the delicious jellied meat smells. I shouldn't have done it, because now that smell is bouncing around inside my olfactory chamber, amplifying the aroma, making it even harder for me to resist. My stomach rumbles. I can't hold out much longer, just as I couldn't stop myself on my very first guide dog assignment from following a man with a Big Mac. The problem was that the blind lady I was leading wanted to go in the opposite direction and I left her stranded in the middle of a zebra crossing. Understandably, I was relieved of my duties. The lady was rescued by a passer-by, but I live every day with the shame.

This is my chance to redeem myself. I can resist food. I can!

No, no I can't.

I have to prove Rose is right.

No, I can't just sit here.

I stand suddenly, pick up my bowl, tip the contents onto the ground and then hold the bowl up to Leach, pushing it into his groin. At least the bowl tastes good: my tongue is secretly enjoying the gravy and jelly residue on the rim.

'Well, I'll be!' says Leach. 'I never thought I'd see the day.'

Rose doesn't hesitate. She knows my resolve won't last. She takes the bowl from my mouth and points to the words *Paddy's Place*.

'Monty can identify Paddy's killer. That's what he's trying to tell you. When we find Yelong, I should bring him into the station.'

'You can't be serious!' Pearl says.

Leach holds up his hand to shut Pearl up.

'I don't know about that, but if Salt's killer is stalking you, then I want you staying with friends or family for the next few days. I can't have you out here alone. He's killed twice and could come back.'

'Sir, I'll be fine here. I have Monty to protect me.'

She glances down at me. My job done, I've discarded the bowl and am devouring my reward.

Leach jerks his chin at the house. 'You don't even have window locks. No Rose, it's too much of a risk.'

'I'm not leaving.'

Leach sighs loudly. 'Okay, okay. I'll send a squad car around to keep an eye on things.'

'Thank you, sir.'

'You're mates with PC Salisbury, right?' Before she can answer, he continues. 'I'm sure he won't mind keeping you company tonight. Good to have a second person in the house.'

Rose goes red-faced. 'I don't need a babysitter, sir. Please don't bother him, he's got a young family.'

'It's not up for debate.'

Chapter Thirty-Seven

Joe Salisbury is assigned babysitting duties. I like Joe. He always gives me a good scratch under my ears whenever we meet. The bad news is that he is likely to be a light sleeper, used to waking at the slightest sound from his six-month-old son. This could be a problem.

As SOCOs dust the house for fingerprints and take photos, I sneak out and leave wee-mails warning my investigative partners not to show themselves tonight. I also ask our doggie neighbours to sound the alarm if they notice a man near Duckdown Cottage with the distinctive smell of burnt sage (that's what funny cigarettes smell like to me), malaria, pus, and possibly a stinky tofu smell like rotten eggs. As scents go, that's a pretty noxious pong and, in the dog world, as good as a perfect fingerprint.

Leach and the pampered pooch have gone. At last, the SOCO team leaves too. The study is off limits because that's where the intruder left a mess. There's crime scene tape across the door.

Rose makes a tuna pasta bake with cheese on top. I've

never seen a live tuna but I'm told they're huge. Somehow they get squeezed into small circular tins. A smattering of pink flesh falls to the floor and I lick it up quick smart. Delicious! I sit in front of the oven and watch the grated cheese bubble away as it cooks, wondering why big'uns watch TV when this is so much more interesting. Rose is flushed in the face and keeps checking her watch. She puffs up the sofa cushions (never seen her do that before), wipes the kitchen table obsessively (never seen her do that, either), goes upstairs and reappears in different clothes. And I've never seen her in a dress. What is going on? It's a wrap-around one and she fiddles with the ties around her waist. She opens a fresh bottle of white wine and drinks half of it 'to calm her nerves'.

Why is she nervous of Joe?

Joe arrives in Nike trackie pants and sweatshirt, ready for a long night, and refuses the wine Rose offers. He asks for coffee instead.

'I'm so sorry, Joe. I told the boss I didn't need protection. This was his idea. Not mine.'

'I know, and it's fine. Sarah sends her love, by the way.'

'Please send mine back. And how is baby Daniel?'

Rose serves the pasta bake with a green salad. Joe tucks into it with great gusto. Rose barely touches hers. He talks happily about his son and shows her photos on his smart-phone. She coos and smiles but I know she's stressed. Something is wrong, but I don't know what it is. They leave the dishes in the sink and move to the sitting room.

'So what about you?' asks Joe. 'Do you want children?'

Rose turns beetroot. She puts her feet up on the sofa, creating a space between them. 'Need to find a man first.'

'So is there anyone special?'

She laughs. 'Come on, Joe, I'm wedded to the job. You know that.'

'But life's about more than that.'

'You know me. I'm the shy girl who goes to parties and gets all tongue-tied when nice blokes talk to me. I spend the rest of the night sitting in a corner until some drunken idiot knocks into me and asks if I want a shag. At which point I leave. Alone.'

Joe is dipping a biscuit into his mug of coffee. A chunk breaks off and floats on the surface. I lick my lips.

'You deserve to meet someone nice.'

'How about Larry?' she says, laughing. 'He asked me out for a drink the other day. He's the best offer I've had in years.'

I tilt my head, confused. Surely she doesn't mean that? Chicken-whippet man?

Joe laughs too. 'I think you can do way better than him.' He sips his coffee. 'Rose, I hope you don't mind me saying this but you look great in dresses, so why don't you wear them more often?'

'At work, you mean?'

'Nah, you know what I mean. You've got a great figure but you hide it all the time.'

Her mobile rings and she dives at it like Betty pouncing on a food scrap. From the colour of her face I suspect she's relieved to be able to change the subject. It's Malcolm, the vet: I'd know his voice anywhere. My hackles go up. He's a nice man but I don't want to go back to that place.

'Hi. Hope you don't mind me calling,' Malcolm says, 'but I wanted to check in on Monty. How's he doing?'

Perhaps I've misjudged him. What a nice thing to do! I

must remember to give his hand a lick next time I see him.

Rose moves the phone from one hand to the other, shaking away the tingles. Now I am really confused. She does that when people are lying. Why else would Malcolm call?

'He's doing well, thanks, considering what he's been through. I guess you heard he chased an intruder away today and hurt his wrist a bit, but it seems to be fine now.'

'Yeah, Joe told me all about it,' says Malcolm. 'He's a brave dog. You're lucky to have him around.'

I lift my head high. What a great day! Everyone likes me!

Rose frowns at Joe and gives him a questioning stare. Joe doesn't look up from his mug and suddenly seems fascinated by the biscuit bits floating there.

'I didn't realise you knew Joe,' Rose says to Malcolm, then gives Joes a little kick in the hip.

Joe looks up, shrugs, and makes a 'What?' gesture.

'Yes,' says Malcolm, 'we were at school together.'

Silence. Awkward.

I'm listening to Malcolm but I find myself watching Joe's body language. Joe looks like a dog who stole the Sunday roast and has been caught in the act.

'Well, thanks for checking in on Monty,' Rose says. 'If he limps tomorrow, I'll make an appointment.'

'No need for an appointment. Just give me a call and I'll fit you in . . . I mean him in.' There's another awkward pause. 'And how are you? It must have been terrifying.'

'I'm fine, thanks, it's just creepy knowing a stranger has been through my things. It's good having Monty and Joe here.'

'Well, let me know if you need anything. Anything at all.'

'Um, thank you.' Another pause. 'Er, goodnight then.'

She ends the call and shakes her head.

'What did you say?' she asks Joe.

He's now looking one hundred per cent guilty hound: head down, eyes down. If he had a tail, it would be tucked between his legs. No response. I almost detect a whimper.

Rose picks up a cushion and starts to hit him with it playfully.

'You're trying to match-make, aren't you? Come on, confess!'

The six-foot-three giant pretends to cower in one corner of the sofa. I want to join in the game so I get up and bark, trying to grab the moving cushion with my teeth.

'Not so much match-make as just open lines of dialogue.'

'Lines of what? You cheeky git. Did you tell him I was single?'

'Well, he asked. I wasn't going to lie.' He is still receiving blows from the cushion. 'And you once told me you'd thought of becoming a vet, so you've got something in common.'

Rose drops the cushion and looks suddenly serious. Her blue eyes are no longer smiling. 'Please don't, Joe. I just can't do this. I always muck it up. Please, don't encourage Malcolm.'

'Okay, okay. I won't,' he replies, his hands raised in surrender. 'But he likes you, regardless.'

Neither of them has noticed that I am having great fun unpicking the cushion stitching with my teeth. I pull off a tassel, spit it out and get my teeth around another one.

'Oh Monty, stop that,' Rose calls.

I look up, a red tassel dangling from my mouth. But this is the game, isn't it? Kill the cushion? And I'm doing a great job of it too.

'Leave it,' she says and gently takes the cushion away from me. 'Well, I'm off to bed. I'll let Monty out.'

I do a pee in the garden and then settle on my doggie duvet. I'm relieved to see her laptop is still on the kitchen table. The killer didn't take it. So what did he come here for?

'There's a spare room. Comfy bed,' says Rose to Joe, who's almost finished the washing up.

I hope she removed those spooky dolls with their big glassy eyes.

'No, I'll use the sofa. Best I'm downstairs in case he comes back.'

'Are you sure?' He nods. 'Okay, I'll get some bedding.'

I hear creaking floorboards as she goes upstairs to collect a duvet, sheet and pillows, then brings them back down. I hover at the sitting-room door.

'And help yourself to anything you want during the night – coffee, biscuits, you know. Well, goodnight, Joe.'

She hesitates and then hurries upstairs.

Joe sits on the sofa and turns on the TV. I lie at his feet and we watch a DVD about big'uns with long canines who bite necks. Seems Rose has a whole collection of vampire movies. I bare my teeth at the screen but Joe reassures me they aren't real.

Chapter Thirty-Eight

There is a black ribbon tied to my collar. Rose wears a black suit she keeps in a plastic cover for special occasions. Her skirt is already coated in my fur which means it looks more badger grey, but she doesn't seem to mind. She leaves me in the car with the windows partially open. Cold air creeps inside.

We are early. It's a crisp morning. The sun is watery in a dreary sky. Droplets of condensation run down the inside of the window. My hot breath forms a minuscule cloud around my muzzle as I pant and fidget. Rose has dropped her car keys twice and, as we drove here, she fiddled with her ponytail constantly. She's as agitated as I am. Through the smudged glass I can just make out an old church with thick rough-hewn beige stone walls and arched stained-glass windows. There's a square bell tower with a pointy spire and a cross at the very top. A gravel path leads uphill to a stone entrance with its own little roof and archway. Gravestones, thick with moss or eroded with age, stick up through the grass, leaning at odd angles as if bent by the burden of centuries passing.

Some are newer and cleaner. I recognise a white marble cross at one corner of the graveyard. Paddy came here regularly to leave flowers for his dead wife, Emily. He talked to the cross with her name on it as if she were standing in front of him. I never understood what he was doing but I knew he was sad. So I'd sit next to him as he knelt by her grave and eventually I would snooze, the low rumble of his voice somehow soothing.

Rose has been inside the church. Now, she opens the car door, clips on my lead and walks me up the path towards the stone archway framing oak double doors with ornate black hinges that remind me of swallows flying in opposite directions. Both doors hang open. She has told me that today is Paddy's funeral, but I am not sure what that means exactly. I overtake her, desperate to see Paddy again. But once we reach the entrance, I stop. I am afraid.

'It's okay, Monty. Let's go inside.'

My nerves have got the better of me and I need to pee, so I cock my leg on an eroded stone pillar.

Rose peers into the church to check the vicar hasn't seen, then strokes my head. We take three steps forward and hover just inside. The walls are pale and bare and the wooden pews look hard and severe. The temperature suddenly drops and I sense that many dead people have been through here. I pull back on the lead.

'No need to be afraid. You want to see Paddy, don't you? He's over there.'

She looks down the aisle towards an odd-shaped, polished wooden box with a lid that is open at one end. It is raised up on a stand and has glistening brass handles. Standing next to this box is the vicar in his black and white robes and curly red hair who looks at me warily. I have met him before, on Paddy's visits to Emily's grave. He would watch us from a distance, as if waiting for the right moment to ask Paddy not to bring me here, but he never plucked up the courage.

'The vicar's given special permission for you to see Patrick before the funeral starts,' Rose says to me in hushed tones. 'He's in the coffin, Monty.' She points at the long box. 'You have to promise me you'll behave and not wreck anything. Promise?'

I stop pulling and wait. She holds me on a tight leash as we walk down the aisle. Apart from the vicar, there is nobody else around. White lilies in vases adorn the nave, their sweet perfume overpowered by a combination of damp earth, brass cleaner and some kind of chemical that gets stronger the nearer we are to the coffin. But I can't smell Paddy. Or can I?

Yes, yes, I can. I wag my tail so fast it becomes a blur, and sniff the long box.

'Can he look into the coffin, vicar?' Rose asks.

'This is very unusual, Detective Sidebottom. I mean, I haven't asked Rebecca about this. She wanted the coffin open so mourners could pay their respects before it's sealed, but I don't think she meant the dog. I really think it's best if he doesn't.'

No way! If Paddy is in there, I'm going to see him. I stand on my hind legs, so my front paws rest on the edge of the box.

'Oh my goodness!' says the vicar, taking a step back.

I can see into the coffin and there is Paddy. He's asleep. His white hair is neatly combed, as is his grey beard. I'm surprised his hair doesn't stick up at odd angles as it always does when Paddy's had a nap. He's wearing his best suit, the one he kept for conferences. I wag my tail and bark, and lean closer so I can lick his face. I'm so happy to see him. But I pull back, shocked. Something is wrong. His skin smells strange. What is that pungent chemical smell? Why does Paddy smell like this? I snuffle his shirt and realise that only his clothes carry his true scent. I bark. Wake up, Paddy! Please. Tell me what they've done to you.

'No, no, he can't do that,' says the vicar. 'Please, get him down immediately.'

'Get down, Monty. There's a good boy.'

I look at her, desperate for answers and whimper. I don't want to leave my beloved master. I push my nose into Paddy's suit pocket. The folded handkerchief smells as I want to remember him: of musty books and red wine, of fishing gear and flower beds, with a faint hint of liver treats. I imagine I hear his voice as we huddle under an umbrella in the rain, Paddy clutching his fishing rod, waiting for a fish to bite.

'It'll be a whopper today, just you wait. Today's the day,' he'd say, giving me a nudge. It never was a whopper, but that didn't dent his enthusiasm. Or mine.

Rose takes me in a tight hug and lifts my front paws off the coffin edge and onto the cold floor. I struggle and whine but she holds me firmly. I'm trying to tell her that I want to stay close to Paddy. I want to guard him. But she doesn't understand.

'Please, you really must take the dog outside.'

I howl, head tilted back, nose pointing at the cavernous rafters, my voice amplified so the sound of my grief reaches beyond the high ceiling, escaping though the bell tower and open doors, beyond the graveyard and the narrow country lanes, the village green, the primary school and the little shop. I hear another howl joining mine, then another and another, until it sounds as if a pack of wolves has returned to Britain. They cry out in sympathy. Only they fully appreciate the special bond between dog and master.

As a result, I am banished from the church and spend the whole service tied up outside.

The sun is higher now but its warmth on my back does little to break the chill in my heart. I hang my head and tuck my tail between my legs. The mourners have left the church and they, like me, stare into a deep rectangular hole in the ground – far deeper than I could ever dig. Paddy's coffin is sealed and suspended above it. I don't want Paddy to go down there because I'll never be able to dig him out. I strain against my lead, and bark, but Rose keeps a firm hold with one hand and pats my head with the other.

'Quiet, Monty,' she whispers, 'or we'll have to leave.'

The vicar drones on, his voice an interminable, depressing monotone. I hear a big'un sniff. Across the grave, almost opposite me, stands Maria Martinez. Behind her 1950s-style sunglasses, tears drip down her cheeks and onto her tight black dress. She dabs them with a white handkerchief she's borrowed from Deakin Bomphrey, who stands next to her, shuffling uncomfortably, and near him, several people I vaguely recognise from the university. Not far from Martinez, Rebecca's golden head of perfectly styled hair is easily six inches above everyone else. She, too, wears sunglasses but her face is set as hard as concrete. I could almost believe this is a bad dream, and I'll wake up to find I have been muzzle-twitching in my sleep. But Rose's soft warm hand on my head tells me this is horribly real.

Earlier, through the closed church door, I heard Rebecca's voice boom out a eulogy for her father. She talked about his many achievements but said little about him as a man. There was no tremble in her voice or stumbling over words. I wish she had said something about Paddy's kindness and compassion, his patience and his sense of humour. I know how much he missed Rebecca and how he looked forward to phoning her, but she was always too busy to talk for long. Most of all, I wish I could tell Paddy, and everyone here, how much I loved him.

The coffin is being lowered into the grave. I lunge forward. I don't want us to be apart. It takes all of Rose's strength to hang on to me and people stare at us, tutting and frowning. I paw the ground. The coffin has reached the bottom and the straps are removed. Rebecca steps forward and throws some soil onto the coffin lid. She doesn't pause, just turns her back and steps away. The man I recognise as her husband does the same. Nobody else steps forward. I can't bear it. My heart thumps in my chest and my front paws claw desperately at the air as Rose struggles to hold me back. I leap forward with such force, she releases the lead. There are gasps as I stop at the grave's edge and bark my goodbye. I lower my nose, sniff the rich earth, inhaling the memory of this moment. Then I nudge some loose soil into the rectangular hole. It lands with a thud on the polished wooden box. I peer down at it. Everyone is suddenly silent. I lie next to the grave with my nose between my paws.

Goodbye, master.

Chapter Thirty-Nine

The crowd of mourners breaks up. Some dawdle in polite conversation. The vicar consoles Rebecca, who cuts him short and walks off. Others head for the car park with a lightness in their step, relieved such a sombre occasion is over and they can get on with their lives. I stumble blindly between them, head bowed, my lead trailing behind me. I walk like an old dog. I feel like an old dog. Rose keeps an eye on me but leaves me to it. She knows I'm heart-broken.

Dante screeches and I look up, past kneecaps and trouser legs, jackets, coats and talking heads, to the branches of an elm. Dante's black neck is craned forward and down, his beak pointing to a gangly man in a pinstripe suit who is joining the funeral too late. He has a phone to his ear and ends his call as he races towards Rebecca, who has been cornered by Bomphrey and a sobbing Martinez. The arrival's bushy grey eyebrows almost conceal his dark eyes and serve to accentuate his hooked nose. He reminds me of a buzzard I once saw catch a rabbit. I sniff the air in his direction but there must be twenty people between us, which makes it impossible to home in on his scent.

I bark at Dante. 'Is he GN1US?'

'Yes, he just drove up,' he screams.

Rose hears my bark. She's been watching the Rebecca-Bomphrey-Martinez trio. She looks to where my nose is pointing. She gasps and runs towards me, but she is on the other side of Paddy's grave. Hackles up, a low and rumbling growl emanates from deep within me. How dare he come here, a man who threatened my beloved Paddy and may even have organised his murder? I stalk my prey, zig-zagging between the legs of stragglers chatting, my eyes glued on Mr Genius. Someone grabs my collar.

'Don't make a scene, Monty. Fratting is already a suspect,' Rose says into my ear.

I whip my head round, confused. Fratting? I follow her line of vision. When Mr Genius entered the churchyard he almost rubbed shoulders with Rebecca's husband, who is leaning against the perimeter wall, scrolling through his phone messages, very much alone. He and his wife have clearly had a falling out. It suddenly dawns on me that Rose thinks I'm growling at Fratting. I pant in agitation. How can I explain that the new arrival had motive to murder Paddy? I'm sorry for what I'm about to do but I have no choice. I lurch forward with all my strength, almost yanking Rose's arm out of its socket. My collar slips from her hand. I race towards Fratting. I'm almost upon him. He smells of salt and stuffy restaurants and beer. He is not the killer. I collide with his legs and he drops his phone. He stares down at me, eyes wide in panic. I lick his hand and wag my tail. Rose has caught up with me. She takes it all in.

Now for the owner of GN1US.

'Monty!' screeches Dante. 'Move your furry arse! GN1US is walking to his car.'

I spy my target standing next to the red Bentley parked in the church's tiny car park. It's blocking the exit so the others can't leave until he does. His driver's door is open. I charge. Ears back, fur bristling, teeth bared. Rose runs after me. I leap at Mr Genius, who sees me coming from the corner of his eye. He raises his arms to protect himself. I hit him side on and he bends like a willow, landing with a thump on the asphalt. I stand on his chest and growl into his face. I'm not going to bite him. I just want Rose and everyone to know that he should be a suspect.

Somebody strong grabs my collar and I am almost lifted from the prostrate man. I snap my head round and find that the Leach has me. He must have been keeping a low profile because this is the first time I've seen him.

'Keep it away from me!' my quarry screams like a baby, backing away on all fours.

Bomphrey runs over and helps GN1US stand. 'Mr Flay, are you all right?'

'Of course I'm not all right,' Flay snaps, yanking his arm away from Bomphrey. He glares at the Leach, pointing a bony finger at him. 'You stood by and let that maniac dog attack me. I'll have your badge for this!'

All my fight has evaporated. I am bewildered. GN1US smells of sandalwood, golf balls and new leather. He doesn't have a hint of the killer on him. What have I done?

Leach hands me to Rose, who drags me away. I don't resist.

'No harm done, Mr Flay,' says Leach.

Flay stares down at the front of his bespoke blue and white striped shirt that's now decorated with my paw prints.

'That dog's insane. Get him put down, or I will,' he yells.

Rose speaks up. 'I'm sorry about this, Mr Flay. But we have just buried his master. He's understandably upset.'

'Oh for Christ's sake!' says Flay.

He storms off and gets into his red Bentley, then screams like a little girl discovering a big, hairy spider in her lunch box, and jumps out.

'Rat! It's a bloody rat!'

I catch a glimpse of Betty vaulting from the car's footwell onto the asphalt. Flay tries to stamp on her. Dante squawks and dives at Flay, his sharp beak aimed at the man's head. Flay ducks. Dante swoops past him and homes in on Betty. She darts between people's legs. It happens so fast, I don't think they notice she has a plastic security pass in her mouth. Dante grabs the pass from the terrified Betty and shoots up into the sky. To my relief, Betty disappears into the tall grass at the base of the church wall.

Leach looks at Rose. 'What the hell was that all about?'

Rose looks down at me. I do my best innocent-dog face.

Chapter Forty

'You can't be serious!' says Pearl, his tanned face turning blood orange with fury. 'The dog's nuts.'

It's Monday afternoon and I'm held on such a tight leash, I feel like my head is strapped to Rose's thigh. But I don't resist. I know why she has risked her career to bring me to the police station where an identity parade has been organised. Amongst the men on the other side of the one-way glass is Yelong Li. He was picked up in Birmingham on Sunday and, because he's wanted in a double murder investigation, escorted to Geldeford nick.

'Monty is most definitely not nuts.' Rose sighs and looks at Leach. 'We've been through this already, sir. You saw it yourself at the funeral. Monty went out of his way to be nice to Fratting. Clearly Fratting doesn't smell like the killer. Then Monty knocks Flay to the ground. He's the first person Monty's attacked since defending Salt. There has to be a connection between Flay and Salt's death.'

'What a load of bollocks,' says Pearl. 'At least Yelong Li has motive and so does Fratting. Why the hell would Flay murder his star scientist?'

Leach nods. 'I know what it looks like, Rose, but you're assuming the dog knows what he's doing. I think you're assuming an awful lot.'

'So why are we wasting our time putting the dog in with Yelong, if you're convinced Flay did it? Hm?' Pearl looks down at Rose, one blond brow raised.

'Oh come on, guv,' Rose snaps at Pearl. 'Flay wouldn't do his own dirty work, would he? He'd pay somebody else. Especially someone with a grievance, like Yelong.'

'Let's just get on with it,' says Leach.

Rose and I wait until Yelong's lawyer, Mr Penn, joins Pearl and Leach in the observation room, and then we go in. The Legal Aid lawyer looks no older than a school boy with acne, proudly wearing his first, ill-fitting suit.

'So, Mr Penn,' says Leach. 'Detective Constable Sidebottom will firstly view the line-up from here to see if she can identify the man she saw standing over Francis Grace's mortally wounded body in his home on Saturday the seventh of September. Then, she'll take Patrick Salt's dog into the room so he can . . .' Leach clears his throat in embarrassment '. . . sniff the line-up.'

'The dog mustn't be used to intimidate my client. He mustn't touch Mr Yelong.'

Leach nods.

Rose and I stand close to the one-way glass as she scrutinises the nine men on the other side. None are wearing glasses, including Yelong Li who has been asked to remove his. All are dark haired, some clearly hail from East Asia.

They're in T-shirts or short-sleeved shirts. Yelong is number three.

'Number two is too tall and four and seven have the wrong physique.' She glances at Leach. 'Can you ask them all to turn to their left, sir?'

A voice through the intercom system tells the men to turn to their left. Rose peers at the right side of their faces, spending extra time looking at Yelong. From this angle, his red birthmark is hidden.

'I need to go in there, sir.'

I'm also looking through the glass, but I'm searching for tattoos as well as bites. Rose doesn't know about the seven-pointed star tattoo. I zero in on Yelong. Number three. He doesn't have any tattoos that I can see, or bite marks either. We are wasting our time on the wrong suspect.

'Are you sure about this, Sidebottom?' asks Leach.

'Sir, I have to do this.'

'Go on then. But muzzle the dog.'

Oh no. I hate muzzles. Not only do I feel like I'm going to suffocate, I also can't defend myself from attack. But I have to show them Yelong didn't do it. So I wait, patiently, as Rose slides the muzzle over my snout and clips it behind my head. It takes all my will-power not to try and shake it off.

'Remember. Keep the dog away from my client,' the lawyer reiterates.

Pearl sulks in a corner.

Before they change their minds, Rose and I leave the observation room. The men turn their heads when we enter. Their eyes grow wide. A couple step back, including Yelong. I smell perspiration. They see a large muzzled dog and auto-matically assume I'm aggressive.

One man complains, 'Nobody said nothing about a dog. What's he doing here?'

Rose ignores him. Leach booms through the intercom, 'Stay in line. The dog won't hurt you.'

She and I walk past each man slowly. As Rose looks for bite marks, I sniff them. None are right. One man has a bandaged arm and Rose asks him to remove the dressing. He complies. It's a new tattoo but nothing like the seven-pointed star. We get to Yelong and I feel Rose's grip on my lead tighten.

Without his glasses, his birthmark – shaped like a squashed strawberry across his left eye – is pronounced. His fear smells of vinegar and yeast, but otherwise I detect nothing more than washing powder and those really sweet energy drinks. He may have overstayed his visa, but that's all he's done as far as I'm concerned. I am about to lick his hand, but worry this might be misinterpreted. And the lawyer might complain. I decide it's best to show no interest whatsoever in Yelong. So I look away and wait for Rose to move on to the next man. I feel her relax.

When we have inspected each man and seen no bite marks, we leave the room and rejoin Leach, Pearl and Penn.

'Well?' says Leach. 'Can you identify the man you saw standing over Francis Grace in his home on Saturday the seventh of September from this line-up?'

'No, I cannot.'

Pearl leaves in a huff and slams the door.

'Right, so if he's no longer a suspect in a murder case then we're just talking about visa violations,' says the lawyer.

'Not so fast. We still have questions,' says Leach. He turns to Rose. 'Take the dog home and get back here as quick as you can.'

Rose removes my muzzle and I have a big, jaw-stretching yawn. Love that freedom!

Driving home, Rose keeps looking at me in the rear-view mirror.

'If it isn't Yelong, then he's still out there,' she says. 'What if he comes back to the house and hurts you?'

I wag my tail. I want the killer to find me. Let me at him!

'I could ask Malcolm a favour. He might have you for the rest of the day.'

I stand and bark a big *No!* I'd rather take my chances.

'Okay, okay. I get you don't like going to the vet.'

Rose uses her hands-free set to call Ed, the handyman. She asks if he can spend the afternoon at her place. She'll pay. She explains the situation. All Ed has to do is sit inside with the doors locked and watch TV. Ed says he's working, but Finn can do it for a bit of pocket money.

'Does he ever go to school?' she asks.

'Hasn't been well,' Ed replies. 'Nothing contagious, mind.'

Rose hesitates. She's unsure about Finn, but she agrees.

By the time we get to Duckdown Cottage, Finn is lying on the front lawn staring up at the clouds racing by. It's blowing a gale. As the clouds temporarily obscure the sun, Finn flickers from light to shadow and back to light again. He sits up lazily and watches us get out of the car. I race over to him, tail wagging. He doesn't smile but takes me in his arms and we have a bit of a rumble. I am as surprised as Rose.

'Finn, you heard my house was broken into on Sunday?'

We stop our play and he looks up at her. He nods once, merely a dip of his chin.

She glances at his hands resting on my back. The grazed knuckles are healing but scabby and bruised.

'What happened to your hands?'

Finn shrugs. She sighs. This is going to remain a one-sided conversation.

'Can you stay here till I get home around six? If you see anything suspicious, don't open the door. Just call the police. Are you okay with that?'

He just stares at her unblinking. It's as if she hasn't spoken.

Rose sighs. 'I'm sorry, Finn. I don't think this is going to work.'

I do. I lick his face and he laughs. Another first. He grabs me around the middle. I jump on him and he lies back in the grass.

'Why don't you talk?' she asks, and then blushes. 'I'm sorry. How embarrassing. Of course you can't tell me.'

Finn has jumped up and is running around the garden. I give chase.

'Finn! Wait a sec!'

He stops and I pounce on him, wagging my tail.

'If there's an emergency, how can you call for help?' Rose asks.

He walks over and shows her his phone. He clicks to messaging and taps in 999, but doesn't press Send. Rose nods. He can text 999 for help.

'Phone my mobile now, will you, so I've got your number.'

She gives Finn her mobile number. He hesitates, then does as she asks and her phone rings.

'Come into the house,' she says, and we both follow her into the kitchen. 'Help yourself to food.'

In the sitting room she hands him the TV remote control.

'Please bolt the door when I leave and keep the windows shut.'

He switches on the telly and is immediately in a world of his own.

Rose hesitates, looks at her watch and then races out of the back door. I hear her mobile ring as she walks away.

'His jacket?' she says. 'I'm on my way.'

Chapter Forty-One

Rose drove as fast as she could, but had to slow to a crawl for the many blind corners on the meandering single-track lane that ended at Sandyheath Common. She pulled into the car park of a thatched pub called The Three Weeds where an incident response vehicle and an unmarked white Ford Focus were parked alongside a muddy, blue Land Rover Defender. She guessed the latter belonged to the publican.

Rose had always loved the tranquillity of the heath with its sandy scrub, vibrant bursts of purple heather and dark clumps of majestic pine trees. She would listen to the wind whistle through the branches and hear the skylarks sing, inhaling the cleansing scent of pine. During the week, only dog-walkers and horse-riders tended to wander across its two square miles. But now all she could hear was the loud rumble of the fire engine and shouting, and smell the acrid stink of smoke.

She found the partially burned silver Ford Fiesta in a natural dip, surrounded by trees, now scorched, the branches blackened.

The fire was out and SOCO was swarming around it like ants at a picnic. Varma saw her approach and waved. His neatly pressed, olive corduroy trousers were tucked into green Hunter wellington boots and he wore an olive Barbour jacket. Rose was still in her smart black suit. But her wellington boots were el-cheapos she'd bought on eBay. She'd ordered standard grey, but received post-box red. She felt like Paddington Bear.

'Saw you coming a mile off,' joked Varma, looking at her boots.

'Going shooting with the gentry, are we?' she teased back.

Only the blue crime-scene booties, pulled over the soles of his wellingtons, spoilt the look.

'Touché. So how was the funeral? I hear Monty went for Flay.'

'Yes, sarge,' said Rose, pulling booties over her wellies. 'It makes me think he's had something to do with all this.' Rose looked around the scene. 'The fire didn't really get started, did it?'

The front of the car was charred and buckled, the front seats melted, but flames hadn't reached the rear. 'Was it reported missing?'

'Yes, this morning by a Mrs Granger,' said Varma. 'Said she got back from a business trip to find it gone. The publican from The Three Weeds saw smoke at three-oh-nine this afternoon. She managed to put the fire out quickly. She's over there.'

Varma pointed to a heavy-set woman in a navy blue quilted jacket talking to Pearl. There was a red fire extinguisher on the ground next to her.

'You've found the jacket?' she asked.

'Come with me.'

Rose followed Varma to a trestle table. On it, a number of items had already been neatly bagged and labelled.

'Look at this,' Varma said, handing her one of the bags. 'Found in the boot.'

Rose peered through the clear plastic at a torn and stained black cotton jacket.

'Should get the DNA back in a few hours,' said Pearl, making her jump. She hadn't seen him approach. 'One of the birds in the lab is doing me a favour.' He tapped his nose and winked.

'Dave, you might want to see this,' called Jemma, the crime scene manager, dressed head to toe in white cover-alls, holding up a glasses case in her latex-gloved hands.

They joined her.

'Where did you find it?' Pearl asked.

'Under the driver's seat. Blackened, but Polo Ralph Lauren. Nice brand.'

Jemma opened the case. Inside was a pair of bifocals with tortoiseshell arms. She held them up to the light. There was an almost perfect fingerprint on one of the lenses.

'Good work, Jemma,' said Pearl. 'I want to know whose fingerprint a.s.a.p.'

'I can hazard a guess,' she replied, with a cheeky grin. She removed a lint cloth from the case, revealing a business card belonging to the managing director of Flay Bioscience, Chadstone Flay.

'Well, I'll be buggered!' said Pearl, glancing at Rose. 'Looks like Flay has some explaining to do.'

Day-time TV sucks. Really. Soaps, advertorials and talk-shows. Why do big'uns like to watch other big'uns being nasty to each other? I just don't get it. Finn has left the TV on with the volume up high, but he's playing a game on his smartphone which is making loud pinging noises. I have offered him Duckie several times in an effort to get him to play with me again, but he is transfixed by the game. With nothing to do, I dwell on Paddy's funeral and feel down-in-the-dumps. I don't like to think of him down there in the dark and all alone. I head out to the kitchen to sniff my bed. Ah, yes, that's better. I deeply inhale Paddy's scent and wallow in fond memories for a while until I need a pee. The back door is shut and I know I shouldn't open it, so I'll have to ask Finn to let me out.

Back in the living room, he is facing the mantelpiece over the fireplace gazing at the framed photos. His smartphone is abandoned on the sofa. There is a message. As he can't see me, I read it.

'Where are you? Headmaster furious. Your review went ahead. Duncan's black eye still bad. His father wants you expelled. Contact me urgently, Anna.'

I stare at Finn's bruised and cut hands. He picks up a framed photo of a proud and happy Kay as a young police-woman, shaking a senior officer's hand and smiling at the camera. I know this photo well. I've studied it, amazed at how alike Kay and Rose look: the same heart-shaped face and pale blue eyes. He moves towards the window to see the image better. Then I notice Finn's expression. Unblinking, all-consuming, cold-eyed hatred. It radiates from every fibre of his body. He is shaking. He grinds his jaw and raises the frame as if he is going to throw it to the floor. I step back and bark. *Leave Rose's things alone!* He looks at me and I see a destructive fury in the bottomless black holes of his eyes that I've only ever seen in a dog that's been chained up all its life. I bark again, baring my teeth, and he places the photo back on the mantelpiece. I keep a safe distance, no longer sure if Finn is friend or foe. We stare at each other. He clenches and unclenches his fists, but I hold my ground. He looks away first, whispering 'No,' over and over as he hugs himself. Slowly his breathing quietens. But I am on my guard.

By now I am desperate to do a pee so I lead him to the kitchen door and bark. He seems relieved that's all I want. He keeps a safe distance from me but opens the door enough to let me out. The wind shakes the trees' branches and hurls leaves in my face. Finn shivers and shuts the door. Oh well. I think I'd rather stay away from him anyway. Why did he react like that to Kay's photo? I cock my leg at the birdbath and then trot off towards the pond for a spot of duck-chasing to relieve the tension.

But where are the ducks? No quacking. No splashing. No complaining.

It's very quiet. Too quiet.

They were there earlier. I hope I haven't pissed them off. Ducks don't mind goading others, but they don't like copping it. When Rose and I were leaving for Paddy's funeral this morning, one of the ducks called me a 'pretty boy' because of the black ribbon on my collar. That made me mad. I was wearing it in honour of my beloved master. So I charged at her and managed to pull out some of her tail feathers. Still, it normally takes more than that to scare away a feisty mallard.

Oak leaves blow in the wind and skip across the lawn towards the hedge at the bottom of the garden. I try to trap them with my paw. But the novelty of this game wears off quickly. Because of the wind direction I don't pick up the delicious smell of raw beef until I'm right next to the hedge. Little meat balls are scattered across the grass. I can't believe my luck. I sniff the one nearest to me. It smells slightly unusual, a little sweeter than I'd expected, but who am I to turn down a free meal? I lick my lips.

'Stop!' someone yells.

Oh no you don't. You're not having my meat balls. I open my jaw.

'It's poison,' screams Celeste, her wings flapping furiously as she races towards me.

I sniff it once again.

'Monty, he's trying to kill you,' she calls and lands, puffing and panting, on the bridge of my nose. 'Don't touch it!'

'It smells fine to me.'

Exhausted and out of breath, Celeste slides off my nose and into the grass. 'I've been trying to get your attention,' she gasps. 'Through the sitting-room window.' She catches her breath. 'But you didn't hear me.'

Ah, Finn has the TV up very loud.

'The killer's here!' she pants.

I do a one-eighty and face the house, ears forward, listening, on hyper alert.

'Where?'

Celeste points. 'In the house.'

I stare at her horrified, recalling the hatred on Finn's face. I feel sick to my stomach.

Chapter Forty-Two

'The boy? Finn?' I yelp, my panic rising. 'But he doesn't look like the killer.'

I know Finn has been badly treated. He reminds me of a dog who's been beaten repeatedly. Aloof. Wary. Distrustful. It's safer that way. He's also angry. If you get too close, he attacks, blindly, savagely. But a murderer?

Celeste shakes her head. She's still breathless. 'No. Look. Ladder.'

I look up. No ladder at the back, so I race down the side of the house. A ladder leans against the wall of the upstairs bathroom. The lead-light casement window is wide open. The killer is inside.

I sprint towards the sitting-room windows and slam into them, paws on the glass. Finn is sitting on the sofa facing my way but he's mesmerised by the game he's playing on his phone. It's as if the earlier incident over the photo never happened. He has his back to the sitting-room doorway. He doesn't look up. I bark as loudly as I can, frantic. But even I can hear the screaming row between two women coming from the TV.

Standing behind Finn is Paddy's masked killer and he has a full wine bottle in his gloved hands. I'm clawing at the window, growling madly. I see the man raise the bottle above his head. I yelp like a scalded cat. It's enough to get Finn to crane forward so that the bottle hits the back of his head at an angle and thuds into the back cushion, unbroken. The blow knocks Finn out. He collapses forwards over his knees. No! I hurl myself against the window pane trying to break in. It cracks but the criss-cross of lead holds the glass in place.

The intruder looks up at me, down at Finn who doesn't move, and then races to the kitchen, still clutching the bottle by its neck. I hear the scrape of the back door bolt. Now I have no way of getting inside. I hear kitchen cupboard doors slam open, food cans hit the floor, then fabric tearing and my heart almost stops. No, he can't be. Not my bed. Don't destroy my bed! All my memories of Paddy!

I dash to the kitchen window and stare in. He has ripped my bed's cover and is now using a knife to cut into the duvet inside. Why? Why is he doing this? I snarl and bark, foaming at the mouth. Then I see Betty poking her nose out of her hole.

'Stop him!' I call. 'Betty! He's the killer!'

He is ripping the stuffing from my bed, then suddenly stops. In his hand is a black and silver USB stick. Was that in my bed?

'Is that Paddy's?' Celeste asks, legs glued to the window pane I'm staring through.

'Yes. Paddy must have hidden it there. I knew there was a lump, but it didn't bother me.'

'That's why the killer keeps coming back. He wants that USB,' she says. 'Your master was a very clever man. He knew the best place to hide it was in the one place that held all your memories – your bed. He knew you'd guard it and keep it safe.'

'But I'm not keeping it safe!' I howl. 'Betty!' I shout, but I've lost sight of her. 'Don't let him take that black and silver thing. Betty!'

The intruder screams and slaps his ankle. He drops the memory stick. Betty has her teeth embedded in his flesh. She lets go and falls to the floor, then scoops up the stick in her mouth and runs as fast as her little legs can muster. The killer tries stamping on her, so she zig-zags to avoid his boots. She is almost at her hole in the skirting board when he slams his foot down in front of it, blocking her path. She charges off towards the doorway leading to the hall. The killer grabs a frying pan and smashes it down on the hall carpet, only missing Betty by a whisker.

I'm desperate to help. I claw at the kitchen window. Betty deflects to the lavatory.

'No!' I bark. 'He'll corner you.'

But she can't hear me. I catch a glimpse of her cowering behind the toilet pipes. The killer takes the toilet brush and pins her against the wall with it. I can hear her pitiful screams. All of a sudden I spy Celeste. The lavatory has one of those old fashioned wall vents that's basically a few bricks missing and a fancy wrought iron grate. She has flown through the grate and is heading for the man's masked face. She's so small he doesn't even notice her. I watch in amazement as she unzips one black boot and releases a toxic stink. The killer is leaning over Betty and his body blocks my view but from his jerky movements, I guess he is trying to grab the stick. He reels back at the stench.

'What the . . . ?' he says.

But Celeste's attack is too late. He shoves something in his trouser pocket. The USB stick. In his other hand he has Betty, by the tail. She is struggling to get free and squealing in terror. Celeste unzips another boot, desperately trying to distract him. This time he sees the ladybird and swats her away. I'm horrified – has he killed Celeste? Then he drops Betty into the toilet bowl, shuts the lid and flushes the toilet.

I shriek.

I am so stunned, I miss a few seconds and then hear the front door kicked open. I sprint around the corner, determined to stop him. He is waiting for me. I expected him to swing something at me and am ready to attack his arm. I don't expect to be sprayed in the face. I turn my head and look down just in time but the pain in my eyes is excruciating and it feels as if my nose is on fire. My eyes are streaming and I'm blind. It's as if he's thrown chili powder. I yelp in agony. I rub my face in the grass, frantic to stop the burning pain. The man kicks me and runs away. I hear Dante land next to me, drawn to us by the commotion.

'What can I do?' he asks.

'Follow that man,' I say between sneezes. 'We have to get that stick back.'

Dante is gone in a few flaps of his wings.

I am finding it hard to breathe and my eyes are blurry but I stagger into the house.

'Follow me,' says Celeste.

'You're alive!'

I can't see her so I follow her voice.

'We've got to help Finn. And find Betty,' I splutter, tears streaming.

I bump into the hall table. I manage to open the toilet seat with my nose, but I can barely open my eyes so I call out blindly.

'Betty! Are you in there?'

'Oh no,' whispers Celeste. 'She's gone.'

'We'll find her. We'll search the sewers.'

'But Monty. She'll have drowned.'

'No, not Betty. Rats have survived flushings before.'

I lurch into the sitting room. The back of Finn's head is bleeding badly but because he is slumped forward the blood is pooling at his feet. He's breathing. He needs an ambulance.

I sneeze several times and wipe my paws across my eyes. It doesn't help much because they are big and clumsy. But time is running out for Finn. His smartphone is on the floor. I slide the pad of my paw across the phone and it comes to life.

'Now for the difficult bit,' I say. 'If only I had Betty.'

After several attempts, I am finally into Messages. I can barely see the tiny screen and hope the number I have touched three times is a nine. But my pads are too big and Celeste tells me I keep hitting the wrong number. Eventually I succeed. But texting is something I have never done before. I attempt to write, 'Ambulance Duckdown Cottage Farley Green.' But I keep activating the wrong keys and it doesn't help that everything appears smudged through my stinging eyes. His phone has some kind of auto-guess function that guesses words, which helps me complete the message. After what seems like an eternity, I touch Send.

Meanwhile, the blood pool below Finn's head gets bigger.

Chapter Forty-Three

Two paramedics lift Finn into the ambulance. He is whiter than I've ever seen a big'un and his eyes are closed. His skull is in some kind of protective casing. The ambulance leaves, siren on full bore.

We are outside the front of the cottage. Rose sits cross-legged on the grass and mechanically wipes my eyes with wet cotton wool, even though Malcolm has said it won't reduce the pepper spray's sting, which, thankfully, is subsiding anyway. The Leach stands close, the ends of his camel-colour trench coat flapping in the wind.

'What in God's name was he doing here?'

Who does he mean? Not me, surely? I live here.

There are SOCOs milling about everywhere; the kitchen floor is a mess of dented food tins, burst treats packets and my dog bed stuffing that blows around like dandelion seeds; the sitting-room carpet has a bloodstain larger than my food bowl; and the driveway looks like a car sales yard with a Peugeot 308 in police retroreflective livery, Leach's unmarked silver Astra and Varma's white Ford Focus, as well as the

SOCO van. But Rose sees none of it. Her eyes are glazed. Nor does she hear her boss or register his sharp tone. She drops her hand into the bowl of water and mistakenly tips it over. She doesn't notice.

'Rose!' he says, louder.

She looks up at Leach as if she doesn't know him.

'What was Finnegan Toyne doing in your house?'

Rose frowns. 'Who?'

'Finnegan Toyne. The boy.'

'Oh you mean Finn. Keeping an eye on Monty.' She blinks, as if she isn't actually sure, but then remembers. 'He was house-sitting until I got home.' She drops the soggy cotton wool on the grass and raises a wet hand to her mouth. 'Oh God! I never thought he'd get hurt. I thought he'd be safe inside. I really did.'

She covers her face. Leach kneels next to her, his stocky legs and over-sized calves putting way too much pressure on his trouser seams. I watch the stitching, fascinated, as it stretches to bursting point.

Pearl walks out of the house, but for once keeps his mouth shut. Leach shakes his head. Pearl disappears back into the hubbub.

Leach touches Rose's shoulder. 'Does the name Toyne ring a bell?' he asks, as if talking to a sensitive child.

'Toyne?'

Rose's eyes open wide and her mouth forms a perfect O. It's as if she's seen a ghost.

'He can't be,' she says.

'He is. You didn't know?'

She stands abruptly and peers in through the sittingroom window.

'Uh, careful. Don't touch the glass,' Leach says.

I join her, wondering what she's looking for. Her eyes wander to the mantelpiece and the photo of Kay in her police uniform, the very photo that sparked so much fury in Finn.

Rose suddenly turns around and leans forward, clutching her stomach as if in pain. She crouches down and curls into a ball on the grass, groaning. The yoga–practising ducks call this position the child's pose. But they do it in silence and find it relaxing. I have never heard Rose make noises like this before. Her anguish is intense. I lick her hand and whimper.

'Oh my God! What if he dies? The sole survivor,' she whispers.

'If he does, it's not your fault.'

I bark once in agreement.

'Rose, I want you to look at me,' Leach says.

She lifts her head. I look at him too. This is clearly important.

'Finn is dangerous, and if I had my way he'd be behind bars.'

'But Kay thought he was innocent.'

Leach sighs loudly and stands up. His joints crack. 'Look, considering Kay's involvement in the case, even if it is cold, I think it's best you stay well away from him. I mean it. No hospital visits either.'

She doesn't respond. He waves over the second team of paramedics. 'Look after her. She's in shock.'

His mobile phone rings. He answers it. It's brief. He then yells for Pearl. Rose comes out of her ball and looks up, like a hedgehog checking that danger's passed. The paramedics ask her questions. She ignores them. I stay close, keeping a protective eye on her.

'Right,' says Leach to Pearl, 'Forensics have just confirmed the blood on the jacket from the silver Ford Fiesta matches the DNA from the fabric in this dog's mouth.'

Five big'uns look at me. I'm not sure which one I should stare back at – now I can see straight again – so I go for the alpha of course, the Leach. I sit proud, head up. That's my piece of fabric! My bite!

He continues. 'We've also got confirmation the glasses found in the car belong to Flay. We'll have a warrant within half an hour. I want his home and office searched. I want all of Salt's files and emails. Dave, you and I are going to Flay's house. We know he's home. It's time that condescending tosser gave us some answers.'

'Should we warn the Chief?' Pearl asked. 'Given they're mates, and all that.'

'Oh, no. I don't think so,' says Leach.

'Be careful, sir,' Rose says, 'He has to have an accomplice and we don't know who he is.'

It's like someone has switched Rose's brain back on. The colour starts to return to her face.

Leach laughs. 'I can handle myself, Rose. You look after yourself.'

'I knew that toffee-nosed git was hiding something,' says Pearl.

Rose and I snap our heads round at the same time and both stare at him, stunned at his lie.

The paramedics try to lead Rose to the ambulance.

'I'm fine. Really.' She stands up, a little shakily. I stand too, ready to go where she goes.

'What can I do, sir?' Rose asks.

'Nothing.'

'Sir, I'm feeling much better.' She looks at the paramedics. 'Thanks for your help, but you're wasting your time. I'm not going with you.'

Leach sighs. 'Then the best thing you can do is take your dog and go stay with a friend. I'm ordering you to have a few days off.'

'No way,' Rose blurts out.

Leach squares up to her. 'That's an order, Sidebottom.'

'I'm sorry, sir. I don't mean to contradict you. But Flay was my suspect. So, naturally, I want to be involved, sir.'

I'm so happy to hear Rose stick up for herself that I bark in support.

Pearl scowls at me. 'Shame those poisoned meatballs didn't work,' he mutters.

'Shut up, Dave!' says Rose 'If it wasn't for this dog we wouldn't be able to link Flay to the killer or have the knife that killed Grace!'

Dave opens and closes his mouth but says nothing. I aim a low growl in his direction.

Leach steps in. 'Rose, you're a key witness now. And your home's been invaded twice. I order you to step away.'

'Please, sir, give me something to do.'

Leach hesitates. 'Christ!' he says, shaking his head. 'Okay, go with Varma to seize the laptops and data from Flay Bioscience and the university, and get them to the e-Crime unit.'

Rose looks disappointed. She's got the tedious job, whereas Leach and Pearl are to arrest the mastermind behind a double homicide and an attempted murder. The light goes out of

Rose's face for a moment. She takes a few deep breaths and nods, resigned.

'Will do, sir.'

My stomach churns. I don't like the idea of Rose going to Flay HQ. Who knows where that killer is hiding? What if she comes face-to-face with him and doesn't realise?

Leach and Pearl drive away.

Varma wanders over. 'It sucks, doesn't it?' he says, gesturing at the departing Astra. 'But we all know you worked out the Flay connection. Not Dave.'

While she's distracted, I search for Celeste and find her peering into a street drain.

'Seen anything of Betty?'

'Afraid not.' She screws up her face. 'Disgusting work, but needs must.' She flies up into the air and then down through the sewer grate.

'Celeste, wait! Heard anything from Dante?'

'Not a dicky-bird,' she replies, popping back out of the grate.

'I'm going with Rose to Flay's company. I want to keep an eye on her. Something's not right. When I get back, I'll help you look for Betty.'

Celeste stares at me hard, still hovering above the drain. 'Monty, you're not going to like this, but the chances of Betty still being alive are slim.'

I shake my head. 'No way. She's tough. She's a survivor. We just have to find her.'

I hear a tap of claws on the road. It's an odd rhythm. One, two, three, pause. Then I hear puffing and blowing like an old steam engine. Celeste ducks into the drain for safety.

'Jake!' I call out, as his scarred face appears around a corner.

From front on, his wide set shoulders obscure his missing back leg.

'All right, Monty,' Jake says.

'All right, Jake.'

'Got some news.' He pauses, scowling at the police car. 'Is them the cops?'

'The killer came back. Almost murdered a boy.'

Jake seems unfazed by this news. I might just as well have said, No, just the dustmen collecting rubbish.

'Right you are then. That gang, the one with the seven-pointed star tattoo, they have a couple of lock-ups on the Truscott Estate.'

'Great work!'

Excited, I wag my tail so fast an empty chocolate wrapper gets sucked into the downdraft.

'Drug trafficking's their game,' Jake says. 'Rumour is they also grow cannabis locally. Under them hot lamps. Their cover is importation of medical and lab equipment. The drugs are hidden inside the equipment.'

'Monty!' Rose calls.

I thank Jake and run to Rose's side. She opens the door to a white Ford Focus. Varma clutches the keys.

'He can't come with us,' says Varma.

'Sorry, Kamlesh. I'm not leaving him again.'

'But he's hardly alone,' says Varma, gesturing to the SOCO team swarming the place.

'And when they all leave?' Rose shakes her head. 'Look, I'll drive myself if you don't want him in your car.'

'Okay,' says Varma. 'Why don't you pick up the warrant for Flay Bioscience and I'll take the university? As soon as I've finished there, I'll join you.'

'Sounds good,' Rose replies.

I don't think that's a good idea at all. There's a connection between this drugs gang and Flay Bioscience that I can't quite put my paw on. Until the killer is caught, I don't want Rose going there without back-up. So I try to herd Varma towards Rose's car, a bit like I've seen Sheepdogs do.

'What's he doing?' Varma asks, doing a little jig to get away from me.

'I guess he wants us to get moving. Come on then, Monty. Let's go.'

No, that's not what I mean. I take the corner of Varma's Barbour jacket in my mouth and tug.

'He's ruining it. Get him to stop,' shouts Varma.

'Monty! Leave it!'

I have no choice but to let go. I give up on Varma and run straight past her into the house. There is something I have to bring with me. Just in case.

Chapter Forty-Four

Hong Seok-Cheon handed the USB to his employer and was glad to be rid of it. Time to get paid and get the hell out of there.

It had all sounded so simple. Ten thousand pounds for one dead professor and some data. An old man. An easy hit. And his client was a dealer well worth keeping sweet. Well connected, and selling shitloads of drugs to university students. So he'd taken the job.

Hong had killed before. Rival gang members. Part of his initiation into the Death Stars. He'd clubbed his first victim to death and then pissed on the sixteen-year-old's body. Marking his territory. The next guy had been tougher to get. Lee Min-ho. A snakehead. Well protected. But there's one place where they all relax – the toilet. So he knifed his target sitting on the crapper. He smirked. He'd never forget the startled look on the fat slob's face when he kicked in the stall door. After that, he'd got his big break: go to England. Set up a front for their drug smuggling operation. Lab equipment. He'd leapt at the chance.

But this hit had become way more complicated than expected. He'd known about the dog but assumed it was a spoilt stupid thing. One kick and the piece of shit would run. But it didn't. It came after him. And kept coming. Who'd have thought?

He watched as the memory stick was plugged into a laptop and its contents scrolled through. Words, equations, numbers. Blah, blah. Graphs, more numbers. Boring. But somehow valuable.

'Good,' said the recipient.

'I want my money.'

'Not until I've checked it thoroughly.'

His head throbbed and he was close to throwing up. Another wave of dizziness hit him. He swayed in his seat, his clothes soaked with sweat, and gripped the underside of the chair with his one good hand. He bent his head slowly to look at his bandaged arm, swollen to twice the size of the other, and oozing pus. That dog! He'd bide his time and when the cops had grown bored of the Salt case he'd find it and kill it slowly and painfully.

'Hey! You got antibiotics?' Hong asked.

He received a tut of annoyance. 'When I'm finished.'

The antibiotics he'd taken hadn't done any good. But what did he expect, given it was past its use-by date? He wiped his soaked forehead with the sleeve of his good arm. This infection was almost as bad as the malaria he'd suffered as a child.

Hong didn't like waiting. He didn't like being told what to do. But right now, he was too weak to do anything about it. He couldn't go to a doctor or a hospital because the cops would be looking for someone bitten by a dog. And he was here illegally.

His employer hit the delete key and watched as the yellow progress bar inched across the screen until the entire content of the USB was gone for ever. The last remaining copy of Patrick Salt's paper on killer bees was destroyed.

'Just to be sure, this is getting incinerated.' The USB is dropped into a pocket. 'Right, let's get your antibiotics.'

Hong glared at his employer's back, but found it impossible to keep anything in focus for long. A cabinet was opened and a syringe filled from a glass bottle.

'Now, roll up your sleeve and lie down here.'

If he lay down for a few minutes, perhaps he'd feel better? The room was spinning. The needle stung as it entered his arm. At first the coolness of the solution felt good. Surely, it would sooth his fever? But as he looked up at his employer's face, his heart beat faster in panic. The smile was fake and the coal-dark eyes looking down at him were filled with a controlled fury, like a cobra waiting to strike.

'You shouldn't have stolen the Shilin Cutter. Stupid, very stupid.'

When scouting out Salt's house, Hong had glimpsed the blade through the neighbour's window. Back in Seoul, only red poles or above had Cutters, gang members who'd earned the right to them. It was time he had his own. He was better than a 49er, a lowly soldier. But the old man had hobbled into the room as Hong jumped out of the window, and may have glimpsed him the night he stabbed the Professor. That's why Grace had to be eliminated. His employer almost totally lost it when he'd broken the news. Those dark eyes had flashed with an uncontrolled rage then. Yelled. Called him a retard, an amateur, and worse. A neat slice across the throat would have put an end to it. But he wanted payment.

Hong tried to sit up, but his strength was gone. Surprisingly strong hands pushed him back down and held him there, hands covered with surgical gloves. No fingerprints. No skin residue. He struggled, but he felt as feeble as that scrawny old man, Grace.

'All you had to do was find the USB and kill Salt. Make it look like a robbery. I gave you everything. Salt's address, his routine, the likely hiding places for the USB. I even handed you the perfect fall guy for the "robbery" – Larry Nice. But you couldn't even manage such a simple job. What do we have instead? Two, maybe three bodies, and way too much evidence left behind.' His employer leaned closer. 'All of it pointing to you.'

What was in that syringe? His eyelids were so heavy. He could no longer lift his arms. He fought off the urge to sleep. If he fell asleep, he was lost.

The phone rang.

'Hello?' A pause. 'Security? What do you want?'

His cry for help was little more than a mumbled dribble. His jaw and tongue wouldn't move. Nobody heard. Hong lay still on the gurney, his eyes wide with terror.

'I need five minutes. Then escort them in. And don't let them out of your sight.'

Chapter Forty-Five

The detective chief inspector kept his finger on the brass doorbell of the four million pound, gated-community mansion. The portico was bigger than Leach's spare bedroom and a Florentine-style lamp hung from its ceiling large enough to cause a power-cut. Behind him, lit by blindingly-bright security lights, was a horseshoe shaped driveway in crushed quartz, a perfectly manicured lawn, and in its centre a circular stone fountain with water nymph holding up a scallop shell. Surrounding the six-bedroom, six-bathroom house, with garage space for four cars and a staff annexe above, was a coiffured yew hedge to block prying eyes.

'How dare you!' Flay growled at Leach. 'And you!' he said to Pearl. 'Leave that alone!'

Pearl let go of the pointy end of a tall rosemary topiary tree cut to resemble a corkscrew. Flay then scowled at the security guard whose job it was to keep the great unwashed masses from his home. Which included the police.

'And you can say goodbye to your job, you idiot,' Flay

shouted at the guard, who was fat and fifty and had flaky bits of pie crust stuck to his lower lip.

'But Mr Flay. They're the bill. They insisted,' the guard simpered, knowing he'd never land such a cushy job again.

'Oh piss off back to your hut!' Flay ordered.

The man almost fell over as he backed down the marble steps.

'This is harassment. I'm calling my lawyer,' Flay said, blocking the entrance.

'This is a warrant to search your house and workplace.'

Leach held it up, so close to Flay's face that the wet ink of the Judge's signature might rub off on his beak of a nose. Flay snatched it and squinted.

'Lost your glasses, sir?' Leach asked.

'Yes, as a matter of fact I have. I have a second pair in my study. Wait here.'

'No, sir, we're not waiting. We're searching your house right now,' said Leach, barging in.

Before Flay could open his mouth, police officers swarmed through the door. Their heavy boots on the Classico Cream travertine floor sounded like the riot squad had arrived. A chandelier, shaped like a spinning top, hung from the circular ceiling rose that reminded Leach of his dear-departed nanna's paper doilies. Straight ahead, a staircase divided the hall in two, forcing officers to stream either side.

'Is there anyone else here, Mr Flay?'

'What? Yes, the housekeeper.'

'Preparing dinner?'

'Yes, why?'

'Your wife?'

'Um, I don't know. Out at a cocktail function, I think.'

'Children?'

'Boarding school.'

'Sir, I need you to sit down and please don't touch anything.'

'I'll do no such thing. This is *my* house!' Flay yelled after Leach as the detective strode into the study. Polished oak floors, oak panelling on the walls, oak desk and marble fireplace with a family photo hung above, in an ornate gold frame as wide as the mantelpiece.

'Wait! That's private!' Flay scurried after him.

'I'll need keys and entry to your safe.'

'How do you know I have a safe?'

Leach glanced at the framed photo above the mantelpiece. 'A man like you?'

'I'm not doing anything until I've spoken to my lawyer.'

'Okay, call your lawyer. One call, that's it.' The wide-set detective took one menacing step closer to the willowy suspect. 'I won't ask you again, sir. Sit down.'

Flay sat at his carved oak desk with green leather inlay. Leach turned his back on him.

'You!' Leach said, pointing at a police officer. 'Watch him.'

Flay picked up the phone and dialled. 'And keep your people away from my files. You hear?'

'Too late,' replied Leach.

'I'll have your job for this!'

As Leach directed the search from the hall, he heard Flay telling his lawyer to get round there immediately. Then his voice dropped to a whisper. Leach looked round at his murder suspect hunched over the phone, clearly on a second phone call.

'Have detectives arrived?' Flay said.

He clearly didn't like the response.

'You idiot!' said Flay, through clenched teeth. 'Watch her. Make a note of everything she takes.'

'Sir, end that call please,' demanded the officer in the room.

'When I'm ready!' Flay snapped. Then into the phone, 'I don't give a shit about the delivery . . .'

Leach stormed in and cut the connection.

'Chadstone Flay, I'm arresting you in connection with the murders of Patrick Salt and Francis Grace, and the attempted murder of Finnegan Toyne.'

In the dusky light, the Flay Bioscience site looks like a Cold War secret research facility with high electric fences, topped with razor wire. Bleak, grey, low-level concrete buildings seem to squat, terrified in the growing darkness. Except for one building that reminds me of a bone with a sharp, pointy end cutting through the sky. I imagine that's the head office. The site must be the size of a couple of football pitches but there's nothing welcoming about it. It's been designed to keep people out.

I peer through the car's window at a sentry box lit up like the Tardis from *Doctor Who* – Paddy and I used to love *Doctor Who*. We even replayed the old episodes so I could watch K-9 and bark at him in support. I pick up the distant smell of gorse and heather with the occasional smattering of silver birch from the open heathland surrounding the site. I feel uneasy. I can't escape the feeling that the security guard, a bruiser of a man with a flattened nose like a pug, is stalling us. He moves as slowly as an old woman I once saw doing Tai Chi in a park, yet I can hear his heart pumping fast and he smells like sour milk which tells me he's agitated. I wish Varma was here, but he's gone to clear out Paddy's office at the university. What's worrying me is that even though Chadstone Flay, aka, Mr Genius, is being arrested, the accomplice is still at large. Where is the man with the seven-pointed star tattoo and a bite wound?

Rose is expecting to simply pick up Paddy's files from his lab. But the fur all down my spine is up on end and I can't keep my paws still. I glimpse a dark bird in flight leaving the site. Could that be Dante? I bark, calling him back.

'Dante! Over here!'

'Quiet, Monty. Otherwise he won't believe you're a police dog. Now, be good,' Rose says.

So I watch the bird fly away in the direction of Geldeford.

We're following the guard's little white Skoda Citigo down a meandering road to the laboratory where Paddy sometimes worked with Dr Martinez. His car moves so slowly I could walk faster. Rose told a little white lie, claiming I'm a police dog, because the security man refused to let me through. She glances round at me, her ponytail swinging like a fox tail.

'He's what I call a Job's Worth,' she says and smiles, then looks out of the windscreen at the rear-view lights we're trailing.

The road takes us past fields growing crops, then at least a dozen glasshouses, each one the size of a tennis court. I hear the buzz of many thousands of bees and, as I peer into the darkness, I see what look like hives inside the long glass structures. We ignore a left turn that leads to the delivery docks and a storage shed. The road meanders by breeze-block, hut-like buildings, all linked by covered walkways. A red-brick chimney stack, as tall as Nelson's Column, is belching out smoke that appears a pale grey against the blackening sky. But it doesn't smell of firewood. It smells like overcooked pork and singed mattresses, and I sneeze. I don't like it.

In a building not far from the chimney the lights are on and somebody in a white coat is waiting for us at the door. Because of the brightness of the interior light behind them, I can't make out who it is. The security guard parks and gets out.

'I'm sorry, Dr Martinez, but she insisted,' he says, pointing at Rose.

Something definitely doesn't feel right. Everyone is tense, even though they're pretending to be relaxed. I ready myself to jump out of the car. But Rose doesn't open the door. Instead she walks over to Martinez, arms wide, as if she were greeting a friend.

'Maria. I'm sorry to disturb you, especially so late. But we have a warrant and I'm to seize all of Salt's documents in hard and soft copy. Including work produced with you. Here's the warrant.'

Rose's stance is relaxed. She's not expecting resistance from Martinez, who gives the document a rudimentary once over.

Martinez smiles. Oh boy, it's like a crocodile yawning. What a huge mouth! But she seems friendly enough.

'You're alone?' she asks. 'I thought these things were always done in pairs.'

She shrugs her shoulders as if she doesn't really care. Yet, I think she does. She scans Rose's face, her eyes wide and alert.

'DS Varma is on his way, but I expect this won't take long. I'll probably be done by the time Kamlesh gets here,' Rose replies.

'Come through,' she says, beckoning Rose inside.

'I'll just get my dog.'

Martinez's response is abrupt. 'No, no dogs. This is a sterile area. He'll have to stay in the car.'

Her smile has gone and her big hooped earrings swing as she shakes her head.

No! I must keep Rose safe. She's my master. I must protect her. I bark and paw at the window.

'Can I tie him up outside then?' Rose asks. 'He may need to pee.'

Martinez hesitates, then I see her glance behind Rose at something in the distance, just for a second. Rose doesn't notice as she has the light in her eyes.

'I suppose so, but can we get inside? It's freezing out here.'

My night vision is better than Rose's. I look in the direction of Martinez's glance. There is a white Ford Transit van parked at the loading dock. I can just make out Hong Lab Equipment written on the rear doors in black. It's the symbol painted above the words that gives me a jolt. It's a huge black seven-pointed star, with gold edging. Their logo. I dash from one window to the other, sniffing the air, desperate to smell the van driver, but it's futile: Rose's windows and doors are shut. What did Jake say about this gang? They smuggle drugs inside lab equipment. My heart races as if I'm running uphill, the fur along my spine bristles and I let rip with one hell of a bark.

'Quiet, Monty!'

Rose opens the car door and I leap out before she can block my exit, and I hurtle in the van's direction. But the security guard is too quick. He grabs my collar, yanking me backwards. The jolt is so violent my bark becomes a swallowed yelp as my collar cuts into my throat. I gag.

'Give him to me,' demands Rose, attaching my lead. 'You can let go now.' She glares at the guard, who reluctantly releases my collar. 'What's the matter, Monty?' she asks.

I am still choking as she ties my lead to a drainpipe near the entrance.

'Sorry, Monty. I won't be long. No chasing squirrels tonight.'

My eyes are wide with fear, the whites of them showing. My tail is up and I bare my teeth, but the sound I make is like a petrol lawnmower that won't start. I cough out a pathetic attempt at a warning. I can smell it, now, hovering in the chilly night air, even though the scent of Martinez's musky perfume threatens to overwhelm it. I smell stinky food that's worse than a sewer, cannabis, and that disease, malaria. But most pungent of all is the stench of an infected wound.

The door locks behind Rose.

Chapter Forty-Six

Rose heard Monty's rasping bark as she followed Martinez along a brighly lit, empty corridor. White walls, white doors, pale grey polished concrete floors and the smell of disinfectant floor cleaner. Why was Monty so agitated? Perhaps he didn't like being tied up outside.

'You're working late,' Rose said, hearing nothing but the low thrum of the air-conditioning and the tap of Martinez's red shoes.

'I always do. I often work through the night. I'm lucky. I don't need much sleep.' She smiled at Rose. 'It's nice to have some company, even if it is on police matters.'

Rose felt a slight numbness in her hands but put it down to the heavy evidence boxes she was carrying. She couldn't help but like Martinez. She was always so welcoming. And like Rose, dedicated to her work. Rose didn't have many friends and found herself wondering, when the case was over, if they might meet for coffee or a drink at the pub one day.

'So how did you get the warrant? Mr Flay was very sure you would not.'

Martinez held open a door that led to a large laboratory, allowing Rose to enter first and place her plastic boxes on the floor. She took off her smart black jacket and laid it on a stool. There were two rows of long, white work benches with shelving above, and on that shelving were hundreds of petri dishes and glass jars. A vase of red tulips stood out – that's a Martinez touch of colour, Rose guessed – and photos of her with friends and colleagues. Against one wall were incubators from which came a low and constant hum. Bees.

'New evidence has come to light,' Rose replied, placing her nose near one incubator so she could get a better look. 'I can't say any more.'

There were hundreds of bees. Almost as one, they swarmed onto the glass nearest her, turning the transparent panel black. Their rhythmic buzzing was suddenly much louder. And fiercer. It was as if they were trying to attack her face.

'Don't do that, please' said Martinez. 'You'll make them agitated.'

Rose stepped away, surprised by their ferocity. Unlike many of her schoolmates she'd never been afraid of bees. As a child, she'd often rescued one from a glass of Ribena or if it was trapped inside the house. But they were never aggressive. Not like that. Something else surprised her. She'd expected the lab to smell of chemicals or disinfectant. Not bad eggs. Perhaps it was sulphur?

'Patrick's workstation,' Martinez said, pointing to an impeccably tidy section of the shared bench.

There was nothing personal left: no photos, stress toys, notes with his handwriting on. He'd been wiped clean.

'Have you cleared this area?' Rose asked.

'Of course. Patrick was a lovely man but untidy. My work must go on and I don't like mess.'

Rose noticed *their* work had now become *my* work.

'I thought you said he was meticulous?'

'No, I was always cleaning up after him.'

Rose felt a mild tingling in her feet and hands. But what did it matter if Martinez secretly thought Salt was untidy?

'His filing cabinets? USB sticks?' Rose asked.

'Over there. But we keep very little paper,' she replied, pointing to a red four-drawer filing cabinet. Another Martinez choice, she suspected.

'Did you have access to all of Patrick's work?'

'Of course. We shared everything.'

'Then I'll need to take your laptop.'

'Oh no, please don't. I need it.'

'I'm sorry. This is a murder investigation.'

Rose pulled on disposable gloves.

Martinez leaned against a work bench and gave Rose a big open-mouthed smile as if they were two friends shooting the breeze.

'Rose? Can I call you Rose?'

'Of course.'

'Rose, I'm guessing you think someone at Flay Bioscience killed Patrick. Perhaps you think it is Mr Flay?'

'Why do you say that?'

'It is just a guess.' She shrugged. 'My concern is for the launch of my new honey bee. If Mr Flay is arrested, I have to know the launch still goes ahead?'

'Maria, I imagine that will be up to the company, but if you know something that could help our investigation, you have to tell me.'

Martinez looked at her feet.

'What is it, Maria?'

'It might be nothing,' she replied.

'It does no harm to tell me.'

'I overheard something, okay? Mr Flay, he was very angry with Patrick.'

No tingling. She was telling the truth.

'What did you hear?'

Martinez's eyes darted around the lab. She was clearly very nervous. 'It's better if you ask Mr Flay this question. He is my employer. This is very difficult, you understand.'

'Maria, I need you to tell me.'

'I think Patrick wanted more money. I already tell you this. He told Dr Bomphrey, who told Mr Flay,' she blurted out.

The tingling began again and it spread painfully through her body. From everything she had learned about Patrick Salt, arguing over money just didn't seem in character. He was devoted to saving bees. Nothing about his simple lifestyle indicated he hungered for wealth. Why was Martinez lying?

'Go on.'

'Okay. It was the day before Patrick died. I had just arrived at the university and was walking past the admin building. I heard Mr Flay and Dr Bomphrey talking. They did not see me. Mr Flay said that Patrick had become a liability and needed to be dealt with.'

'Were those Flay's exact words? He needed to be dealt with?'

Martinez nodded.

'Did Patrick put his request for more money in writing?'

'I do not know.'

'Okay, Dr Martinez, I'll need to get a statement from you.' Rose pulled out a notepad and pen from her pocket.

'No, no, I don't want to make a statement. This could get me fired,' she protested.

Rose didn't want to mess this up. This had to be by the book. She dialled Varma's mobile. He didn't answer. She left a message asking him to call her urgently. She tried Pearl, who picked up and she explained what Martinez had just said. She could hear Flay arguing with somebody in the background. It sounded like her DCI.

'Okay, grab her laptop and printouts and bring her in. I'll interview her when I'm finished here.'

Rose explained to the agitated Martinez that she'd have to go to police HQ.

'While I'm filling these boxes, have a think about exactly what you overheard and when. Can you do that for me?'

'No, no, I will do the statement in the morning. Please? I can't leave here,' she stammered. No smile and her neck was flushed with anxiety. 'I have work I must complete tonight. Very important.'

'I'm sorry, Dr Martinez . . .'

'No! Not tonight!' she shouted.

Rose blinked several times in surprise. 'It has to be tonight, Maria. Why don't you keep working until I'm finished here?'

'I need a smoke,' she snapped.

Martinez left. The lab door had glass panels so Rose saw her make a right turn instead of going left. A left turn would take her back to the main entrance. Odd. There must be another exit.

For the first time, Rose began to doubt Martinez. She had a key to Patrick's university office as well as access to his workstation here at Flay Bioscience. She could easily have removed hard copy evidence or deleted data in the password-protected files. It had been her idea to dial 1471 to check the last phone call Salt had received the day of the murder, so that suspicion would fall on Bomphrey. And she had looked pretty pissed off in that photo of Salt winning the prestigious Frink Medal. A framed photo that had mysteriously disappeared.

Martinez had left her laptop logged on. Rose's curiosity got the better of her. She navigated though Martinez's most recent documents and found a draft media release, embargoed until launch day. Rose opened it: Martinez had made some alterations in Track Changes. The one that struck her the most was accreditation. Patrick Salt was little more than an assistant. Maria Martinez was the lead scientist.

Despite the sealed lab windows Rose heard Monty's increasingly frantic barking. He was growing hysterical. What if he was trying to sound an alarm?

Her mouth went dry. Had Martinez envied Salt? Did she want all the glory for the new mite-resistant bee? She was certainly doing her best to implicate Flay and Bomphrey. Was that to throw them off the scent?

Rose walked to the lab door and peered through the glass. Where was Martinez? She opened it and turned right as Martinez had done. A fire exit at the end of the corridor was ajar. She opened it fully, expecting to find the scientist smoking on the other side. But she wasn't there. Rose had passed two other doors along the corridor. She retraced her steps and looked through the glass of the door nearest to her. The lights were out but the sulphurous smell was stronger here. She tried the handle and the door opened. She flicked the light switch and caught her breath. Lying on a gurney was an East Asian man of athletic build, with a bandaged arm. He was out cold. She caught a whiff of something sweet and putrid, mixed in with the sulphur. She gagged. Recovering, she fumbled for her phone.

Rose felt a sharp jab in the back of her neck and spun to see Martinez with the syringe in her hand.

'Night, night,' said Martinez.

Chapter Forty-Seven

I am tied fast.

I have almost choked myself tugging at the lead, but the knot around the drainpipe only gets tighter. I have barked and barked, hoping Rose will come out, if for no other reason than to tell me to be quiet. I am beyond panic. I am panting with terror. I dart back and forth snarling like a rabid dog. Rose is in terrible danger, and she's all alone.

The security guard has circled the Hong Lab Equipment van several times and made a phone call, but he gets no answer.

He clomps towards me.

'Shut up!' he hollers.

I have to find a way to get him to untie me. I look around, searching for inspiration. Wooden windowsill. That'll do. I start chewing the corner. I love biting into the spongy pulpiness of wood but the paint flakes stick to my tongue and taste bitter.

'Oy! Stop that, you stupid dog!'

I chow down on the windowsill and rip off a good chunk. It's rotten and easy to bite through. I spit it out.

'You little shit!'

Not so little, mate. On my hind legs I can place my paws on your shoulders and bite your nose!

He tries grabbing my snout and shoving my face away from the windowsill. But he doesn't get a good hold and I latch my jaws back into the wood.

'Oh no you don't!'

He picks at the dense, taut knot of my lead and yells a variety of expletives that would even shock my duck pals. After much fiddling with his fat fingers, he unties me and drags me away.

'You're going back in her car,' he says, and opens the back door. Rose never locks it. I willingly leap inside. He slams the door shut and taunts me through the window.

'Why don't you chew her bloody seats? Serve the bossy bitch right.'

He turns and stares at the building into which Rose has disappeared. Yes! Go inside! Please help her!

'Shut it!' he yells at me.

I hadn't realised I was barking. He walks away from the building, towards his Noddy car. He just manages to squeeze behind the steering wheel and I watch him disappear into the night.

It's up to me now. The killer's here somewhere and I have to protect Rose. I grip the metal door handle with my mouth and pull. With a click it opens. I nuzzle into the blanket covering the flattened back seats and find Chadstone Flay's security pass. The flat, shiny, slippery piece of plastic, the size of a credit card, is hard to pick up but finally it's in my mouth and I leap from the car.

At the door, I try to work out where to swipe the pass.

I know this is what I have to do to get inside because I've watched Paddy do it many times. I spot a small metal box about half way up the doorframe. The box has a glass screen with a red light behind it. I jump up and try rubbing my pass against the screen. But my jowl hangs over it, so it doesn't register. I drop to the ground and whimper. How can I hold the pass in my mouth and expose the barcode so the entry box will recognise it?

I use my tongue to shift the plastic card to one side so that half of it sticks out. My drool has coated the plastic; I hope it won't be a problem. Paws up on the wall again, I rub the plastic pass against the glass box. I hear a beep and a click and the door swings open. I race inside before it shuts automatically.

My heart is pounding. My first instinct is to race down the corridor baying for Rose. But I think better of it. I have surprise on my side. I drop the security pass and stare down a long corridor with doors on either side at regular intervals. It is very quiet, save for the hum of bees that seems to come from all directions. I prick up my ears and listen hard for Rose's voice. Nothing. I sniff the air. I smell her, though. Maria's musky perfume is everywhere, but as she works here, I guess that makes sense. The smell that hits me like a charging Rottweiler is the pong of bad eggs and the fishy stink of pus. The fur all down my spine sticks up as I lower my head and sniff the floor. I creep forward, all my senses on high alert, and stifle a yelp when the main door clicks shut behind me. I follow Rose's unique scent of vanilla, honey, peppermint and the sea, overlaid with my scent. Yes, mine! I am officially her dog.

I speed up, then slide to a halt on the slippery floor and

backtrack. On the other side of a door I smell both Rose and the killer. I resist the urge to burst in. I need to be cunning. I grab the door handle in my mouth, pull it down and push the door open as quietly as possible. The lab is dark but I can see there is nobody there. Where has the killer taken her? Nose to the ground, I follow their trail to the fire exit. It is shut. I sniff the sliver of a gap at the bottom and know that Rose, the killer and Maria have just been here and are on the other side. I look up at the horizontal bar. Too easy! I jump up and lean forward with my front paws on the bar which drops down. The door swings open and I topple onto an exterior concrete path.

It leads to other hut-like buildings. They are all grey and look confusingly similar. Except for the red-brick building in the distance with the tall circular chimney. Smoke still punches the sky like a grey fist. I smell diesel in the air but the charred pork and mattress smells have dissipated. I guess the incinerator is now empty. All my senses are on high alert. My ears twitch, tuning in to every noise. No voices, just the buzz of the outside lights and the screech of a fox on the heath. I look up at dark windows and peer into the huts' shadows, but see no movement, save for the wind through the grass. I inhale deeply, trying to catch every smell. The dominant one is Maria's: musky perfume, greasy make-up and garlic, so she is easy to follow. Rose's scent is weak, as if her feet haven't been touching the ground. The killer's odour is weak too, which doesn't make sense. Is he ahead of them? I scrape my nose as I race along the path, ignoring a turn that leads to another hut because their trail goes to the chimney building.

I hear the flap of wings drawing near. For a moment, I

think it's Dante. But the cat-like mewing tells me it's a buzzard. It sweeps down to the grass and grabs a field mouse in its claws and flies away, the little creature screaming in terror. I wonder if the killer knows I am hunting him? Or is he hunting me? I peer into the surrounding darkness, then quickly avert my eyes. They shine out like torchlight and could give away my location.

I stand outside the chimney building. The red bricks radiate heat. An engine judders and clanks within. The door is ajar and the interior light slices through the darkness where I'm hiding. I peek in, but hesitate, my face seared by the ferocious heat. Fire scares me. When I was a pup and living with the Collum family, I collided with the fireguard during a game of chase-me-if-you-want-your-sock-back and landed in some burning embers. I'll never forget the pain.

I snort the many conflicting aromas deep into my nose and use my nasal 'echo chamber' to amplify them: vegetable matter, household and chemical waste, dirty bedding, mattresses and clothing, human waste and charred flesh. The over-cooked pork smell now makes sense. Maria's musky perfume is very strong, but the killer's stink of bad eggs and pus dominates. Rose is in there too, although her scent is getting weaker.

My nose is dry and I lick it. Despite the roar of the furnace, all I can hear is my heart pumping blood so fast around my body, it sounds like a drum beating in my head.

I have no idea what to expect. I charge in with the only weapon I possess – my bared teeth.

Chapter Forty-Eight

The savage heat hits me first. Then the roar of the furnace, like an angry brown bear, its huge jaws promising death. The ground vibrates beneath my paws. The enormous red incinerator has a loading chamber big enough to take a double mattress and a hinged electronic lid on top. The machine takes up half the room. I see Rose, head slumped forward, tied around her middle with packing tape to a chair on wheels. She doesn't move. A drop of saliva falls from her open mouth and lands in her lap.

Nearby, on a gurney, lies the man I know is Paddy's killer. I don't need to see the bandaged arm or the tattoo because his scent has led me here. I guess he's Hong of Hong Lab Equipment. His eyes are closed and he lies on one side with an arm dangling off the gurney. I snarl but it's barely audible above the furnace's thunderous clamour. So I bark at him, but he doesn't move a muscle. I don't understand why they are both asleep. I look around for Martinez. Her musky scent is strong but I can't see her. How did she overpower Hong? And why isn't he tied up when Rose is? Has she gone for help? Something is very wrong. I must get Rose out of here.

I nudge her arm. Then harder. She doesn't respond. I look up into her face that's a livid pink against the glow of the furnace. Her eyes remain shut. I whimper and lick her face. 'Wake up,' I bark! Her head wobbles and falls to one side. I can hear her shallow breathing so I know she is alive, but why doesn't she hear me? What has that man done to her?

I pant fast. I am overheating. I clamp my jaw down on the corner of Rose's jacket and tug. It stretches and tears. The chair doesn't budge. I don't want to hurt Rose but she's in terrible danger. So I take her arm in my mouth. I have my back to the door, my front paws forward to give me purchase. I start backing towards the exit. Rose's limp body shifts slightly but the tape holds and the chair rolls in my direction. If I can get her out of the incinerating room, I can drag her along the concrete path to safety.

The door slams shut. I jump, release Rose's arm and spin round, fangs bared, ready to attack. In that split second, I wonder if the killer has woken up, or if Flay – the mastermind of these murders – has arrived to rescue his henchman. I do not expect to see Maria Martinez with a shovel in her hands, raised, ready to strike. The flames behind me dance a livid orange in her dark eyes. I smell her killer instinct.

Suddenly, everything makes sense. Dr Maria Martinez, who my master trusted, who was always so charming and friendly to him, planned his murder and then hired an assassin to carry it out.

'Bad doggie,' she says.

I growl, eyes narrowed, front paws spread wide. I won't go down without a fight.

'You almost ruined everything.'

I crouch low, ready to attack, fangs dripping saliva.

'But this will solve everything,' she says, looking behind me at the incinerator. 'Soon, you'll all be nothing but ash.'

I pounce. It's as if I'm flying through the air in slow motion. Martinez swings her weapon at me, but she's not fast enough. I manage to grab her arm in my jaws and she isn't able to land the blow squarely. It collides with my left hip, not my head. She screams as my teeth rip her flesh. I fling my head from side to side, desperate to inflict as much pain as possible, to rip and tear like my wolf ancestors, to put all my hurt, anger and grief into this one bite. I will not let go. If I do, we all die. The shovel drops to the floor with a clank but she uses her other hand to punch me in the face. She's going to need more than that to make me let go. Then she swings me around, yelling in fury and agony. My back legs find the floor again, but I've lost my balance and she drives me towards the open furnace. I am a strong dog, but on my hind legs I'm vulnerable. I can't get a grip. I'm terrified. It feels as if my fur is on fire. I have no choice but to release her arm, drop to all fours and dash behind the gurney where Hong lies. I pant, desperate to cool down. The heat drains my strength.

Sweat drips down her temples. Her hair has come loose from a clip and strands are stuck to her damp face. Her white lab coat is bloody where I've torn the flesh of her arm. She scowls at me.

'I'm going to burn you alive, you bloody mongrel!'

She darts around the gurney and tries to grab me. I spring

away to the other side. Hong is now facing me and my head is level with his. I bark as loudly as I can. Rose has to wake up. I've run out of ideas. Hong's face twitches and he half opens his eyes. This is bad. If he gets up and works with Martinez to corner me, we're doomed. She picks up the shovel again. She hasn't noticed Hong's movements.

Wake up, Rose! I cry.

'Shut up!' Martinez screams, raising her weapon above her head.

I keep up the noise. Hong's eyes open fully, he blinks several times looking straight at me, then his hand slowly moves into his jeans' pocket. He pulls out a flick knife. He is weak and clumsy but he manages to get it open. Is he going to stab me with it? He rolls onto his back in an attempt to turn and face her. Martinez whacks the side of his head with the shovel. I hear an exhalation and the man stops moving. The knife drops to the floor. I pick up the handle with my mouth. She sees I have it and laughs.

'And what exactly are you going to do with that?'

My hold on the knife is shaky, and it's no match for a heavy shovel. I do the only thing I can think of. I stab Rose in the calf. Martinez is so taken aback she stares open mouthed. Rose jolts awake and yelps. At the back of the chair I try to cut through the tape but I can't hold the blade steady. Martinez has got over the shock and tries to hit me, but smacks the chair leg instead. The chair rolls to one side. Rose stares, bleary-eyed at the blood-splattered Martinez and then at Hong lying motionless on the gurney. I drop the knife in Rose's lap and stand in front of her, teeth bared, ready to defend her to the death.

'Maria?' Rose says, sounding drunk and trying to take it all in. 'What're . . . you doing?'

'I'm going to kill that freaking dog!' screams Martinez.

She takes two steps forwards and swings the shovel at my head with all her strength.

Chapter Forty-Nine

I see the shovel coming at me and spring to one side. I hear a meaty thud and 'Oomph' as the air is knocked from somebody's lungs.

Martinez staggers backwards with Rose's head deep in her stomach, the chair still attached to her back. Martinez drops her weapon as she collapses, winded. *Clank* goes the shovel, then *thud* as Martinez hits the floor. The tape, partially severed, gives way and Rose wriggles free from of her bindings. She staggers like a new-born pup on wobbly legs and puts her hand out to steady herself. Her white blouse is soaked with perspiration. The knife is on the floor. I position myself between it and Martinez, who might be dazed but her hand moves towards the blade. I jump onto Martinez's chest, my face in her face, and I snarl a warning.

'Give me an excuse! Go on!' I say.

'Get him off me!' she shrieks.

'On your stomach! Now!' says Rose, with an authority I haven't heard before. She staggers slightly but her eyes are as clear and sharp as a newly cut sapphire. 'Hands behind your back!'

I move my fangs so close to Martinez, my saliva drips onto her lips.

'Yes, yes, just get it off me!'

I step back and she reluctantly rolls over. I keep guard, constantly growling, watching her every move. Rose pulls handcuffs from her pocket and seizes Martinez's arms, locking the cuffs tight.

'My arm! Your dog bit me.'

'Cry me a river!'

I lead Rose to the man on the gurney. His face and hair are sodden with blood and sweat, and some of his scalp has peeled away. She looks at me.

'The hit man?'

I bark once.

She checks for a pulse. It's faint but there is one. She pulls out his wallet and reads his driving licence: Hong Seok-Cheon. She stumbles outside and gasps at the cold air. She dials emergency services.

'This is Detective Constable Rose Sidebottom. I need immediate back-up at Flay Bioscience, Lyston Road, Geldeford. Maria Martinez tried to kill me and Hong Seok-Cheon. I have both suspects secured. Both need urgent medical attention.'

She looks down at me as she ends the call.

'We did it, Monty. We did it.'

Chapter Fifty

In Rose's opinion The Lord Dudley was exactly how a pub should be: cheap booze, a clientele that didn't try to pick fights with off-duty officers, and hot chips by the bucketload. Unfortunately, because of the log fire, low ceilings, and the exceptional numbers enjoying an evening drink, this well-known police haunt was like a sauna. Rose had made an effort to look smart as she hadn't seen her workmates for a week – at her boss's insistence. When she'd finished her statement and been checked over at the hospital, she'd crawled into bed and slept on and off for twenty-four hours, with Monty at her bedside occasionally placing his muzzle on the bedclothes to check she was okay. Tonight, her long hair hung loose over a figure-hugging pale blue cashmere top. Her blue jeans were tucked into black boots that had a slight heel, but not too much. Anything over two inches and she was likely to end up face down on the beer-stained carpet.

'What you having?' yelled Leach from the bar.

Rose raised her wine glass. 'Already got one, sir. Thanks all the same.'

Leach nodded. 'How about you, Andy?'

'Ta very much, Craig,' said Detective Inspector Morgan, holding up his pint of Guinness. 'Another one of these.'

Rose had been avoiding Andy Morgan from the Drugs Squad since he almost assaulted her in the car park. To her horror, she watched him weave through the throng of sweaty bodies to where she stood chatting with Salisbury and Varma in a corner near an open window.

'Rose!' he called.

'Oh shit,' she murmured.

Morgan pushed into the small group, his black, sweaty T-shirt clinging to his impressive six-pack.

'Joe. Kamlesh.'

Morgan nodded at them, then returned his focus to Rose.

'Thought you'd like to know we found him. Summers was hiding out with an old squeeze in Brighton. You were right.'

'That's fantastic news! Congratulations,' she replied, relieved. 'Cheers!'

They clinked glasses and Morgan emptied what was left of his pint in a few gulps.

'Look,' he said, wiping the back of his hand across the froth stuck to his upper lip. 'I was a bit hard on you over that pub incident. Move on, shall we?'

'Of course. So will Summers talk?'

Morgan nodded. 'Oh yeah, he'll talk.' He gave her a knowing smile, revealing a chipped front tooth.

'There you go,' said Leach, handing her another house chardonnay. It was pointless arguing. She placed it on a nearby table. Morgan took his Guinness from Leach and skulled half of it.

'He tell you they've arrested Ray Summers? Thanks to Hong,' Leach said, jerking his snooker-ball head towards Morgan.

'So he's recovered enough to talk?' she asked.

'You bet,' chuckled Leach. 'Wants to avoid jail time. Gave up Ray Summers and his gang mates. Even a bloody huge cannabis farm not four miles from here.'

'And best of all,' said Morgan, scratching the black widow spider tattoo on his neck, 'we've got a signed confession incriminating the gang lords in South Korea. Even the Dragon Head. The local police are arresting them as we speak.'

'But Hong's a triad. They'll kill him, won't they?'

Morgan shrugged. 'After the trial he's in witness protection. Then who sodding cares!'

'So Operation Nailgun is a big success,' said Leach. 'Thanks to you finding Hong.' He slapped her on the back. Her wine spilled onto her boots.

'Thanks, boss.' Rose blushed. Time to deflect attention. 'So is Martinez still claiming she was trying to save me from Hong that night?'

Leach laughed. 'Even her lawyer couldn't keep a straight face over that gem. Hong made a copy of the Professor's USB. Something to blackmail her with if she didn't pay up. Once she knew we had it, she clammed up.'

'What was on the USB?' Rose asked.

'Proof her genetically engineered bees are aggressive little bastards that swarm and attack. Needless to say, Chadstone Flay's Holy Grail of beekeeping isn't being released.'

'So Patrick was going to scupper her big break?'

'You nailed it,' said Leach. 'Martinez's salary package for the killer bees development included shares in Flay Bioscience

348

which would've been worth a bloody fortune. Salt tried to reason with her and got nowhere. Bomphrey and Flay refused to listen. So he was going to publish in *Nature* magazine. Martinez found out and got Hong to do the hit. Looks like Tweedledum and Tweedledee had nothing to do with the murders.'

'And Martinez met Hong through her drug addiction? Cocaine?' asked Rose.

'Joe been filling you in, has he?' asked Leach, giving Salisbury a scowl for spoiling his story.

'Not at all, sir,' said Rose. 'Just a guess. Martinez was always so unreasonably upbeat. A hyper bunny. And she worked unbelievably long hours, so cocaine wasn't too much of a stretch.'

Leach stared at her for a moment. 'You know, I think we'll make a detective out of you, yet.'

Rose couldn't help smiling.

'She was dealing to fund her addiction,' said Varma, still wearing his suit jacket despite the heat. A trickle of perspiration slid down his right temple. He wiped it away with a cotton handkerchief. 'She had a whole network of students working for her, supplying anything from smack to dope.'

'How could I have been so wrong about her?' Rose asked, shaking her head.

'Hey, she fooled everybody,' said Varma.

'She only lied about small things,' said Salisbury. 'Things easily missed. And she was right about Bomphrey and Flay. They did argue with Salt about the dangerous bees, and chose to ignore him.'

'So the Professor never asked for a raise?' she asked.

'Nope,' said Leach.

'And Rebecca? Back in Australia?' Rose asked.

'Yup,' said Leach taking a swig of his beer. 'Thank God.'

'And her husband?'

'That man's life isn't going to be worth living.' Leach chuckled.

Varma filled in the details. 'Rebecca found out about Matilda Rutter. She's made it her mission in life to destroy him.'

'That's one scary woman,' said Salisbury.

'And for once in his life Larry Nice was innocent. Who'd have bloody thought!' said Leach.

'Hong did a pretty good job of framing him, sir,' said Varma. 'Had us all going there for a while.'

'Yeah, but it won't be long before he's back in the nick for something or other.' Leach frowned and combed the crowd. 'Where's Dave? Thought he'd be here by now.'

'Said he had a date,' said Varma.

Salisbury and Rose exchanged knowing looks. Pearl didn't want to celebrate her success.

'And here comes yours,' said Leach nodding towards Malcolm, waving at them across a sea of heads, his short black hair neatly gelled and his shirt crisply ironed.

'He's not a date,' Rose blurted out, going beetroot. 'I didn't know he was coming.' She flicked an accusatory look at Salisbury.

'Not me,' he said, raising his hands in submission.

'I invited him,' said Leach, winking at Rose.

Chapter Fifty-One

Wooferoo! Life couldn't be better!

I have my nose out of the car window, sniffing all those rich foresty smells zooming by, my ears flapping in the wind. I bark a friendly greeting to every dog, squirrel, bird, sheep and cow we pass. Maybe even a cat or two – in error naturally.

Rose glances at me in the rear-view mirror. She looks and smells different, mainly because she is covered in make-up that makes her eyes and lips seem bigger, thanks to that woman with all those little coloured pots and powders at the breakfast TV studio in London. Rose was nervous, so I was nervous too and started chewing the corner of a couch on the set which seemed to upset a few people. Everything settled down once I had a rawhide bone in my chops. I sat at Rose's feet as the cameras rolled looking every bit the loyal hound and she did all the talking. Let's face it, I'm hardly going to tell my own tale. Except to you, of course.

'So Monty,' Rose says, smiling at me. 'How do you like the fame?'

Me? I'm not the famous one. Rose is. Although when our photo appeared on the front cover of *OK!* magazine, they called me the Dogtective and now when people pass us in the street, they point and stare and say, 'Isn't that the Dog-tective?'

I wag my tail as I detect duck poo, stagnant water and the honeyed sweetness of clover. We pull into Duckdown Cottage. I leap from the car and run in circles through a purple meadow that was once a lawn, occasionally dashing towards Rose so she can try to grab me. She laughs.

'Pleased to be home, hey?'

You bet!

She kneels next to me and gives me a hug. I lean into her and lick her hand. We're a team now and this is my home.

When Rose told me that Rebecca was putting Paddy's house on the market – and I realised that meant selling it – I was very down-in-the-mouth. I couldn't even eat break-fast and spent the day curled up on my patchwork dog bed. Luckily, Rose had managed to sew it back together for me. That day, not even the ducks could get a rise out of me. When I went into the garden one of them pecked my tail and I didn't even give chase.

'Boring bastard,' the duck griped, pooing in front of me and waddling off.

Rose took pity and drove me round to Paddy's place so I could sniff all my favourite spots one last time. We walked along the riverbank together and she threw a stick into the river so I could go for a swim. I left a final wee-mail on the garden gate, asking the next canine to look after the place for me.

Time to make some new favourite spots.

'I need to get out of this gear,' she says, moving the wheelbarrow so we can walk down the side passage – the front door was damaged by Hong so a screwed-in plank is now holding it in position. Rose goes inside to change clothes, but I lie in the tall grass and enjoy the mellow autumn sunshine and a nice chewy stick.

'Hey there, handsome!'

Celeste hasn't spoken to me since she heard about my TV gig. I think her proboscis was well and truly out of joint. She lands on a dandelion flower like a circus performer lowered into the ring. I remember not to breathe all over her as I know she won't like rawhide breath.

'Good to see you, Celeste.'

She contemplates me for a moment.

'I think you should run your own PI agency, Monty. I'll stick to what I do best – insect crime. You focus on solving the crimes big'uns can't. That way, there should be more than enough work for both of us.'

'You're not upset I've been on TV, are you? That's all about Rose, not me.'

I realise I have a bit of chewy bark sticking out of my jowl. Not a good look. A quick lick, and it's gone.

'I admit, I was a bit jealous,' she said, crossing two of her six legs. I notice the new red boots she's wearing. I suspect she bought them for her TV interview that never happened. 'But my business is booming. The news has spread far and wide of my brilliant strategy to capture Martinez and her assassin, Hong.'

'Glad to hear it. But I don't want to run a PI business, Celeste. There was only one crime I wanted to solve and it's done now. I can move on.'

She opens her wings and lifts into the air so she's hovering at my eye level. 'I think cases will find you, Monty. I think this is where you move on to. Good luck, and leave me a wee-mail if you need my help.'

'Wait! How is Four doing?'

'Very happy,' Celeste replies. 'New home, new family. Doesn't seem to need her cold-water bottle these days.'

Paddy had left details of his new hives in Pirbright Woods on the same USB stick as his research condemning the killer bees.

'Gotta fly. See you around, big boy!'

As I watch Celeste dart off, I feel a tug on my tail. I look round to find a bloated and out-of-breath Betty. Her stomach is blown up like a puffer fish.

'Hold on a mo,' says Betty between pants. 'She's claiming the credit for *your* strategy, is she?'

'It doesn't matter, Betty.'

'It bleedin' well does. You solved the crime. Not her. And it's important you know it, Mr Monty, 'cause she's right about one thing: you should run a PI agency. You'll be bloody brilliant at it.'

I sniff the air as I consider the idea. I'm distracted by Betty, who falls backwards and can't right herself because of her distended belly.

'Betty, what have you eaten?'

She struggles to sit up. 'After my near-death experience I've decided to live life to the fullest, every day. And that includes cramming as much food into my gob as possible.'

'So what was it? A melon?'

After much huffing and puffing, she sits up. 'Very funny, mate. There was a jam doughnut in the larder that seemed kinda lonely.'

She has sugar on her whiskers. In fact, it's all over her head like dandruff. 'Played that game wiv it. You know. Eat a doughnut without licking your lips. Impossible, of course. The sugar tickles.'

She pulls her whiskers near her mouth and sucks off sugar grains one at a time. It's hard to believe that only a week ago my rotund friend survived her toilet flushing because she was slim enough to squeeze through the crack in the sewer pipe caused by the willow's roots, and then strong enough to dig her way to the surface. Just as well Rose never got around to fixing it.

I hear a clank and then a heavy thud from inside the house. I sprint into the kitchen and up the stairs before Betty can roll onto all fours. On the landing, I find a metal ladder that leads to a hole in the ceiling and through that hole, dust drifts down like snow.

'It's filthy up here,' I hear Rose say. She coughs.

I bark.

'It's okay, Monty,' she calls. 'I'm in the attic.'

Yes, but what are you doing up there?

I place one paw on the stepladder and peer up through the trap door, nostrils quivering, but I only get the occasional glimpse of Rose as she shifts battered old suitcases and cardboard boxes. Conflicting smells reach me, each telling their own story: aniseed, olive groves and sun lotion; muddy walking boots and oilskin coats; garlic, red wine and that runny cheese that melts in your mouth; and, less pleasant, the antiseptic and boiled cabbage smells you get in hospital. My ears twitch at the scratching and scraping.

The soles of her trainers appear on the top rung of the ladder. She climbs down, carrying a cardboard archive box with a label stuck on the side. Her blue eyes are bright with eagerness.

'There's loads more up there. Tons of them,' she says, as she places the dusty box next to me and sits, cross-legged on the landing carpet.

I sniff it. I pull back. Decaying rose petals, cigarette smoke and black coffee. There's something else smoky in there I can't identify. Rose fiddles with the tape sealing the box, then pauses.

'This is the one, Monty. The case that killed Aunt Kay.'

I read the handwritten label. It says 'Toyne family murder' and the date. It identifies DI Kay Lloyd as lead on the case. The word 'Unsolved' is printed in capitals on the lid.

She carefully removes the tape, lifts the lid and looks inside the box. The first item she takes out is an A3 manila envelope filled with photos of a house fire. My tail droops, my ears flatten, as she flicks through the images of the gutted and blackened remains of a family home. Worst of all is a photo of a scared little boy. I recognise Finnegan Toyne's dark eyes, but they are wide with horror and his grubby cheeks are damp with tears. I think of him, now fifteen and lying in a hospital bed, in a coma.

'This is our next case,' Rose says, looking at me. 'We owe it to Finn.'

I bark in agreement. From the bottom of the stairs I hear an excited squeak and then an almighty burp.

Acknowledgements

Some years ago, I was visiting a dear friend in Ireland. She introduced me to a beekeeper, Tim Rowe, and it was his love of, and concern for, the honey bee that inspired this story. Those who know me won't be at all surprised to read that our Golden Retriever, Pickles, is the inspiration for Monty, but the idea for this dog detective series predates Pickles. In 2006, my husband and I were staying at a holiday house in Farley Green. As we watched TV one evening, I discovered a squirrel peering through the window, twitching its tail aggressively.

'Bet he's a spy for the BBC TV licensing department,' I said, pointing at the squirrel.

The cottage owner's dog chased it up a tree, barking excitedly, tail wagging. The squirrel peered down at the dog, squeaking, as if they were engaged in an argument. So, the notion of a story about a dog who helps a detective solve crimes that otherwise wouldn't get solved, was born. Thankfully I have a husband and friends who embrace my crazy ideas and laugh with me, as I hope you, the reader, have done. My husband, Michael, is my first editor and my greatest support and I thank him from the bottom of my heart.

I cannot thank enough Sussex CID's retired detective chief superintendent, David Gaylor. David has been incredibly generous with his time and any deviations from correct policing procedures or terminology are my decision. All the characters, including those on the Major Crime Team, are entirely fictional. Veterinarian Steven Cooney kindly answered my numerous dog-related questions. Again, any deviation from reality is down to me.

Monty And Me wouldn't be in your hands if it wasn't for the wonderful people at HarperCollins, in particular my publisher, Katy Loftus. Thank you, Katy, for embracing this story with such passion, and for your guidance and support. I've loved working with you. Thank you also to the sales and publicity teams at HarperCollins, who do an amazing job. My literary agent, Phil Patterson from Marjacq Scripts, is the best agent any author could wish for. Phil championed this book with great gusto and good humour. I know of no other agent who sends out emails with the subject 'Woof! The dog has gone for walkies.' I also want to thank Kirsten Nägele from Heyne, Random House, for publishing *Monty And Me* in German.

And finally, a big thank you to you, the reader. If you would like to stay in touch with Monty, you can find him at www.MontyDogDetective.com.